EVERY MOTHER'S NIGHTMARE

by

Charles Bosworth, Jr.

AN ONYX BOOK

ONYX
Published by the Penguin Group
Penguin Books USA Inc., 375 Hudson Street,
New York, New York 10014, U.S.A.
Penguin Books Ltd, 27 Wrights Lane,
London W8 5TZ, England
Penguin Books Australia Ltd, Ringwood,
Victoria, Australia
Penguin Books Canada Ltd, 10 Alcorn Avenue,
Toronto, Ontario, Canada M4V 3B2
Penguin Books (N.Z.) Ltd, 182–190 Wairau Road,
Auckland 10, New Zealand

Penguin Books Ltd, Registered Offices:
Harmondsworth, Middlesex, England

First published by Onyx, an imprint of Dutton Signet,
a division of Penguin Books USA Inc.

ISBN 0-451-40537-4

To Tyler and Stacy—so loved, so missed.
Two hearts touched briefly in life
Joined forever in death.
To murdered children everywhere,
Killed by the evils of society
And by justice denied.
May they finally rest in peace
To John, for getting justice.

—Mari Kane and Jude Govreau

FOREWORD

This is the true story of every parent's worst nightmare and how it was visited on two women in the same terrible moment. It recounts how that horror was just the beginning of a journey no one should have to take. But more and more travellers are finding themselves on that road, woefully unprepared for the obstacles they are about to encounter. The two women who have made this voyage hope this book will serve as a road map. They cannot make the trip painless and they cannot prevent the violence that will force other parents to follow them. But they can point to the dreadful hurdles that will arise along the way. And for those who must follow them, perhaps knowing what they will find will make them better prepared to overcome barriers they never imagined they would face.

This book has been assembled using a variety of contemporary notes, police reports, records, and court transcripts to provide a basis for the true story it tells. The author also has drawn on the memories of many participants and observers who reconstructed events and conversations as accurately as humanly possible. Every attempt has been made to resolve differences in recollections and to present the most factual account. In some cases, differences have been noted and left for the reader to consider.

A great number of pseudonyms have been used to protect the identities of people who revealed information that could embarrass or compromise them, their families, their friends, or others. The real names of the primary characters have been used, but many others are pseudonyms that have been chosen randomly by the author and bear no connection to real people who may have similar names. An asterisk marks the first reference to each fictitious name.

The author wishes to thank a long list of people who

shared their time, their memories, and their most personal thoughts to assist in the preparation of this book. Jude Govreau and Mari Kane spent countless hours reliving the most painful days of their lives, and doing so with grace and strength. Their families and friends offered their time and assistance as well: Racheal Nichols, Bob Kane, Pat and Joe Indelicato, Rick Pashia, and Jackie Corey.

A special debt is owed John Appelbaum, who spent hours going through the massive details of the trial and was never too busy to help. Prosecuting Attorney George McElroy's cooperation also is appreciated. And special thanks go to the police: Captain John O'Rando, Lieutenant Tim McEntee, Captain Ed Kemp, Detective Bob Miller, Lieutenant Bill Baldwin, Captain Wally Gansmann (ret.), Lieutenant Leo Burle, Deputy Doug Casteel, and Sheriff Walter "Buck" Buerger (ret.).

The assistance of defense attorneys Clinton Almond and Marsha Brady is greatly appreciated.

I want to thank my editor, Michaela Hamilton, and her staff at Penguin USA for their continued direction and support. And, once again, I offer my sincere thanks to my agents, Arthur and Richard Pine, for their expert counsel and efforts on my behalf.

CHAPTER 1

The almost crippling fear of storms had swept across her only after she had settled in the rolling hills of Jefferson County just south of St. Louis. Jude Govreau had lived all over the country—from Florida to California, from Colorado to Virginia—and never had she found any menace in the thunderclap or lightning flash. But her journey to the Midwest had been accompanied by angry storms and even the terrifying funnel clouds that she knew could deliver devastation and death. And now, in her suburban apartment in Fenton, Missouri, Jude would feel her throat begin to close as soon as the sky darkened. The storms that never had given her a moment's concern now sent her into a frenzy. She often led her children to refuge in the basement as soon as the wind began to blow. She fortified a closet with a chair, a television, and an ashtray—the necessities for a safe room designed to protect her against a life-threatening assault. Nightmares about tornadoes would ruin her sleep, always bringing along a haunting vision of an ominous man dressed in black. A gathering storm could send her over the edge, and she even resorted to tranquilizers to dull the edge of the terror.

She didn't seem the type of woman to be threatened by something so seemingly mundane as the weather. A tall, lanky blonde, she carried herself with a leathery attitude that proclaimed she could handle anyone and anything through sheer will and a streak of eviscerating candor. Her brown eyes could narrow into a glare that warned others that she had been tempered in the fire of a hard life and she would take no abuse from anyone.

But as her fear of storms grew into a phobia, Jude Govreau realized she needed help and turned to a Catholic priest. She had been a devout Mormon, but this priest was an experienced counselor and she needed his wisdom. During a year of sessions, he concluded that she was not afraid of storms; she really was afraid of the violence they represented. She had good reason to abhor violence; her past had seen enough to frighten anyone. Her childhood—so often the genesis for such suppressed dread—had been difficult, but not violent. As an adult, however, she had suffered at the hands of an abusive husband while enduring the deaths of two unborn children. She finally had fled from him, fearing for a long time that he would find her and her children and the violence would start again. Now, in Missouri, she hoped she was free of such brutality. Her life still wasn't perfect, but she had three daughters and a solid relationship with Rick Pashia, the man who now slept in her bed. Here, she prayed, only the storms threatened violence.

When the thunder jolted her awake at seven o'clock on Thursday, August 7, 1986, she suppressed her natural response. At that moment, her need for sleep was more powerful than her phobia. The night shift as a bartender in the Soulard area of south St. Louis was piling years of fatigue onto her thirty-eight-year-old body. This morning, she could sleep for another two hours, and she resolved not to let the rain rob her of that rest.

She forced her thoughts away from the rumbling in the already stifling air outside and quickly assessed the morning from her makeshift bed on the sofa. The infant girl she was watching for a vacationing neighbor still slept peacefully in the playpen nearby—the reason for Jude's night on the couch. She knew her fifteen-year-old daughter, Stacy Price, had left the apartment a few minutes earlier for her babysitting job with three-year-old Tyler Winzen in an apartment across the street. Jude didn't know Tyler's mother, Mari Winzen, very well; the women had met only once, three weeks ago, when Mari came over to confirm Stacy's new job at $70 a week. Mari was attractive and seemed quite nice, and obviously was very concerned about the way the last baby-sitter had treated her son. Jude knew from Stacy that Mari kept an immaculate and nice apartment full of plants. Stacy had been bringing Tyler back to Jude's at breakfast time each day, and Jude had become quite fond of the precious little boy. But their arrival was still two hours away, and no one else was stirring in Jude's apartment yet. There was indeed time for more of the sleep Jude needed so badly.

The young woman in the apartment across the street already was awake and was beginning her day with little regard for the rain or thunder. Mari Winzen was not a morning person, but she had begun to find new joy in shaking off the sleep and preparing for work in the kind of routine so many found depressing. Mari had never been so happy. At thirty-two, Mari, a petite redhead with a fiery nature befitting her Italian heritage, finally was finding the strength to prevail over some terrible times. She had turned her back on a life that surely had been killing her. She had divorced Steve Winzen and fled the trailer park where they had battled through an unhappy marriage. She had ended another destructive relationship that began after that. She was winning the battle with a ruinous addiction to Valium. She was holding down a good job at an electronics company and was enjoying the work.

And best of all, she was finding complete fulfillment raising her son, Tyler. He was a wonderful, amazing child, and he made every day a joy. Her success with Tyler soon would earn her the return of her older son, Brian. The thirteen-year-old had been staying with his grandmother while Mari got on her feet, and now she was ready to bring him home to complete her family. She had reached deep inside and mined the courage to live with a new independence and purpose. She was learning that life really was worth the effort.

And she was enjoying the company of one of the sweetest young girls she had ever met. Stacy Price, her new babysitter from just across the road in the Stillbrook Estates apartment complex, had quickly become a welcome addition to Mari's morning. The bubbly teenager would arrive promptly at 6:50 A.M., slip in quietly through the door Mari had just unlocked, and then appear suddenly in the bathroom as Mari applied the finishing touches to her hair and makeup. Stacy would perch on the edge of the bathtub and chatter away; the little brunette could talk incessantly about anything, and Mari loved the sound of the happy voice. Stacy had replaced Bobbi Turner,* the girl in the apartment upstairs, whose performance as Mari's baby-sitter had deteriorated beyond tolerance. Mari had fired Bobbi and persuaded Stacy to watch Tyler until she started high school the end of the month. It was working out well, just like the rest of Mari's life.

She had met Stacy's mother, Jude Govreau, only once. Jude seemed nice enough, and Stacy showed the signs of a careful and proper upbringing. Mari felt only comfort and confidence as she headed out the door each morning for work, leaving Tyler still asleep in Stacy's care. Stacy would pull the blanket and pillow out of the hall closet and sack out on the sofa until Tyler awoke about nine o'clock. Mari kissed Tyler's forehead as he slept, and then she headed for work. As she closed and locked the door behind her, she thought again how good life was. She didn't even mind the run to her car in the rain.

Jude Govreau was awakened again about nine o'clock by the telephone, a call from the baby's vacationing mother to say she would return that evening. Jude had begun her morning routine when she realized at about ten o'clock that Stacy and Tyler had not arrived for breakfast as they usually did. Jude called the apartment across the street, not particularly upset when no one answered. Stacy often took Tyler to visit one of several neighbors in the building. When another call about fifteen or twenty minutes later went unanswered, Jude sent her youngest daughter, ten-year-old Racheal, across the street to check. Racheal returned to say that there had been no response to her knock on Tyler's door and she had been unable to locate Stacy at any of the neighbors' apartments.

Jude sighed and sent Racheal back. This time the girl rang the doorbell: no answer. Jude ordered her back a third time with instructions to see if the door was open. Racheal was out of breath when she returned. She had gone into the apartment and called for Stacy, but no one was there. She heard a loud and startling "click," became frightened, and ran out.

Jude still wasn't too worried. Surely Stacy had taken Tyler to visit the Turners*. Even though Stacy had succeeded Bobbi Turner as Tyler's baby-sitter, the girls still saw each other frequently. Stacy really preferred to avoid

Bobbi, but couldn't hurt the feelings of the girl, who still followed her around and seemed to want her company. Stacy was like that—so kindhearted. Surely Stacy had popped into Bobbi's apartment with Tyler this morning. Jude piddled around in the kitchen for a few minutes more and, about ten-thirty, headed to Tyler's apartment to check for herself. She was a few steps into the hallway before she realized she didn't know where she was going. She had to go back and ask Racheal for the apartment number. Then she strolled across the street and knocked on the door: no answer. Reluctant to barge into someone else's home, Jude hesitantly opened the door and leaned in. There was no response to her call for Stacy.

Jude pushed the door open wide, stepped into the apartment, and took a quick look around the small, meticulously kept living room and the kitchen that opened behind it. The television to her left was on with the volume almost too low to hear; the man on the screen was a curious shade of green. A blanket and pillow still lay on the sofa, and one end of the coffee table in front of it appeared to have been bumped a little out of line. As she stepped into the center of the room, Jude looked at the large rattan "papasan" chair Stacy had talked about. Odd, Jude thought, that there was no cushion on the wooden frame.

She called for Stacy several times as she walked through the room and turned right into the small hallway that connected the two bedrooms and the bathroom. Tyler's bedroom was empty, his bed unmade. A large potted corn plant sat in front of the open window in his room, and the rain splashed in. Strange way to water a plant, Jude thought absentmindedly. She peered into Mari's room; the bed was made and the room was as neat as a pin.

The door to the bathroom was closed; not surprising, given Tyler's childish penchant for closing and locking doors. But then Jude noticed the light shining under the door from inside the bathroom. And she realized she could hear the familiar and sometimes maddening sound of the water in the toilet running.

For the first time, Jude allowed her mind to acknowledge that something was wrong. For the first time, she began to feel the fear.

"Stacy? Tyler? Are you in there?"

She looked at the doorknob, but couldn't touch it.

A crash of thunder outside shuddered through her body. For what seemed like hours, Jude stood in the little hallway and stared at that doorknob, unable to touch it. She could hear her own labored breathing. The storm raged outside, the light glared under the door, and the water in the toilet ran unrestrained. And she couldn't touch the doorknob.

Finally, she backed away and then walked quickly out of the apartment. She pounded on the Turners' door across the hall, raising Bobbi's mother, Brenda*.

"Brenda, I can't find Stacy or Tyler. Have you seen them?" Jude asked urgently.

"No, I haven't seen them this morning."

Jude had to ask. "Do you know if Mari keeps her bathroom door closed?"

Brenda Turner was puzzled by the question, but shrugged and said, "I . . . don't know."

Jude turned, closed Mari's apartment door, and ran back toward her own apartment. She began to cry as she crossed the street, and the tears were flowing freely by the time she charged into her bedroom and roughly shook Rick Pashia from his sleep.

"Rick, Rick, I know you're going to think I'm crazy or I've watched too much TV." Jude's words were tumbling out urgently. "But I can't find Stacy or Tyler, and Mari's bathroom door is closed. I'm afraid to touch it. Something's wrong, Rick. Something's really wrong."

Despite Jude's fear of storms, Rick knew she usually didn't scare easily and the tears meant she was really frightened. Still groggy from too little sleep, he scrambled out of bed and into his jeans, T-shirt, and shoes. They hurried back to Mari's, and Rick charged into the apartment. Surely she was just being paranoid, he thought. He grabbed the doorknob, but turned to Jude and said, "It's locked." Jude told him to look on the frame above the door for the key, and then she decided to go around the back of the building in case she could see through the bathroom window. As she peered into the kitchen and realized there was no window into the bathroom, she muttered, "Dammit," and turned back toward the front of the building.

She ran back into the hallway, but stopped in her tracks. Rick was leaning against the doorjamb, his eyes wide and bulging, his face almost gray, as if he were about to pass out. The look of horror on his face was unlike anything Jude had ever seen. She walked slowly toward him.

"Rick, Rick!" she said, her voice rising to a scream. "Tell me they're not in there!"

He looked weakly at her and mumbled, "Jude, they're in there. They're in the bathtub. We have to call the police."

Jude put her hands over her ears as she screamed. The voice seemed to come from someone, somewhere, else. Oh God, she thought, Stacy was dead. Somehow, her beautiful daughter was gone. Jude had just grounded Stacy for being out too late. Had she killed herself over being grounded? My God, it had just been for three weeks! This had to be another of her vivid nightmares. Surely she would wake up soon. As she battled this flood of paralyzing thoughts, one more pushed through the panic.

"Rick, not the baby, too?" she screamed. He nodded. Tyler was gone, too.

He nodded again when she asked if they were in the water. "Please, Rick, get them out of the water!" she begged.

She leaned toward him and began to strike out at him. He caught her hands and pushed her back, pinning her against the wall. Jude didn't know where the screams were coming from, but they were constant and piercing. From the jumble of thoughts, Jude could only ask, "Was there blood, Rick? Did you see blood?"

"There wasn't any blood, Jude. I didn't see any blood."

As she slid down the wall, reality blurred into a series of disjointed images. Jude was on the floor in the hall and then in the Turners' living room, where Rick was trying to hold her down and Brenda kept trying to cover her with something. The temperature and humidity were sweltering, and this woman apparently was trying to smother Jude with a blanket. She felt as if she were suffocating amid the screams and the heat. Her eyes were pinched closed and she could feel herself slamming into the furniture as she writhed on the floor. She could hear Brenda on the phone talking to someone, but who?

Then the paramedics were over her, strapping an oxygen mask to her face and strapping her to the stretcher. She begged them not to tie her down and she screamed that she could not breathe as the mask covered nose and mouth. She was carried into the rain and heard herself shrieking for them to get the water out of her face. The rain—the storm—was battering her, and she couldn't bear it. Time meant nothing amid these disconnected moments. She was in an ambulance and then suddenly in the hospital emergency room. A nurse above her head was asking repeatedly if she was allergic to any medicines. Jude was able to mumble that she couldn't take codeine, Talwin, or Demerol as they gave her an injection they said would calm her down.

But a new storm was blowing in, and the force in it was not wind or lightning or thunder. It was anger. Raw and pure. Uncontrolled and unfettered by any religious inhibitions or the training she had received from the Mormons. No, this all was God's fault. He had let this happen; He had allowed her precious daughter to be taken away by some yet unknown power that must have been greater than His. Surely a good and just God would not have let this happen. She heard herself screaming words that moments before she would have found unthinkable.

"God, you bastard," her voice shouted to the heaven that she always had believed was out there somewhere. "I hate you, you bastard. God, you bastard! I hate you! I hate you!"

Within minutes, the drug started to calm her, and she felt some of the fight slipping from her body. For the first time since she had looked into Rick's gray face, Jude felt her vision returning. She turned to her right and saw a priest standing there. Perhaps this was a sign from God. At last, she thought, He had sent someone to offer comfort and explain how this had come to pass. She thought again about heaven. Surely, in the midst of all of this confusion and pain, there could be some comfort if Stacy was in heaven. As Jude had done when the fear of storms seemed overwhelming, she now turned to a priest for help.

"Father," she pleaded, "tell me Stacy went to heaven. Please tell me she went to heaven."

The man of the cloth looked at her and said coolly, "If she was a good girl."

The rage erupted again. God had let this happen, and His priest had just spit in Jude's face. She had begged for reassurance of her daughter's salvation and this priest had given her juvenile dogma. How could he put such a ridiculous condition on eternity for Stacy's soul? How could he threaten to withhold heaven from the victim of such a cruel act? How could he compound this injustice on earth with damnation from heaven? Jude pulled a hand free from the straps and struck angrily toward this man as others tried to restrain her.

"You bastard!" someone was screaming again. "You bastard!"

Mari Winzen was having a fairly typical morning at work, highlighted by an invitation from coworker Bob Kane for a weekend picnic at a park along the Mississippi River in neighboring Illinois. Bob had taken Mari out once and they had had a good time. Now, he suggested, they should take Tyler and enjoy the picturesque drive up the Great River Road between the limestone bluffs and the river that sparkled in the sun. It sounded great to Mari.

She still was thinking about that when she got a call from her upstairs neighbor and best friend, Carol Brinkley. Carol was going through a difficult time after the collapse of a romantic relationship, and her odd request on the phone didn't set off the alarm it should have. She needed to talk to Mari about something, Carol said, and she wanted Mari to put her boss, Barney Lewis, on the line, too. Mari shrugged and stepped into Barney's office. "I think Carol has man trouble, Barney. She wants you to get on the line with me so she can tell us something."

"Mari," Carol began tentatively, "something bad has happened. You need to come home."

As Mari Winzen's mind recoiled from the message, the facts Carol was describing became strangely twisted. Mari thought Carol was telling her that Stacy had been found tied up in the bathroom and Tyler was missing. Mari was sure Carol said she was getting dressed to go look for Tyler.

Mari remembered saying only "I'll be right there," as she hung up the phone and then went berserk. She was screaming that someone had kidnapped Tyler. Why would anyone kidnap her child? She had no money; she had nothing of value. What could kidnappers want from her? In her frenzy, Mari even clawed a coworker's face as he tried to calm her down.

Barney and another friend at the office, Cathy Lewis, took Mari to Cathy's car and sat her in the front seat. Barney jumped into the back as Cathy climbed behind the wheel and started the thirty-minute drive through busy city traffic to Mari's apartment. Mari was nearly hysterical, berating Cathy for driving at the speed limit and not streaking through the bumper-to-bumper traffic that was even slower because of the rain. All the while, Mari repeatedly asked who would want to take her child. "I hope he's okay," she said again and again. Cathy nodded her reassurance, but Barney said nothing. Stacy must have been raped, Mari thought aloud. The intruders must have tied her up and escaped with Tyler. They had to find him.

When Cathy finally turned onto Stillbrook Drive and crested the hill near the apartment building, Mari was shocked to see the street filled with emergency vehicles. The flashing red and blue lights on the rescue trucks, ambulances, and police cars added a new urgency to Mari's fears. The car had barely stopped when Mari blasted open the door and exploded through the crowd of neighbors and others who had gathered in front of her building. She was stopped at her door by a huge uniformed police officer who stood stiffly in front of her apartment like a robot.

"Did they find Tyler?" she asked the officer. "Is he okay? Did they take Stacy to the hospital?"

The cop showed no emotion as he looked down at the tiny woman and responded flatly, "I'm sorry ma'am. They're both deceased."

Mari stepped back. Deceased. He'd said "deceased." With all of the emotion of a mannequin, he had said "deceased." She couldn't have heard correctly.

"You mean dead?" she asked in disbelief.

"Yes, ma'am, they're both dead," he said with no change in his voice.

The possibility that Tyler was dead had not entered Mari's thoughts until then. But this cop was saying it with such unemotional finality, such detached bluntness, that it must be true.

Carol Brinkley was approaching as Mari turned to look for help from someone. Carol put her hands on Mari's shoulders as she began to scream, "Tell me no, Carol. Tell me this didn't happen. Tell me no."

Carol hugged her and said, "Mari, I can't tell you that."

Mari Winzen collapsed, sliding to the floor at almost the same place occupied some time earlier by another distraught mother. Rick Pashia was leaving the building to follow Jude to the hospital when he heard these new screams. He had seen the arrival of the tiny woman he believed was Tyler's mother, and now he knew she had learned the horrible truth.

The feeling began at Mari's feet and moved slowly toward her head, as if she were being encased in concrete. This must be shock, she thought. She was in physical shock as surely as she was in emotional shock.

A plainclothes detective squatted down beside her.

"Ma'am, I know this is hard for you, and I'm sorry to bother you now. But do you have any idea who could have done this? Is there anyone you can think of who would want to harm your son and the baby-sitter?"

The suggestion inherent in that question slowly sank in on Mari. The police thought someone had "done" this to Tyler and Stacy. Did that mean someone had killed them, on purpose? The idea rocked Mari almost as hard as the news that her son and her new friend were dead.

"You mean they were *murdered*?" she asked.

"Yes, ma'am. And time is very important right now. If you can think of anyone who might have done this, we need their names now."

Mari buried her face in her trembling hands and felt the tears on her cheeks. Tyler was dead? Stacy, too? Murdered. This couldn't be happening; it couldn't be real. No, please, God. She looked up again at the detective. She couldn't even focus on his features, almost as if he had no face. Nothing registered as Mari's mind tried to outrace the reality that was setting in.

"Mrs. Winzen," he said again softly, "can you think of anyone who would have any reason to do this?"

Who *could* do this to Tyler? she was wondering. No one could *want* Tyler or Stacy dead. They were such innocents. The killer had to be someone who had something against her. Surely this had to be Mari's fault in some way. She thought first of Jim Daniels,* whom she had thrown out of her apartment and her life just a year earlier. He was a clinical psychologist and had seemed so wonderful when they met and began dating. Later, she learned that he was a married fraud, and she threw him out.

"Jim Daniels," she told the cop. "I lived with him here for a while until I found out he was married and had lied to me. He's the only one I can think of."

Another detective leaned over and said, "There's someone named Lester here to see you."

Mari turned to look down the hallway and felt some comfort when she saw the familiar face of Lester Howlett, one of her ex-husband's best friends. When Mari and Steven Winzen lived in a mobile home in Fenton, Lester and his wife had lived across the street. The couple had become good friends, and Lester and Steven had remained close over the years. The link even went beyond that as Lester, now divorced from his wife, lived in apartment across the street from Mari.

Mari scrambled to her feet and ran to her friend. She threw her arms around his neck and cried, "Oh, Lester, they killed Tyler. He's dead." Surely she could find some comfort with this man she felt really loved Tyler, too, and could share this crushing grief.

But Lester just stood there, as if he were stone, while Mari hugged his neck and wept against his chest. When he didn't return her embrace and offered no comfort, she stepped back in surprise and looked into his face. There was no emotion there. Was he in shock, too?

"I know how to get a hold of Steve in Las Vegas," Lester said flatly. "You want me to call him?"

"Yes, I guess you'd better," Mari said softly. If only he had held her, she thought. She needed him to hold her.

Carol Brinkley guided Mari away and Lester left.

"Come on, honey. Let's go upstairs to my place. Let's get away from this. I called your parents and they're on the way."

Mari slumped to the floor in Carol's living room, pulled up her knees, wrapped her arms around them, and began to rock slowly back and forth. She was not crying now. She should be, she knew; she wanted to. She desperately needed to release the agonizing hurt she felt inside. But she couldn't cry. She was numb, and she didn't really have a clue to what was going on. None of this could be real.

CHAPTER 2

Deputy Doug Casteel stepped into the small bathroom, hoping he was prepared mentally for what he knew was the scene of a murder. In the radio message a few minutes earlier, the dispatcher had cited the seldom-used code for a homicide, and Casteel had tried to get ready for what he might encounter when he arrived at 200 Kimberly Manor Apartments, Apartment C, Stillbrook Estates Drive. After almost five years on the Jefferson County Sheriff's Department, he had seen a half-dozen or more murders and even more fatalities on the highways. The carnage was part of the job that cops had to toughen themselves against, and he knew going in to be ready. But there was no way he could have steeled himself for what awaited him here. Across this little room, in a bathtub full of water, were two children.

Stacy Price's body was facedown at the back of the tub, her dark hair fanned out and floating, almost filling the right end of the tub under the faucet. At the other end, her knees were bent and her bare feet extended into the air. Her right arm was pinned under her body, but her left arm was bent back and turned at the elbow so that her hand rested across the small of her back at the waistband of her white shorts. Casteel winced as he noticed the three small flowers embroidered on the hip pocket. The back of her white T-shirt was bunched up to the bottom of her bra and appeared to have a design featuring the Van Halen rock band.

Next to her, at the front of the tub, was Tyler Winzen, faceup and just slightly below the surface of the water. His eyes were nearly closed and his skin was pale against his brown hair. He still wore blue-and-white pajamas. His left arm crossed his body and his forearm rested on Stacy's shoulder. In a heartbreaking sight, Tyler's hand had a grip on some of Stacy's hair.

Casteel looked into the toddler's face and the image burned itself into his memory. He thought he could see the terror the child must have felt as his life ebbed away in that bathtub. Others would believe later that they saw only peace in that face. But that was not what Casteel detected.

On the floor in front of the tub was a huge blue cushion that had covered the bodies in the water. Russell Million, the assistant chief of the Springdale Fire Department, had been the first officer on the scene, and he had thrown off the cushion so he could check the victims for vital signs.

As Casteel looked at the sterile but horrific scene, he knew he had just walked into the biggest case of his career. Only one course made sense: He secured the apartment to preserve evidence and placed an immediate call for a supervisor.

Lieutenant Ed Kemp was shuffling papers in his office at the sheriff's department in Hillsboro on that quiet, drizzly, muggy morning when the dispatcher buzzed. Days like that usually meant a few traffic accidents, but little else. That was okay; as shift commander, he always had plenty of paperwork to do. He didn't expect the dispatcher to say that Deputy Casteel had just called for help, reporting that there were two kids' bodies in a bathtub.

"What?" Kemp sputtered. "In a bathtub? Did they drown? Was it an accident? Electrical? What happened?"

"I don't know, lieutenant. Casteel just said there were big problems and he wanted a supervisor there as soon as possible."

That was good enough for Kemp. Casteel was one of the best young officers he had ever known—cool and calm and thoroughly professional. If he said there was a problem, by God, there was a problem. Casteel didn't shake easily and he didn't cry wolf.

Kemp's guts warned him this case was going to be something extraordinary. Casteel's message implied this was a double-murder, unusual in any area. And murders usually happened at three o'clock in the morning, not in broad daylight. They didn't usually happen at home and they almost never involved kids—especially two kids.

The lieutenant asked Captain Bimel Wheelis to accompany him to the scene, and the two men sped off in Kemp's car for the twenty-minute drive through the Jefferson County countryside. Kemp—a huge man at six foot three and three hundred pounds—chewed up the two-lane black-tops through the rural areas as few others would dare. As the big Ford blasted along at eighty to eighty-five miles per hour, Captain Wheelis nervously reminded Kemp that speed wouldn't count if they didn't get there alive. Kemp grinned and shrugged; he already was driving slower than usual because of the wet roads.

When Kemp walked into the apartment, he was struck immediately by how immaculate it was. Nothing was out of place and there was no evidence of a struggle. Another glance around. Okay, one corner of the coffee table in front of the couch had been bumped out of place by a few inches; the round impression from the normal location of the leg showed in the carpet. A rumpled blanket and pillow meant someone had been sleeping on the couch. Other than that, the living room and the kitchen were spotless. He had been right about Casteel; this was as pristine a crime scene as Kemp had ever found. The deputy had given the cops a good jump on collecting whatever evidence was left behind.

Kemp stepped into the bathroom doorway and noticed first the vapor still rising off the surface of the water. My God, he thought, that water must have been scalding when it was drawn if it still was hot enough to generate vapor now. He checked the faucet; the single-handle control was cranked all the way over to "hot." Being careful not to step on any potential evidence, Kemp edged closer to the tub and took a long look at the scene that would haunt him, just as it would every cop who walked into that room that day.

This definitely was murder, and damn the person who could do this to two kids. He swallowed hard, thinking about his stepdaughter and stepson at home, the kids he had loved and raised as if they were his own. Kim was thirteen and Greg was sixteen, too close to this girl's age for Kemp not to feel this down deep as he looked into the water.

Children. There were no more purely innocent victims than kids. Adult murder victims often had done something questionable that led to violent ends. They shot off their mouths in a honky-tonk or let alcohol override their sense in some way. Maybe they just ignored the obvious danger of being on the wrong side of town at two in the morning. But kids never did anything to deserve this. They were the only real innocents. They had their whole lives ahead, until some crazed adult ended it all. Working on kid murders was worse than working another cop's murder, Kemp thought. At least cops killed in the line of duty knew what they were getting into; it came with the badge. You pays your money and you takes your chances; that was his philosophy for dealing with the danger. Cops always worked hard to find a buddy's killer. But nothing hit cops harder than the murder of a child. There was no greater loss and no greater abuse of innocence.

And in that bathroom that day, there would be no John Waynes. Every cop who walked in left with a tear in his eye and a vow in his heart to get the monster who did this.

Kemp talked to Captain Wheelis, and they agreed that this was too big for the department. Calling in the St. Louis Metropolitan Major Case Squad quickly was the only move that made sense. The special unit was made up of the best investigators from the departments across the region—including Kemp—and could descend on a crime scene with a crushing assault, throwing manpower, expertise, and technical assistance at a case in those crucial first hours before the trail got cold. Kemp called Sheriff Walter "Buck" Buerger and passed on the recommendation. The sheriff agreed with his men's recommendation without hesitation.

Captain John O'Rando of the St. Ann Police Department had been on the Major Case Squad since 1972 and had been a commander for several years. When the call came in about noon that Thursday, he was startled to hear that it was a double homicide and the victims were kids. He pushed an emotional reaction aside for now and drove to the Fenton Police Department, the location closest to the scene and the best place to set up a command post. From there, he would hand out assignments as the squad members reported in. It would be a few hours before he went to the apartment. He knew no one would touch the evidence or the bodies until the commander arrived. All regulation, all standard procedure, for the Major Case Squad.

Detective Bob Miller of the Arnold Police Department was off duty and visiting his sister when he heard the call for the squad over her police scanner. He had been with the Arnold police for four years and had spent twelve years with the St. Louis County Police Department before that. He had handled three or four murders, mostly with the Major Case Squad, including the cases of the pizza-delivery girl who was stabbed twenty-seven times and the woman whose dismembered body was scattered over several counties. But this would be the first time he had drawn the assignment as crime-scene technician. He had been trained well for the job and would be responsible for gathering the evidence; he would be in full command of the scene.

Miller made a quick trip to his station to pick up his equipment. Arnold Detective Greg Happel also was called out and accompanied Miller on the fifteen-minute drive to Fenton. They met Lieutenant Kemp in the parking lot, and he escorted them into the apartment as he gave them a brief description of what awaited them.

"We've got two kids in the tub," Kemp said in a voice that barely masked his anger and disgust. And in the style that everyone who knew him had come to expect, he added with that familiar edge in his voice, "This is one sick puppy to do this to kids."

They stood in the doorway for a minute, trying to adjust to the scene in the steamy bathroom. Happel shook his head. "I've got two boys about this age. I can't take this," he said as he walked out. Miller wanted to leave with him, but knew he couldn't.

The officers began the photography, with Miller using the videocamera and Happel handling the 35-millimeter to record the outside of the apartment building. Then they moved inside for a detailed examination of the apartment. The photography hadn't caught much. A vague footprint was pressed into the grass outside Tyler's bedroom window, and the screen was torn along the lower edge of the frame. It could have been a red herring, a poor attempt to manufacture a point of entry to suggest a break-in. But it would fool no one. That tear hadn't been used to get in or out of the apartment. And the footprint was little more than a depression in the wet grass, certainly not enough to identify the shoe that made it. It probably had nothing to do with the murders.

Inside, there seemed to be little else of evidentiary value in the living room, kitchen, or bedrooms. There were no marks on the only entry or exit—the front door. No forced entry anywhere. Little was disturbed in the tidy apartment. The coffee table was nudged over a bit and the curtains at the kitchen window apparently had been pulled closed, loosed from the ties that had held them back. The blue cushion found in the tub had come from the chair in the living room. Miller figured the killer had used it to hold down the victims, perhaps while he was drowning them. Maybe he didn't want to have to look into those faces. Maybe he just wanted something to cover the bodies or weigh them down after the deed was done. Who could tell now?

So Miller returned to the bathroom. The water in the tub still was hot, and he could see an area on Tyler's arm where the skin was damaged from the moist heat. After all those years as a cop, he still couldn't get used to things like this. Tyler and Stacy almost seemed to be embracing, clinging to each other in death. It wounded him, and he thought of his grandkids who were about that age, but were safe and sound at home.

Someone really had a heart full of hate for these people to have murdered them and left them like this. Who could want to do this to kids? Maybe the girl's boyfriend? No, probably not. The boy probably wouldn't have had to die unless it was someone he knew. Maybe he walked out of his bedroom to see Stacy's murder and the killer, and then he had to die. Miller was running through the obvious scenarios, but it was hard to look for logic in the murders of such babies.

He began to look at the bathroom and plan how to process it. There was some trash in the center of the floor; the waste can probably had been kicked over accidentally. The water supply to the toilet was running, and that might signal that something had stopped it up. But the first order of business was to look for fingerprints, and his first target was the sliding glass doors on the tub. They were pushed all the way to the left now, but it seemed likely the killer had put his hands there at one time or another during the terrible assault. Miller pulled the fingerprint powder and brush from his kit. Lifting fingerprints off those doors could blow this case wide open, right away.

The officers were arriving at the Fenton police station, and the squad soon would be at full strength—twenty detectives for the squad and the use of another ten officers from the sheriff's department. Captain John O'Rando began drawing up teams—usually one veteran detective with one less experienced. That was how the squad groomed its investigators. They all learned from the best on their way up.

The first step was to canvass the neighborhood in case another resident had seen something. With the dense population in an apartment complex, that was a time-consuming job. But it was important, because such complexes provided a lot of people with easy access to the scene—good potential for witnesses. Next would be interviews with the parents. As inconceivable as it might be, they had to be considered primary suspects at the beginning of such a case. Look at the in-laws before looking for outlaws, as the saying went. Then came the acquaintances. What about Stacy's boyfriends? People she knew from school? Could there be a drug connection with Stacy, a common factor in crimes involving teenagers these days? O'Rando started sending out the investigators. There was no time to waste in a case that he knew soon would be drawing the media like flies.

By the time he was ready to check the scene, it was about four o'clock. The tall, lean O'Rando—his black hair and thick mustache adding to his solemn appearance on the job—obviously was in command as he entered the apartment. The other detectives gave him the respect and deference due his position, and him personally as a detective, as soon as he walked in. His eyes tried to capture everything that might be important as he scanned the small, orderly rooms. There wasn't much to retain, until he got to the bathroom. The bodies still were in the tub, and he felt the full impact of the sight. How could anybody do this? He stood in shock for only a couple of seconds, and then he pulled his wits back to the job at hand. He was in charge and he had no time for the luxury of an emotional reaction, even when his insides were churning. He had been a cop for seventeen years and he never had seen a younger murder victim than Tyler. This one would stay with him a long time, and he knew he wanted to look back and know it was solved when the Major Case Squad brought the killer to justice.

CHAPTER 3

The tranquilizers had taken effect, and Jude Govreau was edging back from the brink of hysteria where she had teetered since she looked into Rick Pashia's face in that apartment doorway some two hours ago. As the reality sank in, she began to beg. Please, she entreated the doctors and nurses, please untie her and let her go home to look after Racheal and little Ashley, the baby she was watching. They were fine, Rick said; they were staying at Brenda Turner's apartment.

"Oh God, no," Jude erupted again. "They're still in the building? Get them out, Rick. The killer still could be there."

"It's okay, Jude. Calm down. The police are there. Everyone is safe. It's okay."

Before long—it only seemed like days strapped to that gurney—Jude was released from the hospital. As Rick helped her to her feet, a sweet nurse gently pressed a piece of paper into Jude's hand. "Here. Take this. It might help you." It was the telephone number for a group called Parents of Murdered Children. My God, that's me now, Jude thought.

On the fifteen-minute drive home, she sat with her knees pulled up and her feet tucked under her on the seat. She buried her forehead against her knees and cried. This couldn't be real. Stacy couldn't really be dead and gone, never to brighten Jude's life again with that wonderful smile and that gentle, loving personality. And Tyler was gone, too. That precocious grin and that bright little mind, all gone. These kids couldn't have been there one second, so alive and vital, and then gone just a moment later. It wasn't fair. After everything Jude had survived, this blow wasn't fair. Was there no justice in this life?

When they reached Stillbrook Estates, the street was filled with police and reporters and spectators. Squad cars were parked every which way. Rick helped Jude out of the car and supported her as they walked into their building, accompanied by stares from some of those who had gathered across the street to watch the activity. Jude collapsed into a chair at the kitchen table, and Rick fixed her a soda as she cried. Brenda Turner soon arrived to assure Jude that Racheal was fine, staying now at the apartment of another neighbor, Mary Planbeck; Ashley had been picked up by her parents. Brenda joined Rick and Jude at the table. She wasn't exactly a welcome guest right now, but Jude was too weak to protest the invasion of privacy.

Then the questions that had begun swirling in Jude's head came tumbling out. She had to know what Rick had seen and what had happened while she was out of her mind. Rick cried, too, as he described finding the bodies. No, he hadn't seen Stacy's face. She was fully clothed, so she probably hadn't been raped. Jude was grateful for that much. Stacy was so modest; at least she had not suffered the humiliation of a sexual assault and her body had not been naked for the police and the others to see.

There was no blood, either, Rick said. Tyler didn't look as if he had been brutalized; in fact, he didn't really look dead to Rick. He seemed so peaceful, as if he were sleeping. Rick's first reaction when he stepped into the bathroom was to grab Tyler's forearm to lift him from the water. But the skin on the little wrist had slipped, actually pulling loose from the flesh under the force of Rick's grasp. That was when he realized he was too late. It was over; the kids were dead. And it obviously was no accident; Rick knew immediately they had been murdered. He thought there was a sleeping bag over the bodies, but Brenda told him it was the cushion from the rattan chair.

Rick said Brenda's daughters, Bobbi and ten-year-old Ruthie*, had run into the apartment after Jude's screams brought the Turners into the hall. Rick had chased them out, but not before they had seen what was in the bathroom. The struggle with Jude had followed that, with Rick and Brenda's husband, Jack Turner,* wrestling Jude from the hall into Brenda's apartment to try to restrain and calm her. Brenda had tried to put a wet towel over Jude's forehead, but that had sent Jude further into panic. As Jude scooted furiously around the living room with Rick and Jack in pursuit, Brenda had called the police. It had been an incredible struggle for everyone as they tried to control Jude's thrashing and screaming. Jude remembered flashes of that, but not much.

Racheal came home later, and she and Jude locked their arms around each other as they cried. Racheal pathetically described how she had heard Jude screaming, but didn't know what had happened. Brenda had broken the news to Racheal that her sister was dead.

The telephone had begun ringing off the hook as word spread and Stacy's shocked friends began to call, many of them hoping the rumors were wrong. Rick and Jude talked to as many as they could, but it was so painful and so confused. What could they tell these kids about their wonderful friend? Who knew what had happened?

Some reporters knocked on the door during the afternoon, and Rick turned them away as politely as possible. It was after four o'clock when the police arrived to interview Jude and check Stacy's room for anything that might be helpful. The two detectives made their apologies, and Jude took them to Stacy's room, where they went through the remnants of her young life, even her wastebasket.

The television, Jude's omnipresent companion, was on softly when the five-o'clock news began. The lead story was the murders of Stacy and Tyler, accompanied by live shots from the scene. Jude was shocked to see the kids' bodies— one covered by a blue blanket and one under a red—carted out on gurneys. That was just happening now? Jude gasped. The bodies had been there all this time? She had assumed they had been removed much earlier. The blue blanket obviously covered a larger body with the knees bent. Oh God, Jude cried, that's Stacy's body. As the camera panned across the scene outside the apartment building, Jude was even more shocked to see a distraught Racheal standing near the ambulance, crying in Mary Planbeck's arms.

But before Jude could run to Racheal's aid, the anchorman announced that the children's bodies had been found in scalding water. Jude's fury exploded again.

"He burned them? The son of a bitch burned them?" she screamed. Her tirade brought the police out of Stacy's room, and Jude screamed at them, "Why would he burn them? My God! He burned them?"

Rick was just as shocked. He didn't remember the water being that hot when he reached for Tyler. It had seemed lukewarm, maybe even room-temperature.

As the pain seared itself into Jude's heart, she began to feel a new anger, raw and powerful. She already had recognized the anger at God, that He would allow this to happen. But this new detail of her daughter's death had actually given life to something inside Jude. She was beginning to think about the killer, the depraved person who had done this. Who and why? In her mind, it had to be a man. She had suffered at men's hands before, and she knew the violence they were capable of inflicting on others. Now, she swore, this man would be caught and punished, made to surrender his life for what he had done to Stacy and Tyler. She vowed to see this man executed.

The police began their interview with Jude as she calmed down again. She described her daughter as a sweet, innocent girl with a cheerful disposition; a good student who hung around with equally good kids and had no questionable acquaintances. There was no drug use or sexual adventures that could have led to this, Jude assured the police.

The only person she could offer as a potential suspect was her first husband, the father of her oldest daughter, sixteen-year-old Johnna. He had beaten Jude and then vowed to find her after she fled from him in Virginia. He had been in prison last time she'd heard. Maybe he had been released and had kept his promise to track her down. He was not Stacy's father, and maybe he had exacted his revenge against Jude by taking one of her children. The police promised they would check him out. When they did later, they learned he had been dead for some time—a fact that neither surprised nor saddened Jude.

Then Jude remembered something else, something recent. Just the day before, Stacy had told her mother about getting a series of strange telephone calls while she was baby-sitting at Tyler's apartment. The guy on the phone was "being ignorant," as Stacy had put it. When Jude dragged the story out of her, Stacy said the guy had asked if she wanted to "screw," and she hung up on him. He called back and asked the same question, and she screamed into the phone before slamming it down again. After Tyler woke up and Stacy got up from her nap on the couch, the guy called again and said, "I waited until you got up before I called back." That had bothered Jude; it meant the guy somehow had seen Stacy's movements, almost as if he was stalking her. Jude told Stacy to get Tyler and come home if the creep called again.

Jude also told the police about her phobias—her fear of storms and water, and of choking. Odd, she said, that those horrors would be visited on her daughter this way this very morning. The police seemed intrigued by that and even asked if anyone else was aware of Jude's rather specific and somewhat unusual anxieties. No one that could be a threat, she answered.

But she also became the first to mention an angle the police would find most interesting. Jude quoted Stacy as saying that she was pretty sure Steve Winzen was into drugs—she thought he did marijuana and maybe even sold it. Mari had made some comments to Stacy about Steve's marijuana activities contributing to the failure of their marriage. His looks and manner had frightened Stacy, and Jude warned her not to stay at Mari's after he arrived there. Jude had only seen Steve once—the day Mari visited Jude to finalize the job for Stacy. Steve had come to Jude's apartment looking for Mari, and Jude had immediately disliked him. He certainly didn't seem like the kind of guy who belonged with someone like Mari. He stood about five eight or five nine and weighed more than two hundred pounds, much of which he carried in his belly. He had long black hair and a mustache, and hid behind wire-rimmed sunglasses. Jude even found his voice irritating as he made an angry reference to Bobbi Turner and then told Mari to get home. Jude's embarrassed guest made her apologies and left. The police found all of this quite interesting.

They seemed sympathetic when Jude asked if there would have to be an autopsy of Stacy's body, but they explained that it was required in a homicide. Jude began to lose control again as she pleaded with Rick, "Please don't let them do that to her. Don't let them cut her up. She's suffered enough already." But the police said firmly, "It's the law."

After the detectives left, Jude turned to Rick and announced, "We have to get out of here. I can't stay here anymore. I can't live here now. I can't spend another night here."

Rick nodded. "We'll go to my place. It's okay. We can stay there."

Jude and Racheal threw a few things together and left before dark. The reporters and the crowd still were gathered across the street, and the television cameras captured Jude's departure.

She had a stop to make on the way. They drove to the group home for girls in nearby Florissant, where her daughter Johnna had been staying. She and Jude had been going through serious problems and this arrangement was best for everyone. When they pulled up in front, Johnna was waiting for them. Even at sixteen, she was perceptive enough to know that something was wrong from the way everyone at the home was acting, but no one would tell her what was going on. She ran toward Jude screaming, "Where's Stacy? Where's Stacy?" Jude tried to be gentle as she broke the news, but Johnna turned and ran. Jude had to chase her down. "Please, Johnna, I need you now. You have to help me get through this," Jude begged.

Johnna agreed to stay with Jude for a while. But Jude feared for the girls' lives. Was the killer out to exterminate her family? Was he looking for them, to kill them, too? She decided to take Johnna and Racheal to the home of the woman they called Grandma, the mother of Jude's former boyfriend. Surely they would be safe there. Then she and Rick drove to his home, where Jude spent the first of many sleepless nights.

She felt so helpless as she sat there in the dark. She had given birth to Stacy, had cared for her, had fed her, had given her baths, had disciplined her, had done the million little things parents must do. And now she had no control over what happened to her daughter. She had been murdered brutally and was about to suffer the violence of an autopsy, and there was nothing Jude could do. She had no say in any of this. In fact, she was only beginning to realize how few rights she had in what would be done in Stacy's name over the next several years.

She and Rick talked for hours. Who? Why? How? There were no answers now. Jude would get them, but there were none now. This was terrible for Rick, too. His son also was fifteen and had grown close to Stacy on the weekends when he and his two sisters stayed with their dad. Rick's daughters were thirteen and nineteen, still so close to Stacy's age that this seemed to threaten them, too.

Sometime between three and four in the morning, Jude curled up on the floor and just cried. She could not sleep and she would not rest. But she could cry, and she did that for hours.

She would swear that it stormed and rained on each of the next fourteen Thursdays.

Mari Winzen could hear her father's rage even before he walked through the door of Carol Brinkley's apartment about noon Thursday. Tears already were running down Joe Indelicato's face as he walked in and saw his daughter curled up, rocking back and forth on the couch. To Pat Indelicato, her daughter had never seemed so small as she did at that moment, almost as if she had become a tiny little girl again.

"What the hell happened?" Joe boomed as Mari ran to him. She almost collapsed halfway across the room, and Joe caught her in his arms. "What kind of bastards could do this?" he demanded angrily as his daughter almost disappeared into his embrace.

"Thank God you're here," Mari said as the tears started again. She had not been able to cry for what seemed like hours, until her parents walked in. Her father's Italian temper was engaged, but her Irish mother was in control. Pat Indelicato knew someone had to take charge, and, if necessary, she would fight off her own unbearable pain and do it. She had nearly fainted when Joe called and broke the news to her while she was on duty as a psychiatric nurse. Pat was under the mistaken impression that Stacy had killed Tyler and then committed suicide. Pat was furious at this girl's mother for letting such a troubled teenager babysit a vulnerable little boy and then take his life in this disturbed and tragic act. What a terrible waste, Pat fumed.

But she knew she would have to stay strong when her husband's anger seemed to be taking over on the drive to Mari's. Joe was shouting about the "goddam barrels" in the highway construction zone and was nearly frantic as they arrived. The crowd of spectators outside parted, as if they recognized the wounded grandparents arriving in the midst of this tragedy.

Joe was demanding to know what had happened, and Mari could say only that she had heard someone in the crowd of police officers, paramedics, and firefighters say the children had been drowned—murdered. She knew their bodies had been found in the bathtub, but she knew nothing beyond that.

Pat realized her impression had been wrong. Stacy was as much a victim as Tyler. Lord, this was a double murder. This was not random; it was not accidental. Murder—that word that everyone hears so often but hopes will be warded off through some magic that protects them and their loved ones—had found the Indelicatos. They were not insulated from this violence.

Pat was trying to comfort Mari and Joe when a paramedic's voice outside the open apartment door was heard mentioning that the water had been scalding. In a moment among many that would bind Jude and Mari together forever, Mari now erupted in agonized screams as she grabbed at her father.

"Not hot water! No, no! Don't tell me that! Not hot water!"

Joe flew from the apartment to chastise the officials in the hall to watch their damned mouths. The stunned paramedic and others mumbled their apologies.

Pat also realized from the muffled conversations that Tyler's and Stacy's bodies still were in the apartment. She could not allow Mari to see them being wheeled out. That could push Mari beyond some undefined limit that seemed ominously close for the woman who sat there shivering and sobbing so deeply. It was time for Pat to sweep Mari into the security of her parents' protection, turning back the clock to the time when Mari was a child. "Come on, hon. Let's go home. We have to get you out of here. Come home with me and Dad. Let's go home."

As Mari would for some time, she submissively let Pat lead the way. Mari had indeed become a child again. She could not think for herself or make any decisions for herself. She was too numb, too wounded, too confused. She would follow anyone who seemed to know what to do next.

Mari certainly had no idea. She stood almost like a robot and walked slowly between her parents, their arms enfolding her safely as they guided her to their car outside. Pat wrapped her white lab coat around Mari's trembling shoulders. She looked more like a little girl headed home to ward off a nagging cold in the sanctuary of her own room than a woman who had suffered every parent's worst nightmare.

On the way to the car, Mari saw a crying Bobbi Turner outside the building and went to her. Mari asked if she had seen or heard anything. Bobbi said no; she had no idea what had happened.

Mari couldn't look back at the building as they drove away. She knew she could never go back there, and she felt utterly lost. What would she do now?

After the fifteen-minute drive to the Indelicato house in Ballwin, Mari took her surviving son, Brian, into his bedroom and told him that his half brother, the little boy who loved him so much and had been so close to him, had been murdered. The thirteen-year-old took the news hard. His blond head dropped and he cried. It was the last time he would be able to cry for Tyler for years; another victim.

As members of the huge Indelicato clan began arriving, Pat gave tranquilizers to Mari and Carol Brinkley. Carol went to bed in a guest room and Mari returned to the security of her parents' bedroom. The telephone was ringing constantly, and soon the house would be packed with relatives bringing food and consolation. Aunts and uncles and cousins and friends would crowd the living room and dining room, the garage and basement, and spill over onto the front porch and patio. It was the Indelicato way, the Sicilian way.

Ahead of many of the relatives, the police arrived about four o'clock to interview Mari. Her emotions remained raw and unchecked, but the police were able to get a little useful information from her. As she sat curled up and quivering at the head of her parents' bed, breaking periodically into uncontrolled sobbing, she was able to give several interesting leads to the detectives who perched so awkwardly and self-consciously on the end of the bed.

She thought her former boyfriend, who had lived in the apartment with her, was psychotic and a habitual liar. He had strange flashbacks to his service in Vietnam, talked about having a friend who was killed there, and claimed to have lost a lung to a wound for which Mari had seen no scar. He treated Tyler well, but Mari sensed that he resented how much of her time the boy took. She had run the guy off after she learned he was still married.

He seemed the most likely suspect to her, although there had been an ugly incident with a man who had lived in an apartment upstairs with his wife. He had come on to Mari at a neighborhood party one night and she had rebuffed him; after she went home, she had had to chase him away from her door with orders to stay the hell away from her. A bit later, she had heard the sound of her bedroom screen being torn, and she had been sure it was an angry response by the man or an unsuccessful attempt to get in. He ex-husband, Steve Winzen, had explained the facts of life to the guy in a frank discussion a few days later, and the man had left town soon after that. The landlord had fixed the screen, so it had nothing to do with the tear in the one in Tyler's window today.

Mari explained that Steve Winzen was in Las Vegas with his girlfriend, Patty Garner*. They had been notified and were arranging for a flight home. He certainly wasn't a suspect, Mari added, although she had found some of his friends to be questionable characters. She had decided to hold back from the police one other aspect of Steve's life—his longtime marijuana dealing. She didn't see how that could have any connection to this horror, and she didn't feel like going through all of that now.

But she startled the cops by suggesting that Brenda Turner could have had something to do with the murders. Mari had outraged Brenda by firing her daughter, Bobbi, and replacing her with Stacy as Tyler's baby-sitter. Brenda and Bobbi, both chunky and unappealing, always seemed jealous of the prettier Stacy, and losing the baby-sitting job to her seemed to fuel that hostility from Brenda. Mari said Bobbi had been promiscuous, having sex with a number of young men who included workers at the construction site down the road. Bobbi had even taken Tyler to the apartment of a man across the street and then locked Tyler out of the bedroom while she had sex with the guy. Tyler's innocent description of that bizarre episode had been the final straw, forcing Mari to act on her plans to fire Bobbi. After that, Brenda had not talked to Mari for some time, and had once referred to Tyler as a little brat.

Mari had found other reasons to wonder about Brenda, to speculate that she might even be mentally ill. She seemed obsessed with sex. The first time they met, Brenda had launched into a discussion that ranged from mentions of dildos to the fact that she didn't wear panties. Stacy told Mari that Brenda had once held down a boy who was visiting Bobbi and urged Bobbi and Stacy to pull down his pants.

Brenda also had the unique ability to walk right into any apartment; as the resident manager for the landlord, she had a master key. Several tenants had complained about Brenda's just unlocking their doors and walking in for unannounced visits. That could have explained the lack of forced entry.

So Brenda had something of a motive; she had a bizarre, unpredictable personality; and she had easy access. And Mari offered one more other tidbit that made the mix even more suspicious. Brenda was reading a book Mari had lent her and it included an incident where a woman was drowned in a bathtub.

The cops didn't know it then, but they would find more and equally ominous oddities about the Turners in the very near future.

After the police left, Mari tried to visit with her relatives and friends, but it was almost impossible. The whole situation was unreal. She refused to believe Tyler was dead, to accept that he could have been murdered so heinously in his own apartment on a summer day. She never had even known anyone who died, so how was she to cope with the murders of her son and a young friend she had come to love? She went through the motions, accepting hugs and condolences. But none of this could be true. All she really knew was that she felt this horrible pain and she felt lost. She had been so independent, living in her own home and raising her own family. But now it was all gone—her son, her home, her life. There was no place in the world that was hers.

The evening news bulletins about the murders—obviously television's lead story for the day—sent Mari into a rampage of screams to turn off the TV. She didn't want to see or hear any of this. She finally took one of the many phone calls coming in, only to have a friend ask if she knew who had done it and if the killer had really used scalding water on the kids. Mari threw the phone across the room and fled to her parents' bedroom. She hadn't even begun to think about who or why yet. There was much too much to get through before any of that became important.

Pat Indelicato could tell her daughter was holding reality at a distance—as if she were watching a movie and waiting for it to end. Pat worried about what would happen when Mari realized it wouldn't end, when she really began to feel and to understand what had happened.

Pat also was trying to keep the lid on things in the house that evening. Despite the family's genuine sorrow, the gathering occasionally had taken on something of a festive air as relatives who saw each too infrequently enjoyed each other's company. She was glad when everyone finally left. Pat and Joe joined Mari in their bedroom, and the three of them huddled together on the bed. For Joe and Pat, it brought back memories of happier days when their little girl had climbed into bed with them. But there was no simple joy it in this time.

As they sat there, Mari's croaking voice whispered, "The Sack Man." The pain for Pat and Joe Indelicato was overwhelming. In their family, the Sack Man was the equivalent of the bogeyman or one of the other nursery-rhyme villains who always lurked in the shadows, threatening to snatch a child and run off with him, never to return him to his family. For the Indelicatos, the Sack Man was the faceless evil that parents named in warnings to their children.

"The Sack Man got Tyler," Mari moaned. "I know that's what Tyler was thinking when . . ." She couldn't say it. "My God, Mom, the Sack Man got Tyler."

They didn't say much more that night; they just clung to each other. They may have dozed briefly now and then, but they all watched the sun rise. They weren't even aware they still were wearing the same clothes they had put on a day ago—before their world caved in.

CHAPTER 4

Detective Bob Miller squatted on his haunches on the floor and looked around the bathroom he had come to know very well in just a couple of hours Thursday afternoon. Typical of apartment bathrooms everywhere, it was decorated right out of the pages of a Middle America catalog. The linoleum floor, intended to look like brown quarry tile, was complemented by a tan shag rug notched to fit around the toilet, with a matching mat in front of the vanity and cover on the toilet seat. Dark brown towels hung from the bars on the shower doors and wall. Personal toiletries sat here and there. On the dark wood vanity sat a child's electric toothbrush molded into an Ewok creature from the *Star Wars* movies. One item that stood out painfully was the yellow blanket someone said was the little boy's security blanket; it was on the floor between the tub and the toilet.

But this compact bathroom was vastly different from most crime scenes. Bob Miller couldn't find a single fingerprint anywhere, and it was driving him nuts. The killer had to have touched something. How could there be no prints on the glass doors on the tub? None on the walls or faucet? None on the vanity or the toilet? He had checked everything in that room above the water line in the tub, and found nothing. He had never processed a crime scene that had absolutely no fingerprints. But this place had been wiped clean—top to bottom, side to side. Three empty cardboard rolls from toilet paper had been found among the cotton balls and other bits of trash on the floor, so Miller assumed the killer had used toilet paper to wipe everything down. Flushing three rolls probably had plugged up the toilet, causing the water to run. That was what Jude had heard through the locked door. Bob even dusted the flush handle for prints; clean again.

This guy was very careful and amazingly cool. He had just drowned two children and he was taking a lot of time to remove any evidence—all while the bodies lay submerged in the tub in front of him. He had to be a sociopath; it took someone mighty cold to pull that off. Staying that long in a room with those bodies required a thick skin. To Miller, that nearly ruled out a boyfriend; too icy for that.

And why kill Tyler? What could be the motive for that? He was just three. What threat was he, unless he could identify the killer? So the killer had to be someone Tyler knew. But why had this happened at all? What could demand the murders of these two kids?

Despite the frustrating lack of evidence in the bathroom, Miller was done with that part of his work; he could release the bodies to the custody of Dr. Gordon Johnson, the medical examiner for Jefferson County. As Miller ran the video camera and Captain O'Rando watched, Johnson dragged the bodies out of the water and laid them on the floor. O'Rando was disturbed that Johnson had not spread a sheet under the bodies to collect any evidence, such as hairs or fibers. That could have cost them valuable clues, the captain thought. But he had no right to interfere with Johnson.

The three men then conducted an initial examination of the bodies. They noticed a couple of marks on Stacy's face, perhaps from being slapped. There were other marks around her throat, indicating she had been choked. She might have struggled with her killer, so Miller checked for skin scrapings under her nails; but again, there was no evidence. He covered the hands with plastic bags in case something showed up later. Tyler's body bore no noticeable marks from a struggle, but the skin around his arm and wrist had slipped from the damage by the hot water.

Dr. Johnson zipped up the body bags and enlisted some of the paramedics to help him load them onto gurneys and roll them to the waiting ambulances. They would be driven to Jefferson County Memorial Hospital for the autopsies.

As the bodies were rolled out, Miller felt a chill down his spine. *We've got to get this guy off the streets,* he was thinking. *If he is capable of this, he is capable of anything.*

He may even decide he likes this kind of action. We've got to get this guy.

O'Rando stepped out of the building to watch the bodies being loaded into the ambulances and saw something else that made him wince. In the street nearby, Sheriff Buck Buerger was holding an impromptu press conference. When the sheriff saw O'Rando, he cut short his comments and ended the conference. Buerger knew he had been caught in a stumble. The Major Case Squad always handled press releases when it was conducting an investigation. That prevented the release of too much information or of strategically damaging information at a delicate stage in the case. Buerger would call O'Rando later to apologize. O'Rando understood the need for an elected official to work the media, and he took it easy on Buerger. "I just need to know what you said," the captain explained.

Back inside the apartment, the evidence expert had begun his fingerprinting efforts in the rest of the rooms. He dusted everything from windowsills to countertops to door handles to items on tables. He was desperate, leaving the black powder all over everything. And still nothing useful showed up. There were only the expected smudges from old prints—nothing fresh enough to offer any value.

Nobody is this good, Miller muttered. This guy had to mess up somewhere. This was becoming personal, a challenge from the killer to Miller. A fingerprint would be a real boost for the detectives, a direct link to this creep. If Miller got a print, he got the perp. As the evidence officer, Miller had a chance to put this guy away. But Miller couldn't find a single print. He was beginning to doubt his own abilities. What could he be missing? He dropped into a chair and looked anxiously around the apartment. Dammit. There had to be something there. But where? This place wasn't that big. What could he do now?

It was after ten that evening before he finally packed it in. It had been a long and unproductive day. All he really knew was that there had been no forced entry, the killer had cleaned up the scene, and he probably had loosened the kitchen curtains from their tiebacks to make sure no one saw him through the window while he roamed the apartment. The thumbtacks—one on the kitchen floor and one on the counter near the curtains—proved that pretty convincingly.

Miller would start fresh the next day; maybe things would be different then. But he had to go home with the image of those kids burned into his mind. He was glad his wife, Gloria, was a good listener who understood her husband's job and could ask good questions. Bob Miller already had one big question on his mind: what kind of animal could do this?

At the Major Case Squad's headquarters in Fenton, Steve Winzen had arrived late—about eleven o'clock—for his first interview with the detectives. He had been crying almost nonstop since Patty Garner awoke him with the news from Lester Howlett that morning. At first, Steve thought his son had drowned accidentally. He had called Lester back, only to get the horrible shock of learning that Tyler and Stacy had been murdered. Stacy was a sweet, beautiful girl who had taken good care of Tyler, and her death was a terrible loss. But Steve was barely able to deal with Tyler's death. His son had been a special child, particularly blessed and gifted by God, the only good thing to come from that troubled, doomed marriage; Steve saw incredible potential in Tyler. Ironically, Steve had feared an early death for the boy—a remnant from the haunting loss of Steve's younger brother, Teddy, so long ago. Teddy had died at three and a half of leukemia, and seven-year-old Steve had innocently thought a punch he had delivered to his brother's back one day had something to do with his death. He carried that guilt for years, and even as a thirty-three-year-old father himself, he had worried that there was some link between Teddy and Tyler. Just a few weeks earlier, after Tyler passed the ominous age of three and a half, Steve's father had told him to relax finally—Tyler had escaped the danger zone. And now this had happened. After crying for hours on the delayed flight from Las Vegas, Steve sat with the detectives who were trying to find out who killed his son. "Ask me anything," he said. "I want to do whatever it takes to find out who killed my son."

The police had been anxiously awaiting Steve's arrival from Vegas, eager to see if he could help or if the reports that he was a drug dealer had anything to do with what had happened that morning. The investigators already had checked out his alibi in Vegas, confirming it with the police and hotel there. The long-haired man with the biker looks who arrived for the interview was not the kind of person who endeared himself to the police; they had seen his kind before, and the attitude they perceived in him wore thin fast. But Winzen obviously was distraught over his son's death, and his grief struck them as genuine. He said he wanted to cooperate, but he couldn't veil a subtle animosity toward the cops. The feeling that the investigation had keyed in on him, suggesting that his drug dealing contributed to his son's murder, clearly bothered him.

That resentment was unmistakable to cops like Sergeant Tim McEntee, who had spent eighteen years in the toughest districts in the city of St. Louis and knew violent crime inside out. He had served ten years as a detective, many of them on the Major Case Squad; he even had been a deputy commander. As he looked at Steven Winzen, McEntee wondered what this guy was all about.

Steven openly admitted dealing marijuana for years, but added that he also worked for his father's construction business. He wasn't able to offer much in the way of motives or suspects, but he thought Bobbi Turner's anger at losing the baby-sitting job could have driven her to such a violent act; he also suspected the guy Mari had lived with could be dangerous. The interview gave the police no real help.

Captain John O'Rando's late-night meeting with his officers to analyze the case didn't produce much optimism for an immediate solution. Two dozen officers from eighteen different departments had come up nearly empty. Thirty-six residents of the apartment complex had been interviewed, and the only interesting reports were that several of the women also had received strange or obscene calls in recent weeks. That suggested the nasty calls to Stacy were just that—random calls from a resident jerk with a foul mouth and a lot of free time. The kids' mothers had offered a few leads worth following, but nothing that provided a prime suspect.

Then there were the Turners. They certainly seemed rather strange to O'Rando, even in the moments when he spoke briefly with them in the hallway that day. He wanted each of them interviewed carefully. They warranted close scrutiny.

The only bit of new evidence came from the medical examiner. The autopsy on Stacy's body that evening yielded a cause of death—drowning accompanied by strangulation. There was a large amount of fluid in her lungs, and the tissue in her neck showed hemorrhaging from what the doctor believed to have been hands placed around her throat. There were bruises to her face, forehead, and chin, with particularly large bruises around her left eye and on the right side of her face. There were more abrasions to her right elbow, her knees, and the left side of her groin. There were several contusions and abrasions to her lips, and the doctor noted that she had braces on her teeth. Some of the bruising to her face and scalp was so deep that corresponding contusions were found on the skull, although there were no fractures. She certainly had struggled with her killer, the doctor concluded.

Tyler's autopsy would be performed the next day, and drowning would be set as the cause of death. There were very small bruises on the corner of his left eye, eyelids, and jaw. But he had not been beaten or strangled; he had not been able to resist his killer as forcefully as Stacy.

As the squad broke up so some of them could get a few hours of sleep after two o'clock Friday morning, O'Rando could see the frustration in each officer's face. He felt it, too. Everybody was putting out extra effort because two innocent children had been murdered. Nothing brought out the humanity and dedication in cops as that did. Each cop swore a silent, secret oath to get this killer for Stacy and Tyler, and for their own kids.

Sergeant Tim McEntee felt that pressure down deep. He was hard-core: a big, burly blond with piercing blue eyes and a mustache usually accessorized by a smelly cigar, a saber-edged cynicism that life on the big-city streets had honed, and a "don't screw with me" attitude that suspects seldom wanted to challenge.

But the videotape of the scene in that bathroom reached out and grabbed McEntee when it was played at the meeting that night. The brutality took his breath away and imprinted an unforgettable image on his mind and heart. He never wanted to see the tape again, but it would never leave his mind's eye. For him, it set the tone for the investigation. This murder was face-to-face—no blast from a shotgun at long distance. It was hands-on, and it meant the killer was a cold son of a bitch who could snuff the life out of two kids. McEntee's son was nine and his daughter was six, and he wanted to make sure no one ever threatened them with this kind of violence.

He had been among those canvassing the neighborhood all day, and it had been frustrating to hear "no" repeated at the end of each question. Nothing seen and nothing heard. There was no break-in; there appeared to be no sexual motive; there was little evidence of a struggle; the torn screen surely was staged. The investigation was snowballing to nowhere.

He had helped interview both of the mothers and was struck by how different they were in their grief from the same crime. Mari Winzen was crushed by it, battered almost into unconsciousness. She had retreated into the pain that overwhelmed her. The interview in her folks' bedroom had been among the most excruciating McEntee had ever conducted. Mari had spent much of the time nearly hysterical, sobbing and crying, often barely coherent. What could have been routine turned into a long-drawn-out process as Mari slipped in and out of stories about her son and her divorce from his father. Despite the length of the interview, McEntee made only two pages of notes; there wasn't much of real value in what Mari could offer.

He knew he had seemed gruff, certainly abrupt, and perhaps even unfeeling a few times. When her family suggested the interview could wait until after the funeral, McEntee rather coarsely said that he wasn't going to leave their home until he had talked to her. He had explained firmly that he had to get information from her right then. Solving her son's murder could depend on it, and that was more important than sparing her feelings at that moment.

When he had to push her into reality and press her for answers, he did; and, bless her, she wanted to help. She didn't hesitated to provide hair samples after McEntee explained that they would be used to exclude hers from any others that might be found at the scene. She swore she never would return to her apartment, so McEntee described it to her to see if anything was changed or missing.

She didn't know anything about the torn screen in Tyler's bedroom, only the one already repaired in hers. She had been upfront about her problems—two divorces; a difficult, distant relationship with Tyler's father; several boyfriends over time; and a battle with Valium. But she hadn't mentioned allegations of Steve's drug dealing. McEntee would push her on that later. Maybe she would forgive his pugnacity one day, after the killer was caught. If she didn't, well, that was the price he was willing to pay for doing his job.

Jude Govreau was quite different. The normal grief was there, certainly, but she also was damned angry. She was burning with an almost vicious desire for revenge; she wanted blood. She was getting good support from her boyfriend, and she handled the sensitive questions about her and her daughter's lives pretty well. Jude candidly spoke of her two marriages and her three daughters by different men. And she insisted that Stacy was an innocent, sweet girl who didn't date and certainly had no dark, secret involvement in promiscuity or drug abuse. She wasn't inviting construction workers from down the street into the apartment for quickies. Jude could offer no real suspect or motive, but she certainly wanted to find the guy who had killed her baby.

Jude's sincere description of her daughter left the tough McEntee with a painful image of a girl who would have fought to protect little Tyler throughout the attack, if she had been able.

The Major Case Squad hit the streets early Friday morning, setting up a roadblock outside the apartment complex. Every driver was asked if he or she had seen anything the morning before. But nothing more helpful than a memory of a hitchhiker nearby was offered. Even that would be checked; the hitchhiker would be found later and interviewed.

Some other residents of the complex were being contacted Friday morning, and a couple of them had seen men in the vicinity of Mari Winzen's building; no one seemed particularly sinister, but the investigators would try to track down anyone who had been in the area. A neighbor named Tom Hawkins, who also was a jailer for the sheriff's department, had seen a man in his thirties standing between the apartment buildings at about five minutes after seven that morning. Hawkins had seen the guy around the complex a couple of times before, and they said hi as they passed that morning. The man had brown hair, a mustache, and tattoos on both arms.

Another good account of a man seen nearby had come from Neil Myrick, who lived in an upstairs apartment across the street from Mari Winzen. The report taken from him said he had been looking out his bedroom window at the rain about nine o'clock when he saw a man he thought might have come out of Mari's building. The report quoted a description of a man in his teens or early twenties, six feet tall, two hundred pounds, medium-length brown or darker hair, and wearing a blue speckled T-shirt. Myrick had turned away after seeing the man walk south toward Building 190.

The detectives were talking to as many people as possible that day, looking for anything that might point to a motive or suspect. A man in a nearby apartment at first denied and then admitted having sex with Bobbi Turner. It was his apartment where Tyler had been locked out of the bedroom. That seemed to confirm reports about the previous baby-sitter's promiscuity.

And Stacy's friends were confirming what the police already believed to be true about her: she was a popular, sweet, good-humored teenager with amazingly few problems and a clean record. A onetime boyfriend said he couldn't imagine how anyone could hurt her. Another boy claimed he had heard Stacy say she was afraid of Mari's ex-husband and that she was bothered by the catcalls and whistles of the construction workers down the street.

Bobbi Turner told detectives that she and Stacy had once smoked marijuana; Jude Govreau said Stacy had received counseling after that mistake and it had never been repeated. Bobbi at first denied the rumors of her sexual activity, but then admitted having sex three times with the man who lived in an apartment across the street. She admitted that she had taken Tyler to the guy's apartment on one of those occasions and said another rendezvous had happened in the nearby woods.

When she was reinterviewed later, she told a tale of how she and Mari Winzen went to Lester Howlett's apartment to get the keys to Steven Winzen's mobile home so they could clean it while he was out of town earlier that week. Howlett had asked Bobbi about his keys later, and Bobbi had mentioned that to Stacy. Stacy went to Howlett's apartment to tell him she would remind Mari to return the keys. Bobbi told the police Stacy thought Lester Howlett was very good-looking, for his age. Bobbi thought Stacy would have let Lester, the good-looking family friend, into Mari's apartment without worrying about him.

It would be years before Mari Winzen would hear the story about Steve's keys and deny it completely; she wondered where such a fabrication had come from. She had never had the keys to Steve's trailer and sure as hell would not have cleaned it for him. The only contact she knew of between Stacy and Lester Howlett was when he once asked her for Mari's telephone number at work; Stacy may have gone to his apartment to give him the number later, but Mari doubted it. Mari didn't think Stacy even knew where Lester lived.

As the canvassing continued, the man who used to live in the apartment above Mari described Steve as a biker type who could get loud and violent. Steve had once pushed his way into the man's apartment and threatened him over his untimely use of a vacuum cleaner. That fit with the cops' impression of Winzen.

A woman who had been driving by the apartments told detectives she had seen a slim young man with long, light-colored hair in front of the building where the murders occurred. Lisa Nelson* thought the guy might have come out of the building and seemed to be on drugs. He was carrying something in his right hand, but she couldn't tell what it was. She helped the police develop a composite drawing of the man's face using the Identi-Kit that uses overlays of different facial features to assemble the correct eyes, nose, mouth, and hair. The composite was circulated among the officers.

A woman in a building across the street offered an interesting suggestion for a motive. Ann Meyers* said she thought the murders may have been in retaliation for something related to drug dealing by Tyler's father. She had seen Steve Winzen visiting the nearby apartment of a man named Les and two men she believed were large-scale marijuana dealers.

Sergeant Tim McEntee would pay a return visit to Miss Meyers later, after her name came up in another interview. She confirmed a report that one of her neighbors, Lester Howlett, had tried to assault her sexually two months earlier. She had gone to his apartment after dinner with him and he had suddenly thrown her over his shoulder, carried her to his bed, and tried to take off her clothes. She had been able to roll off the bed and flee the apartment, and had allowed no contact with Howlett since then. Another intriguing story about this Howlett guy, McEntee thought.

In fact, Howlett was on the list of interviewees that morning. The man who had turned to stone when Mari Winzen ran to him for comfort became an emotional jellyfish in front of the cops. He cried off and on as he recounted his actions on Thursday. He had left his apartment early, about six-thirty, to go to a mobile home in nearby Imperial to see a friend, Eugene Fleer. But Fleer hadn't answered the door, and Howlett assumed he had been unable to wake him up. Howlett had gone home and, it turned out, had been the man who had been seen near the buildings by county jailer Tom Hawkins; Howlett remembered saying hi as they passed.

Howlett had gone back to his apartment and slept on the sofa until the maintenance man at the complex stopped by and told him what had happened to Tyler and Stacy. Lester had run to the apartment to see Mari and offer to call Steve in Vegas. Steve's girlfriend had answered the call and Lester had told her what had happened. Steve had called back and said he had booked a flight home for two in the afternoon.

The detectives were surprised when Howlett became so emotional that he was unable to complete the interview. They knew he was a close friend of Steve Winzen's and had known Mari and Tyler well, but his crying and sobbing seemed excessive. He looked fairly tough—only twenty-nine, well-built, six foot two, with dark brown hair and a mustache. But before they could ask him much about his friends or anyone he might suspect would want to hurt them, he was crying so hard—almost hysterically—that they decided to put the questioning off. They asked him to come to headquarters Sunday for a lengthier interview, and he agreed.

But Bob Lutz*, the maintenance man mentioned by Howlett, also had an interesting episode to recount about Howlett. Knowing that Howlett was friendly with the Winzens, Lutz had gone to Howlett's apartment about noon Thursday. Lutz found Howlett sitting on his sofa, readying his arm for an injection of cocaine. Lutz told Howlett what had happened, and Howlett reacted by shooting up, then saying he would go see Mari.

That certainly got the cops' attention. This brutal, cold crime could well be the work of someone on drugs, and Howlett could have been taking a pop to handle what he had just done in the apartment of his friends across the street. Could it also explain why Howlett had become so emotional during his interview with the police? Collapsing in sobs and tears seemed somewhat extreme for this guy, even if he was a close family friend. Was the crime drug-related, as the media always put it? Drugs as a stimulus or drugs as a motive? Either was possible in light of Howlett's activities.

Something else had struck the cops, too. The window at the end of the hallway outside Howlett's second-story apartment looked across the street and directly into Mari Winzen's kitchen window. That offered a unique perspective on the activities in Mari's apartment and could explain the third harassing call to Stacy the morning before, mentioning that the caller had waited until she woke up to ring again.

Lester Howlett had just made the very small list of suspects; in fact, Captain John O'Rando thought Lester probably had just earned the title of "prime."

The cops were anxious to talk to Howlett again on Sunday. No one suspected how that appointment would be broken.

For Jude Govreau, Friday had begun early, too. She started calling the police about seven o'clock to see if there had been any developments in the investigation. She hoped they had caught the guy already, and was disappointed they hadn't. She talked to Captain O'Rando, and he told her the first forty-eight hours were crucial; if the cops didn't break the case then, it could take years.

Most of Jude's day was consumed by two terrible responsibilities, and a drastic step Jude felt she had been forced to take. The responsibilities were the hardest—making arrangements for the cremation of Stacy's body and a memorial service, and making a hurried move out of the apartment and into Rick's house. The other step would come later.

In Jude's family, cremation was the preferred method for ending the body's time on earth—mostly because Jude's mother suffered from a fear of being buried alive. She had insisted that her body be cremated, and even Stacy had expressed a fear of a traditional burial. "Don't put me in the ground and leave me all alone there," she had said. So, just as she had when her mother died, Jude decided again for cremation. She would keep the ashes at home, so Stacy at least would stay close. Others might find that strange, Jude knew, but she didn't care. This was her baby and she had to do what was right for the two of them.

Jude went to a crematorium and picked out the most expensive urn they had; that was the least she could do for Stacy, and she would worry later about how to pay for it. The funeral director explained that he would arrange the cremation when the body was released by the medical examiner; Jude would be notified when to pick up the ashes. A memorial service was scheduled for one o'clock the next day, Saturday, at a nearby Baptist church.

More time Friday was taken up by moving. Rick and some of their friends handled what passed for packing, but really was shoving things into plastic bags and hauling them to the rented truck. Jude had only enough boxes to pack Stacy's belongings, and she did that alone. It was heartbreaking, but Jude hoped she would feel closer to Stacy for it. She even packed the contents of the wastebasket. She was shoving her own clothes into bags later when Rick walked in and spoke to her. Suddenly, Jude heard the screams coming from somewhere again. "How could someone murder Stacy?" the voice was shrieking. Then she realized the screams were coming from her.

After the packing, Rick and Jude made a stop to complete the actions thrust upon them that day: they bought a

.357 magnum revolver at a gun shop. The owner had recognized Jude from the television news and called the police to get the okay before selling her the pistol; the cops approved it. Jude and Rick filled out the paperwork, took it immediately to the Jefferson County Courthouse in nearby Hillsboro to clear the background check, and then returned to the shop to pick up the pistol.

For the foreseeable future, that gun would seldom be out of reach. If the killer was after Jude or the rest of her family, he would have to get past at least six deadly rounds to get them. Jude was terrified that might be exactly what would happen, but almost wished for a chance to look down the sights of that powerful handgun at the man who had killed Stacy. There would be no hesitation about pulling the trigger.

The hours were slipping by in a numbed, confused blur for Mari Winzen. She had no idea what time it was when Steve Winzen arrived at her parents' house Friday afternoon to see her for the first time since their son's death. She was crying almost hysterically as she sat on the patio and looked at this man who had been her husband. When he angrily demanded to know whether the killer could be a construction worker Mari had dated briefly, Mari was outraged. "How do I know it wasn't one of your drug-dealing friends or someone else you know through your illegal activities?" she shot back. They started to go after each other with wild accusations, but Mari's friend Laura Vitale intervened by screaming at both of them. Didn't they realize what had happened and what really was important now? Finally, Mari and Steve set aside their differences, put their arms around each other, and cried for the son they both had lost.

And then Steve Winzen went into a guest room and slept for two hours, until Lester Howlett arrived to pick them up. Howlett again contradicted his cold reaction to Mari, now crying with Steve to mourn Tyler. "We're going to get whoever did this, Steve. We'll get him, buddy," a weeping Lester Howlett kept telling his crying friend. But the inconsistency was lost on Mari; she wasn't even thinking about Lester's peculiar reaction the day before.

Steve was grateful to have Lester with him; he needed a

good friend on this day. It was comforting to be with someone who had loved Tyler so much, too. Steve remembered when Lester's estranged wife had finally agreed to allow him to keep their son one recent afternoon. Tyler and Lester's boy had been thrilled to see each other again and had played together with such joy that Lester had openly wept as he watched them. After Lester called Steve with the crushing news Thursday morning, he had spent the rest of the day reassembling Steve's ailing motorcycle; Lester knew his pal would need some therapeutic time on the road after he arrived home to this crisis. Friends like Lester were important at a time like this, Steve thought.

The cops' perception that the Turner family was on the weird side got more confirmation Friday afternoon. The interview Thursday with this family of recent transplants from Pennsylvania had offered few details of any use to the cops, but had highlighted the rather strange personalities of the Turners. In a follow-up interview, Jack Turner confirmed that his daughter, Bobbi, had been angry for a few days after she had been replaced by Stacy as Tyler's babysitter. But that faded simply to disappointment, and Bobbi had not remained angry. Then Turner startled the detectives by recounting his wife's opinion that Stacy had a crush on him. Nothing had ever happened to suggest that, but Bobbi had told Stacy about Brenda Turner's comments and Stacy had been so embarrassed she stayed away from the Turners' apartment for a while.

Jack Turner also surprised the police by admitting an arrest in Pennsylvania in 1976 for indecent exposure. He said the incident was out of character for him and was the result of his anger and emotional turmoil over his fear that Brenda was having an affair with another man. He got probation and never did anything like that again. The detectives ran a check in Pennsylvania and confirmed the charge and sentence.

The Turners indeed bore watching.

Detective Bob Miller wondered if the bathroom in that apartment was becoming an obsession. On Friday, he finally emptied the bathtub, but only after putting extremely fine filters over the drain to be sure no evidence went down the tubes. All he got for his trouble was some hair. He watched the videotape of the scene again and again. Why was all that trash on the bathroom floor in this immaculate apartment? He even called Mari Winzen to ask her. She didn't know where it had come from; it certainly hadn't been there before. But it did sound to her like two or three rolls of toilet paper were missing. To Miller, that confirmed his suspicion that the killer had used the paper to wipe down the room and then flushed the paper, clogging up the toilet. Mari also said she had indeed kept the kitchen curtains pulled back and tied. Again, Miller's assumption that the killer had closed the curtains was correct. So he knew more about what the killer had done, but none of that got him closer to the killer's identity.

Miller also attended the autopsy on Tyler's body, as he had Stacy's the day before. Both of these procedures wounded him; they were so sad. He bagged the kids' clothes as evidence and took the obligatory photographs.

And then he returned to the apartment. As he sat there in the quiet, searching his mind for some hint of what to do next, he began to cultivate a rather wild idea. A new technique for drawing out fingerprints that regular powder couldn't find had been catching on the last two years; Miller had tried it a few times himself with some success. The item in question was placed in a five-gallon aquarium with a plate holding the contents of a tube of superglue. The glue was then heated with a forty-watt bulb in the closed aquarium. The fumes it emitted adhered to any moisture or oils on the surface, pulling up and preserving every hidden streak or fingerprint in a white, plastic layer of hard glue.

Miller glanced around the little bathroom. Could a whole room be superglued? Why not? It would ruin the room, certainly, but who cared? That was someone else's problem, and Miller's only concern was capturing evidence. He bounced the unorthodox suggestion off some fellow officers and Captain O'Rando, and the answer always came back "Go for it."

With help from his colleagues, Miller sealed all cracks in the room and the exhaust fan with duct tape, squeezed six tubes of glue onto ashtrays, set a lightbulb close by, closed the door, and then sealed it from the outside with more duct tape. He let it cook overnight and then pried it open Saturday morning to see what this massive gassing had produced. Every surface in the room—including the walls, tub, vanity, and mirror—was coated with a sticky white film. Streaks from wiping the mirror were visible now. Water spots on the vanity and toilet stood out clearly. But there seemed to be little else new, until Miller checked the chrome showerhead and found one fingerprint. He looked closely. Yes! It was good enough for an identification. At last, a damned fingerprint. But again, how could this guy be so lucky that he just left one? Miller still wanted to shout for joy. He just hoped this was that missing link he had so desperately wanted. He removed the showerhead and placed it in a plastic bag for the crime lab. At last, some hope.

He looked around the apartment. Could he superglue the whole place? Nah, guess not.

On Saturday morning, after another night of collective mourning by the Sicilian family, Pat Indelicato decided it was time to broach a subject she had been putting off with dread. She turned to her daughter, who seemed to be getting tinier and more helpless by the hour, and said softly, "You know, Mari, we have to make the funeral arrangements."

Mari looked up at her mother with a lost look in her eyes. "Mom, I don't know how," she whispered. "I don't know how."

"We'll get through it together. I've never done it, either, but we'll get through it."

Mari didn't even know if there was any life insurance on Tyler. "How am I going to pay for this?" she asked pathetically. Her parents found a $2,000 insurance policy for Tyler among Mari's papers, and, knowing that would not cover the funeral costs, Mari's relatives guaranteed the balance.

The Indelicatos had been so blessed that they didn't even have a family funeral home; they agreed to a request by Steve's family to use the funeral home of a friend. Pat and Joe Indelicato led Mari by the hand, as if she were the age of her murdered son, and walked in Saturday afternoon to make the arrangements. They weren't sure when to schedule the services, since they still were waiting for the medical examiner to release Tyler's body. So the first chore was to choose a coffin, and the family was shown two in the pitiful size appropriate for a child—a white one with gold handles and a more appropriate metallic blue one with silver trim and handles.

Faced with such a terrible task, Mari and Steve broke down again and cried as they stood surrounded by the coffins. Mari could barely look at the little one she was beginning to realize would hold her son's body. My God, she thought, my child is dead. Tyler really is dead, and I have to do this. She pointed to the blue one.

Would the coffin be opened or closed? Mari insisted that it should remain closed; she knew her sanity could not survive looking at her son that way. Her family had kept secret the funeral director's advice to close the casket. As gently as he could, he had explained to the others that the hot water had not left Tyler's body in a condition to be viewed.

That still did not complete the arrangements, nor did it end the difficulties. The Indelicatos and the Winzens found themselves disagreeing over the location for the burial. Steve and his parents wanted Tyler interred in their family plot. "He's a Winzen," Steve said. But Mari mustered the strength to insist that Tyler would be buried with her family at the Calvary Cemetery in St. Louis. Her face tightened as she turned to Steve. "He's my son and he's just as much an Indelicato as he is a Winzen. He will be buried with my family in the Indelicato plot and that's all there is to it." She couldn't handle much of what was happening, but she knew this had to be done her way.

Rick Pashia was looking into the face of Sergeant Tim McEntee, and the cop's blue eyes seemed to be drilling holes through Rick's forehead. The glare was accusatory, and that was shocking. Rick, Jude, and Racheal had agreed to a request by the Major Case Squad to come to headquarters in Fenton on Saturday evening after the memorial service, even though they were physically and emotionally exhausted. At the small church, people Jude didn't even recognize had offered their heartfelt sympathies. It had been some comfort to see such a huge crowd, and know that so many shared in the loss of Stacy. But Jude was so deeply in shock that she didn't recognize many people who were actually friends. She was surprised and disappointed when Mari didn't attend, but Jude understood how distraught Mari was. She didn't know that Pat Indelicato had urged Mari to stay home. Pat worried that her daughter would shatter if she tried to sit through the service for Stacy.

Some who were there—Brenda and Bobbi Turner—sent Jude into another rage. Bobbi threw her arms around Jude's waist and cried, but Jude angrily pushed the girl away. Jude was convinced the Turners had hated Stacy, and both of them were on the short list of people Jude thought capable of involvement in the murders. She couldn't bear to have them at Stacy's service and was not going to be hypocritical enough to stand for it. She turned and, barely able to contain her hysteria, told Rick to get them out of the church and away from her. Rick ushered the surprised Turners away as Jude struggled to stay in control.

During the service, Jude kept looking at the photograph of Stacy that sat on the table in the front of the church where a coffin would have rested at a traditional funeral. How could anyone have done such things to that face? Then came the songs Stacy loved so much. An aunt of one of Stacy's best friends sang Stacy's favorites by gospel-rock singer Amy grant—"El Shaddai" and "Angels." The memories of Stacy listening to those songs ripped into Jude's heart, and she covered her mouth as she began to sway back and forth. Soon the screams that seemed so far away had started again. Rick hurried Jude to the rest room, where she collapsed onto the floor to rock and wail as the pain tore at her. It was all she could do to get through the rest of the service. The memorial and the gathering of family and friends at Rick's house afterward had brought that intangible mix of comfort and pain, and all of it was so traumatic.

And now, Rick was looking into the hard eyes of Tim McEntee. The cops had separated Rick, Jude, and Racheal, taking each of them into a different interview room after the uncomfortable experience of providing hair samples to check against any hair found at the scene.

Rick was flabbergasted when McEntee read him the Miranda rights. The implication in that was clear; he was being treated as a suspect, and that sent chills through him. And a distinct fear started churning as McEntee leaned menacingly over Rick and growled, "You're our number one suspect. The last case that was similar—the boyfriend did it."

At six foot two and 240 pounds, Rick Pashia was not easily intimidated. But Tim McEntee had done it. Rick was scared, and his stomach was starting to flutter. McEntee probably couldn't have backed Rick down in a bar somewhere, but it was different in this room. Rick was exhausted and frightened, and was starting to think that even Peewee Herman might be intimidating under these circumstances. This blond bear with the badge obviously could cause Rick untold trouble if he really zeroed in on him.

"We've been getting some calls," McEntee was continuing, "that you might be a womanizer and you might beat up women. And that maybe you abused Stacy and she was going to tell Jude on you. That's why you might have killed her. Is that what happened?"

Rick tried to remain calm and answer in a steady voice that wouldn't sound guilty or even nervous. He really wanted to help the investigation, and he guessed it made sense for the police to bear down on him now. He had been expecting some very close questioning, but this accusatory tack had been a nasty surprise. He denied everything, of course. He had dated a few women since his divorce, but certainly was no womanizer. He and Jude had been together for almost two years, he had been married for thirteen years before that, and he never had laid an angry hand on any woman. Had Rick used drugs? McEntee wanted to know. He denied that, too. But how could he prove anything to this cop?

McEntee's favorite interviewing style seemed to be working again. He was the bad cop, and it was a role he relished. It suited him well, and he played it to the hilt. He intimidated with the swagger in his six-foot-three, 275-pound frame, and he punctuated with the stinking cigar clenched between his teeth and protruding from under his mustache. He loved to lean in close to let his smelly, smoky breath offend the subject that much more. And when he cranked up the volume in his booming voice, few people could remain cool and calm.

Rick Pashia was no exception. He was beginning to sweat, and he had done nothing wrong. He denied and

denied, and then McEntee would go over it all again, looking for that crack, that one inconsistency. To Rick, the look
in McEntee's eyes was unmistakable. He seemed to really
think Rick had done it, and he was going to get him, no
matter what. Rick hoped telling the truth would protect
him; it was awfully hard to concentrate on minuscule details
when that powerful presence got in his face. McEntee
stormed in and out of the room, allowing the good cop to
try to put Rick off his guard. But Rick was sure he could
hear voices behind that mirror that hung on the opposite
wall—just like in the movies. Surely there were other detectives watching closely as McEntee tried to sweat a confession out of him.

With McEntee out of the room, Rick turned to the other
cop and asked if the police really were getting calls about
him from people accusing him of the murders. "Yeah," was
the answer. "We're getting some calls about you and the
Turner woman. But you're in the lead."

Jude Govreau couldn't believe her ears. After several
trips through her memory of the events of Thursday morning, the cop talking to her in this little interviewing room
actually had leaned over her and asked the most insulting,
gut-tightening question Jude had ever heard.

"What would you say if I told you one of Stacy's friends'
mothers called us and said you had called her, and had told
her you killed Stacy?"

Jude could not believe it. She never had dreamed she
would be considered a suspect. The victim was her own
daughter, for God's sake. She wouldn't kill her own daughter, and it was perverse beyond contemplation for anyone
to suggest she would. She felt a new pain through her heart.
Oh God, the head games are starting, she thought. She
stared at the cop and said angrily, "I would say whoever
told you that was sick and should be put away."

That didn't seem to impress the detective. "One woman
called and said she was a friend of Stacy's. She thought
Stacy was keeping you and Rick from getting married and
she wondered if you two had something to do with Stacy's
death. We've also had numerous calls saying that Rick was
messing with Stacy and she was going to tell you. That's

why he killed her, and he killed Tyler because Tyler knew him," the cop said.

This seemed worse than the suggestion that she had done it, mostly because Jude could not bear to lose trust in someone else close to her. Rick never had exhibited any violent or abusive tendencies, but she began to let that sliver of doubt work its way into her mind. He was the only friend she had then, and she was going home with him when the grilling by police was done. What if she had been wrong about a man again?

She defended Rick without hesitation, but she couldn't seem to convince the police that he could not have hurt Stacy or Tyler. Jude was getting more and more frightened. The police seemed so sure Rick was involved. Did they know something she didn't?

They worked on her for more than two hours, and she felt weak by the time they said she could go. In the hallway, she saw Rick leaving a room down the hall, and she realized he had been through something similar. He looked almost as deathly gray as he had in the apartment doorway. Racheal, whose questioning by Captain John O'Rando had been kind and gentle, joined them as they left the police station.

In the parking lot, Jude vomited and Rick began to cry. "They said I did it, Jude," he said softly. "I could never do anything like that. They read me my rights, like I was a suspect. I couldn't believe how scared I was."

With his arms around her, Jude looked up and said, "I'm scared, too. Of you."

Rick looked crushed. "What?" he sputtered.

"They said you killed them, Rick. They said you had been messing with Stacy and you killed her to keep her from telling me. They even told me someone called and said I had confessed to killing them."

As Racheal joined in their embrace, Jude and Rick stood by the car and cried. Rick was so shaken he couldn't drive, so Jude slid behind the wheel. As they pulled away, they decided they had to have alibis from that point on if the police were going to treat them as suspects. They drove to his parents' home in south St. Louis County and began the first of many nights spent with friends and relatives. And, no matter where they were, a pistol was always within reach. No one knew what really was out there.

Jude played all the possible scenarios through her head that night. Had Rick really been in the apartment all morning that day? Could he have slipped out without waking her? Was she so sure now that she had seen his feet at the end of the bed when she glanced into the bedroom that morning? She knew these thoughts were ridiculous, but she couldn't chase them away. She felt so alone again. There was no one she could turn to now. Her daughter was murdered and she couldn't go back to her home. She had hidden her surviving children and the cops had accused her and her boyfriend of being the murderers of her own child. How could this be happening?

CHAPTER 5

Lester Howlett was dead.

The news was such a lightning bolt that Captain John O'Rando almost dropped the phone. He hadn't been home very long when his beeper went off about one o'clock Sunday morning; the news from the Jefferson County Sheriff's Department made him shudder. My God, he thought, I'm dead tired and now a prime suspect is dead. What the hell did a third death mean to this double-murder case? Was it a macabre coincidence? A pivotal development that somehow would point to the kids' killer? Or just a terribly confusing addition to this already mystifying investigation? Whatever it meant, the Major Case Squad now had three deaths to investigate, and he knew everyone on the team already was exhausted.

Lieutenant Ed Kemp, still feeling the effects of a rare stop for a few drinks with Bob Miller, ran for the phone that was ringing as he walked into his house; it was O'Rando.

"Guess who died tonight, Ed."

Kemp didn't feel playful. "Don't screw with me, John. I've had a tough night."

"Lester Howlett."

"I said don't screw with me. This is not funny, and it's too late for this."

"It's the truth."

Kemp knew Howlett was being touted by some of the detectives as the lead suspect and was supposed to come in Sunday morning for an in-depth interview because he had blubbered too much when they tried to talk to him Friday. And now he was dead. Something crucial had happened here, and it had to be more than coincidental to the Winzen-Price murders, Kemp was sure.

The page for Bob Miller went off while he was on his

way home, also feeling groggy from tossing back a few with Kemp. He turned around and headed for the new location where he would continue his frustrating service as crime scene technician in this case that had just taken a very surprising twist.

Sergeant Tim McEntee wondered if this was a suicide. Was it too much hope that there would be a suicide note confessing to the murders? Had this doper been overcome by remorse for his evil deeds and taken the most direct way out? That would be a great way to wrap up this awful case, McEntee mused.

But as the cops gathered at the scene, they knew they would have no such luck. Lester Howlett's body lay sprawled on the floor next to a bed in a tacky house trailer at the Spanish Manor Mobile Home Park in Imperial, about six or seven miles from the apartment complex where Howlett had lived and the kids had died. The trailer was owned by an ex-con whose name had popped up before as one of Howlett's buddies—Eugene "Geno" Fleer. The dark, trim Fleer told police he and Howlett had returned about eight o'clock Saturday evening from a visit to Howlett's friends and relatives in Rockford, Illinois. Thirty minutes later, Fleer had gone to Pete Wendler's* house to borrow a television set, and he and Wendler had returned about eleven o'clock to find Howlett dead. Wendler nodded his agreement with Fleer's account of the evening.

The cops already knew Howlett was a cocaine user; the maintenance man had seen that. So there was a good chance that Howlett had either overdosed accidentally, overdosed on purpose to commit suicide, or been the target of a "hotshot"—a massive drug dose administered by someone else as a murder weapon. The last possibility was McEntee's choice. But all three alternatives opened up all sorts of avenues for exploration.

As Howlett's body was taken to the hospital for an autopsy set for the next day, the detectives went to work again. This time, they fanned out through the trailer court, another canvass looking for potential witnesses. But this was Saturday night, and very few residents were home. Those who were had heard nothing at Fleer's trailer. There wasn't much else to do at that hour, so the cops planned to regroup Sunday morning and try to find out what had happened to Lester Howlett.

His distraught parents in Rockford could offer little insight when McEntee called them that morning. His mother had seen him Saturday afternoon and he had seemed in good spirits. His father had feared that Lester was using drugs, and now it seemed confirmed in the worst way imaginable.

The police searched Howlett's apartment but found nothing that told them anything about his death. As they were leaving, they ran into a very drunken man who said he was looking for Lester. When Mark Gerber* said he was a close friend of Howlett's, the police asked him to accompany them to headquarters, for an interview. After getting Gerber's account of his activities on Thursday, they told him Howlett was dead from a suspected overdose. Gerber was shaken by the news, and tears rolled down his cheeks.

"It don't surprise me," he said. "I seen Howlett using cocaine and I had been afraid he was using too much for some time. Me and some of his friends have been trying to get him to quit, but he wouldn't listen."

Gerber was sure Lester had died from an overdose, and he could only think of one person who would want to do harm to him. Gerber had heard on the street that Howlett had been involved in a drug rip-off somewhere in north St. Louis County; the victim was named Dave Helmond.* The police had been called, Gerber had heard, but they hadn't been told the whole story. Could the murders of Tyler and Stacy have been retaliation for the rip-off? the cops asked. Gerber shrugged. "Maybe, but I doubt it."

The autopsy Sunday evening did little to clear up the confusion about the way Howlett had died. There were no signs of violence to the body, which was decorated with a Harley-Davidson tattoo on the right biceps and a flowery design on the other arm. There was no obvious evidence of drug abuse—no notable needle marks from injections and no irritation around the nostrils from snorting. The internal examination by medical examiner Gordon Johnson showed why Howlett had died—he had drowned in his own blood that had filled his lungs. But Johnson said there was no medical evidence to explain that. No heart or circulatory damage; no chest wound; no injury to the throat. Lab tests would be needed for a definitive answer, and that would take a couple of days.

But there were some marks on Howlett's body that interested the cops. The knuckles and middle two fingers on his right hand had been scraped, and the injuries were fresh. The doctor also noted small, healing lacerations on Howlett's lower inside right arm, on the web between his left thumb and forefinger, and on his lower inside left arm. Could those injuries be from struggling with Stacy Price?

And there were two other scrapes, probably three or four days old, that really intrigued the investigators. They were on Howlett's penis. Dr. Johnson called the marks unusual and was unable to suggest what had caused them. But the cops—looking for any connection to the murders—remembered that Stacy wore braces on her teeth. Johnson nodded; dental braces could have made those marks. Had Stacy died when she resisted Howlett's demand for the sexual act of his choice?

Tyler Winzen's wake began Sunday afternoon. Mari and her family spent the morning shopping for their own funeral clothes, and Mari took a long time selecting an outfit for Tyler. But the closer the time to go to the funeral home, the more immobilized she became. She had started to feel as if she were encased in a glass tomb that could be penetrated only by the pain in her heart—real, physical pain from a broken heart. She heard and felt almost nothing else. When she finally eased into the bathtub, she was unable to do anything but sit there and stare at the wall. She had no idea what to do next. Finally, Laura Vitale whispered, "Come on, Mari, you've got to do this."

"I can't," Mari pleaded.

"You've got to."

Laura, proving that true friends will do anything for someone they love, shaved Mari's legs, washed her hair, and bathed her as if she were a helpless baby. Through the fog, Mari remembered how lovingly Laura had held Tyler in the hospital soon after his birth, even before Steve Winzen had held his son; that had irritated Steve. But it seemed right as Mari looked into Laura's face now. Laura was showing the same love for Mari, and Mari would love her forever for it.

But even that couldn't insulate Mari from the trauma of arriving at the funeral home and looking for the first time at the closed coffin adorned by Tyler's photograph. The bouquets of flowers filling the parlor were almost overwhelming. Mari knew what was happening, but she could not accept the fact that Tyler's body was in that box. Instead, she circulated around the room, greeting the hundreds of mourners who filed through. Knowing that there would be another night of visitation at the funeral home on Monday before the funeral on Tuesday, Mari was able to hold off her fears of the inevitable—the moment when she would really have to say goodbye. That was something she could not begin to think about.

Back at the Indelicato house after the funeral home closed, word arrived that Lester Howlett had died, probably of a drug overdose. Mari was horrified. "Everyone I know is dying," she screamed. What a morbid coincidence, she thought, that a friend should die so soon after the murders. To Mari Winzen, there certainly could be no direct link between these tragic events.

Steve Winzen heard about his friend's death Sunday and could not believe he had lost two of the people he loved most in such a short period. The grief was accompanied by a strange foreboding. Would the authorities try to pin the murders on Lester now? His proximity to the scene and the timing of his death certainly made him an easy target. What an appalling thing to do to his buddy.

Jude Govreau gently placed the urn bearing Stacy's ashes on the shelf in the living room on Sunday afternoon. The funeral director had called earlier to announce the urn was ready. After some stiff but heartfelt words of sympathy from the director, Jude carried the urn in the blue velvet bag to the car, where she and Rick sat weeping for thirty minutes before they could drive away. But Jude felt a little better after she had placed the urn on the shelf. Stacy was safe now, Jude thought. The killer couldn't get to her now, couldn't do her any more harm. When they visited a friend later, Jude took the urn. She couldn't risk leaving Stacy's remains unguarded, just in case the killer was watching.

Rick and Jude still were talking late Sunday night when the telephone rang. A friend called to ask if they had seen the news on television—the police were saying an unidentified suspect in the kids' murders had died the night before in Fenton. Jude immediately called the Major Case Squad headquarters; the detective said all he could tell Jude was that the investigators were looking into a suspicious death. Further details would have to wait until they knew more, he said.

The news was unsettling to Jude. Had the killer cheated her again by dying before she could confront him, before she could find out why this had happened? Did this mean she might never learn the truth? That possibility was infuriating. She could not live with that. She had to have justice, complete and sure. The death of this unnamed man, this could-be killer with no face for Jude to imagine and hate, could not thwart her. She would not allow it.

Monday was a very busy day for the Major Case Squad. The first order of business was for its board of directors to approve a three-day extension of the squad's five-day time limit. It was only a formality; no one opposed the extra time to take this investigation as far as the squad could.

Eugene "Geno" Fleer hadn't had much to say to the police at his trailer Saturday night, so he was brought in bright and early Monday for an interview at the command center. The questioning by two detectives began with his activities on Thursday. To the cops, this guy with his raven-black hair swept back meticulously seemed cool and hard, unconcerned as he answered, and clearly not intimidated by them. He calmly explained that he had slept until eleven o'clock Thursday morning and then dropped by Lester Howlett's apartment between twelve-thirty and one. He was surprised to see all the cops at the building across the street and wondered what had happened. He got no answer at Howlett's and was departing when he ran into the maintenance man, Bob Lutz, and asked about all the heat next door. Lutz surprised him with the news of the murders, and Fleer went home. He talked to Howlett on the phone about six o'clock that evening, and Howlett said the kids' bodies had been found in the bathtub. Howlett was upset and said he had hated calling Steve Winzen in Vegas to break the news. Howlett had been on the phone with Steve when Fleer was knocking on the door that afternoon. Fleer drank beer at home alone that evening and turned in about ten-thirty.

Fleer's tough facade cracked a bit when the detectives began pursuing details about his activities Friday and Saturday. He suddenly couldn't remember much and was beginning to seem a little nervous. On Friday, he was at Howlett's apartment for a while and then went to another friend's house. Okay, he mumbled. That wasn't true. He had been at yet another friend's house Friday for spaghetti when Lester dropped by and invited him to tag along on an overnight drive to Rockford, Illinois, to buy cocaine.

That shocked the detectives. Guys like Geno Fleer didn't offer that kind of information to the cops very freely. Where was Fleer going with this?

He said they made the eight-hour drive to the home of a friend of Howlett's in Rockford and Fleet slept there while Howlett left to visit his mother. While Howlett was gone, he bought an ounce of cocaine from an unknown dealer. They drove home Saturday afternoon, arriving in Fenton about eight o'clock, and Howlett stopped by his apartment to pick up a scale and materials to cut the cocaine before he started selling it. They went back to Fleer's trailer, because Howlett said he didn't want to cut the cocaine at his place—with the murders across the street, there was too much heat around. Fleer then picked up his earlier account—he had returned from a trip to borrow a television and found Howlett dead about eleven o'clock. Fleer said he flushed the cocaine down the toilet before he called the police.

He added another detail he thought the police should know because it was so strange. Howlett had said his penis was sore from having sex with a woman earlier that week. That rang a bell with the cops, who knew of Howlett's rather personal injury. Geno Fleer's knowledge of that was interesting. Was he telling the truth, or was he molding a story to fit the facts he knew the cops would have learned?

Drugs. More and more about drugs. During another interview that morning with Steve Winzen, Sergeant McEntee explained that he really didn't give a damn about who was or wasn't dealing drugs. He just wanted to know the truth so he could try to solve this double murder and perhaps learn what really had happened to Lester Howlett. He wasn't looking for anything as small-time as a drug bust; he wanted a murder charge against a child-killer. Okay, Winzen shrugged. He and Lester had sold some marijuana together, but Lester's cocaine use and dealing were totally separate. Steve hated cocaine and had warned Lester about its evil—its victims ended up dead or in prison. Steve especially hated the habit of injecting drugs, and Lester had deferred to that by forgoing his preference for needles in Steve's presence. Lester had vowed he was working on his problem, however, and claimed he was kicking it. Apparently not, Steve said forlornly.

Cocaine—that sent a chill down Tim McEntee's spine. The word was synonymous with "crazy." You never knew what someone whacked on cocaine was going to do. Crazy things. Violent things. Things no one could imagine doing. Things like murdering two children.

Other detectives were finding out even more about Lester Howlett and cocaine that morning. A friend, Billy Schwartz*, knew that Howlett had been occasional roommates with Geno Fleer and Steven Winzen. And Schwartz admitted selling Howlett an ounce of cocaine about once a month. By Schwartz's estimation, Howlett's habit weighed in at $300 to $700 worth of cocaine per day, four or five days a week, and he had other sources. Schwartz knew about the trip to Rockford and had in fact declined Howlett's invitation to ride along. He had been to Rockford with Howlett once and thought he made about two trips a month to pick up the goods. Geno Fleer and Steve Winzen knew all about Howlett's cocaine deals in Rockford and the Fenton area, Schwartz said, and had been present at several transactions.

Schwartz said he had talked to Howlett on the phone the night of the murders; he was mumbling so badly and was obviously so messed up on cocaine that Schwartz ended the conversation and said they would talk later. Schwartz also remembered that on Friday, Howlett claimed to have had such long and energetic sex with a woman he had picked up in a bar two days before that it had left him "raw" and injured.

The drug angle took a more ominous turn when the police talked to Ben Cagle*, another character who drew the detectives into the ever-widening circle of friends and business acquaintances orbiting around Steve and Lester. New names were popping up as fast as the detectives could write them down. Cagle had been the best man at the Winzens' wedding and had spent a lot of time with Steve and Lester Howlett. Cagle had kept his family together when he was out of work by selling a little marijuana he got from Steve. Steve only dealt in marijuana, Cagle insisted, and Howlett handled coke. In fact, Cagle had seen Winzen and Howlett Friday night, and Howlett had been planning to drive to someplace close to Chicago for a cocaine deal the next day. That all fit.

The information got interesting when Cagle said he had been warned by another friend, Don Hopkins*, to stay away from Howlett and Mark Gerber. They had recruited Hopkins to help them rip off another coke dealer and then kill him. The dealer wasn't home, so the plot fizzled. But Cagle later passed the warning along to Steve Winzen.

Cagle said Don Hopkins even claimed to have been the victim of a rip-off by Howlett and Gerber. Hopkins had opened his door one night, expecting a cocaine delivery from them, and instead had a pistol stuck up his nose by Gerber's cousin and an accomplice. They made off with Hopkins's money and guns. According to Cagle, failed drug deals weren't uncommon among this group. In early July, Steve had been trying to buy two suitcases of marijuana from two Mexicans who reportedly ran into trouble at the airport. The delivery never happened.

Amid all of the stories of drug deals, rip-offs, and murder conspiracies, one call to the Major Case Squad about six o'clock Monday focused the investigation in a surprising way. Sandy Barton*, who had dated Steve Winzen and was a waitress at a restaurant in Fenton called the Steak 'N Tail, said she had been driving to work about ten-thirty Thursday morning when she passed the apartment complex where she would learn the murders occurred. She saw an acquaintance, Eugene Fleer, drive an old silver Ford Granada out of the parking lot onto Highway 141 and pass right by her in a hurry.

"He seemed a wreck, out of sorts, as if he had a terrible hangover, and his hair was a mess," Barton said. "Anyone who knows Geno knows that he is immaculate. His hair is always in place, straight out of the fifties, even when he's loaded."

It also seemed unusual for Fleer to be at the complex, since she knew Steve Winzen was out of town and he usually took Lester Howlett with him. She had become quite concerned after hearing that Tyler Winzen had been murdered and Lester Howlett had died—both of them people very close to Steve. Why, she wondered, would Eugene Fleer be coming out of those apartments shortly after Tyler was murdered and shortly before Howlett was found dead?

Miss Barton also offered another interesting observation. "I know Geno is a crazy son of a bitch. I know a girl he went out with, and he terrorized her. I saw him beat the shit out of a girl in front of the Steak 'N Tail last year during the World Series, and it really seemed for no apparent reason."

By nine o'clock, Eugene Fleer was back at the command post for another interview. This time, the cops would be a little tougher on this guy, now a potentially violent suspect who had lied to them. Detective Bill Baldwin and others on the squad watched through the two-way mirror from an adjacent room as Tim McEntee went to work. The first order of business was for McEntee to advise Fleer of his rights and ask him to sign a waiver.

"I know my rights," Fleer said. "I know them well, and they're right there on that poster on the wall, anyway. I learned what to say and what not to say when I was in prison. And I learned what to sign and what not to sign. I'm not signing any waiver. You've always got a better chance of beating any rap if you don't sign the waiver."

McEntee nodded. Now he knew the score, too. This guy was hard-core and would not be shoved around. So McEntee cut to the chase, telling Fleer that the police had a witness who put him at the murder scene within minutes of the killings.

Fleer didn't seem fazed to be caught in a lie. "Okay, I was there. I spent the night with Lester in his apartment. I left the next morning; I don't know what time it was. But I had nothing to do with killing those kids. I wasn't involved in any way."

That denial aside, McEntee was more than a little happy

with Fleer's admissions that he was at the apartments not
only about the time of the murders, but even the night
before. McEntee lived for moments like this. He leaned in
close, his blue eyes flashing; he hoped his stale breath still
carried the worst reminders of the last cigar he had smoked.

"Then why did you lie to us before?" he snarled into
Fleer's face. "If you didn't have anything to do with this,
why did you lie about being at Howlett's apartment that
morning? Why'd you say you were home in bed when this
witness saw you driving out of the apartment complex with
your hair messed up?"

"Because of my record," Fleer said, a hint of nervousness
surfacing now. "I'm an ex-con, and I didn't want to admit
I was involved with drugs. And I don't need to be in an
apartment complex where two kids are murdered. My record alone is enough for you guys to implicate me if I'm
there. I don't need the grief for something I had nothing
to do with."

Too late for that, McEntee thought. Your grief from us
is just starting. And McEntee was beginning to see something else in that face—something quite familiar.

"You don't remember me, do you?" he growled. "Let
me see your shoulder. Pull back your sleeve." Fleer
obliged, and the long, wide scars on his right shoulder were
plainly visible.

"Where'd you get those?" McEntee asked, almost positive what the answer would be.

"You guys shot me," Fleer snapped. There was no anger;
it was just a matter of fact for a guy who lived Fleer's kind
of life.

McEntee had been right. In 1974, when Eugene Fleer
was only eighteen years old, he had been part of a gang of
older men who were pulling robberies around the city of
St. Louis. When the police arrived just in time to foil a
getaway from a pharmacy on Chippewa Street in south St.
Louis that was being hit for drugs and money, a shoot-
out ensued. The robbers took a hostage to try to protect
themselves; it didn't work. Fleer was felled by a blast from
a shotgun, one of the other robbers was killed, and a third
was wounded. McEntee had been among the cops banging
away at the bad guys that day, and his partner had fired the
shot that took out the young Eugene Fleer. Fleer survived

extensive surgery and drew twelve years in prison for armed robbery and assault with intent to kill.

And now, Fleer and McEntee faced each other again. Geno had a ready story. He had gone home after leaving Howlett's that morning, cleaned up, and then returned to Howlett's about twelve-thirty. He was surprised to see all the police cars, but didn't think that much about it. Howlett didn't answer the door, and Fleer was leaving when he got the word on the murders from the maintenance man, Bob Lutz. Fleer drove over to a friend's and spent some time working on motorcycles with him. Fleer made a trip to another friend's house for a while and then returned to the first buddy's to eat dinner and watch movies before driving home.

McEntee pushed Fleer about his activities with Howlett the night before the murder and was surprised when he readily admitted that they had used cocaine. "We did a quarter-ounce. We did trails all night long. I was pretty high. I don't remember much about that evening or early the next morning. By the time I got home later that morning, I wasn't high anymore."

The detectives wanted to know about the night of Howlett's death. Had he told them the truth about that? Fleer shocked them again. "No, I didn't tell you the truth. But I want to get that cleared up right now. I don't want to get caught in a lie and have you guys charge me in those murders because of it."

The trip to Rockford to buy cocaine had been planned for Thursday night, but was postponed because of the murders. They went to Rockford on Friday and bought the ounce of coke from a guy named Al; Fleer couldn't remember his last name right then. Howlett gave Al about $500 in cash and a gold necklace to hold until he got the rest of the money; the cocaine was in a brown paper bag secured with brown tape. They stashed it in the glove box and drove back to Fleer's trailer in Fenton, where Howlett began cutting it, using a bottle of baby laxative powder. About eight-thirty Saturday night, Fleer did a favor for Howlett by delivering some cocaine to a customer, and then he stopped to pick up a television set from Pete Wendler.

"When I got back to my trailer about ten-thirty, Lester was dead. The cocaine was on the kitchen table with the

scale and the cut powder. I didn't see any syringes or anything around Lester. So I hid the cocaine and the scales
under the trailer next to mine. I took the cut powder and
drove back to Wendler's house. On the way, I dumped the
cut powder out of the car window as I drove. I threw the
bottle out of the window somewhere close to Highway 21
and Route 141."

Fleer told Wendler about Howlett and then asked him
to agree to a story for the cops to reduce any suspicion
that Fleer was with Howlett when he died. Wendler agreed,
and they drove back to the trailer, stopping along the way
to call the police and report Howlett's death.

McEntee pushed again. "Where's the cocaine now,
Geno?"

Without hesitating, Fleer said, "I took it back to my
trailer and hid it in the insulation in the bottom of the ice
box. I put it there after the deputies left Sunday morning.
The scales are in the cabinet in the kitchen."

While Fleer was feeling so cooperative, McEntee gave
him a "consent to search" form, hoping he would agree to
let the police search his trailer for the cocaine and scales.
But Fleer got tough again. He didn't have to sign anything.

"No, you don't," McEntee drawled. "You don't have to
sign anything. You have a right to talk to your lawyer and
your family about it if you want to."

Fleer thought for a moment. "All right, I'll sign the form.
I want this settled as soon as possible."

He looked McEntee right in the eye and said, "I'm a
cocaine dealer. I'm not a baby-killer."

McEntee was almost shocked. That kind of candor from
a penitentiary-educated criminal wasn't right, and that
statement was flabbergasting. He was copping to being a
coke dealer? McEntee would have been more comfortable
if Fleer had continued to lie in the face of contradictory
evidence. That was the expected line. But he was trying
too hard to be cooperative now. This honesty didn't fit
Fleer. No, something else was happening here, and
McEntee wondered what it was. Fleer surprised the cops
even more by asking to take a polygraph test on the murders; one was scheduled for the next day.

Baldwin and the other detectives found Geno Fleer as
cold as an icicle. Baldwin didn't think this guy cared about

anything in the world but himself. He didn't flaunt his amazing record as an eighteen-year-old shoot-out veteran, a man who had survived a shotgun blast. But his laid-back style under tough police interrogation gave him away. He was cool—ex-con, tough-guy cool—under a surface that even looked like the classic Mafia type.

But Fleer was being so cooperative now that he agreed to accompany the detectives on a tour of the Howlett death route—to the trailer to find the cocaine and the scales, and to the location where Fleer claimed he had pitched the bottle from the cut powder. McEntee and Bob Miller found the baggie of cocaine exactly where Fleer had promised, hidden in the insulation at the bottom of the refrigerator. And, surprisingly, the detectives found the bottle along the road, right where Fleer said he'd thrown it.

While Fleer was working with the police, other detectives were confirming parts of his story in an interview with Pete Wendler. Fleer had indeed asked Wendler to help him with a phony story about finding Howlett's body. Fleer had left Wendler's about nine o'clock after borrowing the television and then returned at ten. He used the telephone to make a long-distance call—he said to Rockford, Illinois—and then explained to Wendler how he had found Howlett's body. Wendler asked why Fleer hadn't called the police, and he said he was afraid to because of his record.

Wendler agreed to go back to Fleer's trailer and tell the police the men had been together when they found Howlett's body. They called the police from a pay phone on the way. Once at the trailer, Fleer said he had not found any drugs when he discovered Howlett's body. But Wendler thought Fleer seemed to be under the influence then. Fleer said Howlett had been staying with him because Howlett was worried about the Major Case Squad's investigation into the murders and because he owed money to some drug dealers who were the kind of people who would kill you for that. Fleer later confirmed to Wendler that he had hidden an ounce of cocaine he and Howlett had bought in Rockford.

The detectives returned Fleer to the Fenton police station for the night and Tuesday morning charged him with unlawful possession of a controlled substance—cocaine— and tampering with evidence. The charges didn't seem to faze Fleer, as if he had known they were coming from the moment he opened his mouth about the coke. As McEntee escorted Fleer to a cell after booking, the cop made some reference to the murders of these babies. Fleer corrected McEntee: "The girl wasn't a baby; she was a teenager. That's not a baby."

McEntee asked if Fleer had anything else to say. He nodded. "I deal cocaine. I don't murder babies."

Mari Winzen was staring at her baby's photograph atop the small blue coffin Monday evening. That's my son, she was thinking; he's in there. He's dead and he's in that box. He's my son and I want to take him home. Just for tonight, one last time. Why can't I do that? she wondered. Who would it hurt? I'll bring him back tomorrow.

She wasn't aware of the funeral parlor full of people milling about and speaking in hushed tones. All she could hear was her own thoughts about her son. This desire to take him home made perfect sense to her. She knew the funeral was the next morning, and she would bring him back then. All she wanted was one more night with him at home. She walked calmly to the funeral director and spoke quietly.

"Would you please ask everyone to leave. I want to see my son."

The poor man looked stricken. "Mrs. Winzen," he said softly, "I don't think you want to do that."

Mari stepped over to the coffin and glanced nervously around the room. No one seemed to be watching her. She slipped her fingertips under the rim of the lid and lifted gently, checking to see if it was locked; it didn't budge. She had no idea that Laura Vitale's little daughter was watching from the side, wondering in painful confusion what Mari was doing.

Mari felt frustrated as she walked away. Pat Indelicato brought a distinguished-looking man to Mari and introduced him as a psychiatrist whom Pat worked with at the hospital. He gently took Mari's hand and said, "Mari, this pain will never really go away. All I can tell you is that, somehow, it will get better."

Mari looked blankly at him, as if he had just commented on the lovely weather, and said, "Thank you for coming."

She turned and walked away.

The doctor leaned close to Mari's mother and whispered, "Pat, keep an eye on her."

Before long, the funeral director announced closing hour, and the crowd began to drift out. But Mari felt a new hysteria sweep in. "No, no," she began to protest louder and louder. "He's my son. I want to take him home tonight. Please, please. I'm not leaving without him. I want to see my son. I just want him home. Dad's got the station wagon. We can take Tyler home."

Joe Indelicato and other men in the family began to slip quietly around Mari, and the mass of relatives began easing her toward the door as her cries became louder. Bob Kane, the man who had just started dating Mari and had become so fond of Tyler, leaned over and whispered to her, "Mari, just remember Tyler as he was." And then Bob left. He couldn't bear to see Mari go through this.

As Mari was placed delicately in the backseat of her parents' car, she wondered why everyone was resisting her perfectly rational request. "I don't care if he's dead," she pleaded tearfully with her mother. "He's my son and I want him with me."

"I know," Pat whispered. Mari finally had realized this wasn't a movie, Pat thought. She was going home on this last night without her son, and that reality was sinking in. The funeral tomorrow would be worse, but they still had to get through this night.

Once back at home, Mari called Captain John O'Rando to see if there were any new developments and heard yet another shocking revelation. O'Rando told her what he had been confirming for reporters that day—Lester Howlett had been the Major Case Squad's leading suspect and his death was thought to have been a drug overdose. Again, Mari had heard news she couldn't believe. There was no way this man who had been Steve's best friend, this man who she thought she knew so well, this man whose children had played with Tyler, could have murdered her son. She knew Lester was using cocaine. Could that have caused him to do such a monstrous thing? She always had thought of it as such an evil drug and had been glad that Steve seemed determined to stay away from it, despite his marijuana business. Had it turned out somehow that cocaine had pushed a friend to kill Tyler and Stacy?

Mari could feel the strain on the tenuous threads holding her together. Her hand trembled as she called Jude Govreau.

"My God, Jude," she screamed as the threads began breaking. "He killed our babies! They said he killed them!"

"Who?" Jude nearly screamed back.

"Lester. Lester Howlett. He was Steve's friend. He was my friend. He was at my parents' house Friday with Steve, crying and saying how they would get the killer. But the police say he killed them! He overdosed on drugs and he's dead. But they said he killed them!"

Jude had never heard of Lester Howlett, but she knew the police were looking into the death of a prime suspect. Now she had a name, however unfamiliar. There still was no peace or comfort in this. If this Lester Howlett had killed Stacy and Tyler, death was too good for him. Jude's anger still was boiling. If Howlett was the murderer, his death would deny Jude all the answers she needed and the justice she demanded. Why had he killed them? How had he killed them? Was someone else involved? How would she find justice in this kind of death for her daughter's killer?

Jude called O'Rando, and he gave her essentially the same information. It looked like a cocaine OD at the trailer owned by Howlett's friend, Eugene Fleer, another unfamiliar name. The police were checking out Fleer's story and already had caught him in some contradictions. If anything more developed, he would let her know. Jude felt no relief, only a new frustration as she hung up the phone.

And that night, Mari began to have a recurring dream. Tyler's body was at home; she tenderly laid him on the sofa and covered him snugly with a blanket. She knew he was dead, but it didn't matter. What mattered was that he was home, where he was safe.

The preliminary report on Tuesday from Lester Howlett's autopsy confirmed everyone's suspicions: he had had cocaine in his system when he died. More tests would be needed to determine how much and if it was lethal. Even those reports didn't surprise anyone when they came in later showing that there was so much coke in Lester that it tested pure in his urine. Would an experienced user like Howlett make that kind of mistake? Perhaps, if he had been using too much to pay attention. But most of the cops thought the tests strongly suggested that the dose was intentional—a "hot shot" intended to commit suicide or murder. Was he overcome by guilt after killing his friends' little boy and an innocent teenager? Was he only a witness to the murders who planned to tell the police everything he knew the next day? How could anyone answer these new questions?

And O'Rando was warning the detectives not to get too bogged down in speculation about motives in any of the deaths. Sure, motive could be important. But the captain knew playing that game could derail the investigators, maybe even causing them to overlook something that didn't fit with their pet theories. Follow the trail left behind, he told them, not the guesses about which path had been taken.

The detectives also turned their attention to Brenda Turner on Tuesday. All of the cops who talked to her said she was so weird that she worried them; her anger at the loss of her daughter's baby-sitting job was mentioned repeatedly as a potential motive, as weak as that might seem. Mari and Steve Winzen even agreed—a rare event—that Brenda had to be high on the list of suspects. O'Rando decided some innovation was needed here, and he told Detective Bill Baldwin and Sergeant Tim McEntee to ask her to come down to headquarters to look at photos of the scene to determine if anything seemed out of place. That wasn't a tactic O'Rando used very often, but maybe it would shake something loose from Brenda Turner.

The chubby woman with the brown hair flipped through the pictures so unemotionally that the cops were shocked. She asked a lot of direct, technical questions about how the murders were committed, forcing the police to explain that they could not divulge that information. Finally, as she saw the picture of the children's bodies in the bathtub, Brenda choked a little and said wistfully, "I wonder why anyone would do something like that to Tyler. I considered him like my own baby. I used to baby-sit him, and I still watched him sometimes when his mother was gone. My husband and I called him Dedo as a little nickname."

When she saw the photo of the living room, she pointed and said the coffee table had been moved from its usual position in front of the sofa where Stacy usually slept when she first arrived in the mornings. She kept looking at the photo and added softly, "This is where the struggle took place."

"Why do you say there was a struggle? There's been no public statement by the police that there was any struggle," Baldwin said.

Brenda began to fidget a bit, the first nervousness she had shown. "Well, I can tell by the photograph that there was a struggle here before Stacy was strangled."

Baldwin and McEntee looked at each other as the red flags went up mentally. Was this woman betraying too much knowledge of the crime?

"Mrs. Turner," Baldwin said slowly, "I think it would be proper for us to read you your rights under the Miranda warning."

She didn't seem surprised as she listened and readily agreed to sign the rights waiver. As she talked, she made several references to her little Tyler, her little baby, or her Dedo. When one of the cops would mention Stacy's name, Brenda would respond, "It's sad that this happened to Stacy, but poor Tyler."

Brenda looked at the officers. "Do you think I did this? Because if I did it, I can't remember doing it. Do you think it would be possible for me to do something like this and not remember it?"

Baldwin and McEntee were stunned. That was the most bizarre thing either of these experienced detectives had ever heard during an interview. Most cops would interpret it as a subconscious admission of guilt, an invitation to come and get a confession. It certainly didn't qualify as a denial.

"Well, if you find out I did this, I want you to kill me. If I did this, I would want to kill myself."

Baldwin and McEntee could almost feel their jaws dropping open as Brenda went on to describe Stacy and Tyler's morning routine in detail. She added that she had a key to all of the apartments so she could assist the owner if there were problems. In return for that and for vacuuming the hallways, the landlord gave her a rent reduction of $20 a month.

McEntee looked directly into Brenda Turner's face with his piercing blue eyes. "Brenda, did you kill Tyler and Stacy?"

She sat silently for what seemed a long time. Slowly, she said, "I don't think I did. I loved Tyler and Stacy. There would be no reason for me to do this." And then she added, "But if I found out I did, I would want to be killed."

O'Rando couldn't drop the pursuit of this suspect here. Brenda agreed to a polygraph test that afternoon.

After that incredible interview, the police asked Jack Turner to talk to his wife. He called later and said even he had some suspicions about her. She had been acting oddly since the murders—sick to her stomach, nervous, and on edge. She had seen a doctor, who had prescribed some medication. When Jack brought up the murders, she said, "Do you think I could do that? You shouldn't love me if I did this. If I did it, I can't remember it."

Other interviews continued Tuesday with tidbits coming in here and there to paint a more detailed picture of this group of people who seemed to orbit around drugs. John Cass* had taken in Eugene Fleer as a roommate off and on for the last four years, and Fleer's most recent stay had ended the month before when he moved into the trailer in Imperial. Fleer was a neat and clean person whose major fault seemed to be a propensity to beat up women when he lost his temper. Fleer had visited Cass the day of the murders and had called Howlett from Cass's house. Cass spoke to Howlett on the phone, and he seemed groggy, as if he had just awakened. Howlett mentioned Tyler and said, "I loved that little boy just like he was my own."

A part-time marijuana dealer, Richard Zobrist*, offered another odd story. Howlett's sister had told Zobrist that on Thursday, just after the murders were discovered, Howlett had given her an envelope containing all of his photographs of his children and asked her to keep them for him.

While he was laid off as a construction worker, Zobrist supplemented his income by selling marijuana he got from Steve Winzen; Zobrist had met Howlett through Steve. Zobrist had heard through a friend that a man named Dave Helmond sold marijuana he got from Howlett, and there was a rumor that Helmond had been ripped off to the tune of $16,000. Zobrist remembered that Howlett seemed to be spending a lot of money about that time. Another of these vague stories about drug rip-offs, but Zobrist had offered the same name Mark Gerber had listed as the victim. This had to be checked out, the cops knew.

In Rockford, Illinois, Lester Howlett's cocaine source was eager to cooperate once the cops explained that his drug business was the last thing on their investigation agenda; if Albert Farley* didn't have anything to hide about the murders, surely he would want to help. He got the hint and began to tell what he knew. He had gone to high school with Howlett in the Rockford area and had met Steve Winzen and Eugene Fleer through him. Farley had indeed sold Howlett an ounce of cocaine on Saturday, as he had twice before since July 4. On Saturday, Howlett was short of cash to pay for the coke, so he gave Farley $500 cash and a gold necklace worth $1,500 to hold until he could pay him off. Farley said Howlett's death couldn't have been caused by bad coke; Farley had snorted a couple of lines from the same batch he'd sold to Howlett. Farley said Howlett had called Thursday afternoon to make arrangements for the deal and had told him about the murders. When Howlett called again later, he'd said the kids' bodies had been found in scalding water.

And then Howlett asked if Farley thought that would get rid of fingerprints.

What an interesting question, the detectives thought.

The Indelicato house was quieter Tuesday morning than it had been since this began. Everyone moved about without talking, solemnly going through the motions of getting ready for the funeral. Pat thought her daughter was slipping back into denial as time to leave drew closer. Mari wanted to cry, but the tears had stopped again as she thought about what lay ahead.

The funeral mass at St. Vincent de Paul's Catholic Church in south St. Louis was packed, and the priest who had baptized Tyler wept as he gave the eulogy. Jude Govreau, Racheal, and Rick Pashia sat quietly some distance behind the family. Jude felt the pure agony of the first real funeral service she had ever attended. Jude had stood outside and watched as a limousine arrived and delivered the wobbling Mari, clad in black and almost hidden by oversized black sunglasses. Mari came directly to Jude, and the women hugged, feeling this new bond of death they had yet to realize would connect them for life. They cried as they held each other, and then Mari's mother and father almost carried her into the old cathedral. Jude was glad Mari had so many of her relatives around her; Jude knew what it was like to face this without any blood family for support and comfort. And for the first time in her difficult life, Jude really felt as if she knew what someone else was feeling.

As a singer strummed the guitar and sang, Jude looked at the religious statues and the figures of angels that adorned the sanctuary and her questions about where Stacy was at that moment overcame her. She began to cry so pitifully that a woman sitting in front of her turned and took Jude in her arms. Jude accepted the comfort from this complete stranger; any comfort was welcome.

To Mari, this church service was another unreal episode. She still had no sense that she was attending her son's funeral, and she couldn't believe that she had no tears. She always had been critical and suspicious of women who weren't crying when they were interviewed on television after their children had died. Now Mari understood.

The procession to the cemetery was impressive. Cars lined up for what seemed like miles, and Mari's cousin in the police department arranged to close a section of Interstate 70 to accommodate the column of mourners. And, as there had been at Stacy's memorial service on Saturday, plainclothes detectives mingled with the crowd to watch for anyone suspicious.

At the cemetery, Mari and the Indelicatos stood looking at the grave where Tyler's body would be laid to rest. The hole, Pat Indelicato was thinking as the graveside service ended; the Sack Man had taken Tyler and put him in a hole. It was hot and muggy, but Pat and Mari stood with their arms around each and shivered. Mari began to feel the pain of leaving Tyler for the last time. She cried then, but there was no relief from the ache to hold her son again.

Her father, devastated that he could do nothing to help his own child, almost carried her back to the limo.

Eugene Fleer calmly said no twelve times as Officer Dennis McGuire of the Arnold Police Department ran the polygraph test Tuesday afternoon. In the small room in the motor home that served as the Major Case Squad's mobile command center, McGuire had interviewed Fleer and hooked him to the polygraph. McGuire ran three tests, each time asking if Fleer knew who had killed Tyler and Stacy, and if he had killed them. Had he been in Mari Winzen's apartment on Thursday? Had he run hot water over Tyler's body? Had he cleaned up a drug-injection "outfit" after he found Lester Howlett's body? Had he purposefully lied to McGuire about anything? Twelve times Fleer said no calmly and firmly.

McGuire's conclusion was just as clear. On all three tests, Eugene Fleer showed no signs of deception. "Evaluation of the resulting charts indicated to this examiner that Mr. Fleer was being truthful with his responses to the relevant questions," McGuire wrote in his report.

That evening, McGuire wired another suspect to the machine; this time, Brenda Turner answered thirteen questions. Did she know who killed Tyler? Did she drown him in Mari's apartment? Was she angry enough at Stacy to kill her? Did she strangle Stacy? Had she taken any drugs in the last twenty-four hours? Was she under a doctor's care for any mental disorder? No, she said repeatedly.

And Dennis McGuire came to the same conclusion. There were no signs of deception; his opinion was that she was being truthful.

So much for polygraphs, O'Rando thought. He didn't like them. You couldn't use them in court, and they usually were inconclusive anyway.

Brenda Turner was as strange as they come, and she had motive and opportunity. She had looked awfully suspicious for a while, but O'Rando just couldn't see her as the killer. Some of the elements were there, but it just didn't gel.

To O'Rando, that seemed to be the story on everyone in this whole investigation.

CHAPTER 6

The shock to Mari Winzen that accompanied the news that Lester Howlett was a prime suspect doubled with the disclosure that his body had been found in Eugene Fleer's trailer. Was it another bizarre coincidence that Lester Howlett had arranged for Mari to meet Fleer at her apartment just two days before the murders?

This new bombshell exploded on Wednesday, August 13, after Mari had mustered all the strength she could find to go to the Major Case Squad's motor home in Fenton for an extended interview the day after Tyler's funeral. She still could not find a way to cope with what was happening. Earlier that day, sitting on the patio with Carol Brinkley, Mari had wanted nothing more than to find a way to disappear, perhaps even slipping back into the painless fog she knew she could create with enough Valium. "I'm going to stay straight until I get my son taken care of, and then I never want to be straight again," Mari had said through the growing anger and pain. "If this is what being straight gets you, I don't want it."

But she had agreed to meet with the police again. With all of the information coming in about the drug business that surrounded this case, the police hoped Mari might have additional details and be able to help them put things into perspective. Mari couldn't believe it when the police told her where Howlett had died. And the police were equally surprised when Mari told them about her recent introduction to Eugene Fleer.

The events of the week had begun Monday the 4th, when she called Lester to ask him to drive her to an unfamiliar location Tuesday night. She had to attend a special class as punishment for a regrettable shoplifting incident that occurred while she was taking too much Valium and had too little cash—she had light-fingered a steak for Tyler. Mari was terrible with directions and feared she would be unable to find the class; an absence would compound the error she was trying to erase. Lester readily agreed to help out, but called Tuesday morning with a problem. He had an unexpected chance to see his kids that night and wanted to send a buddy—Eugene Fleer—as a stand-in. Mari knew those opportunities had been rare amid the wrangling between Lester and his estranged wife, so she let him off the hook. But she was concerned about going with Fleer. She had seen him once with Steve and Lester, and she commented to Steve that the guy was "scary-looking, like a murderer or a hit man for the Mafia." Steve had shrugged that off casually: "That Geno Fleer. He's okay." On Tuesday, Lester vouched for Fleer by asking rhetorically, "Mari, would I let you go with anybody who would hurt you?" It was her turn to shrug, and she accepted the last-minute substitution. After all, Steve had always said she could look to Lester for help if she needed him. And Lester had always made her feel secure in their friendship.

The conversation ended Tuesday morning with two questions from Lester that she hadn't thought much about at the time.

"Would it be all right if Geno took your car tonight?"

"Sure."

"By the way, what time do you usually go to work in the morning?"

"Oh, about five after seven."

Geno Fleer arrived right on time at five-thirty on Tuesday. Stacy was there to baby-sit, and Brenda and Bobbi Turner were visiting, too, when Fleer knocked on the door and let him in. Stacy was doing the supper dishes as Tyler sat on the counter beside her. As Mari gave Stacy some last-minute instructions, she noticed Fleer's coal-black eyes staring intensely at her son. The gaze was so direct and powerful that Mari stopped in midsentence and looked at Fleer.

He sensed her concern and said, "Man, that's really an incredible kid you and Steve have there."

Mari's apprehension melted into a mother's pride as she smiled. "Oh, thank you."

Mari handed Fleer her key ring as they walked into the

parking lot. The thirty-minute drive was quiet, and Mari glanced at the man behind the wheel. He was dark and handsome in a mysterious, almost dangerous way. His eyelashes were so long they seemed to brush his eyebrows. His thick black hair was brushed back, and he was clean-shaven. His white T-shirt was tucked into his blue jeans, and his whole appearance was neat and clean. This guy is really good-looking, Mari thought.

He didn't seem to want to talk, and Mari's attempts to generate conversation were received without much enthusiasm or reciprocation. She told him he looked like the Italian singer Gino Vannelli, and he said his mother was a full-blooded Italian named Vitale. Mari chimed in that she was Italian, too, but the chitchat died out anyway.

They arrived at the class thirty minutes early, and Mari signed in. Geno suggested they get a soda until class began, and they drove to a Steak 'N Shake restaurant down the street. The conversation still was sparse, but Fleer was extremely polite. He lit her cigarette and opened doors for her, and insisted forcefully that he would pay the check when she offered to pick it up. When they drove back to the class, Geno smiled and said he would be waiting.

But he wasn't in the car when she came out ninety minutes later. As she stood there looking around, Fleer walked out of the rest room at the service station next door. The Geno Fleer who slid behind the wheel then was a markedly different man. His face was red and his neck was flushed. He was so talkative that Mari wondered what could account for such a dramatic change in personality. She thought she detected a little mark on the inside of Fleer's left arm and wondered if his visit to the rest room had been to shoot up.

He shocked her by turning suddenly and volunteering, "You know, I've been in prison before."

That was not really what she wanted to hear from this somewhat alarming character. "Oh, really? What for?" she asked, trying to sound casual and unconcerned.

"Armed robbery."

"Oh." Mari felt frightened then. This was not exactly normal conversation, and she was getting concerned about this strange man. She reminded herself that Lester and Steve had said Geno was okay. He rambled on about being on parole and trying to get a job with his father's roofing company. They hadn't gotten along well in the past, but they were trying to start over. Geno said he wanted to get away from Steve and Lester because they were selling dope.

"Did you know about that?" he asked.

"Not really. I really don't want to know. But I do know that Steve is not a good person to be around if you're trying to straighten out your life."

The drive home was uneventful. When he shut off the car in the parking lot, he handed her the keys and smiled.

"Thanks, Geno. I sure appreciate your help tonight."

"Okay. No problem."

And then he was gone, walking off toward Lester Howlett's building across the street. Stacy and Tyler were fine, and Mari put her son to sleep with a bedtime story. The next day was marked only by the three obscene calls Stacy got that morning. She didn't seem frightened when she told Mari about it, and they laughed about the heavy breather who had nothing better to do. Stacy watched Tyler again Wednesday night so Mari could go to the final class alone. When Mari returned, Stacy and Tyler had gone to a friend's home with Brenda Turner. They came home later, safe and sound.

Everything seemed normal on that rainy Thursday—until she got the call about midmorning that destroyed her life.

The police were fascinated by her account of her acquaintance with Geno Fleer. And it dawned on her then that Fleer had had possession of her keys for ninety minutes while she was in class. He easily could have had copies made and could have used one to walk in her front door Thursday morning.

All of this was hitting Mari as a blinding revelation. She had been sure that she somehow had to be the cause of Tyler's death. Surely it had been her former boyfriend or a neighbor who had a grudge against her. But the police had confirmed her ex-boyfriend's alibi, and the neighbor upstairs had checked out, too. She had felt lost when they told her that earlier. If they hadn't been revenge against her, the murders didn't make sense. She desperately needed to make sense of this horror.

And now the police were saying the most likely suspects

were Lester Howlett and Eugene Fleer, the men brought into the lives of her and Tyler by Steve Winzen's drug dealing. She felt a new outrage growing at Steve. Had his dealing and his cocaine-sniffing buddies taken the only thing in her life that really mattered? Was Mari as much a victim as Tyler and not really part of the cause?

Mari told the police that she had known all along that Steve Winzen sold marijuana. That was his only business as far as she knew. She had been able to live with it because she knew he was so opposed to cocaine dealing; he only handled marijuana, and that seemed less offensive and dangerous to Mari. Their marriage had disintegrated for many reasons, but she said the final straw came when she learned Steve had cut a marijuana deal right in front of her older son, Brian. That was the push she needed; she moved out and began a divorce that took two years to finalize.

The police asked Mari to name the people she considered suspects. For the first time, Mari put Lester on the list, and she cried. "Normally, I'm sure he wouldn't do such a thing. I know he loved Tyler. But drugs make you do crazy things. I know. Maybe he did drugs Thursday and went crazy. And there's more that makes me think he could have done it. He just asked me Tuesday what time I usually left for work, and when I ran to him Thursday outside the apartment, he wouldn't even put his arms around me. I needed comfort from him as a friend, and he was just cold. I didn't really think that much about it then, but now it makes sense if he did it."

Then Mari mentioned Brenda Turner. She had to be on the list because of her anger and bitterness when Bobbi lost the baby-sitting job. Brenda had been hateful to Stacy over it, once telling Mari, "Damn Stacy. I don't ever want to speak to her again." Mari even remembered Bobbi recounting how Brenda once flew into a rage when they lived in Pittsburgh and punched Bobbi in the face for no reason. Brenda later mentioned it, too, but said she only slapped Bobbi for talking back. Brenda once dragged Bobbi across the street by the hair after learning she had been watching dirty movies.

And then there was Geno Fleer. Mari didn't know much about him, but found him rather scary. He had had access to her door key, and, beyond that, Stacy might have let him in because he had just been introduced as a friend of Lester's. Geno had to be on the list, too.

As the interview ended, Captain John O'Rando asked for a very difficult favor. He wanted Mari to go back to her apartment with the detectives to see if she noticed anything they had missed. The thought of going back was excruciating, and Mari resisted. But O'Rando explained that no one else could inspect the apartment the way she could. Bob Miller was going crazy trying to determine if he was missing something, and Mari was the only one who could say for sure. Finally, she agreed; maybe it would help the police find the killer.

But she didn't find much of real value. The coffee table was moved slightly, the rattan chair was pushed back against the wall, and the blue cushion had a new tear in it. There were new scrapes and some spots of an unknown substance on the wall behind the chair. There was a similar spot on the wall behind the couch, and none of the spots had been there before. The now-open blinds in Tyler's room had been all the way down and closed when she left, and the rip in his screen was new. A large stuffed animal sitting on the bed usually was kept on the other side of the room. She had worried that Tyler would suffocate under it while asleep, so she moved it every night. Now she wondered if its location back on the bed meant it had indeed suffocated her son under the killer's hands.

The first and only return to the apartment was as awful as Mari had feared, and she was distraught by the time she got home. She felt so lost again. Her instincts had been totally wrong, and now it appeared that her husband's drug dealing had led, at least indirectly, to the murders of Tyler and Stacy, maybe even by a man she counted as a good friend. Mari had nothing to cling to.

Her mother suggested they pass some time addressing thank-you cards, but Mari knew she couldn't face that yet.

"I don't want to do this now, Mom. Someone killed my son, and no one is doing anything about it." Pat could see more anger brewing behind Mari's eyes. "I've always been told that nothing bad would happen to me. But now my son is dead, my home is gone, and no one can do anything about it."

Then Mari saw it—the 8 × 10 photograph of Tyler on

her parents' shelf. She took the picture to her bedroom, cuddled it against her for a few moments, and then placed it gently against the pillow and covered it with the blanket. She finally felt as if she had Tyler with her again. It was a delusion, of course, but it made sense to her. And she kept Tyler's photograph in bed with her for weeks. As long as she had that, she almost could pretend she still had him.

If drugs had played as big as role in this case as it seemed, the police wanted to know everything. Had there been a rip-off that made revenge a motive for murder? Detectives quickly tracked down the reputed dealer, Dave Helmond, and learned he had indeed been robbed at his home on July 13. And Helmond admitted that he had bought marijuana from Steve Winzen through Lester Howlett. But Helmond insisted he had no idea who had ripped him off. He had answered a knock on the door only to be overpowered by a man who pushed in, pistol-whipped and kicked him, and held the gun to his head while demanding to know the location of the cash and jewelry. The stocky, scruffy man hiding behind large sunglasses even put the gun to the head of Helmond's two-year-old daughter and threatened to kidnap both of his children if Helmond didn't comply. He finally led the man to a box that contained $4,000—the down payment on a new house, Helmond insisted—and the robber escaped with the money, five gold chains, and an AR-15 semiautomatic rifle. Neighbors later said they had seen three men in a maroon Chevy parked outside Helmond's house about the time of the attack.

Helmond had alibis for Thursday morning and Saturday night, and they checked out. If he had plotted or arranged any murders in revenge for this robbery, he wasn't tipping his hand to the cops. They didn't see him as a very likely murder suspect, anyway.

Steve Winzen knew about that rip-off, too, but he hadn't told the cops. Lester tipped Steve about it the morning after it happened, but denied any role. Dave Helmond called Steve later and said he suspected the attack had come from Jefferson County; Steve promised to look into it. Over the next week, Lester finally broke down and admitted he had planned and executed the robbery, accompanied by Eugene Fleer and a third man. Steve tried to reach

Helmond to tell him he had been right and to clear himself from suspicion. Although Lester said the money was already gone, Steve planned to try to help Helmond recoup his losses. But Steve couldn't reach him; Helmond's phone had not been repaired since the robbers cut the line, and a couple of stops at Helmond's house failed to find him. Steve and Patty Garner left for Las Vegas on Saturday, August 2, and he planned to renew his efforts after his return, planned for Friday, August 8.

The Major Case Squad's investigation wasn't going very well, time was running out, and frustration was mounting. Even getting an interview with the owner of the apartment building turned out to be troublesome. The man refused a polite request to come to Major Case Squad headquarters. He was too busy and he had nothing to say. He made it clear he believed he was politically connected to enough people to override any cop's orders. But O'Rando wanted to know who had access to the building, such as maintenance workers or repairmen, and anything else the owner could tell the police. He certainly wasn't a suspect, but his aloof, evasive, and uncooperative attitude needed what cops liked to call "a station-house adjustment." He probably was more worried about being liable to a huge civil suit for damages by the victims' families than he was about helping catch the killer. So, O'Rando dispatched Sergeant Tim McEntee and Lieutenant Ed Kemp—the two biggest, most ornery men on the squad—with orders to do whatever was necessary to bring in the reluctant landlord.

The man was dressed in satin shorts when he answered the door at his beautiful home on a hillside in an exclusive subdivision. He wasn't happy to see the two grinning hulks standing there with badges in their hands, and he made it clear he still had no intention of going anywhere with them. Kemp gritted his teeth and said sarcastically, "Well, sir, we're investigating the murders of two children, and you may have information that could be useful. We have to insist that you come with us."

"Well, I'm extremely busy today."

McEntee stepped quite close to the man and growled, "You will come with us now or we will return very soon with a warrant for your arrest issued by a judge and we will haul you to jail."

"What happened to the Constitution?" the man sneered.

"I just suspended it," McEntee snapped.

"What are you guys, the world police?" the man mumbled sarcastically as he picked up a *Bon Appetit* magazine to read on the ride in. "Now I know why kids don't like you."

"Yeah, I'm your worst nightmare—a bigot with a badge. I'm just a detective from the slum district in St. Louis and you're welcome to call my chief and complain if you like. But you're coming with us now."

Kemp looked at the satin shorts and the effete magazine, and felt embarrassed to be hauling this guy into the station in front of his colleagues.

Later, McEntee and Kemp would agree they kind of liked the "world police" title. They'd have to remember that; they might want to use it themselves sometime.

The man confirmed that he had given Brenda Turner a $20 break on her rent to be building caretaker and that she had a master key. She often told him what was going on around the building and what the residents were saying about him; he couldn't offer much useful information beyond that. But at least he had learned about cooperating when asked so politely by the Major Case Squad.

By eight o'clock Thursday night, August 14, the squad had followed up ninety leads in the Winzen-Price murders and the death of Lester Howlett. Some crime lab work was pending, but everything else was done. Garbage collectors and school-bus drivers had been interviewed. Everyone who worked with Mari and Jude or knew them very well had been contacted. Teenagers who knew Stacy had been pumped for information. Long shots had been followed and hitchhikers had been found. The cops had traced an obscure trail through a maze of drug dealers and cocaine addicts and rumors of rip-offs and robberies all the way to Rockford, Illinois. One worrisome suspect had been charged with cocaine possession and surely would take a fall for that. But the Jefferson County prosecuting attorney had looked at all of the evidence and had come to the same conclusion the detectives had reached—there wasn't enough to file charges against anyone on anything.

John O'Rando studied the final report written by the squad's report officer, Tom Deakin. The eighteen pages laid out the facts and the investigation well, ending with some conclusions: that the primary suspects, excluding the late Lester Howlett, were Brenda Turner and, perhaps, Eugene Fleer; that all available leads had been followed; and that any further investigation was within the scope of the Jefferson County Sheriff's Department.

At eight o'clock, O'Rando signed the report and inactivated the Major Case Squad. Its investigation was over. The squad had a clearance rate of about 85 percent, and it was tough to walk away without an arrest. O'Rando knew it was maddening for all of the two dozen detectives who had worked so hard and so long. But O'Rando's heart ached for the mothers, and he hated to fail them. He had come to know both of them well over the last eight days, and he felt their pain and their anger. He regretted not being able to deliver justice for them, and for those kids.

Bob Miller felt terrible, too. He had packaged all the evidence he could find, including a piece of wall where a small spot showed up behind the chair. He had done everything he could, including the destruction of the bathroom in a desperate attempt to turn up something. Maybe that one fingerprint from the showerhead would lead to the killer once it was matched. Maybe something else would turn up on this Geno Fleer character. But Miller could still see those kids in the bathtub; that sterile, clean scene that would haunt him. Now he had to fold up his tent and walk away, and it felt terrible.

Tim McEntee hated the feeling of utter failure that he took away from this case. He and most of the detectives didn't want to quit, and they knew they would be checking in on this one from time to time, even on their own time. His consolation was knowing that the squad was turning over enough information to Jefferson County detectives to make the case if they got one little break, one little tidbit that might come in later.

Bill Baldwin always kept in mind that the Major Case Squad had no magic wand to wave for mystical results. The detectives still were just cops doing their jobs the best they could, usually working a lot more hours than they got paid for. They got a little more respect as part of the squad, and that sometimes opened doors faster. But they couldn't perform supernatural feats. This case proved him right. They seemed to have most of the pieces—Lester Howlett, Eugene Fleer, Brenda Turner, Steve Winzen, drug dealing—but they couldn't put the puzzle together.

Ed Kemp had never known frustration such as he felt with this case. If he never worked another child-murder case, he would be grateful. He approached his job in a case like this as God's agent. We work for God, he would say. No one else has the right to take a human life, and it's our responsibility to solve it when someone does. But it hadn't happened here, and Kemp was disappointed. And he would take something else with him—something beyond the memories of those kids in that bathtub and the violence that accompanied their deaths. His mind had seized upon that single-handle faucet in the shower. His instincts said the killer may not have intended to use hot water. He may have just cranked the handle all the way over to get as much water in the tub as fast as he could, not realizing he had shoved the handle to the hot side. From that day on, Ed Kemp vowed never to have a single-handle faucet in his house. To this day, every time he checks into a motel, that is the first thing he looks at. And he always thinks about Tyler and Stacy.

No one was more upset when the Major Case Squad disbanded than Mari and Jude. They had been disappointed—almost disbelieving—when the squad failed to develop a solid prime suspect. The women had been talking to O'Rando and the detectives as often as possible, and Eugene "Geno" Fleer was the name usually mentioned. He already faced drug charges, but there obviously was no real optimism that something would develop to justify murder charges against him. No one seemed sure what to make of Fleer, and Mari and Jude couldn't convince themselves that Lester Howlett had done it. In fact, they couldn't really find a motive among any of the few suspects developed by the police—other than the anger and resentment they knew was harbored by Brenda Turner.

The cops were trying to be upbeat, giving the women assurances that none of them would rest until the case was solved. But there was too much uncertainty as the investigation changed hands, and probably speeds. Surely, the women thought, the pace would slow as the Major Case Squad departed. Sheriff Buck Buerger's department certainly couldn't keep up the tempo set by the squad, nor did it seem likely the deputies could accomplish what the squad could not. The mothers were losing faith in the system, and their contact with officials in the sheriff's department had not impressed them so far. With so many misgivings came the nagging fear that the children's murders never would be solved. Neither woman thought she could live with that.

CHAPTER 7

Stacy Price loved the rock group Duran Duran and named her cockateel Simon, after the lead singer. Tyler Winzen knew all the words to every Phil Collins song and could rewind cassette tapes to exactly the spot where his favorite number started.

Stacy was crazy about animals and wanted to be a veterinarian. Tyler was fascinated with driving, steered the wheel on his toy dashboard all the time, and even had an ignition key for his tricycle.

Stacy made the world's best brownies. Tyler hated vegetables.

Stacy had new dental braces. Tyler didn't understand why she needed "bracelets" on her teeth because she already was beautiful.

How do you describe two children who were alive and happy and loving and so full of promise one moment, and then gone forever in the time it takes for a summer thunderstorm? How do you convey their importance to their families or tell the world what it lost or preserve their memories forever?

And what brought them to the place where those lives ended?

The small apartment at Stillbrook Estates in Fenton had meant a new start for Mari Winzen.

She was born Maria Indelicato on May 3, 1954, the first child of Joe and Pat Indelicato. They lived in St. Louis until Mari was five, when they moved northwest to a new suburb called Berkeley. Joe, a welding foreman at a refrigeration company, and Pat, who raised the family at home during those years, had two more children—a son three years younger than Mari and a daughter six years younger. Joe was very Italian and raised his children in a strict, traditional manner that meant no dating as young teenagers. He once drove down the street secretly watching Mari and sprang from the car in anger because a boy was walking her home from school. Mari chafed under rules that rigid and complained that her boyfriends were afraid to come to her house.

She met a friend of the neighbors when she was a senior in high school and they were allowed to date. Fred, a tool-and-die maker, was two years older and drove a hot Dodge Challenger. Early that spring, he asked her to marry him as soon as she graduated. Despite her parents' insistence that eighteen was too young for Mari to wed, the ceremony was held just after graduation in June 1972—from graduation gown to wedding gown in a week. Fred's well-to-do parents provided a rent-free apartment in a remodeled two-family building in St. Louis and, as a wedding present, let Mari carpet and furnish it as she wished.

The freedom she craved had arrived. And, eleven months later, so did their baby, Brian. The pregnancy had been unplanned, and Mari was emotionally unprepared. By the time she was in her sixth month, the fantasy had evaporated. She was eighteen, married, pregnant, immature, and miserable, and she realized she did not love the man she had married. When Brian was six weeks old, Mari took a job as a secretary in a real estate office with some girls she had known from high school. The others had a blast going out after work, partying, and dating; Mari went home to her infant and her husband. The marriage disintegrated. They separated in May 1974 when their son was a year old; Mari and Brian moved back to her parents' home.

Over the next couple of years, Mari fell in with a pretty fast crowd. Her parents baby-sat Brian while she spent many evenings out with a gang that thought popping Valium was the cool thing to do; she joined them and occasionally took a few hits from a marijuana cigarette, too. In 1977, Mari and Brian moved into an apartment with a girlfriend who had a son about the same age. But Mari soon slipped into the easy, convenient habit of leaving Brian at her parents' about half the time.

In 1979, Mari attended a small party and met the host, Steve Winzen. Even though there was some pot-smoking, Steve angrily threw out a couple of the partygoers when he found them snorting cocaine. That impressed Mari, who thought cocaine was an evil well beyond Valium or marijuana. Mari and Steve began to date, lived together for a while, and got married in March 1980. Things were great. Steve worked for his father's construction company, and Mari worked for a truck-leasing company. They rented a townhouse and Brian moved in with them. Steve and Brian got along well, and Steve coached the boy's soccer team. Mari and Steve decided to have a child, and when she became pregnant, they moved to a house they rented, with an option to buy, in another St. Louis suburb, Maryland Heights.

Tyler Patrick Winzen was born on December 29, 1982. But by then, Mari and Steve had begun drifting apart. Steve was laid off and Mari was staying home as part of her plan to be a full-time mother until Tyler started first grade. They fell far behind on their bills, and Mari sank into depression. After years without drugs, she started taking Valium again. When they had to move from their house, Steve's father lent him enough to buy a house trailer in Fenton, a small town just across the line in Jefferson County. To support his family and pay back his father, Steve moved up from selling an occasional bag of marijuana to selling as much as he could. And he made a new friend in the man who lived in a trailer across the street—Lester Howlett. The men started hanging out together while Mari spent more and more time with her friends. Soon the Winzens were married in name only, openly dating other people. And they spent a lot of time fighting. When Steve sold some marijuana to someone in the trailer, right in front of Brian, the ten-year-old had seen more than he cared to and moved back in with his grandparents.

That was a wake-up call for Mari. She was tired of coming home and finding Steve's friends lying on her bed, stoned and crushing out marijuana cigarettes on their jeans. She was taking up to fifty Valium a day, and she knew it all had to stop. In the spring of 1984, she started attending meetings of Alcoholics Anonymous. She met Carol Brinkley there, and the two became good friends; eventually,

Mari accepted Carol's offer to become roommates in her apartment at Stillbrook Estates at Fenton. Mari and Tyler left Steve, and a divorce followed. Steve fought for custody of Tyler, and some nasty allegations were thrown back and forth in court. But in the end, the judge awarded Tyler to Mari.

Everything got better after that. Mari became a true believer and faithful practitioner of the AA program. She turned her life over to God, kicked the Valium, got a job with a radio and electronics company, and could feel herself becoming a better person. When an apartment below Carol's opened up, Mari moved in and invited the man she had been dating—a clinical psychologist—to join her. Things seemed fine until she learned he was married. She threw him out and felt better about that, too.

Tyler also was settling down. He had become hyperactive after Mari left Steve, obviously feeling the effects of separation from his doting father. Steve paid child support promptly, never missed his regular visits with Tyler, and was an excellent father; the bond remained strong. After a while, Tyler finally began to adjust to the change.

By the summer of 1986, Tyler had become an extraordinary little boy. He was several months from his fourth birthday, but already he could print his name, read and write his ABCs, read a few little words, and carry on amazingly mature conversations. He did so well in preschool that the teachers moved him into the class for five-year-olds to give him more of a challenge. He had walked and talked early, and Mari knew every mother wanted to think her child was special. But strangers would approach her in stores to tell her how beautiful her brown-haired, blue-eyed little boy was. Tyler never met a stranger; he was open and friendly and assertive, and never hesitated to speak his mind. His wide smile lit up his mother's world.

Steve Winzen also found something phenomenal in his son. Tyler loved music, his father's passion. The child's favorite song was the Moody Blues' "In Your Wildest Dreams," and that would endow it with special meaning for Steve forever. When Tyler was three, he began describing a relatively insignificant gathering of friends and family, offering great detail about who was there, what they wore, and what they said; Tyler was remembering perfectly an evening from nearly two years ago. Steve was shocked as he realized his son had nearly total recall. Wonderful things surely were ahead for this young man.

Mari also spent hours enjoying Tyler. They watched movies together, and she read to him. Once, as they lay on the floor side by side to watch the movie of Stephen King's *Cujo,* Tyler delighted Mari by vowing that, together, they would fight off any attack by such a ferocious dog. As he sat mesmerized by the action on the screen, he told his mom, "We'd kick him and hit him and bite him; we wouldn't let him get us."

She loved to watch him as he listened to tapes of Phil Collins on his cassette player. When he got a rock stuck in the assembly, Mari had a coworker, Bob Kane, fix it; she brought Tyler to work to thank Mr. Kane. Mari had a crush on Bob, and this favor helped open the lines of communication. They had a date or two in late July and early August.

Mari decided to give Tyler a summer vacation from preschool; he was bored and she hoped some time off would reenergize his batteries. Through her neighbors Brenda and Bobbi Turner, Mari had met a nice teenager, Stacy Price, who lived across the street. She seemed quite responsible and had a lot of experience caring for her younger sister, Racheal. Mari asked Stacy if she wanted to baby-sit for Tyler over the summer, but Stacy didn't want to be tied down. So Mari somewhat reluctantly gave the job to Bobbi Turner. Mari's hesitance proved to be grounded. Tyler soon became hyperactive again and seemed to have lost his happy disposition. He even drew blood when he bit a neighbor girl, a habit Mari had broken him of long ago. When Bobbi called Mari at work to tell her about the incident, Tyler was crying so hard that Mari knew something was wrong. Little Tyler even pleaded over the phone, "I want my brother, Brian."

Mari began checking on the job Bobbi had been doing over the last month and wasn't pleased with what she learned. Even Stacy Price confirmed that Bobbi had not been doing a very good job with Tyler. And, in addition to failing to attend to Tyler's needs, Bobbi had been taking him to the apartment of a young man across the street and locking Tyler out of the bedroom while she and the man were inside. For Steve and Mari, that was the final straw. On a Friday in mid-July, Mari fired Bobbi. She turned to Stacy again, almost begging her to fill in for the last few weeks before Stacy started high school. Stacy agreed; she could use the money for new school clothes.

Tyler perked up almost immediately after Stacy took over. His sunny personality bounced back, and he really took to his new sitter. Stacy did an excellent job taking care of him, giving him the time and attention he needed; she actually enjoyed playing with him and doing what he wanted to do. She also took care of the apartment, and Mari even paid her something extra each week to give the place a good cleaning.

Stacy had a sweet combination of naiveté and maturity, and Mari enjoyed her company. But when Mari got home at night and Stacy wanted to tell her about the day's events, Tyler's impatience for his mother's attention would come out as he admonished, "Stacy, don't talk-lock-lock." Nobody knew where that phrase came from.

The next several weeks were fun. On Saturdays, Mari took Tyler, Stacy, and Racheal to a nearby swimming pool. Stacy had occasionally talked about a boy she had a crush on, and they once encountered him at the pool. Stacy didn't think it was funny when Mari and Racheal pushed Stacy's raft into the boy's in an attempt to stimulate some action between them.

Tyler's playful obsession with driving everything got him in trouble once. He and Mari were sitting on the porch waiting for Carol Brinkley so they could go on a picnic. When Mari stepped back into the building to check on Carol, Tyler hoped into the car, turned the keys Mari had left in the ignition, and then slipped the gear shift into reverse. At a slow idle, the car began backing out of the parking space. Mari stepped out of the door just in time to see Tyler crying as the car rolled backward across the street and slowed to a stop just in front of the window of the apartment where Stacy lived. By the time Mari pulled him safely from the car, she was too scared even to chide him.

Tyler and Brian had become exceptionally close; Tyler worshiped his older brother, and Mari was sure Brian was about ready to move back in with her and his brother. That really would complete her family and her happy life.

Stacy and Brian also became friends because of his regular visits to Mari's apartment. The possibility of a budding romance between them was fun to contemplate. They even decided to go on a date to the movies together. Mari planned to drop them at the theater on Saturday night, August 9, 1986.

It wouldn't happen.

Jude Govreau moved into Stillbrook Estates with her three daughters in 1984, the most recent stop in an unsettled life spent searching for something better.

She was born Judith Phipps in Vallejo, California, on April 5, 1948, to an Italian mother and a Native American father who was in the navy. She had an uneventful but odd childhood as she moved from city to city across California, attending six schools by the time she was ten. She had few friends and stayed to herself; she was the girl who was last to be picked for sports teams. She never liked school, although she was a solid B student.

The family, which included a sister who was ten years younger than Jude, moved to Pensacola, Florida, when Jude was ten. Her father, who had always been away at sea before, drew shore duty and suddenly was around the house. But he remained a stranger; he paid little attention to the children or his wife. He never gave them a dime for an ice cream cone. "Go ask your mother" was his uninterested response. He never asked about school; he never talked to his children at all, unless it was to ask someone to bring him something, perhaps a warm, wet cloth for his head when he was suffering from a migraine headache. He wasn't abusive; he just wasn't interested. Jude never saw her parents kiss, and they didn't even sleep in the same room.

Her father showed some interest, however, in the woman who owned the duplex where they lived and who inhabited the other side. He helped her with chores and even had his daughters do her dishes and laundry. The girls suspected something more was going on, and they were right. Jude's mother finally asked for a divorce in 1960, and it was the only time Jude had seen her father show any genuine emotion; he never spoke a word to his wife, but he cried. He later married the landlady.

Jude's mother moved with her daughters to Norfolk, Virginia, where she had worked as a barmaid during World War II. She went back to her former profession, leaving twelve-year-old Jude to care for her sister. Jude never went back to school after that. Education wasn't important to her mother, anyway, and she could afford to send only one of her daughters. Jude's sister liked school, so she was the one. Jude was thrilled, although she regretted it later. After her mother became pregnant in 1962, Jude got another little girl to care for.

In 1966, at the age of eighteen, Jude married a young man named Dean Price, a welder who lived next door. They moved into an apartment a few blocks from her mother, and Jude continued to take care of her youngest sister; the middle girl had married at fourteen and moved away. Jude had been married to the welder for four months when his parole officer knocked on the door; Jude hadn't known Dean had served five years in a federal prison for the theft of a government check-writing machine and the forgery of thousands of dollars in checks. Dean said sheepishly that he had intended to tell her someday.

The abuse began unexpectedly not long after that. He slapped her around with a folded newspaper after she accidentally plugged up the kitchen sink. She accepted his apology and his promise never to do it again; they kissed and made up. But the violence remained a constant as his drinking increased. He was drunk one night when he accused her of cheating on him; she actually had been to the grocery store, where he had sent her. Dean beat her for two hours, breaking her jaw and her ribs. After four days in the hospital, she went back to him. She had nowhere else to go. There weren't any shelters for battered women then.

She got pregnant a year into the marriage. When she was seven months along, Dean knocked her down the stairs because she was going to take thirty-five cents out of his change bank to buy cigarettes. She began hemorrhaging vaginally, but the doctors tried to delay any drastic steps. Her daughter was born prematurely three weeks later and lived only fifteen minutes before dying of what the doctors said was a concussion and fractured skull.

She got pregnant again about six months later and miscarried at three months. She was pregnant a third time when Dean threw a fork across the room and stuck it in her buttocks because she wouldn't hand him a towel. That, finally, was it; she left him but waited more than three years to get the divorce. Her daughter, Johnna, was born in February 1970. Dean later went back to prison for destruction of private property and had been paroled again when he died in a head-on collision with a tractor-trailer truck. But Jude wouldn't find out about his death for three years, and then only when she had a desperate reason to search for him.

She moved to Ohio with a new boyfriend in late 1970 and found herself in a new nightmare. He started using drugs, and eventually she fled back to Virginia after he pulled a loaded pistol on her. She didn't know she was three months pregnant when she left. Stacy was born on May 13, 1971, and Jude gave her the Price name.

She went through two brief marriages to sailors in 1972 and 1973. The second lasted barely a month. She threw him out when he started to hit Stacy because she was crying; she wrote him a "Dear John" letter when he went to sea the next day.

While Jude was looking for a better choice as a mate, she also was exercising her absolute opposition to any war and, specifically, the war in Vietnam. She traveled to protests across Virginia and even helped hide young men who were dodging the draft. She didn't believe in sending America's children to kill Vietnam's children. It was an extension of her nonviolent philosophy.

One of the men she had hidden during that period renewed their acquaintance later, and in 1974, Jude and her two daughters moved with him to his hometown of Fort Collins. Unfortunately, he just disappeared after she told him she was pregnant. When the baby was born in December 1975, Jude named her Racheal and gave her the name of Jude's third husband, Nichols.

The four females moved to Flat River, Missouri—not far from St. Louis—in 1976 with a man Jude had met in Colorado. She got a job as a quality control inspector at a Zenith television plant; he stayed home and watched the kids. Jude's search for some stability led her to the Mormon church in 1977. While she was laid off and drawing unemployment, the church asked her to provide a temporary home for two children from a troubled family. A social worker suggested that Jude apply to become a licensed foster parent, and within weeks, Jude had become what she was told was the first single foster parent in the state of Missouri. She opened her home to twenty-seven children during the next four years. This new effort taught her that her compulsion to try to restore emotionally damaged men and save children in crisis must come from some sort of Florence Nightingale complex.

And in 1980, she took a fourth husband, a butcher she had met through the church. He gave her the name Govreau. That marriage ended the next year, and she swore it would be her last.

Jude began working as a barmaid at Tucker's in October 1983; she was ready to graduate from bartending school when her mother died in Virginia and Jude had to make a last trip to the state where she had spent so much of her life. But the new job and a refund from the IRS helped Jude move to a new apartment at Stillbrook Estates in March 1984. She had met Rick Pashia just before that, and they had started dating.

Stacy, then thirteen, had been baby-sitting for a couple of years and was much in demand because of her love of children and her mature approach to the job. She was good with the kids, teaching them the ABCs or other lessons while still finding time for the fun activities they enjoyed. And the parents liked her because she had taken the time to learn how to handle police or fire emergencies, as well as how to administer first aid. And she was conscientious about taking care of the homes where she worked.

But there was a fun side to her, too. She was so outgoing, so bubbly, that everyone loved her; she had lots of friends and a reputation as something of the class clown. Jude would learn later that her daughter's friends were more devoted to Stacy than she could have imagined. She was turning into a beautiful young woman, five foot three, 110 pounds, with a pretty face and long brown hair. She tried out to join several of her friends as a cheerleader at Ridgewood Junior High School in Fenton and was crushed when she didn't make the squad. But she was a standout in the girl's glee club. She had a beautiful voice and loved to sing the songs made popular by one of her favorite performers, Amy Grant. Stacy also attended a Baptist church with a friend and took her religious convictions very seriously. They seemed to complement the nonviolent lessons being taught at home, which she took very seriously. She wouldn't even hit kids back if they struck her.

One of Stacy's great joys was riding the horse owned by a neighbor who often took her to the stable. Stacy loved animals and would become hysterical anytime she saw one suffering in the slightest. She was especially critical of anyone who was cruel to animals, and that concern drew her toward a career as a veterinarian. She wanted to make animal's lives better.

Stacy had taken to her new job baby-sitting little Tyler Winzen with enthusiasm and joy. She would bring the toddler back to Jude's every day, and he would entertain them all with his amazing mind. Every time he walked in, he would greet everyone happily, but would save his best for his buddy, Rick Pashia. Tyler would announce, "Hi, dude," and then exchange high-fives. He loved Stacy's kitten and often talked about his dad's cat.

Tyler excitedly told Jude how he had driven his mother's car "all by myself." When Jude said he must have been scared, he said he was, but only because he didn't have his seat belt fastened. Another time Tyler noticed Jude's rowing machine standing up in the corner and said ominously, "Oh, you've got a spanking machine." No, Jude explained, that was an exercise machine. Tyler insisted, however, that it was for spanking. He stood in front of it to demonstrate how the extended arms would swing around and deliver the punishment as he whacked himself on the bottom with his hands. Where did he come up with these things? Jude laughed in amazement.

Jude often took her daughters and Tyler swimming or to the movies during the day, before she went in for the night shift at Tucker's. Tyler even accompanied them when they went to Stacy's dental appointment for the installation of Stacy's braces. He usually would fall asleep in the chair, curled up on his knees with his rear humped into the air.

As the summer began to fade, Jude could see Stacy's

growing excitement about starting Fox High School at the end of August. Jude was so proud of Stacy as she watched this girl becoming a young woman. There was so much to look forward to—first dates, proms, college, marriage. Stacy's life would be so much better than her mother's, Jude knew.

CHAPTER 8

Captain Wally Gansmann stared as the videotape flickered
its harrowing images across the screen. In his twenty-one
years with the Jefferson County Sheriff's Department, he
had never handled the murder of a child and had never
witnessed anything like the scene rolling across the television now. He had heard some of the scuttlebutt during the
Major Case Squad's investigation—about the bathtub,
about how ghastly the murder of the children had been.
But he couldn't have envisioned this scene in his grimmest
imagination. Even though he had been a member of the
Major Case Squad for years, he wasn't on this case, and he
had kept it at arm's length. He hadn't asked about it and
he hadn't read the squad's written reports. If the squad
couldn't bust this one, it would revert to the sheriff's department. If that happened, Gansmann wanted a fresh perspective when it got dropped on his desk.

And now it had arrived. After eight days on the trail,
the Major Case Squad couldn't break it. So, on Friday,
August 15, the foot-high stack of documents had been delivered to Gansmann as the chief of the detective section
for Sheriff Buerger. Gansmann sat and watched the tape
Bob Miller had made in that bathroom. Like all of the
badge-carrying fathers who had seen it firsthand or had
watched the tape, Gansmann felt the tightness, the anxiety,
and the outright fear that anything like this could happen
to children in the county where he had raised his own.
Somewhere in his community was a beast who could inflict
that kind of death on two kids. He still was out there, free
to threaten or kill others unless the sheriff's department
could find him and bring him in.

Gansmann had heard the name of the lead suspect, this
Eugene "Geno" Fleer. Some of the narcotics detectives

said they had heard him mentioned a time or two around the fringes of the local drug trade. But Fleer was not considered a well-known quantity in police circles, and that was a little unusual for a person suspected of this kind of brutality.

After Fleer, the late Lester Howlett remained a suspect. Brenda Turner's name got mentioned; there was even some suspicion about the maintenance man at the complex and a worker or two from the nearby construction project. Gansmann waded through the huge pile of paperwork, trying to digest all the names and relationships and nuances that had frustrated the Major Case Squad.

Lieutenant Ed Kemp and others from the sheriff's department who had worked with the squad were confident something would break loose someday and the murders would be solved. Killings this controversial, magnified by Howlett's subsequent and mysterious death, would generate a lot of talk on the street, and some of it was bound to find its way to the police. Something would turn up someday, everyone was sure, and this bad guy would get what was so deservedly coming to him.

Gansmann had passed that optimistic view along to Mari Winzen and Jude Govreau, two of the most disturbed survivors of murder victims he had ever encountered. All the detectives who had talked to them offered similar assessments. Jude's grief was heightened by anger and a taste for revenge as strong as anyone had ever seen. There was no doubt that she would be unrelenting in pushing the police for a solution. Mari's sorrow was so overwhelming, everyone thought, that it would be difficult for her to deal with much beyond the pain of living each day. But Mari had called Gansmann for updates a couple of times already, so it appeared she was going to stay in close contact, too. He told both of the women that every lead would be followed and every witness or suspect would be questioned closely. He promised the sheriff's department would not slide this case onto the back burner.

He even was willing to try something rather unorthodox. Two weeks after the murders, Gansmann and his detectives wired a cooperative Steve Winzen so they could eavesdrop on a conversation he was about to have at his trailer with Eugene Fleer. Out on bond from the cocaine charge now,

Fleer was going to drop by to try to clear the air between the men. Gansmann and his squad hoped Fleer might say something that would reenergize the investigation.

Steve hadn't considered Fleer a leading candidate as the killer, but he was reconsidering in light of the intense interest by the police. As Steve waited for Geno to arrive, he felt a slight tug he recognized as fear. He knew Fleer was capable of startling violence. That, in fact, was the way the men had met about two months before the murders. Steve had stepped out of a tavern to the crack of knuckles smashing into jawbone and the whump of blows to the belly. He turned to see a man knock a woman to the parking lot pavement and then savagely kick her. Steve ran over and shouted at the man, who turned with such a wild, enraged look in his eyes that Steve was unnerved. Steve told the man to leave the woman alone, and the man muttered something about Steve being next. But then the man turned and ran away at full speed. The woman was battered and bruised, but said she had just met the guy and wanted nothing more to do with him; she wouldn't press charges.

Later that night, Steve and Lester Howlett were inside getting a bite to eat and the woman-beater joined them at the table. Lester introduced the man as a friend, Geno Fleer; Steve told Lester what had happened and then left. Over the next few weeks, Fleer began to turn up at Lester's regularly, and Steve would avoid him or leave. Fleer even apologized to Steve one night, saying he had a problem with women and was working on it. Steve never liked Fleer, but tried to tolerate him as a friend of Lester's.

And now, as detectives hid in another room and listened, Winzen and Fleer sat down to talk. Fleer said nothing to incriminate himself in the murders or Howlett's death; he assured Steve that he wouldn't do anything to hurt him or Lester. But Fleer said he knew Lester Howlett had been behind the rip-off of Dave Helmond. Howlett had tried to get Fleer involved, but he begged off; his robbing days were over, he said. Fleer's story remained fairly consistent with what he had told the police in his final version of those events, but Steve thought he detected a few contradictions as Fleer went over the same stories. All in all, the conversation was disappointing for Steve and the cops.

* * *

The days and emotions remained jumbled for Mari and Jude after the Major Case Squad departed.

Mari's family and coworkers assembled by Bob Kane had hauled everything out of her apartment under the supervision of Pat Indelicato, who continued to fill the role of director among the cast of lost souls. Pat had cringed as she tore down the yellow crime scene tape stretched across the doorway and stepped into the apartment where she had last seen her grandson alive. She knew it would be painful, but she could not begin to prepare herself for what she would see. The place was covered with black fingerprint powder and strewn with used rubber gloves, and a square of the wall had been cut away behind the sofa. All of Mari's lovely plants were dead. The sight of the brown, shriveled stalks and branches that had been so green and alive under Mari's loving care almost took Pat's breath away. Death is all over this apartment, she thought. But she stepped in and felt nothing; no fear, no sadness, no anger. She realized she was in shock, and the best thing to do was finish the task and get the hell out of there.

She hurriedly filled boxes with Mari's belongings and Tyler's toys—the hardest part of the job—and then opened the bathroom door. She took one look at the high-water line in the bathtub, turned, and walked away. She collected Mari's towels from the hallway linen closet and was surprised they seemed damp. Later, she would wonder if the moisture had really been evidence that the killer had cleaned up the bathroom with them and then returned them to the closet. Had someone done something that calculating, or was that warped idea proof that her mind was as injured as her heart?

Mari arrived as the work was underway and the yard was littered with her possessions; Pat met her outside. Mari cried as she mumbled, "I don't know what to do, Mom. I can't stand any more of this. My son is gone. My home is gone. What did I do to deserve this? What do I do now?"

Pat gave her the only answer possible: "Go home. We'll handle everything."

As the relatives finished cleaning out the apartment and prepared to leave, a police officer assigned to watch over the effort offered Pat a tip.

"Don't throw anything in the Dumpsters," he said softly.

"Why not?" was her puzzled response.

"Souvenir hunters."

Oh, God, Pat thought, this world really is getting sicker. That afternoon, Pat could feel her family deteriorating. Mari was overwhelmed by it all; she simply had no tools to deal with the pain, no defense mechanisms to handle this turn in her life. Pat sent her to the store for some milk—an effort to give her something to do—only to have her return in tears and recount how she had been standing in line when she automatically turned and began searching the store for Tyler. It had taken a couple of seconds before she realized Tyler was not there and that even something as simple as picking up a gallon of milk never would be the same.

And Joe was absolutely devastated. As he sat in his favorite chair, Pat curled up in front of him and laid her head on his knees. The tears flowed as she whispered, "Joe, I feel so bad."

His voice was flat as he said, "I can't help you, Pat. I can't even help myself."

She had never heard anything like that from this strong man. She realized then that Joe somehow felt he had failed his daughter and the honor of his family. He had talked to the police and been told, essentially, that unless he could give them the name of a suspect, there wasn't anything he could do to help. The police also had implied that they were watching the Indelicato family closely, just in case any of the relatives had thoughts about vigilante justice. Pat realized that Joe was feeling completely helpless. There was nothing he could have done before or could do now, of course. But that feeling of failure was the burden he carried through this.

The next Friday, August 15, Sergeant Leo Burle—who pronounced the "e" at the end of his name—had visited Mari to discuss the case. As she showed the detective from the sheriff's department to a chair on the patio, she thought he was a curious-looking man—in his fifties, medium height and build, with a mustache and a high forehead that abruptly exploded into a shock of thinning, graying hair combed into a high pompadour at the crest of his head. He seemed nice and told Mari how sorry he was about her loss. He explained that he would be the lead detective on the investigation for the sheriff. He vowed to find Tyler's killer if he had to work day and night. He told her to deal with him directly from now on, and even gave her telephone numbers for his office and home.

Sergeant Burle told her some war stories about his many years as a cop and even slid back the cuff of his slacks to show her the pistol tucked into his short dress boots. Although she thought it was a little overdone, she found his stories kind of exciting, almost like the stuff she had seen on TV cop shows. Burle asked some basic questions about the case, breaking no new ground. He told Mari the detectives were looking closely at all of the suspects and he was confident something would break eventually.

Over the next week, Leo Burle became Mari's knight in shining armor. She just knew he was going to deliver the revenge she lusted after. They talked daily, and Burle assured her everything possible was being done. Sometimes she called him at home in the evenings and they talked for two hours. Burle stopped by frequently, and they sat on the patio. She shared all of her feelings and fears, her suspicions and hopes, and he listened intently. He gave her some welcome tidbits about the investigation, but warned her not to repeat them because he wasn't supposed to tell her. Yes, Eugene Fleer remained a suspect, as did Brenda Turner; Lester Howlett probably had been involved somehow. This was more than any other cop had told her, and she appreciated being kept informed. After all, as the victim's mother, surely she had a right to know; only Sergeant Leo Burle had been willing to give her any information.

He punctuated the conversations with more anecdotes about his career. He had arrested the famous madam of Jefferson County who ran massage parlors that were fronts for prostitution, and she had offered him sex to let her go. Mari remembered the highly publicized case and Burle's role in it contributed to his growing stature as her larger-than-life hero. He explained the inner workings of the sheriff's department; he described how the department worked with the prosecuting attorney, and what kind of evidence was needed to get charges. Mari felt as if she were really getting behind-the-scenes information. With this inside view, Mari began to feel as if she were living in a television show, and it was fascinating.

Mari was less than surprised when Burle suggested they go to a nearby Denny's Restaurant for coffee one evening. By then, she thought getting out for a few minutes might be beneficial and she felt more comfortable with her own personal detective. They had coffee and everything went fine.

They even went out for pizza one Friday night, and Burle told Mari the police were convinced Fleer was the killer and they strongly suspected Howlett was involved. Burle said those suspicions were backed up by the cocaine deals in Rockford and the reports of rip-offs among dealers. Mari hoped all of this meant the investigation would lead to a murder charge soon.

Pat Indelicato was less enthusiastic, however. She thought Leo Burle was eyeing her daughter like a junkyard dog sizing up a bone. But anytime Pat brought up her concerns, Mari dismissed them with the tone of a teen-aged girl who had just been asked to the prom by the big man on campus.

Before much longer, when nothing happened in the case, Mari lost confidence in Burle and his investigation. She began to suspect that he did, indeed, have other interests where she was concerned. Their relationship deteriorated and the regular visits by Burle ceased.

But Sergeant Burle denied any interest in Mari beyond the boundaries of the investigation. He said he spent a lot of time with her, including trips for coffee or pizza. That was standard procedure in such a case; after all, she was the mother of the youngest victim and the ex-wife of a man whose drug dealing could have been a motive. But that was as far as it went, Burle said.

Over the next few weeks, Mari's emotional condition deteriorated. She went back to work three weeks after the murders, before she was really ready. She cried more tears than she thought was possible, but there was no relief in that and no hiding from the pain. She had died and gone to hell, only to find out that hell was living what was left of her life. Her world had exploded and she was left with the shattered remains. She didn't even know herself anymore; as much as her life had changed, so had she. She was taking an occasional tranquilizer, but she promised her-

self she would be careful not to slip into the habits that
had sent her over the edge before.

She still couldn't stand to drive her car by herself, and
she couldn't listen to the radio because so many songs reminded her of Tyler. One day her color vision simply disappeared. The world became black and white and shades of
gray—almost as if her vision were reflecting the reality in
her life. But, amid the rest of her troubles, it didn't matter;
so what, was her apathetic response. And if all of that
didn't convince her she was losing control, her body added
the insult of an occasional loss of control of her bladder.
She was thirty-two years old and she was wetting her pants.

She was even beginning to have vague, subtle thoughts
about how easy it would be to die and leave all of the misery
of this world. One day in mid-September, as she drove home
from work, two voices began whispering to her. The first
urged her to drive into a brick wall or a bridge abutment.
"Just slam into it," the voice murmured. "There won't be any
more pain. You won't even have to think about all of this
anymore." As she started to accelerate, the other voice
warned, "No, Mari. Don't do it. You can't do that."

She pulled over and buried her face in her hands. Her
head hurt so badly she wanted to scream. She began to
sob as she pulled away and drove directly to St. Anthony's
Hospital. When the clerk in the emergency room asked if
she wanted to be admitted, Mari nodded. She couldn't do
this alone anymore.

The weeks since the murders had left Jude Govreau just
as adrift. She and Mari hadn't talked much. In one phone
conversation, Mari and her mother angrily complained
about Howlett's appearance at the Indelicato house that
Friday to pick up Steve Winzen. Mari nearly spat venom
as she described how Howlett had sat there and cried and
carried on about Tyler's death. "He was in our house all
day, and he's the bastard who killed Tyler," Mari snapped.
But Jude usually couldn't reach Mari when she called; her
mom usually said Mari was asleep.

The women had shared another insult and injury, however. Within a few weeks of the murders, they both received bills for $165 from the Jefferson County medical
examiner's office for the body bags used to remove their

children from the apartment. The invoices sent Jude and Mari into orbit. Their kids had been murdered in a crime the police couldn't solve, no one would give them any straight answers about the case, they weren't allowed to see any of the police reports, and now the county wanted them to cough up $165 apiece for body bags. Joe Indelicato and Jude placed outraged calls to the medical examiner's office, and the issue was never brought up again.

Although the incident infuriated Jude, it was a minor addition to the ordeal. She had been unable to sleep more than three hours a night because that was when her mind attacked her the most viciously, sometimes playing images of how Stacy must have looked in that bathtub. Jude's only rest came in the occasional nap in the afternoon. The more time passed, the more Jude realized Stacy was never coming home. After a while, it didn't even help to play the mind game Jude had developed to try to fool herself into thinking that Stacy was away at college and would return in a few weeks.

Jude called the police every day, but seldom got anything more than "We're following every lead." Eugene Fleer had been released after his family posted $1,000 in cash to satisfy the $10,000 bond, and the police really had not much more to say about him. Captain Gansmann had met with Jude and Rick and told them the police strongly suspected, but couldn't prove, that two men—probably two big men— had been involved in the murders. She rotated calls through all the detectives, but most of them were reluctant to discuss the investigation for fear Jude or Mari might leak sensitive details to the press and blow the case.

Jude managed to pry occasional bits of information free, however. One investigator told her Fleer had lied about being at Howlett's the morning of the murders. Another had explained Fleer's alibi of borrowing the television the night Howlett died and suggested that Fleer had hidden the cocaine in the refrigerator in an attempt to protect it from any drug-sniffing dogs that might be brought in. Sergeant Burle suggested Fleer might have switched the piles of cocaine, letting Howlett snort from the pure cocaine while thinking he was using what he had already cut with baby laxative; that could explain the overdose by such an experienced doper. Jude was surprised Fleer had given up the cocaine to the cops so easily later; she assumed he was trying to deflect suspicion in the murders by cooperating in the drug case. In the daily journal she was beginning to keep, she developed a list of every lead or suspect she heard mentioned. But there seemed to be no real direction to the investigation.

In addition to the bill for body bags, every contact Jude had with Dr. Gordon Johnson, the medical examiner, frustrated her. He couldn't tell from the bruises whether Stacy had been strangled from the front or rear—an important fact, Jude thought, suggesting whether Stacy had trusted the killer enough to turn her back on him. He had concluded that Stacy was nearly dead when she was placed in the tub. She had struggled; the bruises on her forehead and the scrapes around her mouth could have resulted from being beaten against the bottom of the tub. He said her fingernails had been bitten too far down to recover any scrapings of skin from the assailant; Jude knew Stacy never chewed her nails. And Jude was furious later when she heard Johnson had not placed the bodies on a sheet when he dragged them from the tub. All in all, the medical examiner's performance didn't impress her any more than the record established by the police.

But those bits of information intensified her curiosity about the killer's anger. Why had he abused Stacy so badly? Why had he felt compelled to beat and strangle and drown her? Jude knew her daughter would not have resisted. She was a nonviolent, physically passive girl who would have been too terrified to fight back. Why would someone unleash such fury on this teen? If the motive was sex, surely there would be other clues—clothing in disarray or something. What possible motive was there to kill two children that way?

Without promising leads in the investigation, Jude could find nothing to hang on to as she was buffeted about by each day's routine of tears and insomnia. She wasn't sleeping and she wasn't eating and she could find no relief from the pain; she could only cry. And her phobias were finding new ways to work on her. The rain made her crazy, sending her into uncontrollable sobs and panic attacks; it seemed to arrive every Thursday, without fail. And now she couldn't even run water into a bathtub. Once, she and Racheal had tried to clean the bathroom and were crying in each other's arms instead when they heard the telephone ring. When they couldn't find which phone was ringing, they became convinced it was Stacy's portable phone in the bedroom where they had set up her furniture and belongings. But that phone wasn't plugged in, and Johnna said, "Mom, it's Stacy calling from the grave." Jude insisted it was nothing more than some kind of electronic interference, but they packed the phone in a box and took it to the basement, never to be opened again.

A week after the murders, Jude returned to the 6:00-P.M.-to-1:30-A.M. shift behind the bar at Tucker's. She didn't feel ready, but she couldn't afford to miss any more paychecks. She tried to look as presentable as possible that first night. She fixed her hair, but there was little she could do about the obvious loss of weight and the dark, sunken eyes that returned her stare from the mirror. She was shaking so badly that she had to make three passes before she was able to keep her purse from falling off the bread rack, where she kept it in the kitchen. When she walked into the bar, every face turned toward her and the place was dead quiet. She felt as if she had leprosy and the curious public were looking for the scars. She reached deep inside and found a cheerful, "Hi! How's everyone doing?" That seemed to ease the tension—for the others—and she managed to accept several expressions of condolence without coming unglued. But many times she had to flee secretly into the bathroom to cry.

Most of the customers and coworkers respected her privacy, and she found it hard to forgive those whose comments ripped open her wounds. One woman suggested Jude console herself with the knowledge that it could have been worse. "Worse? How?" Jude demanded angrily. Well, Stacy could have been mutilated, was the awkward response. Really comforting, Jude thought. Another woman said that at least Stacy was in a better place and at peace now. "How do you know that?" Jude almost shouted. "She's not at peace. She died violently and terribly. Just because she's dead doesn't mean she's at peace. How can anybody whose life ended like that be at peace?"

Over the next few weeks, many of Jude's customers wanted to talk about the case and ask what she had learned about the investigation. Many of them were sure Lester

Howlett was the killer. Jude even learned to talk about it without crying. She tried to make it just another conversation, just another trip through the same dialogue.

She found that she was unable to stay in the house alone during the days. She had spent more than $1,200 to install security bars on all of the windows, a metal frame around the sliding doors, and two deadbolts on the front door. But even if she had designed a safe house, she still couldn't feel safe. When Racheal returned to school and Rick was at work, Jude would leave the house until it was time to pick up Racheal. She spent her days wandering through Kmart or the malls, or having a soda at Rax or Pizza Hut. When she returned home, she usually had a neighbor go in and check the house first.

Much of the time, Jude found herself walking through a fog. As she prepared to write a check at the grocery store once, she genuinely could not remember her name. She froze for a moment, fearing she finally was losing her sanity. The killer finally had done it; he had taken her daughter and now he had taken her sanity, too. She looked at the puzzled cashier and then mumbled that she had the wrong checkbook as she fled from the store.

Life at home sometimes was as difficult. She found herself setting a place for Stacy at the table most of the time, as if she could not admit that it was no longer necessary. When the meal was ready, Jude usually called out the habitual "Girls," unable to admit that only Racheal was there to answer the dinner bell. Jude once dissolved into uncontrollable tears after she made Stacy's favorite breakfast before realizing she was not there to enjoy it.

Jude started trying to eat again after a couple of weeks, only to throw up most of the food again. She was careful to stay away from alcohol, even beer; she knew it was a depressant, and God knew she was depressed enough already. She wondered how the world could go on, flowers blooming and the sun shining, when her world was dark and full of terror. Surely she would die of a broken heart, she thought; but no, it would not be that easy. The panic attacks began within weeks, sending pains across her chest and down her arms. When she did sleep, she often would awake in a cold sweat with her chest tight and her breathing labored. After an attack on the way to work, she drove to a hospital emergency room. A doctor checked her heart and attributed the symptoms to stress. He finally persuaded her to take a mild antidepressant, and that seemed to help a little. Then she became convinced she couldn't die. Her body would keep going until she got the killer, and because she had to be there for Racheal.

Racheal was having similar problems, waking up a lot at night, crying and frightened; Jude would move her to a pallet on Jude's bedroom floor. Racheal returned to school in September, and Jude took her to the bus stop each morning to see her off safely; there would be no more naive assumptions about the simple things in life. Jude warned school officials to watch over Racheal and not allow her to be approached by anyone claiming to be a relative or friend. Amid all of that, Racheal amazingly resumed her record of making straight A's. She had to learn to deal with the whispers—"That's the girl whose sister was murdered"—as she walked down the halls. Some of her friends seemed perplexed about how to deal with her, as if she had some terminal communicable disease. She hated these new problems, but she realized she could do little about how other people dealt with her. She was bothered more that the TV and newspapers always referred to Stacy as "the baby-sitter," without using her name. She was a person, Racheal protested, not just some anonymous "baby-sitter" whose identity had disappeared behind a shorthand description. She was a real person—a daughter, sister, and friend who was sorely missed by many.

Racheal's worst times came at home. She had to listen to Jude's incessant telephone calls looking for information about the murders. And Jude realized after a while that she was relentlessly questioning Racheal to see if she had remembered anything new that might help the investigation. Jude seemed to be at her all day every day, passing her growing obsession down to her daughter. It hurt to admit, but Racheal probably was better off at the baby-sitter's where she stayed after school than she was at home with her possessed mother.

In September, Jude decided to offer a reward for information, as they always say, leading to the arrest and conviction of the person or persons responsible for the murders. There seemed to be no movement on the case, and Jude hoped waving some cash at it might shake something loose. She could only afford to put up $500, but she thought anything would be better than the nothing that was happening. If the $500 didn't spur any interest, she thought she might add more to it later when she received the $2,000 death benefit from Stacy's life insurance policy.

Jude checked with several charitable organizations to see if any would be willing to lend its name, sponsorship, and tax-exempt status to the effort. When she had no luck, she decided to call Child Find Missouri, an organization dedicated to locating missing children. She had contacted the Child Find offices in the St. Louis suburb of Maplewood about a year earlier when Johnna was missing from the group home. Jude feared she had been kidnapped, and the staff at Child Find sprang immediately into action. Within two hours, fliers with information about Johnna were being circulated throughout the area. Johnna, it turned out, had run away, and she was located in three days. But Jude had been impressed by the dedication and quick response of Child Find. She remembered she had talked to Margaret Baxter,* the executive director—a short, thick woman with sandy blond hair and a ruddy complexion. Jude called her again.

Margaret was even more receptive than she had been a year ago, and readily agreed to lend Child Find's tax-exempt status to Jude's reward campaign. She turned Jude over to Jackie Corey, one of her chief assistants, and told Jackie to take care of her. Jude and Jackie made a solid connection from the start and would become good friends. Jackie and Margaret explained that Child Find's primary goal was to locate missing or kidnapped children. But after Jackie Corey had talked to Jude a couple of times, she knew she would do anything to help this wounded mother find her daughter's killer.

Margaret Baxter added that since children still were at risk from a killer on the loose, Child Find would add $2,500 to Jude's seed money, set up a trust fund at a local bank to accept donations to the reward from the public, and help publicize the whole thing. Margaret knew some of the local reporters and would arrange it all.

Once again, Margaret was riding to Jude's assistance. Jude didn't have many friends or relatives backing her up, and she knew nothing about dealing with the media. She appreciated Margaret's efforts more than Margaret would ever know. This woman seemed so professional, so knowledgeable, so together—so powerful compared to Jude, who felt so powerless amid all of this pain and confusion.

As the women discussed their plans, Margaret suggested a news conference to announce the reward, spiced up with appearances by Jude and Mari to decry the lack of progress in the investigation. Margaret guaranteed a good response; the press would be hungry to interview these women, who still had never commented publicly on their children's brutal murders. Despite some nervousness about such a performance in front of reporters and cameras, Jude realized it could generate some needed publicity and restore an urgency to the investigation. But there was a big hitch; Mari had called her a week earlier with the news that she was hospitalized for an emotional breakdown. Would Mari be up to facing reporters asking how it "feels" to be the mother of a murdered child and to know that the case remained unsolved? Jude's concern was justified. Mari's reaction was indeed less than enthusiastic: she wanted nothing to do with that kind of pressure. Jude would have to be the spokeswoman for both of them, Mari said flatly.

Even the psychiatric ward at the hospital wasn't prepared to deal with Mari and the realities of her life. Group therapy was pointless. She wasn't going to get anything beneficial out of listening to one woman worry that her dog was sick, another complain that her husband didn't show her enough attention, or another one bemoan her childhood in a dysfunctional family. To Mari, none of that approached the burden she carried or gave her any insight into how to bear the load. She wouldn't even participate in the group conversation; she was afraid an honest account of her life would blow the others away. Her psychiatrist was nice and sincere, but he wasn't able to deal with the depth of Mari's grief. A lot of the staff talked to her, and were genuinely interested in helping, but they didn't know what to do for her either. No one there was equipped to solve the problems of the person she had become, the person she thought of as "the homicide survivor."

She was able to connect somewhat, however, with her roommate. This suicidal young woman had suffered some of life's cruelest blows. She had watched her father shoot and kill her mother and sister, and then himself—a scenário that pushed her to a suicide attempt. The trauma in her life and in Mari's actually created a link between them, and they both found some comfort in that.

The only good thing to come from her time in the hospital was the opportunity to be alone for a while on neutral ground—free from the almost smothering protection of her parents, the persistent well-meaning advice, and the crushing assault of everyday life. She had become a misfit out there. She was afraid people would pity her, and she didn't want that. She was beginning to think she really just wanted to be left alone with her grief. She decided she would take a small apartment near her job and spin a cocoon around herself. She would work and huddle alone in her apartment, and repeat that every day until her time on earth was over. She really didn't even want to be here anymore, but she had to be until she died. So she would work and hide in her safe room. That was the only way she thought she could cope with what had happened and how she felt. Strange, she thought, that someone else had murdered Tyler and she got the life sentence.

Sergeant Leo Burle had called her at the hospital a couple of times to chat and had even dropped in to see her. He stopped by one Sunday, but surprised her when he explained that this was an official visit. She felt a brief surge of anticipation. Had something finally broken? But then Burle explained that Geno Fleer's trailer had been vandalized and the police believed Mari had done it. She was speechless and had to suppress an urge to laugh.

"I wish to God I could tell you I did it, Leo, but I didn't."

"Look, Mari, we know you did it and we really don't care. Nothing is going to happen to you. We just want you to admit it so we can clear it up."

"Leo, I didn't do it. Fleer probably did it himself for the insurance. I swear, Leo, I didn't do it."

"No, Fleer didn't do it himself. We know that. We don't care if you did it, we just want to clear it up."

As Burle left her room, it was obvious he didn't believe her denials. She still found it funny. She wouldn't have minded if someone had torched Fleer's trailer. But she hadn't done it; that was the least of her concerns right now.

* * *

After Jude called to propose the joint media appearance, the idea haunted Mari for days. Here was a chance to tell everyone about the pain that wouldn't end, about the ache for her lost son that dragged her down every second of every day, about the anger at the killer who had done it and the disappointment that the cops had not solved it. The people out there needed to know all of that, and maybe it would touch a tender nerve in someone who knew something. Maybe it would bring forward someone with that one tip that would expose the murderer. Mari didn't want to peel away the layers of her soul that way, to put herself and her grief on display; her doctor and family advised against it, too. But she finally decided to take this next, painful step. She called Jude back and agreed to participate in the news conference.

Margaret Baxter arranged it all, adding it to the poster that Child Find already had issued featuring large photographs of Tyler and Stacy, announcing the reward, and asking for calls to its offices or the sheriff's department.

Jude and Rick picked up Mari at the hospital on Tuesday, September 30, and drove to Margaret's office for the event. For the first time, the two women had a chance to really talk to each other. They shared their pain and frustration, and their anger that the killer had not been caught. In fact, they agreed, the cops weren't even showing them enough compassion or respect to keep them informed about the investigation. The deaths of their children—their flesh and blood—had precipitated this, and Mari and Jude felt they were being treated as outsiders who had no interest in what was happening and no business asking questions. They seemed to have no rights; that made them angrier and caused them more pain than anything but the murders of their children.

When they arrived at the Child Find office and Mari was introduced to her host, she found something vaguely troubling about Margaret Baxter. But Mari was more concerned about how this news conference would go, and she and Jude soon found themselves sitting in front of a battery of reporters, pleading through tears for help from the public to solve the murders. Mari's anger and frustration gave her a new voice, and she heard herself answering questions and expounding in detail. She even disclosed that she had suffered what she described as "just about a nervous breakdown."

"Maybe through offering the reward, we can get this cleared up," she was saying as the reporters scribbled away. "There is a killer loose. People don't seem to realize this. Is it going to take another child being murdered to make them become aware? For seven weeks, there has been absolutely no publicity, no coverage. We've got to make the public aware. I have an older child. Stacy's mother has two other children. We're very frightened."

Then she fired her first public salvo at the sheriff's department. "I don't feel like they're doing enough. Its been eight weeks and they have no evidence, no suspects. I personally do not know what they're doing. I call them every day and they're always waiting on something. And they're not doing anything."

To a reporter from the *St. Louis Globe-Democrat,* Mari also talked about "the Sack Man." A fun family tradition had been destroyed and her father couldn't even say those words anymore because Tyler really had seen the Sack Man.

Jude told the reporter about her loss of appetite and sleep, and her grief at never being able to watch Stacy leave on a first date, dress for a senior prom, graduate from high school, or bring Jude's grandchildren into the world.

As Margaret Baxter had predicted, the press was eating it up. Talking to the newspaper reporters had been one thing, but now Jude and Mari were told that Rick Edlund, a reporter for KSDK-TV, the NBC affiliate in St. Louis, wanted them on camera for a special interview. That terrified them. Jude still feared that someone was targeting her family, and she worried that appearing so brazenly on television might draw a bull's-eye on everyone's forehead. They finally decided to grant the interview only if they were filmed in shadows to mask their faces. Edlund agreed, and the women were impressed with how sensitively and kindly he dealt with them during the interview. From the dark that fell across their faces, Mari and Jude ripped into the police again. Mari caricatured Sheriff Buck Buerger and his men as "Deputy Dawgs." Why don't they chase leads instead of following leads? she asked sarcastically.

Buerger was contacted by reporters for a response, and he predictably disagreed with the mothers' views on the investigation. The children had not been forgotten; his detectives were following every lead and doing everything they could. They had solved 95 of the 102 murders in Jefferson County in the twenty-two years since he became sheriff; that was an incredibly high clearance rate and proved that his department could perform. He also mentioned that Lester Howlett's death made it more difficult to get answers; one important source of information had been silenced permanently. But if Howlett was the murderer, the detectives would prove that. If someone else had killed the children, the police would find him, Buerger swore.

After the women's interview was broadcast on TV and the stories appeared in the newspapers, Mari got a call in her hospital room from an irate Leo Burle. How dare she do that to him? he fumed. He had cared for her, tried to help her get information, and even visited her in the hospital. And that was how she repaid him? His own men were giving him flak over her comments. Mari snapped back that he actually had done nothing to catch her son's killer. She screamed that she had meant every word she said to the reporters, and then she slammed down the phone. But that surge of fury was soon followed by a wave of overwhelming fear. What had she done? She knew that would be the end between her and Burle. Had she destroyed any chance of getting the police to find the killer?

Jude also was on the receiving end of Burle's anger when she talked to him later. Hoping to convert the situation to her advantage, Jude explained that she had not been the one making the critical remarks about the police; she hoped maybe that would get him to confide in her. But he was in no mood to be friendly. Neither woman could keep her mouth shut, he snapped, so he wouldn't tell either of them anything again to keep from endangering the investigation. Jude would take great pains for several weeks to smooth things over with Burle.

Bob Kane had become Mari's closest confidant. He had visited her often at her parents' home and in the hospital, always there to listen without being judgmental or overbearing. Mari appreciated that kind of friendship. And Pat

Indelicato was grateful to see a man spend time with Mari, and keep his hands off of her.

On a visit to Mari at the hospital one Sunday in mid-October, Bob convinced her to join him for a motorcycle ride through the fall weather. The wind in her face felt good as they drove through Babbler State Park, and she closed her eyes. She rode that way for a long time—listening to the hum of the motor, feeling the sun on her face, and hearing the leaves blow across the road. She began to feel some peace. For the first time in more than two months, something felt—almost—good. When she thought of Tyler, the agony still was unbearable. But she could feel something else now, too. It felt right to be there with Bob. When she opened her eyes, she felt almost reborn. Her color vision, gone since those dark days after the murders, had returned. She could see the palette of hues in the fall foliage, and she suddenly felt alive again. Perhaps, after all of this time, the terrible shock was beginning to wear off. But there was something else, something spiritual. Being with Bob felt very right.

CHAPTER 9

Margaret Baxter had become a valued friend in ways Jude Govreau never could have imagined, and Jackie Corey was teaching Jude amazing methods to get information other people didn't want her to have. The women talked almost daily, and Jude often visited her new friends at the Child Find office in Maplewood. Margaret seemed as dedicated to finding the killer as Jude was and promised that Child Find's resources were at Jude's disposal. Margaret and Jackie even called in two private investigators they thought might be able to do what the police couldn't. Margaret highly recommended these former Major Case Squad detectives. She said she had used them to help get kids out of a cult in South America and they were so good they provided protection for the executives of a well-known international corporation headquartered in St. Louis.

The men visited Jude and spent a few hours learning the details of the murders. They carried themselves well, exuded confidence and competence, and seemed more intense than most of the police officers Jude had met. The investigators said they would take any case unless it involved dirty cops or the Mafia. They promised to check things out for a few days and call back. When they did, they told Jude flatly that there was nothing they could do; they would not take her case. The police were doing everything they could and these detectives didn't really want to get involved. They wouldn't be more specific about their reasons, but they would need $500 to cover their phone bills, mileage, and other expenses.

Jude was disappointed, but not terribly surprised. She paid the fee; they apparently had put in the time. But she was confused and couldn't help but wonder about their refusal to take the case. They had said there were only two reasons they would turn one down, and she wondered whether this case involved dirty cops or the Mafia. She had a hard time seeing this as a Mafia case; she had never heard of a mafioso immersed in the worst kind of organized crime suddenly becoming a child-killer. Beyond that, she thought ruefully, both Tyler and Stacy were part Italian, and that made them even more unlikely victims for a Mafia hit. Although the private detectives never would tell Margaret Baxter or Jackie Corey what was going on, Margaret speculated there must have been some Mafia involvement to scare off men she knew to be tough, hardened pros.

Jude was getting used to that kind of disappointment; the same scenario was being repeated often. She would receive gracious and promising offers of help, but nothing ever materialized. After the reward was announced, a man in his seventies who was an experienced investigator called and offered his assistance for free. He went to Jefferson County and talked to the detectives at the sheriff's department, but called Jude later to say they wouldn't cooperate with him and there was nothing he could do. A probation officer who worked with sex offenders said she would see what she could find out and would even try to meet with Eugene Fleer; Jude never heard any more from her. Jude talked to several well-known detectives in the St. Louis area, and they were free with their time and advice. But nothing they suggested worked, and their promises to check with the detectives from the Major Case Squad and Buerger's department yielded little of any use.

A veteran investigator from the St. Louis Police Department chatted with Captain John O'Rando and reported back to Jude that O'Rando suspected Brenda Turner was the killer. That reinforced one of Jude's suspicions, especially since she learned that the Turners had moved out of the St. Louis area a few weeks after the murders. No one seemed to know where they were, and that bothered Jude, too. All of this worry about the Turners planted a seed in her mind that would germinate there for some time before blooming later into a bizarre scheme.

Jude and Mari had talked to each other very little since the interviews in October. Mari even had refused Margaret's request for a donation toward the reward fund, drawing a crack from Margaret that Mari must not be too interested in finding the person who killed her son. Mari retorted that she just wasn't interested in doing it Margaret's way. Mari hoped that Jude understood; the problem was Mari's personal reaction to Margaret, not the goal. Mari simply found something objectionable about Margaret—something phony or devious, perhaps—and Mari was terribly uncomfortable with Margaret and her tactics. Mari asked Jude to handle that aspect of the case; Mari would find another course.

The rest of October, the month that began with the interviews, was a very strange period.

Eugene "Geno" Fleer walked into a Jefferson County courtroom in Hillsboro and entered a guilty plea to one count of possession of a controlled substance—the ounce of cocaine he and Lester Howlett had picked up in Rockford. Fleer had made his deal with prosecutors, and he would be sentenced a few weeks later to four years in prison. Jude and Mari weren't sure what to think about this new entry on Fleer's record. They feared his imprisonment could dull whatever edge remained on the investigation into the murders. In fact, some of the detectives whom the mothers were talking to almost daily even commented that Fleer wasn't going anywhere now, so they didn't have to worry so much about him. The cops promised to keep tabs on Fleer while he did his time and to keep the women informed in case something came up. But Jude and Mari knew better than to count on that; they hadn't been able to learn anything substantive about the murder investigation, and it wasn't likely they would hear what went on behind prison walls.

And the women wondered if Fleer had gone to prison for his own safety. Was he afraid to be on the streets, a target for the kind of revenge rumored to be behind the murders? If the deaths of Tyler and Stacy were some kind of drug hit gone wrong—an apparently popular motive in some speculations—was Fleer worried that he would be the next victim of vengeance? Was he going to hide behind bars long enough to let this cool off? Was he trading a couple of years in prison for his own skin? Even some of the police admitted wondering if he was trying to take the heat off by copping to the drug charge.

In October, Jude attended a meeting of the organization called Parents of Murdered Children; she had kept the phone number the nurse had so thoughtfully pressed into her hand in the emergency room the day of the murders. She had talked on the telephone several times to the woman who had founded the group as a way to help grieving parents handle their overwhelming grief. The woman even put Jude in touch with the mother of a nine-year-old girl who had been murdered in a bizarre case. She and Jude talked often, and that helped Jude see that people could find a way to survive the loss.

But attending the monthly meeting for the first time was different. Sitting in the circle of bereaved parents, Jude was unable to find the strength to introduce herself or tell the others what had happened; Rick Pashia had to do that. There was so much pain in the room that all Jude could do was cry as she looked from person to person, realizing that each of them had lost a child in the cruelest manner possible. She would go back for three or four more meetings, finding some comfort among people who understood what it was like to pray to die. She listened to one man and woman tell about the murders of their three children, and wondered if she ever would learn to handle it as gracefully as they had. But she finally had to stop going to the meetings. It just hurt too much.

Late in October, Mari ended her thirty days in the hospital, returned to her parents' home, and tried to resume some kind of life. Although her boss had fired her while she was in the hospital, he kept sending her paychecks, and he gave her job back when she got out. She really didn't feel any better and was still battling the sorrow and the anguish and the depression. But she had needed the time away from everyone, and she hoped she had exorcised the worst of the demons.

She began to wonder about that, however, as Halloween neared. That had been one of Tyler's favorite holidays, and it would be the first one Mari would endure without him. As the time for trick-or-treating approached, Mari thought a lot about the activities the year before. Tyler's Grandma Winzen had made him a clown outfit, and he had sat patiently while Mari applied the appropriate makeup, holding his chin in her hand as she drew on the clown face. What a big boy he was getting to be—a little man, she had thought lovingly. And he had been thrilled to knock on the doors and hold up his plastic pumpkin to collect the goodies. It had been the first Halloween in which he could really participate. And now, Mari was haunted by the fact that it had been his last.

When her friend Laura Vitale called to ask if Mari wanted to go trick-or-treating with Laura and her kids, Mari exploded. She screamed into the phone, demanding to know how Laura could do something so cruel. Mari threw the phone across the room and ran, leaving her father to soothe poor Laura; she was stunned to have a gesture of kindness blow up in her face.

Thanksgiving was no better. Mari left the dinner table when her father began the holiday prayer. "Am I supposed to thank God for killing my son?" she asked bitterly.

In the first week of December, Mari and Jude met at a candlelight ceremony sponsored by Compassionate Friends—another organization formed to help parents recover from the deaths of their children. Standing in the large crowd in a synagogue, Mari stared at the huge board covered by photographs of the lost children—including Tyler and Stacy. As Mari watched grown men sob uncontrollably, she felt as if her heart were being ripped out. She never could go back.

Christmas crumbled in a fiasco, too, with everyone's efforts to make it joyous failing miserably; Mari cried all day. She thought of it as "black Christmas." The only bright spot in the day came when Bob Kane dropped by that evening to give Mari a diamond necklace.

Once again, Bob was there when Mari needed him most. He was was waiting for her in January, too, when she decided she had to leave her parents' home. They were smothering her with their care and concern, treating her as if she were a two-year-old again. She understood why they were doing it, but she still had to get away before she atrophied beyond restoration. Pat and Joe Indelicato understood as well; it had been difficult for them, too.

Bob offered her a spare room in his apartment—strictly as a rental agreement—and the idea felt right immediately. Mari moved in and soon realized she and Bob were falling deeply in love. As the next weeks and months passed, Mari would find some measure of contentment. She and Bob often sat together and talked about how wonderful these new feelings were; something greater than the two of them was making this happen, Mari was sure. She mused that someone must be sprinkling "magic dust" over them. Being in love with Bob couldn't take away the pain of Tyler's absence, but Mari tried to accept it for what it was. Eventually, they began to talk about marriage, and Mari hoped the cloud was beginning to lift.

But the gloom of August 1986 came back with a vengeance in March 1987. Mari was listening vaguely to the television tuned low for background noise when she heard an announcement about a program on child-murder cases. When she turned to look at the TV, she was shocked to see her son's face—the face that she had missed so terribly. She exploded into tears and began to tremble, almost as if she had been blown back in time to that hallway outside her apartment that awful morning. She felt crushed as everything rushed back in an overwhelming wave of pain and anguish. Within minutes, she had called her doctor and was on her way to pick up a new prescription for Valium. As she took the first pill, she started down a road that would carry her even farther back than the shock of that television program and would transport her even farther away from the recovery she had sought so desperately.

Within weeks, she was taking too many Valium—sometimes ten a day—and the drug was doing its job too well. Everything in her world was now dull and gray, and she managed to function at the flattest level possible. She quit her job and sought refuge in her home—a move she would recognize later as a dreadful mistake. She began reading books about real-life crimes, often comparing the suffering described in those stories to her own.

But she fell hardest into the clutches of a new obsession. She had remembered seeing a Clint Eastwood movie called *Sudden Impact* about a rape victim who exacted her own lethal vengeance on the pack of creeps who had assaulted her and her teenaged sister, leaving the younger victim catatonic and institutionalized. The woman hunted down each rapist, lured him to a secluded location, and then shot him to death. She even performed what a movie detective called "a .38 caliber vasectomy" on one of them. Mari rented the movie, watched it repeatedly, and then bought her own copy to watch for hours and hours. Mari found this woman's revenge—justice, it seemed to Mari—not only appealing, but the only fair and proper way to deal with people who had inflicted such torment on their victims and then eluded the police and courts. Mari longed to deliver that kind of retribution to the person who had killed her son and her young friend. She sometimes believed she could feel the gun in her hand and could see the bullets tearing into the killer's heart. Finally, Mari thought, she had found the way to do what the police obviously could not.

Pat Indelicato felt chills as she watched Mari sit mesmerized in front of the television. Her daughter seemed to disappear into the world inside that screen as *Sudden Impact* played over and over. Mari was so lost in the fantasy that she wasn't aware there was anyone else in the room. There was only the woman avenger stalking and punishing the offenders—Mari's choice over reality. Pat understood that Mari wanted to write a finale to her own movie. If this slim blond woman portrayed so vividly in the movie could do it, Mari could, too.

In April, Mari started working three days a week for Laura Vitale's catering business. Although that occupied some of her time, Mari still had too much left for watching television, taking Valium, and getting lost in her pain and agony. One small victory brightened things for a while. When the cemetery operated by the Catholic Church announced a new policy that would allow only a flat marker on Tyler's grave—not the two-foot marble headstone Mari had chosen—her father rode to her rescue. Joe Indelicato finally had found a battle he could fight for his wounded little girl. Joe and Mari appealed through all possible channels in the church, eventually taking their case all the way the St. Louis archdiocese, and they won. Pat Indelicato had stayed out of it; this was something Joe and Mari needed to do together. With this victory, Joe had restored his honor and dignity, and Mari beamed the day her father took her to pick out the monument they had won the right to place at her son's grave.

Mari had come to think of this as essential to her sanity. That headstone was one of the few physical reminders she had left that Tyler Patrick Winzen had ever lived. As time passed, Mari began decorating the headstone on holidays and often left little gifts there on her frequent visits throughout the year. If others found this strange, that was their problem. She found that it preserved a closeness to Tyler; it helped bridge the distance put between them by a stranger. Only a parent who had made a trip to a cemetery to share a holiday with a child would be able to understand what Mari Winzen needed to keep her sanity.

Mari and Bob also started house hunting. After a month, Mari visited a subdivision nestled into the hills off Manchester Road in St. Louis County. When she opened the door to a split foyer, she knew she was home; this was where she and Bob were supposed to be. They bought the house in May, got married in June, and moved into their home in July. Surely, she felt, her love for Bob and the satisfaction of a new home would help rebuild her life.

On July 6, 1987, Jude Govreau began doing volunteer work for Child Find at the agency's new office in Clayton, one of the well-to-do suburbs in the western sprawl of St. Louis. On Mondays—her day off from her bartending job—Jude dressed like a serious businesswoman and went to the Child Find office to help in any way she could, mostly answering phones or stuffing envelopes seeking contributions to the organization. Much of her time was spent, however, sitting in Margaret's private office, discussing ways to solve the murders. Working there was a way to stay involved with this small circle of people who had taught Jude so much, especially Jackie Corey. She had shown Jude how to keep tabs on Eugene Fleer, making series of phone calls to the Missouri Department of Corrections to find out where Fleer was doing his four years on the cocaine charge. The detectives at the Jefferson County Sheriff's Department thought Fleer was in the maximum-security prison in Jefferson City, but Jackie and Jude learned that he had been moved to the medium-security prison there. Jackie taught Jude how to pose as Fleer's aunt and make regular calls to the prison to check on her "nephew." Jude was shocked at how easy it was and how readily prison officials told her that her nephew was doing well.

Jude, Margaret, and Jackie had spent the spring beating the bushes for new ways to keep the investigation alive. In

March, they arranged another interview with reporter Liz Irwin, whose stories ran in both the *Jefferson County News Democrat* and the *Journal.* Margaret told Liz that the $3,000 reward announced in October had not brought a single tip, not even a prank call. So, Jude explained, she and Mari had put up $500 for any "valuable information" on the case. It didn't even have to lead to an arrest. Jude begged anyone who knew anything to come forward.

"For every minute they are silent, another child may be in danger," Jude said in Liz Irwin's story. "I just feel that there has to be someone out there who has information. If it's money they want, we'll scrounge it. If that's what it takes, somehow, someway, we'll raise it."

And, as she always did, Jude tried to remind everyone that real people—two innocent children—had been murdered viciously, taken forever from their families. "Stacy was a funny, bubbling girl full of life and dreams," Jude cried. "People keep telling me to remember the good times, but it's the horror that she went through that stays in my mind. The hardest thing is knowing that the pain was there and there was no one to help her. I don't think the baby realized he was being murdered, but my daughter knew."

The Child Find group also called in Ellen Jaffe, a consumer-rights reporter from KMOV-TV, Channel 4, the CBS affiliate in St. Louis, to do a story on the insensitive body-bag fee charged by Jefferson County. After Jaffe's story ran, Jefferson County revoked the ordinance setting the fee and vowed never again to assess a murder victims' survivors.

In late May, Child Find sponsored an observation of National Missing Children's Day with a gathering on the lawn under the Gateway Arch on the St. Louis riverfront. High school bands played, mimes entertained, and the line of dancing cheerleaders from St. Louis's professional soccer team gyrated for the crowd. And then a thousand balloons, each containing the name and picture of a missing child, were released for the winds to carry past the gleaming arch. Jude told reporters how Child Find had helped her, and she pleaded with a congressman from St. Louis to sponsor legislation giving more rights to crime victims and their families. The Rev. Martin Braungardt of Festus offered a prayer, reminding everyone that his seventeen-year-old daughter, Diane, had been missing for two months without a trace. Her fate remains a mystery today.

As the first anniversary of the murders approached, Jude and her Child Find mentors found themselves planning new strategies on several fronts. Despite the popular opinion that Geno Fleer was the prime suspect, Jude still had a strong suspicion that Brenda Turner, and perhaps Bobbi, had played some role. Even Captain John O'Rando listed Brenda among his chief suspects. Jude didn't want the Turners to fade too far from view, so she, Margaret, and Jackie decided to see if they could find them.

Jackie confirmed that Jack Turner still worked at an automobile plant in Fenton and learned through a friend at the post office that the Turners' mail had been forwarded to a town in Pennsylvania ten days after the murders. Working the phones some more, Jackie found the telephone number for Jack Turner's sister in the town. Margaret called, pretending to be a reporter doing an update story on the murders, and was pleasantly surprised when the woman volunteered Brenda's home number.

Margaret applied the same ruse in a call to Brenda, who was willing to say only that the year since the murders had been difficult for her family. "By the grace of God," she said, "the kids and I have made it through." She referred other questions to her attorney back in St. Louis and hung up.

Jude was astounded, and the odd comments made her even more suspicious. She wondered what Brenda knew about "the grace of God." Jude's growing doubts about the Turners left her even more frustrated. If Brenda was the killer, how would they ever prove it? Wasn't there some way to drag a confession out of this peculiar woman? Did Bobbi, or even her little sister, Ruthie, know anything? Would they talk? Jude didn't know what to do with these hunches, but she filed them away to let them bubble. She had no idea of the direction they would lead months later.

A call from the sheriff's department on July 30 seemed to confirm Jude's worst fears about the police investigation. A detective asked Jude and Rick to come to the station to be fingerprinted and then asked if Jude, by some chance, had a set of Stacy's fingerprints. Jude was stunned. After fifty-one weeks of supposedly intensive investigation, the police were just now asking for the adults' fingerprints and were admitting they didn't even have Stacy's? Amid everything else the authorities surely had done to Stacy's body in the hours after the murders, they hadn't taken her prints? Fortunately, Jude had a set of her daughter's prints that had been taken at school, so she complied with the request and tired to channel her skepticism into something beneficial.

After all, there were other concerns to be attended to the first week of August 1987. Jude, Margaret, and Jackie began to implement their plans for the anniversary, designed to draw as much play in the press as possible. Perhaps a series of events on that occasion would shake something loose. Mari declined an invitation to join with the others, saying she still couldn't face that kind of exposure. They would have to mark the sad day without her. She and Jude had been talking more often, however, and Mari had visited Jude on May 13 to bring flowers for what would have been Stacy's sixteenth birthday. Jude looked at the petite woman and decided the stress was taking a terrible toll on her; she seemed to have aged ten years, Jude thought. She was disappointed that Mari still could not find the resolve to back up the efforts Jude thought were so important. But Jude had no way to know just how deeply Mari had sunk into a morass of grief, obsession, and Valium.

A news conference at Child Find headquarters was set for August 6, 1987, to announce an increase in the reward to $10,000, to issue a new edition of the poster bearing the kids' photos and announcing the higher award, to renew criticism of the pace of the investigation, and to disclose a couple of surprises. One thing that would not be disclosed was the lack of money to pay the higher reward. Margaret had proposed upping the ante and had dismissed Jude's worries about the money by saying no one ever had to pay these rewards, anyway. They really were just an attention-getter designed to produce publicity about the cases in hopes someone would come forward with something useful. Jude shrugged and went along with the plan; after all, that was "the word" from Margaret, and Jude usually deferred to her friend's expertise. Anyway, Jude decided, she would be glad to do whatever was necessary to raise the additional money if someone earned it.

Without revealing too much about their plans, the women also invited the police to attend the news conference, promising it would be an important event. Sergeant Leo Burle and Captain Ed Kemp attended for the sheriff's department, and Sergeant Tim McEntee represented the Major Case Squad.

After Jude told the reporters about the higher reward, she blasted the sheriff's department for failing to make an arrest after a year. And she zeroed in on what she thought was a major—and missing—piece of evidence. What had happened to the fingerprint that was found on the showerhead? she demanded to know. After a full year, it still had not been identified, and she saw that as a symbol of the cops' failure to give this case the attention and energy it deserved.

Her criticism seemed to take Burle and Kemp by surprise, and they staunchly defended the investigation. Burle explained that every lead that developed was being followed and the small amount of evidence collected—including the fingerprint—was being examined by the Missouri Highway Patrol's crime laboratory, as well as the FBI lab at Quantico, Virginia. The FBI had, in fact, used the evidence to develop a psychological profile of the killer that the sheriff's department was applying to the investigation. Lester Howlett's death and possible connection to the murders still were being examined, Burle said, but there was no solid evidence incriminating Howlett. Burle even added that a high number of potential witnesses in the case were involved in some form of criminal activity themselves, and that made them much less cooperative with the police.

Although Kemp was not participating directly in the investigation, he was confident all of that was true. He told the media that the FBI even had used new technology— scanning a fingerprint with a green laser to make it more identifiable—in hopes of matching it to a suspect. And, although he couldn't tell the reporters, he actually thought Captain Wally Gansmann was obsessed with the Winzen-Price case. To Kemp, that meant that Burle would be working hard on it, too, since Burle was Gansmann's right-hand man and chief assistant. Despite all of that, Kemp under-

stood Jude Govreau's emotion and frustration; her criticism
was just misdirected, he thought.

Then Jude announced the rest of the plans assembled by
her, Margaret, and Jackie. At ten o'clock the next morning—Friday, August 7, the first anniversary of the murders—Jude would hold a memorial service outside the
apartment building where the horror had begun. And then
she and Child Find would sponsor a picket line around the
sheriff's department in the Jefferson County Courthouse in
Hillsboro. The demonstration would be another attempt to
remind people that someone had slaughtered two innocents
and was still out there somewhere while the police mumbled about following leads.

As the news conference ended, Child Find distributed
fliers with pictures of the children, an account of the successful effort to rescind the fee for body bags, and a poem
written by Jude entitled "In Remembrance of Stacy and
Tyler."

My heart is filled with sadness,
My mind is torn with pain.

I often sit and wonder,
Will I ever see you again?

I miss the laughter, the sparkle in your eyes.
We never really had a chance to say our last goodbyes.

I miss the wrinkle of your nose,
The smile upon your face.

But now a million tears will come,
And none can take your place.

The pain and fear you had to bear,
I sometimes wonder. Does anyone care?

Taken away so young and good.
Oh God, I wish I understood.

I pray you are walking on streets of gold,
For in your arms, a tiny boy you hold.

A beautiful boy with eyes of blue,
So full of life, just like you.

Left behind, so many tears
Of joy and laughter through all the years.

Even though we had to part,
Stacy and Tyler remain forever in my heart.

I see a face I can no longer touch,
Of a child I love so much.

The next day was hot and muggy, a typical August morning in the St. Louis area. Jude and about twenty friends gathered solemnly outside the apartment building on Stillbrook Estates Drive to remember and mourn Stacy and Tyler. Jude cried without stopping during the ceremony, which marked the first time she had returned to the apartment complex since she fled it the day after the murders. As she looked at the door that led down that hallway to Mari's apartment, Jude felt her throat tighten, and she wondered if she was about to collapse again, just as she had one year ago, almost to that very minute. She wished Mari had felt up to joining them that morning to honor their children. Mari explained on the telephone the night before that she just could not do it. She had been back to the apartment once, with the police, and she didn't think she could ever go back again. Mari was glad Jude had called, but going back there was too much even to contemplate. Mari's reaction bothered Jude, but she tried to understand.

As the small crowd stood close together in the hot sun, they spoke quietly about their loss and angrily about the lack of an arrest. They carried a poster with Stacy's picture and played her favorite tape of songs by Amy Grant. Jude, Racheal, Rick, and Stacy's friends wept and hugged each other as they wondered aloud how a year could have passed since that day.

And then most of the group took the peaceful demonstration to the courthouse. They decorated utility poles around the building with yellow ribbons in memory of Stacy and Tyler, and marched along the sidewalks as people going by stared. Jude, Racheal, Jackie, Margaret, and others carried signs that Child Find had made bearing the children's photographs and reading, "Who Murdered Stacy Price? Who Murdered Tyler Winzen? Don't You Care?" Another sign was an enlargement of the reward poster Child Find had circulated.

They marched for two hours in temperatures that reached 102 degrees. The merciless heat and humidity and sun got to Margaret, and she had to leave. But the others pushed on, hoping Sheriff Buck Buerger or some of the detectives would have the grace and courage to come out and talk to them. Jude understood that the police probably were unhappy with the picketing, perhaps even personally insulted. But they should come out and discuss it with Jude and the others, who had a right to some answers. Jude was owed that much, she was certain. But no one from the sheriff's department or any other office came out, leaving Stacy's heirs to parade around the building in a nearly silent protest.

As Jude made the circuit around the building, sign in hand, she explained her obsession to reporter Liz Irwin: "If I have to do this every day until the day I die, I will. I see it as trying to keep this from happening again. It's a cry for justice. It was such a senseless crime. If it's never solved, there is such a thing as a perfect crime."

Thirty miles north, in St. Louis County, Mari Kane spent the day in tears.

CHAPTER 10

The face that stared back at Jude Govreau from the framed canvas was supposed to be her daughter, but it was not the beautiful girl she remembered. The finished painting was a very poor likeness of Stacy and a deep disappointment to Jude. She had supplied photographs and paid a pretty penny to the company that promised a faithful oil portrait. The salesman delivered the finished product to Jude as she stood behind the bar at Tucker's on the evening of September 2, 1987, and her heart fell. The wonderful keepsake and touching memento she had envisioned arrived in the image of someone Jude had never seen before.

She lifted it across the bar and was about to stash it out of sight when she heard a startled gasp from a woman seated a few stools down. "Oh, my God! That's that babysitter who got killed," the woman sputtered in such shock that Jude was almost too unnerved to react. She didn't know this customer. How could this woman whose eyes flashed so wide know Stacy well enough to recognize a terrible painting of her?

"How do you know?" Jude asked in disbelief.

"I know the guy who killed her."

Jude almost leaped down the bar. "What do you mean, you know the guy who killed her?"

The woman looked directly into Jude's eyes and asked, "Do you know a guy named Geno Fleer?"

Jude sucked in her breath, and her mind warned her to move cautiously. "I don't know him, but I know *of* him. What do you know about him?"

The woman's mouth almost clanged shut, and she began to cry as her hands covered her face. She obviously had said more than she wanted to, more than she should have, and she would clam up completely if Jude didn't play this right. Her years behind the bar had taught her how to deal with this situation, and she poured the sobbing woman a very stiff Kahlua and cream. Drunks always talked, and Jude knew what she had to do to keep this amazing opportunity from slipping away. Getting results took several drinks and Jude's best barside manner, but slowly the woman began to open up. She wouldn't reveal her identity, but through almost continuous tears she explained that her sister, named Ginger*—a dancer at a club in nearby Arnold—had dated Geno Fleer's brother for three years. The tempestuous and often violent relationship ended when Ginger's boyfriend was killed in a motorcycle crash in early 1986.

But through this close link to the Fleers, the woman had heard a detailed version of what had happened in Mari Winzen's apartment on August 7, 1986. As Jude kept sliding loaded drinks in front of the woman, she began to recount what she insisted were the facts.

"Geno and Lester Howlett were doing coke and Geno decided he was going to go mess with Stacy. He took some coke with him and went down and knocked on the door. Stacy let him in, because she knew him. She met him when he took Mari to that meeting."

Jude's heart was starting to race. This woman already had revealed an amazing knowledge of the situation; she had heard a solid story from someone who knew more than the news media ever had reported. Did she really know the truth? Was Jude finally going to learn what had happened and who had done it?

"When he got in, he tried to make Stacy do some coke so he could get into her pants. She didn't want the coke. Then he made a pass at her and she got scared. She said she didn't want any coke and she wanted him to get out. He got mad and slapped her in the face, and she started screaming. He got even madder and he really started slapping her around. The little boy came in and he was crying because Geno was hurting Stacy. Geno dragged her into the bathroom and strangled her and killed her. He killed the boy, too, because he was crying and he saw what happened."

Jude was crying and trembling by the time this woman finished her terrifying description of how death had come to Stacy and Tyler. The story tore into Jude; if it all was true, they had died as horribly as Jude had feared in her worst nightmares.

"Lester went over to stop Geno, and he saw what happened," the woman continued. "He didn't do anything to stop it. But Lester was going to tell the police later, and that's why Geno killed him. Geno's girlfriend knew all about what happened; he told her."

Jude looked intensely at this woman who knew so much. "Were you there? Did you see this? Were you in that apartment that morning?"

"No, but I know what happened."

"How? How could you know all of this?"

"I *know*," was the firm answer.

Jude began to cry harder, and she fought to hold back the sobs that could telegraph how vitally important all of this was to her. "Will you tell the police? Please, let me call the police."

"No, no!" the woman said as panic edged into her voice. "He'll kill me if I tell."

"Who?"

"Geno. He knows where I live. He knows my sister. He'll kill me."

"Please, go with me to the police," Jude begged. "I'll give you money or buy you drugs—whatever you want. Just go to the police station with me."

"No, he'll kill me. I'll see if I can get you some more names of friends of Geno's who might talk to the police to get the reward. I'll call you back later and let you know. But I'm not going to the police."

Jude had overplayed her hand with the booze, and she had to escort her staggering source into the rest room so she could expel the alcoholic truth serum. The woman kept crying as she worried that Geno would kill her, and Jude kept pleading for her to repeat her story to the cops. Finally, the woman fled the bar.

Jude was left to deal with a rush of emotions that night. There was the excitement of knowing she might have happened onto the key to the mystery. There was the ache of knowing that Stacy and Tyler might have died as violently and painfully as Jude and Mari had feared. There was the worry that this woman might have disappeared into the night, never to be found again. Jude slept even less than usual, and made an early and excited call to the sheriff's department the next morning. Her fantastic tale got a lukewarm reception, however, and a detective mumbled that he would see what he could find out.

Jude could not rely on the same answer she had heard so often; she decided to become the dedicated detective this case needed. Through the kind of telephone lead-chasing Jackie Corey had taught her, Jude began with a call to the club where the mysterious woman's sister worked. Jude was thrilled when she reached Ginger, opening the door to another slick technique learned from Jackie. Jude introduced herself and asked innocently, "Do you have a sister named Angela Downs*?"

"No, I have a sister named Barb Canton*," was the reply.

There was the name of the elusive source. Barb Canton. Jude's ruse had worked. But Ginger guessed who Jude was and broke more startling news to her. Stacy had baby-sat for Ginger about four years before the murders, while Ginger lived behind the apartment where Jude lived at the time. Ginger was dating Geno Fleer's brother then, and Stacy probably had met him. Jude was aghast and wondered if her daughter might even have seen Geno Fleer years before the murders. Ginger believed Geno was the killer; his brother had beaten her often and had threatened to kill her and her kids if she left him.

Jude could not contain her excitement. She called Captain O'Rando and filled him in, adding that the detective in Jefferson County had not seemed very interested. O'Rando arrived later with a police officer from Arnold, and they spent several hours taking detailed notes on what Jude had heard. O'Rando promised to check it out completely. Jude's hopes soared. Had she finally solved the murders herself?

But, as she had learned with every other lead over the last year, this was not to be. O'Rando called back in a few days with disheartening news. They had found Barb Canton and interviewed her extensively. She knew nothing; she had heard a lot of intriguing speculation and street talk, but none of it could be confirmed, and O'Rando could see no way to pursue what he assessed to be no more than rumor

and innuendo. It might be true and the police would keep
it in mind, he said, but there was no way to prove any of
it now.

Jude tried not to crumple under the weight of unrealized
hope. Later, she cried harder than she had for some time.
She had been so close, she thought. "I'm so sorry, Stacy,"
she whispered.

But there was no time to dwell on failures. Jude decided
to turn her attention to the fingerprint that had begun to
drive her crazy. Jackie had a friend who was well placed
in the Missouri Highway Patrol, although he had no connection to the crime lab. Jude took the long shot and called
the source, dropped Jackie's name, and asked if there was
anything he could do to hurry up the analysis of that
damned fingerprint. The friend promised he would check
into it. Jude thanked him, but assumed his good intention
to help would join so many others paving the road to, in
this case, nowhere.

She was shocked when he called back in three days and
delivered. She finally had the answer, but it was not what
she had hoped. The fingerprint was Stacy's. Not only did
Jude still not have a clue to the killer's identity, she now
had significant evidence that Stacy had fought her attacker
all the way to the end, all the way into that bathtub. She
had been upright when the killer got her to the tub—not
unconscious and near death. The image of a struggle before
Stacy was forced into the tub added another dimension to
Jude's nightmares.

Detective Bob Miller—the man whose lonely dedication
to finding some kind of evidence in that bathroom had
touched everyone—was as disappointed as Jude. His superglue technique in that almost sterile bathroom had
yielded this one fingerprint, and he had hung his hopes on
it. When he heard the news, he felt even worse than the
day he had had to walk out of that apartment for the last
time. He and the Major Case Squad had done their best,
and it hadn't been enough. That hurt, and he couldn't find
any way to make it right with himself, the two women left
behind, or those kids in that bathtub.

As the fall of 1987 dissolved into winter, Jude Govreau
and Mari Kane found solace only in action. They were talk-

ing on the phone more often, partly because Mari had so
much time on her hands at home. The bond between them
seemed to be getting stronger, even though they often
snapped and growled at each other. On one occasion, when
Mari became almost irrational, Jude wrote in her daily journal that Mari was really "losing it." Mari often reacted
angrily to what seemed to be Jude's unwillingness to talk
to her. They often couldn't stand each other because of the
different ways they handled their grief. But around those
moments, they shared a bond that could be understood by
no one else in the world. Each of them realized that no
one knew how she felt except for the woman on the other
end of the chain forged in the heat of their children's
deaths. Neither of them could think of her own child without thinking of the other child who died in the same place
at the same moment. Even though the victims were a little
boy and a teenaged girl, in their mothers' minds they had
become like twins. That was the term for children born
together; what else could you call children united so intensely in death? So, when one of the mothers needed the
other, she was there. It was not a matter of choice; it was
a matter of fact.

The mothers also were sharing tips and hunches and rumors and new names to add to their lists of people who
might know somebody who knew somebody who had heard
something. They each made call after call trying to find
that magic bit of information. They followed every piece of
hearsay, no matter how bizarre. They checked on a report
that a man—possibly gay and the owner of some statues at
a posh hotel in downtown St. Louis—had supplied drugs
to the murderer; dozens of calls failed to turn up any such
person. They actually had a name for one suspect who supposedly had been fired from the police force in Chicago or
a suburb, but calls throughout that area failed to find anyone who had heard of such a man.

Some of the leads were so ridiculous they should have
been rejected out of hand, but the women refused to let
anything slide. A tipster who called Child Find said her
daughter had a friend who had a friend whose uncle by
marriage knew who had killed the kids. Even Jude and
Mari realized that one would be tough to follow and gave
up after several calls.

They often conferred with Captain John O'Rando, and he always took the time to talk to them. They liked, trusted, and respected him, and felt in turn that he really cared about them and the kids. Although he told them he was angry that they were conducting their own investigations—which he feared could screw up the cops' efforts—he still checked out some of the dead-end tips, reported back to them, and tried to salve their disappointment with reassurances that the police would nail the killer eventually. That promise was not simply appeasement; he knew some new names and possibilities had popped up, and they all pointed toward Eugene Fleer. People who might have been afraid of Fleer were growing more comfortable with him behind bars, and they were starting to talk. O'Rando even thought an arrest might be within reach, with a little push.

At a meeting of the board of directors for the Major Case Squad in late fall, O'Rando pulled Sheriff Buck Buerger aside and suggested that a formal request for a special review would be looked upon favorably by the directors. The sheriff agreed and made the request through channels. The board approved it in December, and O'Rando spent a few weeks clearing his desk to give himself time to command the effort. On February 22, 1988, he began a three-day reactivation of the Major Case Squad. Jude and Mari were ecstatic. Surely this meant something was about to happen.

O'Rando's first step was to check into a man named Jim Main*—another of the people Jude and Mari had heard about. Main had told Jefferson County detectives that Fleer had lived with him for almost three months after the murders and sometimes offered his own theories about what had happened. Fleer believed the murders were the result of a drug deal that went sour, Main remembered. And he provided more tantalizing details about those conversations when the Major Case Squad visited him. Some of the things Fleer said had bothered Main. Although Fleer always couched these conversations as theoretical, Main had the nagging suspicion that Fleer knew too much. He could be offering insightful speculation, or he could be revealing the truth that only someone who was there would know.

And an odd incident stood out in Main's memory. After they had been talking about the murders one evening and

Main had excused himself to take a shower, Fleer crept into the bathroom, reached through the shower curtain, and grabbed Main. The bizarre move had scared Main, despite Fleer's laughter at what he said was just a joke. But Main wondered if he should read something more sinister into it. And Main clearly was nervous as he sat with the detectives and recounted Fleer's descriptions of how the murders must have occurred.

"The baby-sitter was watching TV and somebody came to the door, and she knew them," Fleer had said. "She let them in; they talked. A little hanky-panky went on and she got pissed off. He beat the shit out of her, and the kid came wandering out of the bedroom in his pajamas. The kid was killed because he knew or could identify the guy."

Main looked at O'Rando and asked whether the girl had been beaten or drowned. O'Rando shook his head; he never gave a witness that kind of information. Main shrugged. He had asked because he remembered Fleer saying the killer must have used his bare hands and that the girl's esophagus was destroyed. O'Rando nodded casually, disguising a flash of excitement. Why would Fleer say that unless he had felt Stacy's throat in his own hands and had known the power he applied?

Main said he had asked Fleer why someone who had killed the girl would take the time—increasing the risk of discovery—to kill the little boy and then submerge both of the victims in a bathtub of water. Fleer had a quick answer: "To cover their ass. They would have to cover every step, every trace, to make sure there would be no evidence. They would have to cover their ass by wiping everything off."

And then Fleer added, "Hot water takes impressions off the skin."

There it was, O'Rando thought. The simple explanation for perhaps the most grotesque act in this terrible crime. For the first time, O'Rando had heard the obvious conclusion offered by someone with a unique perspective. And O'Rando's guts told him Main had heard it from the guy who had done it.

Main also said Fleer claimed the police had shown him photographs of the crime scene. O'Rando perked up as soon as he heard that; he knew no one had seen the photos but Brenda Turner. He had a strict rule against that tech-

nique except on rare occasions. Everyone who worked for
O'Rando knew that was prohibited, and Fleer's claim made
it likely he was groping for a way to explain why he knew
so much; that was another indication of guilt, O'Rando
thought.

When Main brought up Lester Howlett's death, Fleer
said he was sure Howlett had not committed suicide but
had been murdered.

Main also offered a revealing look at Lester Howlett's
demeanor twenty-four hours after the murders. Main had
stopped by an automobile repair shop owned by mutual
friend Henry Garcia the morning after the bodies were
found and was surprised to see Howlett sitting on the floor
of the garage crying as he read the newspaper. "I let Steve
down," Howlett was moaning repeatedly. When Main offered him a drink to calm him, Howlett responded, "I'm
never going to drink or do drugs again."

O'Rando wondered if Howlett's behavior could be
chalked up to normal grief at a friend's loss or if this man
was suffering pangs of conscience for what he had allowed
to happen and perhaps even witnessed.

Main's memories still left room for someone to interpret
Fleer's comments as the theorizing of an interested ob-
server to murders that hit close to home. But the next witness catapulted Fleer into a more suspicious role. His
former girlfriend, Carol Thompson*, told detectives of a
party at Main's house one night when Fleer said he, Howlett, and Steve Winzen had been involved in a drug rip-off
in Illinois; Fleer believed the murders were revenge by the
victimized dealers. They had killed Steve's son in retaliation
and killed the baby-sitter because she was a witness. When
the use of hot water came up, Carol remembered, Fleer
quickly explained that hot water eliminated fingerprints.

Carol Thompson believed Fleer had murdered the children, and she buttressed that with some frightening firsthand knowledge of his capacity for violence. When he
thought she had received a phone call from an old boyfriend, he went berserk, ripped off his clothes, and began
to beat and kick her; he even tried to smother her. When
she reached for a nearby semiautomatic pistol, he took it
away from her, stuck the muzzle against her chest, and
ordered her to take off her clothes. She was too scared to

respond, and Fleer pulled the trigger. The gun failed to fire—to Carol's relief and Fleer's surprise. Fleer looked at the grip to discover there was no clip. Frustrated by that, he dragged her to the kitchen, beating her and ripping off her clothes along the way. He grabbed a knife, but before he could use it, the police pulled up outside, and he fled. Hours later he called to apologize, saying he realized that sometimes he would "snap" when he became angry. He could never remember what he had done in that condition, but he would be sure he had done something wrong.

Among the others interviewed during the new investigation were two of Fleer's old friends—both of whom had done some time with him while he was serving his sentence on the drug case. David Powers, an armed robber, remembered that Fleer had a reputation for beating his girlfriends and for "snapping" into a rage at any time; he would become a violent man who could easily kill someone. In prison, Fleer seemed extraordinarily worried about the kids' murders and talked almost incessantly about them. He fretted over and over that the police would try to pin them on him, but tried to reassure himself by saying all the evidence was circumstantial and all the witnesses were dead. Powers said Fleer mentioned that the victims were beaten before being strangled and drowned, and Powers thought he had never read or heard that before.

The other inmate, Mike Delmar*, had known Eugene Fleer since the terms they served together in a juvenile center fifteen years before. In prison, Fleer never confessed to the kids' murders, but when Delmar asked Fleer if he was involved, he never denied it. Delmar thought that was strange; no one wanted to be tagged as a baby-killer, especially in prison.

The police got one more tasty tidbit from another of Fleer's friends, Tom Hudson*. Fleer also had lived with Hudson for a while after the murders and had said he was sure they were "a professional job." Fleer based his conclusion on the killer's decision to submerge the bodies in hot water to be make certain there were no fingerprints left behind.

O'Rando looked at this new round of incriminating interviews and concluded there still was not enough for murder charges. After three days of renewed investigation, even more fingers pointed at Eugene "Geno" Fleer. But it was all talk and hunches; no solid evidence had emerged. Once again, John O'Rando had to walk away from the Winzen-Price case without closing the book.

He tried to be optimistic when he talked to Jude and Mari, and they tried to keep their hopes alive despite this newest disappointment. But that was even harder when they learned that in the middle of the squad's three-day return, Fleer had been transferred from the prison in Jefferson City to St. Mary's Honor Center, a halfway house not far from downtown St. Louis. After serving fourteen months of his four-year term, Fleer was within six months to a year from parole—a thought that sent new tremors of anger and fear through the women's hearts.

As it soaked in, the idea that Fleer was approaching release pushed Mari even deeper into the emotional danger zone created by her new addiction to Valium. Instead of acting as a tranquilizer and moderating her moods, the drug left her cranked up and running at full tilt. She longed to become an apathetic zombie with dulled senses. Instead, she was hyperactive and short-tempered, flying off the handle at Bob and Brian for no reason. The anger she could not resolve was unleashed at the people she loved the most, and she couldn't hold it back. She would talk for hours, often keeping a fatigued Bob awake until four in the morning. She couldn't sleep, because the psychological movie projector switched on as soon as she closed her eyes. Scenes she imagined from the murders flashed across the screen in the back of her mind, playing mercilessly over and over. She learned to hate the night, because the sleep that should have been a safe haven had become yet another time of torture. She had to take more and more pills to knock her into an unconscious stupor just to get some rest. It wore on Bob, too. He spent much of his day worrying about what Mari was doing, and hoping she would not be in some new, even higher orbit when he got home.

Fleer's transfer to St. Louis caused more turmoil, and led to a desperate, demented plot for which Mari even enlisted Bob's help. The Kanes spent night after night staking out the halfway house, parked on the street in a seedy, dangerous part of town, hoping to spot Fleer as he returned by the mandatory check-in time of ten o'clock. Wearing a baseball cap and turning up her collar to conceal her face, Mari slumped down in the car and clenched a baseball bat in her hands. If they could get Eugene Fleer alone on the dark streets, the Kanes had vowed, they would beat him to death before the state could free him to devastate more lives. To Mari, inflicting a painful death on Fleer by her own hand would be nothing less than justice. To Bob, the destruction of Fleer seemed a small price to pay for Mari's salvation. Her psychosis had begun to wear off on him, too. He often dreamed of dragging Fleer into the woods, stringing him up, and letting Mari inflict what damage she would to the man she was certain had killed her son.

But night after night, the avengers huddled in their car and watched the center's residents arrive just before ten o'clock. They never even caught a glimpse of their prey, and wondered if they could really have carried out their murderous scheme even if they had come face to face with a defenseless Fleer. They soon were glad they never had a chance to find out. And when she looked back later from a saner place, Mari would realize God had protected the Kanes from a greater evil.

But she would have to go miles and climb mountains before she reached that place. She encountered one of the obstacles as she innocently talked with her sister on the telephone in her kitchen one afternoon. In midsentence, Mari collapsed to the floor in violent convulsions. Bob rushed to her and pushed a spoon wrapped in a towel into her mouth to keep her from swallowing her tongue. He had seen an epileptic seizure once before and feared that could be what was causing these furious spasms jolting through his wife's body. But as the attack finally subsided and Mari began to relax, Bob was sure he knew the real cause. She was taking huge amounts of Valium, and he had feared something disastrous was about to strike. He knew her body could withstand the effects of that many pills only so long before it rebelled.

When she had recovered enough, Bob sat her down at the kitchen table and demanded they have the talk he knew had been overdue for a long time.

"Mari, you've got to get off the Valium. You know that's what caused this attack. It's going to kill you if keep this up."

"You don't understand, Bob," Mari snapped angrily. "It wasn't your son who was murdered and taken away forever. You don't know how that feels. Everyone thinks they do, but they don't. No one can really know until it happens to them. Everyone tells me time heals all wounds and that the grief will get better. But it doesn't, and I have learned that it always will be there. I have to do this, Bob. I need the Valium. I don't want to be straight anymore. It's not worth it. I got straight and did everything right, and my reward was Tyler's murder. If that's what being straight gets you, I don't want it. What would happen if I got straight now? Would someone kill my other son?"

Bob was angry, too, and he refused to back down or let Mari cloud the truth. "Being straight didn't kill Tyler, Mari. Some creep killed Tyler. Eugene Fleer probably killed Tyler, and it had nothing to do with you being straight. It had to do with him being a scum and a drug dealer. You've got to get off the Valium or it's going to kill you, too."

"You just don't understand."

Bob understood. He knew how badly Mari hurt and suffered and grieved. He shared in that loss, too, as much as possible for someone who wasn't Tyler's parent. But Mari's pain didn't excuse the drug abuse, and he was going to do everything he could to stop it before it killed the woman he loved. Playing detective, as he had seen Mari do so often in her search for Tyler's killer, Bob checked for the doctor's name on the label of one of her prescription bottles. My God, he thought, this guy is doling out one hundred Valium tablets a week to her; she could be taking fifteen a day. Bob angrily called the doctor and insisted he stop prescribing this drug to a woman who had had to go to Alcoholics Anonymous once before to kick the habit. The doctor replied that he had given them to Mari to stop headaches and that he would continue the medication as long as she needed them. Bob would not be deterred; how would the doctor like it, Bob asked, if he submitted to the state medical board all of the prescription bottles Mari had collected with the doctor's name on them, along with an explanation of Mari's addiction and record at AA? Would the doctor want to explain these heavy Valium prescriptions for a former addict? All right, the doctor agreed; no more Valium.

Bob relished this victory and hoped he could persuade

Mari to use the opportunity to get clean again. She didn't tell him she already was getting concurrent prescriptions for Valium from two or three other doctors. She had always been amazed at how easy it was to get all the Valium anyone could want and more than anyone could need.

As Mari feared she was losing her grip on reality and what was left of her life, Jude was headed toward a different kind of catastrophe. She struggled to get through each day and at night often sat and cried as she poured her heart into the thoughts she recorded in her journal.

"I would give anything just to have Stacy back again, to see her face and hear her voice, to put my arms around her and tell her that I love her. Where was God? Where is God? Where was He for her? She loved Him. She trusted Him and me. Where were we when she needed us? I am so sorry, Stacy, that I wasn't there. I love you.

"I often sit and ask the question, 'Why?' Why our children? Why my child? She was so young and beautiful, so full of life. Why so much suffering, so much pain, so much fear? Was she just too special for this world? Is there really a place of peace and beauty and happiness? Or is it just that we need there to be so we can deal with our loss? I get no comfort in thinking she is in God's arms in a perfect place. She should be her with her family, who loved her most."

Jude looked for ways to fight back. She even talked to an attorney about filing a wrongful-death suit against Fleer, seeking monetary damages from him on the grounds that his unjustified actions had taken her daughter's young life and had deprived Jude of Stacy's company for decades. That surely would generate a lot of publicity and might even shake loose some valuable tips, Jude thought. But the attorney told her there was almost no chance for success with a suit against someone who had not been charged in the case. And a judge might rule that a suit filed on such a slender thread was frivolous enough to justify an order for Jude to pay Fleer's attorney fees. Taking such a chance could actually prove to be counterproductive.

To keep going, Jude invested most of her emotion in the relationship with her Child Find saviors, Margaret and Jackie, who soon took her into their inner circle. Margaret surprised Jude one afternoon by handing her a stack of business cards that read, "Jude Govreau, Director of Children's Rights"—her first business cards and her first title. At a Child Find picnic for kids, Margaret shocked Jude again by presenting her with an award—a wooden plaque with a beautiful painting of a rose and the inscription "Because You've Touched Our Lives." Not only was Jude learning how to fight for her sanity through the search for Stacy's killer, but she was finding a place where she felt she belonged. Margaret had some idiosyncrasies, but Jude could easily overlook them. And she was spending more and more time with Jackie as she became as much a friend as tutor.

Jude's all-out determination to find the killer and her alliance with Child Find led to a new series of reckless and potentially dangerous activities. As she became more active in her investigative efforts, she began to worry more about the safety of her family, Rick Pashia, Mari, and anyone else who was asking questions about the murders and Eugene Fleer. Jude had been getting a lot of hang-up calls for months—sometimes forty a day—and she wondered if the harassment was a serious message rather than a childish prank. Even Rick worried that the killer might try to eliminate these amateurish civilians who were playing detective. They had to laugh when Sergeant Tim McEntee called Jude early in 1988 and said he had been on a routine visit to prison to question an inmate when he had encountered Fleer. Fleer said he was afraid of Jude and had heard rumors that she had put a contract on him among the inmate population. Jude acknowledged that the thought had crossed her mind, but she still found some grotesque humor in the suggestion that Fleer spent his time in prison worrying about danger from her.

Jude and the others were convinced they had reason to worry about a visit in the dark. She feared being caught in the wrong place at the wrong time—alone and vulnerable— and the .357 magnum revolver she kept at home was to big to conceal when she left the house. So she and Rick bought sleek .38-caliber semiautomatic pistols and carried them at all times. Matching his and hers guns, they joked sardonically.

Rick had been drafted as an operative as Jude became

the hardest-working private detective imaginable. While she worked the telephones, he worked the streets, following her tips and hunches. He often was glad to have the pistol tucked away when he ended up in some less than respectable locations. Acting on another long-shot tip to Jude, he spent a number of late nights hanging out at a topless bar across the Mississippi River in the little town of Brooklyn, Illinois. Although its population of a thousand was black, its only industry was owned by whites who sold white flesh to white customers at topless clubs, massage parlors, and porn shops. There was little violent crime associated with the night spots that had sprung up almost in the shadow of the Gateway Arch. After all, the cross-section of mostly white construction workers and businessmen from across the St. Louis area who drove into Brooklyn for some raunchy recreation couldn't be worried about being waylaid. But still, Rick was uncomfortable getting to and from the area and asking odd questions in his search for a biker bartender who supposedly knew something about the murders. Rick never found the bartender. He suffered the same result after several nights at a rough tavern in Jefferson County searching for a guy who was supposed to look like singer Kenny Loggins. Despite the frustration and the danger, no lead could be left unchecked.

The most surprising effort by Jude and her cohorts came up in April 1988. Although the spotlight was on Eugene Fleer as the prime suspect, Jude and Mari couldn't shake their suspicions about Brenda Turner. They had passed on their concerns in several telephone calls to the police in the little town in Pennsylvania where the Turners had settled and had briefly considered going there to see if more could be learned. Their interest really was piqued when Mari impulsively called Brenda one afternoon to see if an unexpected blast from the past could shake anything loose. But Brenda remained as enigmatic, and suspicious, as ever. In a bizarre stream-of-consciousness dialogue, she said she had helped Stacy get to heaven. "I may have murdered them in my heart, but not in deed," she murmured. She speculated that Tyler would have fought a woman who attacked him and said she often lay awake at night wondering if she had done it. She said Bobbi had decided never to have a

best friend again for fear she might lose her as she had
lost Stacy.

Jude's belief that Brenda was mad as a hatter was reinforced by her ramblings, and Jude rankled at the woman's
insistence that Bobbi and Stacy were best friends. That was
not true; Stacy tolerated Bobbi's following her around only
to keep from hurting her feelings. Jude thought about the
times Brenda's comments had hurt Stacy and Tyler. Jude
could find no way to believe that someone so hateful, jealous, and vicious could be ruled out as a suspect.

The call intensified Jude's frustration. How could the
truth about the Turners be learned? If Brenda or Bobbi or
little sister Ruthie could be isolated and interviewed, would
they reveal more than they would say on the phone?

As ideas and impressions about the Turners were batted
back and forth by Jude, Jackie, and Margaret, someone
suggested gong to Pennsylvania for a face-to-face meeting.
They could stake out the Turners' house, wait until Janet
and her husband were gone, and then descend on Bobbi
and Ruthie. Jude and the others had a hunch the girls might
spill what they knew under the right circumstances and
away from their parents' influence. The Child Find crew
would plead with the girls to tell whether their mother had
committed the murders. If that failed, putting them on an
airplane and bringing them back to St. Louis for interrogation by the police might work, too, the women mused. It
wouldn't really be kidnapping, if the girls more or less
agreed to come back with them.

Jackie saw the danger in the plan immediately and suggested calling in the family services department in Pennsylvania before taking such extreme action. The child welfare
workers could mediate a meeting with the Turner girls and
provide official sanction, Jackie counseled. But Margaret
preferred the less complicated, more direct approach. She
decided the plan would be carried out by her and the private investigator they had worked with.

On a warm spring day, the three women went to the
bank so Jude could withdraw $900 and convert it to travel-
er's checks for the mission to Pennsylvania. Margaret's
tendency to waffle at the last minute surfaced again, and
she decided Jackie and the detective should make the trip.
As the next two days passed, Jude developed serious sec-

ond thoughts about the whole idea. The police really could make a case that this was kidnapping, she finally realized. She told Margaret of her worries, and Margaret readily agreed. In fact, Margaret had discussed the plan with Captain Wally Gansmann at the sheriff's department, and he had nearly exploded. He couldn't believe the women had even discussed such a thing, and he warned them it was illegal. He angrily rejected Margaret's odd suggestion that he deputize them to legitimize the plan. Margaret returned Jude's money, and Jude sighed in relief that the whole scheme was aborted.

But a different kind of crisis surfaced before long. Despite the continuing success of weekly bingo games that brought in $3,000 to $7,000 every Saturday night and provided most of Child Find's income, the organization began to have financial problems. Margaret explained it to Jude as a temporary cash-flow crunch caused by a delay in an expected cash grant. But the inconvenience became a crisis, and Jude learned that the telephone company was about to disconnect the phones because of a delinquent bill for $8,000. Jude knew that Child Find could be destroyed by the loss of its lifeline for the investigators who lived on the phone chasing leads on missing children. Although she was strapped for cash, as always, she offered to lend Child Find $1,800 she kept in a special account from Stacy's life insurance proceeds, the fund from which Jude hoped she would pay the reward when someone solved the case. As important as that was, Jude was willing to lend it to Margaret if it would keep Child Find and the phones going. Margaret cried in protest, saying she couldn't take Stacy's insurance money. But Jude insisted, and Margaret acquiesced with gratitude.

The next day, Jude was stunned to see what would be only the first of a series of newspaper and television accounts of an investigation into allegations of mismanagement at Child Find—and Margaret Baxter was at the center of the controversy. The story in the *St. Louis Post-Dispatch* on May 17 said the Missouri Department of Revenue was investigating charges by at least three former employees at Child Find that an average of $1,000 a week from the bingo games had been unaccounted for, that Margaret had used Child Find money to pay for her son's car repairs, that she had charged personal and business expenses on the same American Express card, and that she had intercepted cash donations to pay for expenses such as lunch and gas.

In the newspaper story, Margaret denied doing anything wrong, although she agreed that there was a grain of truth to some of the allegations. She explained that she regularly took the bingo proceeds home in her briefcase after the games on Saturday nights, but did not count or touch the money until she went to the office on Monday mornings to turn it over to the bookkeeper. She had used $1,000 in Child Find money to repair her son's car, but that was because it was used for the group's business. She had racked up personal and business expenses on American Express, but the bookkeeper was supposed to separate them. And she had tapped the cash donations, but only to provide expense money to other workers—never for herself.

Margaret told the reporters the charges against her were the griping of disgruntled employees trying to discredit her and Child Find's work. "I haven't done anything wrong," she said. "You've got a lot of people here saying crazy things. I'm innocent."

Jude was shocked to see such allegations against a woman she had trusted so implicitly, and she felt sure they were false. Jude was confident Margaret would not violate the trust she seemed to take so seriously. When Jude talked to Margaret later, that was the tack her friend took. She urged Jude to believe in her and help Child Find weather this storm.

But the allegations mounted over the next few days. Local police chiefs told reporters they had quit working with Child Find because of tactics they felt preyed on parents' fears about child abductions and misled the public about the scope of the problem. The Better Business Bureau said it had received numerous complaints about fundraising campaigns by telephone solicitors. Child Find of America charged that the unrelated organization in Missouri had tried to make money off the national group's name. The national clearinghouse for missing children that was established under federal law disclosed that it had briefly removed Child Find from its referral list in 1986 because of its handling of cases, especially its taking sides in parents' battles over custody of children. Employees reported that Child Find used most of its income from bingo to pay staff salaries, a violation of state law. Even the claims of assistance in more than a thousand cases of missing children were called into question; one staff members said the number really was ten to fifteen in 1985 and 1986.

On Thursday, May 19, the State of Missouri shut down Child Find's bingo games, effectively cutting off the group's income and ending its operations. And the U.S. Justice Department announced it would conduct a special audit that could lead to an order for Child Find to repay a $25,000 federal grant it had received a year earlier.

At an all-night board meeting that evening, members could find no basis for continuing their service with Child Find as it collapsed under the weight of the allegations. At four o'clock Friday morning, Jackie Corey submitted her resignation and those of the other five staff members.

On Friday, the telephone company disconnected service to Child Find, leaving Jude to wonder what had happened to her $1,800. She had no choice but to tender her resignation, no matter how reluctantly. And she told a reporter, "I do not feel that Margaret has done anything wrong. I know that Margaret never took a dime for herself, ever."

Jude heard from Margaret a few more times, and she always denied any misconduct. But the events of late May had destroyed what Jude had thought was a warm and caring relationship. And the Missouri attorney general's office once called Jude to ask about the $1,800 she had lent Margaret. She explained the purpose of the loan and it was never mentioned again. Eventually, the state and federal governments completed their investigations without taking any action against defunct Child Find or anyone associated with it. The justice department cleared Child Find of any wrongdoing.

Jude never saw her $1,800 again. But she had lost much more than money. She had lost the woman she had thought was her best friend, and had lost the ability to trust. She felt stupid and marveled that she could have been so blind. Once again, she felt completely forsaken. "But I won't quit," she wrote in her journal. "No one can stop me. I will go on searching for the answer. I don't care if everyone turns away."

* * *

Mari was tired of the same answers from the police. Every time she talked to a detective, she heard the lame excuses and sorry explanations: the cops were positive that Eugene Fleer was the killer, but the prosecuting attorney's office said there wasn't enough evidence to file a charge. In August, Mari decided to go directly to the source; she called Jefferson County Prosecuting Attorney Bill Johnson and asked for a meeting with him and the police. Johnson didn't have much to say about the case and wouldn't even offer his opinion on the evidence, but said he would attend a conference if the police agreed. Sheriff Buck Buerger offered no opposition to the idea, and a meeting was set.

Mari was surprised when Jude showed some reluctance to a powwow right then. She feared an inevitably angry confrontation would do the investigation no good. But Mari insisted. "I want some answers right now, dammit. How long are we going to put up with this? They're not doing a damn thing, and they keep giving us the same old excuses. If there isn't enough evidence to charge Fleer, I want to hear it from the prosecuting attorney. And I want to hear the police explain why not and what they're doing about it."

"Okay," Jude said. "I know they're not doing anything. We're the only ones who are investigating this case. We're the only ones who care who killed our kids."

The group met in the tiny office of Captain Wally Gansmann at the sheriff's department. Mari, Jude, and Rick Pashia were not surprised when Gansmann said Buerger couldn't make it. They stared accusingly at Gansmann, Sergeants Leo Burle and Bob Mullins, and Johnson's emissary—a young prosecutor named John Appelbaum whom the women had never heard mentioned before. Johnson couldn't make it either, Appelbaum explained, and he was there to represent his boss.

Mari and Jude glanced knowingly at each other; they could have predicted something like this from Buerger and Johnson. Instead of meeting with the men who made the decisions, they got the same old faces and a new flunky standing in for Johnson. John Appelbaum seemed pleasant and polite enough. But this rookie—a mere kid whose baby face was accentuated by glasses and brown hair—certainly was no match for this double-murder case and the angry

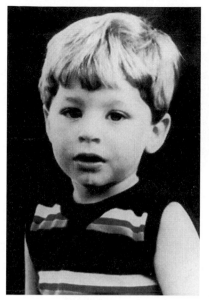

Tyler Winzen, age 3.

Stacy Price, age 14.

Mari Kane's apartment building. Behind the upper center window is
the hall that overlooked Mari's apartment.

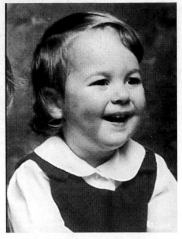

Stacy, age 18 months.
(Olan Mills)

Stacy, in kindergarten.
(Pres-Tige Portraits)

Stacy with her family on her last
Christmas. From left to right: Jude,
Johanna, age 15; Racheal (below),
age 9; Stacy, age 14. *(Rick Pashia)*

Stacy, 11 years old.
(Jude Govreau)

Tyler Winzen, on his last
Halloween, 1985.
(Mari Winzen)

Tyler, 2½, with brother Brian, 11.
(Olan Mills)

Mari Kane helps Tyler
at his first birthday
party. *(Patty Baez)*

Family Portrait taken in 1983. From left to right, front:
Nicholas Indelicato, cousin; Tyler, 18 months; Christy
Indelicato, cousin. From left to right, rear: Brian Kane,
brother; Pat Indelicato and Joseph Indelicato, Mari's parents.
(Olan Mills)

Jude Govreau hugs Stacy's friend, Mike Hardcastle, at the first memorial service. (*Dennis Caldwell, Festus News-Democrat*)

Racheal Nichols hugs Jude's friend, Joellen Scherren, at Stacy's memorial service. (*Dennis Caldwell, Festus News-Democrat*)

Stacy's friends at the first memorial service. (*Dennis Caldwell, Festus News-Democrat*)

Laura Vitale Krueger, left, and Lorraine Lapp, right, comfort Mari Kane during the news conference after Eugene Fleer's arrest. (*Dennis Caldwell, Festus News-Democrat*)

Eugene Fleer at Boone County Sheriff Dept. just after his arrest.
(*Dennis Caldwell, Festus News-Democrat*)

Jude Govreau and daughter Racheal picket the Jeffferson County Courthouse to protest the slow pace of the investigation.
(*Dennis Caldwell, Festus News-Democrat*)

Capt. John Orlando, Chief
Deputy Commander of St. Louis
Metropolitan Major Case Squad.
Orlando was initially in charge
of the murder investigation.
*(Wayne Crosslin,
St. Louis-Post Dispatch)*

Sheriff Walter "Buck" Buerger
of Jefferson County. Buerger
was in charge of the murder
investigation after the Major
Case Squad withdrew.
*(Reynold Ferguson,
S:. Louis-Post Dispatch)*

Former Prosecuting Attorney
George McElroy of Jefferson
County assisted John Appelbaum
with the Fleer trial.
(St. Louis-Post Dispatch)

Prosecutor John Appelbaum
played the key role in getting
Eugene Fleer convicted.
(William Greenblatt)

Jude Govreau, left, and Mari
Kane comfort each other in
the hallway during the trial.
(St. Louis-Post Dispatch)

Eugene "Geno" Fleer leaving
Boone County Sheriff's Dept.
after his arrest.
*(Dennis Caldwell,
Festus News-Democrat)*

The only family portrait of the Kane family since Tyler's murder, taken May 1989. Seated: Bob and Mari Kane. Standing: Brian Kane. *(Olan Mills)*

Mari Kane, John Appelbaum, and Jude Govreau in front of the Jefferson County Courthouse, summer, 1994.

mothers sitting in this room. This was another major disappointment for the women, who wondered why they never got a break.

Mari's contempt for everyone in the system boiled over as she leaned toward Jude, nodded at Appelbaum, and cracked, "Oh, my God, Jude, it's Mr. Peabody. This is par for the course."

Appelbaum ignored the comparison with the cartoon character as Captain Gansmann assured Mari and Jude again that the detectives were following every lead. Then Appelbaum explained apologetically that no one in his office had been assigned to the case. He had never read the police file and knew very little about the murders; he could offer no informed opinion on the evidence. He promised to read the reports and get back to the women as soon as possible.

"That's just the kind of crap we expected," Mari snapped as she drilled Appelbaum with a cold stare. "Two children have been murdered and no one in the prosecuting attorney's office has looked at the evidence? No wonder nothing is happening. Nobody in this county gives a damn about this case but us."

Appelbaum took the barrage of insults calmly and seemed sincere despite the abuse. "Mrs. Kane, the prosecutor's office doesn't really get involved in a case until there is enough evidence to charge. Everyone here agrees there isn't that much evidence yet, so we haven't been very involved. But I promise, I'll review the file and get back to you."

Mari glared at the young man. "I just think our kids deserve better than this."

Appelbaum nodded. "I do, too."

CHAPTER 11

John Appelbaum rocked back in his chair, slipped off his glasses, and rubbed his eyes. After three solid days reading through the two-foot stack of reports and interviews in the Price-Winzen murder case, he had reached an inescapable conclusion. The identity of the murderer was obvious, and Appelbaum wondered why the police had not pushed for charges. The prosecutor was confident that with a little more work by the detectives and a couple of good breaks, he soon would charge Eugene "Geno" Fleer with the sadistic murders of Tyler Winzen and Stacy Price. There just was no doubt in Appelbaum's mind that Fleer was the killer.

Contrary to the snap judgments about John Appelbaum by Mari Kane and Jude Govreau—and despite his boyish appearance—he was no inexperienced rookie or milquetoast Mr. Peabody. True, he was just twenty-seven and had worked in Johnson's office for only a year and a half. But he had served as chief felony prosecutor for the last six months, recognition of the impressive list of convictions he had racked up—seven felony trials in seven months. In fact, he had just won his first murder trial, squeezed guilty pleas from three men in another murder, and had four more murder cases pending. His big win had come in one of the most bizarre murders in county history. Just days before meeting with Mari and Jude, Appelbaum had obtained the death sentence for a man who dismembered his girlfriend, deposited her torso in a trunk, and dumped it along a country road. The man had confessed and led the police to the remaining body parts, which he had stuffed in Hefty bags and thrown into a pond. The 250-pound killer asked a jury to believe he had been defending himself against an attack by a knife-wielding woman; it didn't wash. And the man's horrible crime had eliminated the qualms that the young,

Catholic, pro-life prosecutor had brought to his job when it came to the death penalty. John Appelbaum now believed there were some people for whom death was the only just sentence, and he found room in his religious faith for such retribution by society.

He had become a prosecutor in Jefferson County in January 1987, fresh from law school at St. Louis University and with only a vague recollection of the Price-Winzen murders that had occurred five months earlier. He remembered a mention of bodies discovered in a bathtub three days before he returned from vacation after taking the bar exam. But he hadn't even made the mental connection between the murders and nearby Jefferson County. After he started working there, he had heard little discussion of the case by prosecutors, cops, or anyone else at the courthouse.

Appelbaum began his career trying smaller cases, but soon was getting the important ones. As he spent more time with the detectives and other felony prosecutors, he heard an occasional mention of the double murder of the kids in 1986. Detectives like Leo Burle and Bob Mullins seemed to be checking a lead every now and then, but they didn't ask the prosecutors for advice. The blackboard that displayed the history of the investigation was tucked away in the back room of the detective bureau. There had been leads, everyone said, but nothing solid enough for a charge. Geno Fleer's name was mentioned a time or two, and there were constant complaints that the kids' mothers were media hounds always running to the newspapers and television to pressure the authorities. Appelbaum sensed the cops were just hoping for a break in a case they really thought would never be solved.

The meeting scheduled with the victims' mothers came as a surprise when Johnson announced it to Appelbaum one morning. Appelbaum was not surprised, however, that Johnson would send him to handle it. The message was clear; Johnson wanted his top gun to deal with these women. But the request carried no implication that this meeting was expected to lead to a solution.

The women clearly were upset with the authorities as the meeting opened that morning; to them, every comment from the police or prosecutor was another step in the old runaround. Appelbaum really couldn't blame them, and he

refused to take their comments personally, even their
snippy attacks on him. But even while he was explaining
to the women that prosecutors usually didn't get involved
until there was enough evidence for a warrant, he was
thinking that the prosecutors should have been actively participating in the investigation from the beginning. That certainly was Appelbaum's practice, and it especially should
have been the procedure in a double murder of children.

That conclusion was reconfirmed after Appelbaum kept
his promise and spent three days in the detective division
reviewing the file. Some guidance from a prosecutor might
have brought this case together a long time ago.

Appelbaum had no difficulty seeing that everything
pointed to Eugene Fleer. First, his conduct and comments
during two interviews with the police were contradictory
and incriminating. Innocent people didn't act as Fleer had;
his demeanor betrayed him. When confronted with evidence against him, he admitted in the second interview that
he had lied about several things. And Appelbaum really
was struck by Fleer's off-the-wall comment at the end of
that interview: "I deal cocaine; I don't kill babies." What
kind of mind comes up with something like that as a
defense?

The case against Fleer had improved, too, after the
Major Case Squad was reactivated for three days in February. The information provided by those witnesses painted
a chilling portrait of a man capable of explosive, lethal violence, especially against women and especially when
spurned. Fleer's constant "theorizing" about the case also
betrayed an obsession common among criminals; the urge
to talk about their crimes was irresistible. His need to puff
himself up in front of his friends had loosened his lips
enough to divulge details he shouldn't have known if he
were innocent. And his explanation for knowing so many
details—that the cops had showed him the photos during
his interviews—rang false.

Appelbaum also thought the choice was easy between
the two potential motives offered by detectives—drugs or
sex. This was not a sex crime; the evidence and a process
of elimination made drugs the obvious motive. The case
was surrounded by an aura of drugs. So many people at
the center and so many around the edges were involved in

the drug business that, to secure information, the police had had to explain time and again that they only cared about the murders, not about drug deals. The case was saturated in illicit drugs and the lifestyle that accompanied the drug trade.

The psychological profile that Sergeant Burle asked the FBI to prepare in 1987 fit Fleer perfectly, except for a slight difference in age—a factor the profile said could vary. The killer was someone who probably had dropped out of high school, performed below his potential, and had a spotty work record in a low-skilled job. If he had a car, it was an old, beat-up clunker. Abuse of drugs or alcohol was a serious problem, and the killer probably had used drugs just before or after the crime. He often reacted to stress with an outbreak of anger, and the injuries to Stacy showed anger or fear. He probably had been interviewed by the police already and had been overly cooperative, even though that did not fit his real character. The profile leaned toward sex as the motive, but Appelbaum knew the FBI hadn't seen all the evidence.

The authorities had assembled a biography of Fleer that fit the profile. He came from a middle-class family in the Fenton area, but had started using drugs at thirteen and had run away from home. He dropped out of high school in the eleventh grade and was arrested for misdemeanor theft in St. Louis County when he was seventeen, and just after his eighteenth birthday in June 1974, he and two of his buddies tried to pull off the robbery at a drug store in St. Louis. He and another robber were wounded; the third was killed. Fleer drew a twelve-year sentence. He got his high school equivalency in prison, where he also took some college classes and was trained in small engine repair. After he was paroled, he had a variety of small-time jobs. He had worked most recently as a roofer, but was laid off shortly before the murders. He had an extensive history of drug abuse that had caused him continual problems. He even drove a battered 1976 Ford Granada.

The profile that fit Fleer so well seemed to miss Lester Howlett by a wide margin, Appelbaum thought. Howlett was better-educated, had a better work record, was more of a family man despite his strained marriage, and was nonviolent. The profile wasn't evidence, but it was a good indication to Appelbaum that his instincts and reading of the case were on target.

Appelbaum was not too shocked that the police were unable to construct a convincing case against Fleer. After all, many of them thought Lester Howlett was the best candidate for killer, and his death wrapped up the case neatly. The cops who suspected Fleer had worked hard and followed the leads, but they had never tied it all together. Despite their eagerness, they had lost their perspective as they followed tips down one dead end after another. When Fleer went to prison on the drug rap, the investigation had lost steam. After that, it seemed no one had really steered the cops' efforts.

Appelbaum drew up a short list of chores for the detectives. While he spent more time getting to know every single detail of the case, he wanted the cops to make sure the witnesses still were available and to double-check a couple of items. And he wanted them to check on the 10:26 A.M. collect call to Lester Howlett's apartment the morning of the murders; the call was placed from the same hotel in Las Vegas where Steve Winzen and Patty Garner were staying. Was it a bizarre coincidence or an ominous clue?

If the police could get those reasonable requests done, Appelbaum was sure Geno Fleer soon would take a tumble for murder.

Bob Kane made it clear. "Mari, I'm not going to watch you die. If you keep using Valium like this, I'm going to wake up some morning and you'll be dead in bed beside me. I'm not going to watch and wait for that to happen."

Mari knew she was about to lose her husband just as certainly as she had lost her son. Even through the Valium-induced fog, she knew she was headed down the wrong road and toward a risk of more than the ruination of her own health. Finally, she decided she could not let Tyler's murder kill her marriage to this special man. So, in September 1988, she took a big and very shaky step: she went back to Alcoholics Anonymous. Telling the people there she had slid back into drug use was humiliating—one of the most difficult things she had ever done. And she knew she was not meeting the most-often-cited criterion for AA members; she was not doing this for herself, but for Bob. But she decided her motivation this time was less important than the results.

And she found, just as she had several years before, that she was welcomed to AA with open arms and accepting smiles from wonderful people who offered their help without their disapproval. Finding the strength to live without Valium again was hard and the first month was hell, but she knew Bob was worth it.

Mari's resolve was tested immediately. Eugene Fleer walked out of prison in September 1988 after serving twenty-one months—paroled after less than half of his four-year sentence. The news sent spasms of fear through Jude and Mari and released a new flood of tears. The terror they felt knowing that Fleer was free to roam the streets again dwarfed their apprehension a few months earlier when he had been assigned to a work-release program in Columbia, a hundred miles west of St. Louis. He had remained under severe restrictions then, even though he once showed up in Jefferson County at a restaurant that employed Sandy Barton, the woman whose recollection of him leaving the apartment complex the morning of the murders had been so damaging. But now Fleer really was free, and the fear Jude and Mari had felt before was edging toward panic. After calling Mari with the news, Jude warned Sandy Barton. Everyone connected to this case should be looking over his or her shoulder now, Jude was sure. When she called the police, she was not surprised that Fleer's parole was news to them. That showed just how well the cops had stayed on top of this case, she thought.

Working the phones like a pro, she caromed through the Department of Corrections until she found Fleer's parole officer in Columbia. The man was kind and understanding, and explained that Fleer had been warned to stay in Columbia, where he was working as a drywall installer and living in a duplex apartment obtained for him by his parents. He also had been ordered to steer clear of Jefferson County and anyone associated with the case. If he showed up there, Jude should let the parole officer know immediately. That would violate Fleer's parole and could bounce him right back behind bars.

Small comfort, Jude and Mari thought. The next few

weeks sent them through a jumble of emotions and thoughts. They even attended a meeting of Parents of Murdered Children together, despite the pain that brought. Mari struggled hard to keep the latest setback from sending her back to Valium.

The renewed intensity of feelings brought out by Fleer's release gave new eloquence to Jude as she wrote in her journal: "When I was driving in the truck today, I could see Stacy sitting there, pretending like she was driving and pulling her glasses halfway down her nose, and looking up at me as she so often did. Why did she have to die? So many questions and no one to answer them. So much pain and nothing to ease it. So many tears that can never be dried. Such an emptiness that can never be filled. Such loneliness that can never be put into words. Silent screams that will never be heard."

But the women could not sit by idly. Jude called the police in Columbia and filled them in on Fleer. They might want to know that a man with a reputation for beating young women and suspected of murdering one was a new resident in a city that was home to a campus of the University of Missouri and all those young women students. A detective asked her to send him the newspaper clips so he could start a file on this guy.

Jude also called Sheriff Buck Buerger and asked him to announce to the media that the investigation remained active, despite an earlier comment that he believed the key to the case might have died with Lester Howlett. Jude feared that too many people assumed Howlett was the guilty party and they would not be looking for more clues to the real identity of the man who murdered the children. If Buerger could tie such a statement to comments about Fleer's parole, that might stir the pot enough to bring someone else forward with information, Jude hoped. The sheriff agreed, but Jude never saw any action. She wasn't surprised.

Meanwhile, Mari screwed up her courage and took a more direct—and more dangerous—step: She called Eugene Fleer. When she heard his smooth voice on the phone, she had to fight the desire to scream at him and demand to know how he could have killed her little boy. She had to resist the urge to vomit as she thought that this voice

was probably the last her son had heard as he died so
horribly at this man's hands. But she composed herself
quickly and had to admit that the voice she had heard
didn't sound like that of a killer—however that should
sound. She slipped into her ruse, employing some of the
personal information about this man that she and Jude had
gathered during their investigation. She posed as "Cindy,"
an old friend of his former girlfriend, Carol Thompson, and
said she once had met him at a party. Fleer was polite and
friendly as "Cindy" explained that she remembered him
and wondered if he would like to get together for a pig
roast at the University of Missouri in Columbia. He would
love to, he replied, but he didn't have a car. "Cindy" mentioned that she had heard he and Carol had broken up.
Fleer's voice turned colder as he called Carol a liar and a
cheat; that was why he had slapped her around. "Cindy"
said goodbye with a promise to call again about their get-
together. "Great," he said with obvious enthusiasm.

Bob Kane was upset and Jude was angered by Mari's
covert call and plan. Jude couldn't believe Fleer hadn't recognized Mari's voice; if he had, Mari could have endan-
gered everyone, Jude feared. Bob and Jude pleaded with
Mari to give up the risky idea. It could be suicide, and it
was exactly the kind of step the police said they were afraid
these rabid women could take, endangering any chance of
the real detectives getting enough evidence to charge Fleer
with the murders. Reluctantly, Mari recognized that the
plan was too desperate and abandoned it.

But she didn't stop searching for ways to incriminate
Fleer. In October, on one of the many calls running down
leads, she spoke with a man who confirmed he knew Fleer,
but had little else to say over the phone. So Mari immediately drove to the man's house, only to learn that she had
arrived at the place of business of a ponytailed biker drug
dealer. The man invited her into his front room and, as
Mari stared apprehensively at the rifles and handguns arranged strategically around the room, explained to her that
Fleer had asked for asylum shortly after the murders; Fleer
had been looking for a hideout while all the heat was on.
Mari's new informant recounted how he had pulled a gun
on Fleer and ordered him out of the house. The polite drug

dealer said he had called the police to tell them about the conversation, but no one had ever come to take a report.

The Sunday-morning visit to Jude's home on November 20, 1988, was rare for Mari—a chance for the two women to commiserate over the lack of progress on the investigation. As Mari flipped absentmindedly through the pages of the Sunday *Post-Dispatch,* she was drawn in by a magazine cover story on the special "priority squad" used by the St. Louis police to catch the murderer of a beloved Catholic nun. She took the magazine home and studied it closely. Accompanying the long and detailed story was a photograph of the detectives holding a large photograph of the victim, Sister Pat Kelley. As much as Mari loved the nuns who played such an important role in her church and her faith, she felt pangs of anger and resentment. Why wasn't there a priority squad holding large photographs of Tyler and Stacy? If the police in St. Louis could assign ten detectives to this single murder and get a confession from the killer within days, why couldn't Sheriff Buck Buerger use the same technique in Jefferson County for two children's murders?

The story fascinated Mari as it recounted how Colonel James Hackett renewed the investigation into the rape and murder of Sister Kelly, whose body had been found in the office of an apartment building where she operated a program that helped the poor and elderly pay their utility bills. When Hackett returned to his old post as chief of detectives nine months after the murder that shocked and angered St. Louis, he realized the first investigation had concentrated too hard on an electrician as a suspect and had ignored a likely connection to a similar rape and murder in the same building almost six months earlier. He reopened the case by applying the approach he had used successfully in the past. He pulled together a squad of handpicked detectives—each with a particular strength—and orchestrated an all-out assault, reviewing the evidence from a fresh perspective and looking in different directions. Within a few days, a man who lived in the building had confessed not only to Sister Kelley's murder but to the earlier murder there and two others in the neighborhood.

Why couldn't this approach be used in Jefferson County?

Mari wondered. She called Colonel Hackett and found a sympathetic ear. The veteran homicide detective explained that he had no jurisdiction in Jefferson County, but he graciously offered to call his old friend Sheriff Buerger and offer all the assistance he could to form a priority squad. Mari was pleasantly surprised when she called Buerger and he agreed to a meeting to discuss the idea.

This new development helped breathe some fire back into Mari and Jude's hopes. They had met again with the police and Appelbaum in early November, and the prosecutor had assured the women that he and the cops were making progress toward murder charges against Fleer. They had heard that before, of course, and were careful not to take that kind of talk too seriously. Although Appelbaum would not divulge details, he seemed genuinely concerned about the case; that was something new from the prosecutor's office. Jude still had some reservations about him. After all, she thought he had reneged on his promise at the first meeting to let her read the original police reports. He said he had never promised that and couldn't risk having details leaking out at such a crucial point.

Appelbaum's demeanor made Mari wonder if she had been too hasty in her assessment of the young man. The women's experiences with the authorities had left them skeptical about anyone in the "justice" system. The mothers demanded proof of trustworthiness before they would invest emotionally in anyone. Appelbaum would have to prove that he was different before they would bestow any credibility on him. They would need more than sincere promises. But Mari was beginning to warm to this young man; there was something about him that made her want to trust him.

Appelbaum's busy trial schedule delayed a meeting on a priority squad until the end of January 1989. Meanwhile, special preparations were begun by Mari, Jude, and Jackie Corey. Jackie reached back to a favorite tactic, the same one used on the first anniversary of the murders. The women circulated petitions again, this time calling for a priority squad. Submitting the petitions would help draw the media's interest, Jackie knew, and that always increased the pressure on the police. Perhaps the signatures of hundreds of voters would be more persuasive than the nagging of a couple of demented, obsessed women.

Mari, Bob, Jude, Rick, and Jackie Corey arrived for the meeting on Monday, January 29, with the press corps in tow, all of them looking forward to a well-covered event. But Sheriff Buerger had been around too long to walk into that kind of snare; he wasn't interested in a media circus, and he wasn't about to discuss a murder case in front of the press. He flatly refused to admit the reporters. The women were disappointed, but agreed to leave the press outside. They couldn't risk a cancellation by Buerger at this point. So they crowded into Buerger's office with him, Captains Wally Gansmann and Ed Kemp, Sergeant Burle, and Appelbaum.

The women's opening gambit was dramatic as Mari dropped petitions bearing twelve hundred signatures on Buerger's desk. "Every person who signed these wants a priority squad assigned to this case," Mari said sternly. "These people and the reporters waiting outside want to know what you're going to do about these children's murders. Their killer is out there somewhere, and these people want to know why you haven't caught him." The officers took turns explaining again that the case had never been closed. Every lead that developed was followed; every known witness was interviewed.

After an hour of discussion, Buerger took a promising step. "I don't have ten men to put on this, but I will assign a few men to work exclusively on it for a few days. I don't think they'll find anything new, but we'll see what they can come up with."

Appelbaum winced. He was sure they were close to an arrest without a priority squad, and he feared reeling in Fleer anytime soon would seem to be a response to new pressure from the women, rather than the natural result of long, hard work.

Buerger's promise was more than Jude and Mari had expected, but they weren't about to break into celebration yet.

"I feel sad we even had to ask for it," Jude wrote in her journal that night. "They should have done it on their own. But then, there are a lot of things that should have been done by the police. We have had to push for everything."

*   *   *

In the week after the meeting, John Appelbaum assembled the pieces needed to complete the puzzle. An essential part of the picture was supplied by a convict named Michael Watson, an Illinois man held in the Jefferson County Jail in 1986 for a nasty crime that had crossed the Mississippi River and state lines. He and three other men had kidnapped a man in Illinois, driven to Jefferson County, slit his throat, and left him for dead. He fooled them and survived. The other men drew life sentences, but Watson's minor role got him five years for kidnapping in Illinois and a concurrent term of four years for assault in Missouri. Appelbaum had handled the preliminary hearing on Watson, and first assistant prosecutor David Crosby, faced with a formal demand for a speedy trial and little time to assemble a case, had agreed to the plea bargain.

Watson had told the detectives he had been cooling his heels in the county jail when Fleer was arrested on the cocaine charge after Lester Howlett's death. Watson remembered the day Fleer was sentenced and returned to his cell to boast, "I'll take four years—two years for each life." When Watson asked what he meant, Fleer bragged that he had killed two people and was getting away with it. He laughed and added, "They think Lester killed them, but we both killed them. We beat the girl and suffocated the boy, and then put them in a bathtub of water." Fleer said the girl's name was Stacy and the boy's name was Tyler, and he had taken the boy's mother, Mari, to a school for shoplifters. Fleer told Watson the boy's father was Steve Winzen.

Michael Watson was no choirboy, but his knowledge made him a valuable witness. Appelbaum couldn't choose the kind of people Fleer talked to, so he worked with what he got. And Watson gave him plenty to work with—a confession from Fleer. Appelbaum was thrilled when Burle handed him the note written by Watson as he offered his account of the conversation with Fleer and the accurate information on the murders. Watson wouldn't provide a written or recorded statement, but the details were priceless.

Appelbaum savored the moment, because this case had locked him firmly in its grasp, too. He realized he never

had thrown himself emotionally into a case as he had into
this one. He had handled some brutal, heinous crimes, but
the murders of these children had reached deeper inside
him and touched him in a way the others had not. He
wanted to get justice for the kids whose lives had been cut
so short and for the man who had caused so much pain.

The investigation into the telephone call from the hotel
in Vegas had not been as successful. The hotel did not keep
records of collect calls, and a detective had spent hours
going through the hotel register without finding anyone suspicious. Steve Winzen and Patty Garner denied making the
call; they had been sound asleep in their room until Howlett called them much later with the news.

As the puzzle took shape, Appelbaum asked David
Crosby to meet him for a special session at Leo Burle's
apartment one evening. Appelbaum wanted someone with
a critical and unbiased eye to look at the evidence and
force Appelbaum to make his case. He ran through the
files and reports, explaining how all the facts fit together
and why he was convinced Eugene Fleer was their man.
When Appelbaum was done, Crosby nodded and said,
"Let's charge him." That was music to Appelbaum's ears.

On Tuesday, February 7, 1989—with no small amount of
satisfaction—Appelbaum drafted two counts of first-degree
murder that charged Eugene Fleer with strangling and
drowning Tyler Winzen and Stacy Price. After two and a
half years, the time had arrived for Fleer to pay for what
he had done. Appelbaum informed Bill Johnson about the
charges, got an arrest warrant signed by a judge, and called
Captain Gansmann to quietly plan Fleer's arrest.

Appelbaum slept hardly at all that night, and at four-
thirty on Wednesday morning, he and a team of detectives
assembled at the sheriff's department for the two-hour
drive to Columbia. Captain Gansmann had invited Leslie
Mars—the young reporter from the *Jefferson County Journal* and its sister paper, the *News Democrat*—to make the
trip with them to record the arrest in one of the sheriff's
department's toughest cases.

The entourage drove directly to the Boone County Sheriff's Department to pick up a deputy as official escort for
the arrest in the new jurisdiction. Appelbaum decided to

wait at the Boone County Jail for the police to do their jobs and bring Fleer back there to be interviewed.

Surveillance units outside Fleer's apartment informed the cops that their man was up and moving around. Burle led the team to the small apartment just after eight o'clock and relished the sound when he knocked on the door. Fleer, his hair already combed neatly, showed no hint of surprise when Burle informed him that he was under arrest for the murders of Tyler Winzen and Stacy Price. He coolly and compliantly turned around and placed his hands against the wall to be frisked and handcuffed. Burle glanced around the room—the place was small but exceptionally neat and tidy.

Fleer sat silently on the drive to jail. John Appelbaum got his first look at his suspect as the officers escorted him into an interview room. The cold eyes, the hard face, and the look of arrogance convinced the young prosecutor he had been right—dead right—about Eugene Fleer. Fleer told the police he had nothing to say until he could talk to an attorney; that ended any chance at an interview. But Appelbaum stared at his new target through the two-way mirror as Fleer sat in an interview room with Detective Rich Harris. Fleer's cool facade was showing some cracks; he looked shaken as he sat there, awaiting the trip back to the Jefferson County Jail in Hillsboro. Appelbaum even thought he detected some moisture around those cold eyes.

Just before Fleer was placed in a car, Appelbaum ordered the police to secure him with ankle shackles as well as handcuffs. As Harris snapped the shackles around Fleer's ankles, the detective said, "This might be a little uncomfortable."

Without any hint of a smile, Fleer cracked, "I'm already a little uncomfortable."

Leo Burle drove the unmarked Pontiac; Fleer and Harris sat in the back. The congestion from Burle's raging sinus infection and the wind noise whistling through the windows prevented him from hearing much of what was said behind him. As they turned onto Interstate 70, Burle heard Fleer remark casually that he could see the back of his apartment from there. But Burle didn't hear Fleer later when he turned to Harris and said, "You know, I've still got a lot of contacts in Jefferson County. I heard that you were re-

opening the case. I figured it was just a matter of time
before you guys came to get me." Harris was surprised by
the revealing remark from a tough ex-con who had been
so careful not to say anything before that. The detective
made a mental note to be sure to pass that along to
Appelbaum.

Before Appelbaum left Boone County, he made a call
to prosecuting attorney Bill Johnson. Fleer was in custody,
Appelbaum confirmed, and Johnson could make the series
of important calls.

Mari Kane was on the phone about nine o'clock planning
a shopping trip with a friend when the faint beep alerted
her to an incoming call. With her friend on hold, Mari
answered the other call and was surprised to hear a man's
voice say, "Mrs. Kane, this is Bill Johnson." She felt a slight
beat of anticipation; maybe Johnson was calling to tell her
the priority squad discussed last week had been formed and
was beginning its work.

Instead, Johnson said, "I wanted to let you know that
we arrested Eugene Michael Fleer this morning for the
murder of your son and Stacy Price. We went to pick him
up about five o'clock this morning and he is being returned
to the county jail from Columbia."

The news was almost too sudden for Mari to grasp. As
she screamed and dropped the phone, she realized Johnson
had just delivered the words she had hoped so long to hear.
"Oh, my God," she screamed again and again as she picked
up the phone.

"Mrs. Kane, are you all right?"

"I'm okay. I'm okay. Oh, my God," she shrieked as the
tears began rolling down her face. "Oh, my God, I'm wonderful. Thank you. Thank you."

She still was screaming as she hung up the phone and
then dialed Jude's number. She had to call Jude; no one
else would understand, could share this moment the way
Jude could. Busy signal. Mari kept screaming, "Oh, my
God," as she dialed again and got the pulsing busy signal
again.

Jude was about to embark on a momentous day for
daughter Johnna—celebrating her nineteenth birthday by

starting her first job—when the phone rang shortly after nine o'clock. Jude was surprised to hear Bill Johnson's voice say quite formally, "Mrs. Govreau, I am calling to inform you that we have arrested Eugene Michael Fleer for the murders of Stacy Price and Tyler Winzen."

Jude began to scream, almost the same scream that had come from her that day long ago in the apartment hallway. She remembered telling Johnson to call Mari, but she had no idea at what point she hung up the phone. She just knew that Rick had run down the stairs and she was screaming at him about Fleer's arrest. The news sent chills down Rick's spine; he couldn't believe the moment everyone had longed for had arrived.

Through the sound of her own wailing, Jude thought that Bill Johnson's announcement had been delivered in an oddly formal manner, almost that he would use if he were informing Fleer that he was under arrest. Another surreal moment in this unexpected drama.

Jude tried to calm herself as she dialed the familiar number to Mari's house and got a busy signal. She dialed again and again, not knowing that her soul mate's attempt to reach her was clogging the line from the other end. Finally, Jude heard the ring and Mari's excited hello. As Jude said, "Mari . . ." the other voice shot back, "I know," and the women began to scream in unison. The words were flying back and forth too quickly for either to know who was saying what. "Can you believe it?" they were saying over and over. "They got him. They finally got him. Oh, my God. We finally got him."

Mari Kane felt herself come alive, perhaps the most alive she had been in thirty months. The elation coursed through her and released yet another flood of tears. But it felt good, and Mari did not resist. Then there was anger; but it was a different kind of anger from what she had known for so long. Her fury at the police was being joined by a new focus on Eugene Fleer's face as the last one her son had seen as his life was stolen.

"Jude, I'm going to the courthouse. I have to see that son of a bitch in chains."

"Mari, I don't think they want us to do that."

"I don't care, Jude. That bastard killed our kids, and I

want to see him in chains. We've got him and I want to see him brought in. I want to see his face."

Mari called Bob with the news, but told him not to come home from work. She was leaving for Hillsboro and she would see him later. She drove by to pick up Laura Vitale, who insisted Mari was too emotional to drive. With Laura behind the wheel, they swung over and picked up another friend, Lorraine Viehland. The fifty-five minute drive to Hillsboro flew by, and soon the women were standing in the brutal cold outside the courthouse. A deputy told them it would be about an hour before Fleer arrived.

Jude had changed her mind, and she and Rick were on their way to Hillsboro when a police officer in Arnold pulled them over. Rick was about to offer his unique explanation for his speed when the friendly officer asked about Rick's customized license plate—DAREMO. Rick was confused, but explained that it was an acronym for the first two letters in each of his three children's names—Danny, Rene, and Monica. The officer laughed; it seemed Daremo was his wife's maiden name, and he never had seen it on a license plate before. He had wondered if Rick was an unknown in-law somehow.

Jude couldn't believe her trip to see the jailing of the man who had killed her daughter was being delayed by this cop's small talk about his wife's maiden name and a license plate. Without worrying about being tactful, Jude explained the situation to the surprised officer, who quickly sent them on their way. What else could possibly happen? Jude wondered.

She and Rick soon were parked next to the car containing Mari and her friends. Through the unending tears of excitement, the women chatted back and forth, huddling in their cars for warmth against the biting wind. The time passed slowly, and Mari kept asking the deputies in the sheriff's department for updates on the motorcade headed for Hillsboro. Still an hour out. Thirty minutes out. Fifteen more minutes.

The women wouldn't learn until later that the trip had been slowed by lunch at a Dairy Queen restaurant. Fleer had eaten his burger and fries in the car, but the women still would fume that they were kept waiting in the cold while Fleer got a free lunch.

Mari's excitement as she waited for his arrival was marked by such an edge that Jude exacted a promise that Mari would remain in the car when Fleer arrived. "I promise, I promise," Mari cried in a voice that trembled under the anticipation and emotion. But she and her friends had stepped out of the car to stretch when the squad cars delivering Fleer pulled into the parking lot sometime after two o'clock. As Mari realized the moment she was awaiting had arrived, she leaned forward angrily and screamed, "There's the animal that did this to my son."

Mari's eyes were riveted on the car door as Fleer—now sporting a mustache and a day's growth of heavy beard that seemed to accentuate his coal-black hair—stepped out. Mari didn't even notice the television cameras that converged on Fleer and his police escort, a cigar-chomping Sergeant Burle and Detective Rich Harris. Fleer carried his coat, but the heavy, dark blue sweatshirt he wore made him seem husky and muscular.

By then, Jude and Rick had stepped out of the car, and Jude leaned into Rick's chest for support. She couldn't take her tearful eyes off Fleer, whom she never had seen before but who had become such an important figure in her life. To her, he looked like nothing more than a typical street thug. But he seemed so huge, and Judy's gaze was drawn to his hands cuffed in front of him; they looked immense and powerful. "Oh, God, Rick, Stacy never had a chance," Jude cried. "Look at him. He's the last thing she saw. She never had a chance." This made the violence real again.

Rick stared at Fleer and wished for a few minutes alone with him. He was surprisingly average-looking, but Rick could perceive something threatening below the surface.

As the reporters shouted questions at the center of everyone's attention, Eugene Fleer leaned toward the cameras and—with a look that bordered on a sneer and a voice that struck observers as smug—said, "I'm not guilty."

Mari had charged across the street, her two friends barely able to restrain her as this new anger drove her forward. She had not seen Fleer since he walked away that night in August 1986 after he so graciously drove her to class. But she had spent most of the last thirty months waiting to see him again, dreaming of seeing him in chains on the way to jail. And now her moment had arrived.

As Sergeant Bob Mullins stepped in to be sure Mari stayed well back from the object of her rage, she kept screaming, "You bastard. Look at him. Look at him." Fleer didn't even glance her way as he neared the door of the courthouse. But Mari's fury exploded, and she spat angrily at him. The gesture was spontaneous, and it seemed to convey her disgust perfectly. She wasn't even aware any reporters were there and would be shocked later that night to see her contempt and her every move replayed on the television news.

Appelbaum was overwhelmed by the size of the horde that met the team's arrival. He lagged back and watched the events unfold in the gravel parking lot outside the jail. He saw Mari and Jude almost convulse as their pent-up emotion was released. They seemed to be reliving that horrible day when all of this started. He hoped the arrest after so long would provide some release, some catharsis for these mothers who deserved it so much.

In the packed courtroom for Fleer's arraignment—the proceeding to inform him officially of the charges—the defendant stood before Associate Circuit Judge Gary Kramer and quietly said yes when asked if he understood the charges. From the front row, Mari and Jude gasped and shed even more tears as the judge read that Fleer was charged with strangling and drowning their children; it still was hard for them to hear that put into these official words. When asked about an attorney, Fleer said he would hire his own. The proceeding took only minutes and was strangely anticlimactic after the drama of Fleer's arrival. The women were relieved when the judge ordered Fleer jailed without bond. And before the observers knew it, the arraignment was over and Fleer was being escorted down the hallway and off to a waiting cell.

That did not end the activities, however. The reporters and television cameras crowded into the county commissioners' room down the hall for a news conference with Bill Johnson, John Appelbaum, Leo Burle, and Wally Gansmann. Jude and Mari slipped in and watched with grim amusement as the officials explained why it had taken so long to make an arrest. Reading from a prepared statement, Johnson said, "These charges do not arise out of one large break, but the contribution of numerous leads, many of which came from citizens responding to the sheriff's department's request for information broadcast by the local media."

Gansmann said the priority squad announced only a week before had had nothing to do with the arrest; no one had even been assigned to that yet. The police had known then that they were close to charging Fleer, but they hadn't been able to say that publicly.

Mari felt her anger surging at the authorities again. If the case had never been closed, why were the charges only being filed now? If there had been a dearth of leads for so many months and even years, why hadn't every step of the investigation been traced and retraced until the detectives made their own breaks? How could the murders of two children be put on the shelf, swept under the rug—whichever cliché applied—to await some magical development that would present a solution? If the priority squad was a good idea, why hadn't the police done it before? Why had the mothers had to propose it and demand that it be done? If it had been unnecessary, why had Buck Buerger agreed to do it? If John Appelbaum's assignment to the case had been the decisive factor, why hadn't he been brought in before Mari and Jude demanded another meeting? Mari was cynically confident she knew the answers, but she tried to push all of that aside to relish the reality of these moments.

John Appelbaum was explaining to the reporters that Fleer had been acquainted with the victims, but would offer no more details. He was determined not to discuss the specifics of the evidence. When asked if the pressure by the mothers had had any effect on the case, Appelbaum graciously offered his belief that their efforts had kept the case alive in the media and kept the leads coming in. Mari and Jude grinned at each other sardonically.

Burle confirmed reporters' suggestions that Lester Howlett and the Winzens were connected and that there was some kind of link to Fleer, but he said that remained under investigation as part of the evidence. Fleer had been the prime suspect for some time and the cops had been keeping tabs on him. "It's a very complicated, large puzzle that's taken all this time to piece together little by little by little," Burle said.

Although the mothers were unimpressed by the authorities' pronouncements, one simple statement from Bill Johnson was a thrill: "The defendant faces the death penalty." They had waited thirty months to hear that, too.

Then the press turned to the women. Jude told the reporters it was frightening to see Fleer for the first time and she was struck by what she saw as a total lack of remorse in his face. She was surprised he made no attempt to hide from the TV cameras as most defendants do. She praised the results of the work by the police. "He's a slimeball and I'm happy he's off the streets," Jude said. And she thought to herself that she finally could stop worrying whether he was behind every bush, waiting to kill Racheal or some of the other survivors who could threaten his freedom.

Mari was reluctant to speak to the media gang, but finally agreed to a brief interview. Was she happy that this day finally had arrived? "Yes, we couldn't put this to rest. We couldn't put this behind us. We're never going to get our kids back. I still have to go to the cemetery on Christmas to see my son and send Stacy roses at her house, where her ashes are. It's not going to bring them back. But this man is going to pay for what he did to our kids. Yes, it feels real good."

Later that night, Mari finally agreed to an interview with a television reporter who had camped out tenaciously at Pat Indelicato's house. Mari knew she was saying more than she should to Deanne Lane of KSDK-Channel 5, but she couldn't stop herself; the events of the day finally had released an anger that would not be restrained. She was bitter, she said, that the police had dragged their feet for so long. What about a motive? Fleer could have been stalking Stacy while he was staying with his buddy, Lester Howlett, Mari suggested. Or the motive could be related to a drug deal involving her former husband, Howlett, Fleer, and others.

The interview was an emotional and stressful way to end what had been the best day in a long time. But there was one more event awaiting at home. Steve Winzen called in a rage and threatened to sue Mari, the reporter, and the television station. Mari couldn't find room for worry about a lawsuit now that the man she was so certain had killed her son finally was behind bars.

But the interview had smashed what should have been a moment of relief for a haunted Steve Winzen. Amid all of the turmoil over the investigation and the mothers' efforts, Steve had disappeared. He had retreated into an emotional shell and hidden behind a hostile facade, alienating Patty Garner and just about everyone else. He drank heavily and became someone Patty neither knew nor liked. Even Steve didn't know who he was anymore, and that cast him farther adrift in the misery caused by his son's death. He cried every day; he could find nowhere to put all the love he had for Tyler and all the grief his death had left behind. The police had treated him with no respect. Even the contact Patty made for him at Parents of Murdered Children brushed him off when he called. He had been hurt badly by Lester Howlett's death, too; he had counted on Lester to help find out who had killed Tyler.

And the ultimate insult. The prevailing theory of the murders centered on something he was supposed to have done to cause his own son's death. There had been no connection between his marijuana dealing and Tyler's death, he was sure. And there was no way Lester had killed Tyler—none in the world. Even the injury to Lester's penis had a relatively innocent explanation. Lester had told Steve the wound had been inflicted by a woman with rather active sexual habits. It had hurt like hell, Lester said.

A mutual friend who had seen Lester right after the murders agreed with Steve's analysis. Mary Jansen and her husband had lived near the Howletts and the Winzens at the trailer park; they had seen each other often in 1981 and 1982. A distraught Lester called Mary shortly after noon the day of the murders, and she and her husband went to Lester's apartment. He sat in a chair for two hours, rocking back and forth, asking for updates from Mary as she stood at the window and watched the police activity in front of the murder scene. "What are they doing now?" he kept asking. Mary's instincts told her Lester knew what had happened over there. He wasn't involved and wasn't capable of killing kids, especially Tyler; but Lester knew what had happened. He said only that he and Geno had been high for three days and had just returned to town. They both had been seen outside Mari Winzen's apartment that morning, he added without further explanation. He was a mess for the next two days, and his death seemed to confirm her suspicions. She knew then that he had killed himself or Geno had killed him.

Steve had wrestled with all of that and more. Six months after the murders, he had nearly died from a burst colon. He was convinced he had had a near-death experience and had been allowed to talk to Tyler. His son's voice had come through a cloud and welcomed Steve to a new place. But Steve had told Tyler, "I can't come now. I want to, but I can't. I have a daughter to think about." At that moment, Steve returned to the reality of a hospital room.

And now, on the night when Steve should have been able to take his first deep breath in years and rejoice in the arrest of his son's murderer, he had just watched Mari and a reporter who knew nothing about him destroy him on the most-watched television news show in the St. Louis metropolitan area. His family had seen it; his friends had seen it. How could he face them now? Hell, yes, he was angry.

The next day, Mari decided to make a gesture of appreciation and gratitude to those she had criticized so vehemently in the past—within the past few hours, in fact. She had roses delivered to Sheriff Buck Buerger, his detective bureau, and the prosecutor's office. They deserved that much.

She also visited Tyler's grave to tell him she had kept her promise; justice finally was about to be delivered. She then tried to find some relief from the intense pressure and incessantly ringing telephone with a shopping trip with a friend. But the televised images of her face and actions from the night before wouldn't leave her mind, and she had the paranoid feeling that she was recognized by everyone who looked at her as she walked the mall. After dozens of imagined furtive glances, Mari decided to retreat to the relative safety of her home. She would spend days getting over the feeling that her grief had been supplemented by a new and unwelcome celebrity marked by her unrestrained anger as she spat at her son's killer.

Captain John O'Rando was thrilled to hear that Eugene Fleer finally had been arrested. O'Rando knew the framework had been there, and he was glad the case had come together for Jefferson County. After all the time he had spent with Mari and Jude, all the hours trying to help them understand how this case had to be handled, he was gratified to see this day.

Sergeant Tim McEntee had been briefed on the impending arrest by his buddy Captain Ed Kemp. The news that Fleer finally was in custody was almost anticlimactic after all this time. But McEntee was elated to know his old pal was back behind bars. Everything had poined at Fleer; nothing pointed away from him. Under "McEntee's Code" for marking suspects in his notes, Fleer's name always ended with an exclamation point, never with a question mark reserved for suspects who might be innocent. He fit the profile for this kind of vicious crime, and McEntee too was glad Jefferson County had been able to put it together.

Detective Bob Miller was watching television when he saw the bulletin about the arrest. He was floored. Unless the cops in Jefferson County had more than he had heard about, he didn't see how they could justify charges now. He hoped he was wrong, but he doubted that Geno Fleer would be convicted on the slim evidence the investigation had produced.

Captain Ed Kemp wasn't confident, either. Oh, sure, Geno Fleer knew something about these murders; maybe he even had some role in the cleanup or the cover-up afterward. In fact, Kemp thought Fleer had probably killed Lester Howlett to keep the police from cracking the men's drug ring. But it probably was Howlett who had gone to that apartment for sex with Stacy and ended up killing both of the victims. Kemp just couldn't buy Fleer in that role.

Detective Bill Baldwin phoned John O'Rando and the sheriff's department to offer his congratulations. Baldwin felt joy more than relief. He had no doubt that Fleer was the killer, and he hoped this was the first step down the courtroom aisle that led to the judge's bench where Fleer would be sentenced to death.

The day after the arrest, a saddened woman who remembered Eugene Fleer fondly from high school offered readers of the *News Democrat* a more human face for this accused murderer she had known as Gene Fleer. The photo that accompanied the story set the somber mood as it showed Fleer from the back, sitting in a chair with his head bowed and hands cuffed behind him. The woman told reporter Leslie Mars, "He was a sweet kid. He was quiet, but always restless. We walked the halls together and laughed together. We had a friendship. . . . He knew all the answers in our history class." His friend said Gene had changed in the ninth grade. By the tenth grade, he was hanging around with the wrong crowd, the rough crowd that always was looking for ways to get into trouble. She lost track of him then, but ran into him years later after he was paroled from prison on the armed robbery and assault charges. "He would always be real friendly. And I remember him saying that it was difficult being on the outside. He was having a rough time." After a pause, she added, "This is very hard. It hits home when something like this happens to one of your classmates. He could have had such a wonderful life."

Mari Kane was unimpressed by the sensitive recollections about a young Gene Fleer. She found the memory of his difficulty adjusting to life outside prison walls much more telling. She could still hear his blurted revelation to her: "You know, I've been in prison before."

A few days later, a county juvenile officer approached John Appelbaum in a courthouse hallway and offered another view of the young Geno Fleer—a view born of a unique perspective. "I handled his juvenile case, and he was the coldest, meanest kid I ever ran into. I have no doubts he is capable of this."

CHAPTER 12

Captain Wally Gansmann took the telephone call at his desk on Thursday morning while he still was basking in the glow of Eugene Fleer's arrest twenty-four hours earlier. From the point of view of the officers who worked with Gansmann, he seemed nearly obsessed with the case; to them, it was good to see the work by so many detectives pay off. The sheriff's department had taken some nasty criticism over the lack of progress, even though the officers were confident they had done everything they could. Fleer's arrest seemed to vindicate the investigation and the department. And Gansmann didn't know it yet, but this call was about to heighten that sense of accomplishment.

The caller was a man named Neil Myrick, one of the many people interviewed in the days after the murders in 1986. His memory of seeing a man near the apartment building had seemed relatively inconsequential then. But as he spoke to Gansmann on this day in 1989, Mr. Myrick seemed to be offering a much more useful recollection. He had just heart a report on the radio about an arrest in the Price-Winzen murders. He had taken a good look at the man outside that building more than two years ago, and he was willing to help again if the police were interested. Gansmann immediately sent two detectives to Myrick's office to hear more.

Myrick, a pleasant young man who had lived in an upstairs apartment across the street from Mari Kane's building, told Sergeant Butch Myers and Detective Dennis Lassing that he had been lying in bed about nine-thirty watching the rainy morning outside after his wife had left for work. As he took in the street scene—unusually quiet because the rain had kept away the construction crews—he saw a man jog up to Mari's building and go inside.

Several minutes later, the man came out and jogged around the west side of the building. The man was in his late twenties, with a heavy build and dark brown hair. He was wearing a light jacket over a shirt and shorts, possibly blue.

Myers handed Myrick a sheet of paper bearing six mug shots and asked if he could identify any of them as the man he had seen that morning. Myrick immediately pointed to the photograph marked Number 3 in the upper right corner. "That's him," he said with a nod.

Number 3 was Eugene Michael Fleer. Myers had used a mug shot taken when Fleer was booked on the drug charge just days after the murders. Myrick assured the police he had not seen the television coverage of Fleer's arrest the night before nor the photographs of him that accompanied the newspaper articles that morning. Myrick's selection of Fleer's mug shot had not been tainted; Myrick had not even known about the arrest until he heard it on the radio that morning.

Gansmann and Appelbaum were thrilled; they now had a witness who put Fleer in that apartment building that morning. He had lied when he first denied being in the complex that morning, but was tripped up when a woman saw him leaving. Now he had been snared by another witness, a man with absolutely no motive to lie.

Speculation about whom Fleer would hire as his attorney had run rampant through the courts for a few days before the word came out: Fleer had chosen Clinton Almond and Marsha Brady as his defense team. Appelbaum felt mixed emotions at the news that his adversaries would be the partners with the law office directly across the street from the courthouse. Clint Almond—a wiry man in his fifties—had spent decades cultivating a reputation as a crusty, colorful character with a bottomless bag of legal maneuvers that Appelbaum thought usually were little more than defense tricks—stunts, really. Appelbaum had been the second-chair prosecutor on a murder case against Almond and Brady, and knew them to be wily and resourceful. Appelbaum thought Almond was a master at screwing up the state's case and playing mind games with prosecution witnesses before trial, and Appelbaum really disliked that. But he wasn't intimidated by the old veteran. Almond was the most dangerous before trial; if Appelbaum got to the jury with half of his case, he had a good chance to beat Almond. Appelbaum's string of victories had made him just cocky enough to relish the matchup. Borrowing a cliché from western movies, going against Almond suggested a show-down between the old gun in town and the young hand making his name.

Almond knew both sides of the aisle. He had been an assistant prosecutor in the 1960s and had been appointed chief prosecutor when his elected boss became a judge. However, even though Almond was a Democrat in an over-whelmingly Democratic county, he lost the election to a Republican about a year later. He turned to defense work, developed a high-profile practice with a number of major murder cases, and supplemented that with a nimble partici-pation in politics.

Appelbaum always thought Almond's appearance was just right for the role as quirky defense attorney in a small town. He was slim, and his graying black hair always seemed unkempt because of the hooked strands that slid across his forehead. His voice was marked by a gravelly twang tracing his background to the small town of Herrin in southern Illinois. He had been in Jefferson County for years and fit in well with the rural atmosphere.

Marsha Brady was his younger protégée and partner, and they led an interesting life together from their horse ranch to their airplanes to their ski trips. Appelbaum thought Brady was classier than Almond and a better lawyer on the whole. She knew her way around the courtroom, and Appelbaum thought she was more effective in front of a jury than her partner. And she certainly carried herself with more grace; she was a slim brunette who dressed conserva-tively, usually in tasteful business suits.

In the offices of Almond and Brady, the defense attor-neys prepared for what they knew would be a difficult case. They saw John Appelbaum as an ambitious young prosecu-tor who studied the evidence and made a determination in his own mind of guilt or innocence. Once he landed on guilty, Almond and Brady thought, it made no difference to Appelbaum what means he used to convict. He got tun-nel vision and refused to consider anything that didn't fit his theory of the crime or, especially, that tended to indicate the defendant was innocent. The defenders thought Appelbaum had a habit of leaning on witnesses by explaining that the defendant was guilty and would go free unless they helped.

As they looked at the Fleer case, however, Almond and Brady thought there was even less to point at this defendant than they had imagined. There was not a shred of physical evidence against Fleer, and the circumstantial evidence could just as easily indict Lester Howlett. The former prosecuting attorney, Dennis Kem, had turned the case down back in 1986 before he went on to an appointment as a circuit judge. That it was filed now by his appointed successor, William Johnson, and his assistant, John Appelbaum, seemed the perfect support of the defense attorneys' opinion of the current prosecuting attorney's office.

They found nothing to contradict their impression of the evidence after they interviewed Eugene Fleer. He offered them essentially the same account he had finally given the police and said he had been shocked to be busted for cocaine possession in 1986; he had cooperated so fully on the drug angle because the police had sworn they were interested only in the murder. He had been had, he told his new attorneys. But they really stunned him with their theory that Lester Howlett was the killer. Fleer refused to believe that about his friend, and his indignant reaction to their suggestion struck Almond and Brady as genuine and heartfelt.

Mari and Jude called Appelbaum as soon as the defense team was announced. Who were these people? Appelbaum offered his opinion of his adversaries and said he would have to stay on his toes to counter the tactics he expected from them. The women were finding a new confidence in the young prosecutor, who certainly had taken this case by the horns.

Appelbaum tried to prepare for any kind of assault, and he didn't have to wait long. The first blast came the week after the arrest. An incensed Marsha Brady accused prosecutors of orchestrating a media circus for Fleer's arrival at the jail. Brady told the *News Democrat* that the presence of the grieving mothers, the inquiring reporters, and the prying TV cameras obviously was designed to arouse prejudice among potential jurors, violating Fleer's right to a fair trial. Not since she arrived in Jefferson County in 1965 had there been such a massive explosion of publicity. And she suggested that the lack of significant details about the case suggested it was so weak that prosecutors hoped to convict Fleer in the press before he got to trial.

Prosecuting Attorney Bill Johnson and Sheriff Buck Buerger righteously denied the charges and noted that they had scrupulously avoided discussing the evidence with reporters. They would not try this case in the press, they said, as Brady obviously was. Buerger said he had seen a lot of cases get just as much publicity, and Johnson said he had no control over the actions of the media.

The defense team's opening gambits continued. Before long, Appelbaum received a call from a frantic Jude Govreau reporting that her neighbors had seen a man in a Cadillac driving through the neighborhood and taking pictures of Jude's house. Jude feared it was one of Fleer's friends setting her and her family up for the final assault she had always feared. But Appelbaum was confident he knew what was happening. He had Jude bring in one of her neighbors, and the woman identified a car parked across the street from the courthouse as the one she had seen cruising the area. When the woman described the gray-haired man she said was taking the photographs, Appelbaum figured his hunch had been correct. He called Clint Almond, asked if he had been photographing Jude's house and car, and warned that he would be watching for any more stunts. Almond blew up, railing about false accusations. Appelbaum knew the battle was joined, but he never dreamed how rough and long the road to the courtroom would be.

With the preliminary hearing approaching, Appelbaum worked hard at pulling together a case that would convince a judge that the charges justified a trial before a jury. At a "prelim," Appelbaum's burden was to establish probable cause for the judge to believe Eugene Fleer had committed the crimes charged. The basics of the case had to withstand scrutiny from the defense and the judge. As Appelbaum developed the case and solidified the witnesses, he also worked at forming a plausible theory of a motive. He was not compelled by law to prove a motive, but he knew he would have to offer the jurors a reason for Eugene Fleer to commit this terrible crime. Jurors would have to find some way to explain how a man could do this to children.

And Appelbaum was confident the evidence was strong to support his theory: Tyler Winzen had been murdered in retaliation for a drug deal gone bad involving his father, Lester Howlett, Eugene Fleer, and others; Stacy Price had been killed to eliminate a witness.

Although Appelbaum was unable to present a scenario in detail right then and prove exactly who had done what, he could draw reasonable inferences from all of the witnesses and evidence. Fleer, Howlett, and Steve Winzen obviously were associates in the drug business. The reports of a bad deal involving cocaine from a source in Illinois and the brutal robbery of dealer Dave Helmond in his home were ample evidence of trouble in the organization. Fleer had made many comments suggesting all of that to some of the witnesses, and that lent extra credibility to this theory. Appelbaum deduced that Winzen had made the connection for the bad deal, probably cocaine that was tainted in some way. Fleer had been ripped off, and he wanted to send a message to Steve Winzen and others—nobody did that to Geno Fleer. Killing Winzen's son was the most powerful way to do that. If Fleer would kill a kid, the druggies would say, he would do anything; we'd better not mess with him. And killing Tyler instead of Steve would keep Steve in line as a valuable and money-producing gear in the drug machine. When Lester Howlett—Fleer's partner and perhaps witness to the murders—began to crack, Fleer eliminated him, too.

Appelbaum was certain the truth about what had happened in Apartment C lay in that set of facts. He wondered if average citizens drafted as jurors could find room in their relatively normal psyches for that kind of evil. He would have to convince them that they never could know what went on in the mind of a drug dealer, in the heart of a sociopath willing to make money by selling destruction to others and willing to kill to protect his profits.

As the prosecutor pondered those questions, his case was shaping up as well as he could have hoped. Some new tidbits had come in. One woman had called to offer a startling account of Fleer's conduct at a party in the days right after the murders. He seemed spaced out and looked bad; in a phrase Appelbaum heard often to describe Fleer during that time, the woman said he "looked like the devil." To entertain everyone at the party, Fleer had described being interviewed by the police and claimed they had shown him photographs of the children's bodies in the bathtub. And then Fleer "cackled" a chilling laugh and puffed out his cheeks to demonstrate how the children's faces had looked under the water.

Appelbaum double-checked with Sergeant Tim McEntee and was assured no one had shown Fleer any crime scene photos. In fact, the Major Case Squad hadn't even had the photos back from the developer when they first interviewed Fleer. Perfect, Appelbaum thought. That meant there was only one way Fleer could have seen those grotesque sights he recalled with such glee: he was the one who had put those kids in that tub and looked into their faces.

Not long after Fleer's arrest, Mari Kane came to Appelbaum with another request. She wanted to see the county jail so she could know the conditions under which this man was living. She had never seen a jail before and she needed to know. Appelbaum cleared it with the jailers and then escorted Mari to the door of the cells on the second floor of the courthouse. Mari stepped in alone and was met by an overwhelming darkness and the nasty smell of urine. A jailer pointed her to a corridor lined with cells, and she stepped uncertainly into it. She was shocked to find herself separated from several male inmates only by the bars. But her eyes were drawn away from the men and to the paint chipping off the bars and then to the small cells and crowded conditions. As she walked slowly down the corridor, the men made the predictable sex-laden comments. But she barely heard them and cared even less. She did not see Fleer, but she now knew that he was not living in comfort but in conditions barely a step above squalor, and she was glad.

Jude and Mari's husband were furious when they heard what she had done. Jude was afraid Clint Almond would find out about the visit and somehow use it against the prosecution. "You're going to blow this case," Jude chastised Mari angrily. But Jude also asked later for an account of what Mari had seen.

Witness Michael Watson was developing into something of a problem. Although he had written a note in 1986 detailing his memories of Fleer's confession to the murders, Watson had steadfastly refused to provide police with a signed statement or videotaped account of the conversation. His testimony at the preliminary hearing could clinch it for the prosecution, and a full statement before then was essential. But Watson—a huge but surprisingly soft-spoken man still serving his sentence from the kidnapping and throat-slashing incident—wanted to wait until he was out of jail and clear of any danger as a snitch. In early March, Appelbaum heard Watson had just been paroled from prison in Jefferson City and was headed home to Illinois. Appelbaum dispatched Sergeant Burle and another detective to the bus depot, where they tried to persuade Watson to return to Jefferson County with them to give the statement he had avoided so long. But he still balked; call him later, he said.

Appelbaum's frustrating experience with Watson made him even more interested in calls from a man doing time in a federal prison in Minnesota. Donald Walker,* a Jefferson County native serving a twenty-year sentence for robbing a convenience store and service station in 1985, said he had been an informant sent in by the Secret Service and other federal agencies to get details about official corruption in the county. He had worn a wire to record conversations with anyone who might be involved. He had concentrated on reports of a diamond-smuggling operation, theft and counterfeiting of food stamps, and payoffs from seedy massage parlors. He even ran the Touch of Class massage parlor outside of Fenton and an escort service for a while in the early 1980s.

Walker said he had been awaiting trial on the robbery charges and working the undercover investigation when he was introduced to Eugene Fleer by a bail bondsman. Fleer called Walker and set up a meeting one night in September 1986 in a bar just across the line in south St. Louis County. Walker had not worn the wire that night, because he was hoping to score a deal on diamonds and cocaine without the feds' knowledge. He was met by a drugged Eugene Fleer, who was accompanied by a blonde and was still snorting cocaine and popping Valium as they talked. Fleer got totally wasted, and as his tongue got looser and looser, he started talking about how he had killed two kids. He began to cry as he said killing the girl had not bothered him, but he could hardly stand the fact that he had killed the little kid. He said another guy was involved in the murders and was about to go to the police, so Fleer had given the guy a "hot shot"—a fatal overdose. One more man knew about the killings, too, and that was the purpose of the meeting; Fleer wanted Walker to kill the other man. "There has to be one more killing before the killing can stop," Fleer explained. He offered a payment in diamonds and cocaine. The discussion never went any farther, and because Walker had not worn a wire that night, no recording of the conversation existed.

That information sounded good to Appelbaum, but Walker wanted something in exchange. For his testimony, Walker wanted Appelbaum to arrange a reduction in his sentence. The prosecutor said he could only make his standard offer for a prisoner—a letter to the parole board reporting his cooperation and urging that it be considered when parole came up. That didn't satisfy Walker, and he was unsure whether he would testify without a better deal.

Two important witnesses—two big headaches for John Appelbaum. He decided not to worry about Walker as the June 13, 1989, date for the preliminary hearing neared. He would call Michael Watson as a witness and take a chance that the unpredictable ex-con would take the Fifth Amendment. Even without his testimony, however, Appelbaum was sure the rest of the evidence would carry the day.

The "prelim" already had been delayed while the case was assigned to Associate Judge Robert Curran and again when Clint Almond broke his arm in a skiing accident. But the defense had another surprise up its sleeve when June 13 rolled around. That morning, Almond came into Appelbaum's office, announced that he knew the prosecution had a snitch, and then offered to waive the hearing if Appelbaum would furnish copies of all documents in the case. Done, Appelbaum said. He eagerly traded a free ride past the preliminary hearing in exchange for records he would have to produce later anyway.

Appelbaum called Mari and Jude to inform them about the waiver of the prelim, and had to calm Mari's initially loud and angry protest over another botched event. "No, this is good for us," he explained. "We don't have to have the hearing. I wasn't even sure what Watson was going to say. Now we don't have to worry; we go straight to trial."

Clearing that first hurdle also meant it was time for Appelbaum to keep an important promise to the mothers. He sat down with them in his office and said, "This is the day you've been waiting for." He explained each of the forty bits of evidence and how it fit into his grand design for the case against Eugene Fleer. He sensed the women were not only pleased, but impressed with the strength of the case. And he hoped they understood that Fleer had been arrested at the proper time and only when the evidence against him had gelled. The murder charges had not been the result of the pressure applied by Jude Govreau and Mari Kane.

Jude accepted that; her opinion of the police was so low that she assumed they didn't care what she thought or felt. But Mari never would believe it. She would always remain convinced that Eugene Fleer would have escaped justice and their children's murders would have been forgotten if she and Jude had not become a source of constant irritation and embarrassment to the police.

Two weeks later, Fleer was arraigned and entered a plea of not guilty. He was ordered to stand trial on January 22, 1990. And then John Appelbaum made a formal announcement he had saved for a moment when Eugene Fleer was present in court and could hear it said to his face. Appelbaum notified the judge that the state would seek the death penalty. When someone like Fleer had so ruthlessly taken innocent lives, Appelbaum thought it was important to make the official statement when the defendant could hear the news up close and personal.

The case against Fleer was moving quietly toward trial that summer, but Appelbaum was plunging into another investigation that would be unlike anything he had ever experienced. This new case would hang over his head as he prosecuted Fleer and, in the end, would prove to be completely different than it first seemed.

On July 7, 1989, five-month-old Ryan Stallings fell ill with a strange stomach ailment at his home outside of Hillsboro. Five days later a doctor at the respected Cardinal Glennon Children's Hospital in St. Louis signed an affidavit saying he believed Ryan had been poisoned with ethylene glycol, a substance found in antifreeze. The state took custody of Ryan and placed him in a foster home after he was discharged from the hospital. His seemingly confused parents, Patricia and David Stallings, said they knew of no way their son could have ingested the chemical. On September 4, after a visit with his mother at a state office, Ryan was hospitalized again with ethylene glycol poisoning, and authorities said they had evidence that Patricia Stallings had given him the substance in a bottle when she fed him.

On a warrant approved by Appelbaum and Prosecuting Attorney Bill Johnson, the woman—pregnant with a second child—was arrested at home the next day and jailed on a charge of assaulting her son. Two days later, on September 7, Ryan Stallings died. His death came only hours after John Appelbaum's wife, Carol, had delivered their second child, a daughter. Since Appelbaum would prosecute Patricia Stallings, he had been keeping up with the latest developments by phone from his wife's hospital room, and Johnson told him the charge was being upgraded to first-degree murder. Appelbaum watched the television in his wife's room as Johnson announced the new charge and, as Appelbaum winced, said the state would seek the death penalty against the twenty-four-year-old woman. Wrong, Appelbaum thought. Not every first-degree murder is a death-penalty case, and Johnson still didn't see the difference.

Five months after her arrest, Patricia Stallings would deliver another infant son. No one—especially the prosecutors—could dream how that child would affect the case against his mother.

But the Fleer case would not give Appelbaum much time to contemplate the evidence against Patty Stallings. Appelbaum was taking some time off at home with his wife and new baby on Friday, September 15, when he got a call from a furious Jude Govreau alerting him that she had just spoken to reporter John Auble from KTVI-TV, Channel 2, in St. Louis; he said he was going to interview Fleer at the jail. Jude's anger was shared by Appelbaum, who saw such jailhouse interviews as an outrage. Why should a murder defendant get a free shot to—surprise! surprise!—proclaim his innocence on TV? And why would a sheriff allow his jail to be the setting for such a farce?

Not that Appelbaum was surprised. Auble recently had interviewed another prisoner at the jail while he was awaiting trial on charges of assaulting his wife. Appelbaum had never heard of a televised interview with a jailed defendant, and he hadn't liked it the first time Auble did it. But Appelbaum thought talking to Fleer, the suspect in the murders of two kids, was over the top. He raced to the courthouse in hopes of heading off the ill-advised interview and immediately ran into the reporter in the hallway outside Sheriff Buck Buerger's office. The sheriff already had approved the interview and arranged for it to be held in Captain Ed Kemp's office.

"What are you doing interviewing Fleer?" Appelbaum demanded angrily.

"There's nothing wrong with that," Auble responded.

Appelbaum shook his head. "You'd interview the devil if he'd talk to you," he snapped.

Auble grinned. "Yeah, and it probably would be a great interview."

Appelbaum spun on his heel and went directly to Judge John L. Anderson's chambers to ask for an order prohibiting the interview. Fleer was a jailed suspect awaiting trial, and such an interview generated improper pretrial publicity, the prosecutor argued.

"I don't like it," the judge said. "But the reporter and Fleer have a First Amendment right to do it. It's up to the sheriff to decide whether one of his prisoners can conduct an interview in jail."

Appelbaum couldn't find Buerger, but he went back to Auble and demanded to sit in on the interview. "I don't trust you, and I want to hear everything that's said," Appelbaum insisted. "I don't want to be on camera, but I want to be in the room the whole time." Auble had no objection, and Appelbaum dropped into the chair behind the desk in resignation as Fleer was brought into the room.

Auble and Fleer sat on a couch as Fleer told the camera, "Everybody has had their say. The detectives have had their say. The sheriff's department has had their say. The families of the victims—of course, they're entitled to justice for their children—but they've had their say. So, I'd just like to have my say."

Auble asked, "Your say is what?"

"My say is that I'm not guilty, that I wouldn't allow something like that to happen in any way, shape, or form if I was aware of it."

Appelbaum was unimpressed by the claim of innocence, but the next revelation almost blew him out of the chair. Auble asked about a document Fleer had provided him— a report that showed Fleer had passed a lie detector test in 1986; Fleer claimed the Major Case Squad had told him he'd flunked. He said he was outraged that the police had lied to him about the results of a test he voluntarily took to assist their investigation.

But it was Appelbaum who was outraged now. Auble was publicizing a lie detector test of dubious accuracy that was not admissible evidence in court, and potential jurors would hear Fleer's claim that this helped prove his innocence in a doctored police investigation. What pejorative hogwash, the prosecutor fumed. He even told Auble that the test had been examined by another expert who had said it was poorly administered, had a significant margin of error, and could be interpreted to show deception by Fleer. But Appelbaum refused to discuss the evidence any further; he would not try this case in the media, he insisted.

The final insult arrived when the cameraman swung around to level the lens at Appelbaum leaning back behind Kemp's desk—after he specifically had said he did not want to be on camera.

Auble's story led to the five-o'clock news and opened with a recounting of Appelbaum's unsuccessful attempt to stop the interview while showing the tape of him sitting in the office. Then Auble moved to the featured player, showing Fleer affirming his innocence and charging that he had been misled about the polygraph. As Mari Kane's face appeared on the screen, Auble said she was unimpressed with Fleer's claim of innocence. "We feel the defense attorney is grasping at straws," she told the reporter.

Jude had called Mari earlier with the news of the Fleer interview and Auble's request for reaction from the mothers. Although Mari still was reluctant to talk to reporters, she called Channel 2 to demand a chance to speak for her murdered son. Auble arrived to interview her and seemed very nice; she was grateful for the chance to represent the victim's side—a side too often ignored by all parties in the system.

Auble repeated the interview with Fleer on the news at ten o'clock, but this time showed Jude Govreau responding that she and Mari were confident the prosecutors had "a real good case."

Appelbaum was unsure whether the episode would have any real impact, and he was angry that he had been shown on TV after expressly forbidding that. But he was glad it was over.

Mari and Jude still were furious that Auble was giving such a forum to the man they were certain had killed their children. Their kids had never got to have "their say." Why should Fleer have his say until it could be balanced by the evidence that would be presented in court?

John Auble's piece led to a story in the *News Democrat* a week later that went into more depth on the polygraph issue and quoted Clint Almond as saying Fleer had been so "livid—damned mad" when he found the report in material provided by prosecutors that he demanded to go public with the interview with Auble. The prosecution had a weak case and had completely misread the evidence, Almond insisted. Bill Johnson reiterated the second expert's doubts about the polygraph and scoffed that it was the only thing the defense had found to attack. The case was strong and a jury would decide, Johnson said.

But there would be more from Channel 2. When Jude encountered Auble in the courthouse one day, he asked offhandedly if it was true that the mothers had stalked Fleer. Jude—unaware of Mari's surveillance outside the halfway house where Fleer had been held months earlier—

snapped defensively, "This man stalked my daughter for two days. If I had stalked him, he'd be dead now."

But Auble's assault on the prosecution of Eugene Fleer was just beginning, and even more ammunition was about to be provided by events no would could have imagined.

CHAPTER 13

John Appelbaum spent weeks resisting demands from the defense to disclose the address of witness Michael Watson. The ex-con didn't want to talk to Almond and Brady, Appelbaum explained, and that was his right. Although Watson's residency in Illinois offered him some protective insulation from Jefferson County, the man still was afraid for his safety because he had such damaging information about Eugene Fleer's jailhouse confession in 1986. Almond and Brady thought that was one of the most ludicrous things they had ever heard.

But in fact, Watson still hadn't given a signed statement to prosecutors and was holding back while he sought special concessions. His primary demand was for parole officials in Missouri to apply time he had served in Illinois so his parole would be satisfied sooner. Appelbaum explained that he had talked to parole officers, but that was all he could do. Watson even called Appelbaum once and asked for $100 cash because he was broke. Appelbaum stalled, wondering if he was being set up. Had the call been recorded in hopes of catching Appelbaum in a slip that would play into defense hands? Appelbaum covered himself with a letter to Watson explaining that such a payment would be unethical for a prosecutor and damaging to Watson's credibility as a witness. Appelbaum could connect Watson to social service agencies that might help him financially, but there would be no payment from prosecutors.

By the end of September, Almond and Brady tired of Appelbaum's reluctance and persuaded Judge Anderson to order Watson brought to Jefferson County for an interview. On November 2, Appelbaum and his investigator, Chris Borgerson, drove to East St. Louis and picked up Watson. After lunch at a Chinese restaurant, they delivered the seemingly cooperative Watson to a conference room in the courthouse to talk to the defense team. But when Borgerson left for a coffee run, Almond and Brady disappeared with the prosecution's critical witness. Borgerson made a frantic call to Appelbaum, who began searching for the missing persons. As Appelbaum entered Judge Anderson's courtroom, Borgerson pointed to the stairway leading to the jury deliberation room and said he thought he had found them. Appelbaum took several steps up the stairs but froze when he heard the three familiar voices laughing.

In a few moments that he would regret later, he stood on the stairs long enough to hear what sounded like Watson telling the defenders how he had conned the prosecutors. Watson's value as a witness had just evaporated.

Appelbaum stormed down the stairs and told Borgerson to let him know when they were finished. Appelbaum paced his office in a rage; he concluded that the defense had been in contact with Watson before. Was losing Watson's testimony a fatal blow to the case? Appelbaum had spent months dealing with witnesses who were less than anxious to cooperate. He had had to massage most of them, reminding them that all he wanted was the truth. They didn't have to accuse Eugene Fleer of anything or even believe that he had done anything wrong; they just had to be truthful about what they knew. And now Michael Watson was slipping away during a hidden interview with Almond.

When the defense had finished, it was the prosecution's turn. Appelbaum, Borgerson, and Detective Rich Harris told Watson they knew what had happened, had overheard part of the conversation, and wanted to know the truth. Was Watson's story about Fleer's confession true or was his recantation to Almond true? Harris explained that the police couldn't protect him unless they knew the truth. Appelbaum said he couldn't take Watson into a courtroom to testify against a man accused of a double murder unless he knew the truth, too. Watson hedged, refusing to give them a straight answer. But he was a changed man, now implying that he feared the police and prosecutors. "If you're going to kill me, just kill me now," he kept saying.

Appelbaum finally gave up and made a firm decision— he never would call Watson as a witness. He wouldn't say that to anyone else, but the decision was made. Watson was out.

That afternoon, Marsha Brady called Appelbaum into a conference with Judge Anderson and accused the prosecutor of eavesdropping on the interview with Watson, calling that a flagrant violation of ethics and court orders. Brady said Appelbaum, Harris, and Borgerson then threatened Watson and she wanted to take depositions to establish under oath just what had happened with this critical witness.

When Appelbaum told Harris about Brady's charges, the detective smiled and disclosed a little secret: he had recorded the conversation with Watson and that would prove that Watson had not been threatened. Appelbaum had to grin with embarrassment as he listened to the tape; he seemed desperate—almost wimpy, he thought—as he begged Watson repeatedly to tell the truth. He certainly hadn't bullied or threatened this huge witness.

Appelbaum later provided the judge with a transcript of the interview to prove no threats had been made; the judge agreed to Appelbaum's request to seal the document to keep it from becoming public. Almond got around that later, however, and made sure the transcript got to the press to discredit Watson and, perhaps, Appelbaum. Almond attached a copy of the transcript with a defense motion asking the judge to prohibit testimony by Watson or the other inmate witness, Donald Walker. Watson should be barred, Almond argued, because Appelbaum's unethical eavesdropping had forced the defense to change its strategy and because the prosecutor and police had threatened Watson and his family after he changed his story. Borgerson testified that he had lifted his sweater to show Watson his gun, but only to convince the witness that the authorities could protect him.

The judge should veto Walker's testimony because he had been given too many deals in exchange for his cooperation, Almond insisted. Appelbaum disagreed, saying his only effort on Walker's behalf was a letter to the parole board setting out his cooperation.

Judge Anderson withheld a ruling on whether Appelbaum could call the men as witnesses, but offered his opinion of the young prosecutor's surreptitious listening on the stairs: it may have been ungentlemanly, but it was not unethical or illegal.

Appelbaum felt vindicated, although embarrassed. He certainly wished he had resisted the urge to climb those stairs and listen to the voices coming from behind that door. As he contemplated the odd events, he had to shake his head. He knew Clint Almond's involvement would complicate things, but this case was turning out to have more twists and turns than a bad spy novel.

As the trial date in January 1990 neared, Almond turned up the heat on Donald Walker. The informant was now in federal witness protection in prison, so he was promising his full cooperation. As part of that, he had explained to Appelbaum why he had not come forward earlier with his account of Fleer's confession. Walker had talked to his attorney about it in December 1986, but his attorney had advised him to keep his mouth shut. Getting involved in that case would only bring him trouble; if he was a potential witness in a double murder, the authorities really would screw with him while his robbery case was pending, the attorney said. Then Walker identified the attorney—Clinton Almond.

Another crazy twist, Appelbaum thought. When he told Almond and Brady what Walker would say, Almond replied that he probably would have to take the witness stand to refute Walker's claim. That created another odd problem, Appelbaum mused, if the defense attorney was about to become a witness in his own case.

Appelbaum was relieved when Walker's version was supported by his sister in Virginia, who confirmed that he had told her the same story about Fleer and Almond in December 1986. That provided a concurrent, consistent statement by Walker and helped his credibility considerably. But the woman was reluctant to testify. She worried about her children's safety, even across so many miles. Appelbaum hoped he could reel her in later.

As the trial approached, Almond and Brady demanded an opportunity to take Walker's deposition. At a cost of several thousand dollars to the state, Appelbaum had Walker brought to Jefferson County from the prison in

Minnesota. And then Almond changed his mind; he didn't want a deposition before trial.

Donald Walker's role in the case had drawn different reactions from Mari and Jude. For Mari, it was another incredible coincidence. When she made a long-distance call to Walker's sister in an effort to bring her into the prosecution's fold, Mari learned there was a good reason the name was familiar. Mari had gone to Berkeley Junior High School with Walker more than twenty years ago, and they had portrayed the lead characters in a school play based on the legend of Bonnie and Clyde, the bank robbers played more famously in the movies by Faye Dunaway and Warren Beatty.

After the old connection was learned, Donald Walker began calling Mari to discuss the case and promise his cooperation. From a prison in Minnesota, he made hundreds of dollars in collect calls to her, and they would spend hours going over what he knew. He told of his own exploits as an informant running a massage parlor for people he said were the real power in Jefferson County, and made claims of corruption among high public figures. He described Fleer's confession but always held back what he said was the best evidence. Mari believed Walker's story, just as she believed Watson and as she believed in Appelbaum's ability to recognize the truth when he heard it, even from people like these men. She thought a twenty-year sentence was too long for Walker's crimes, and she was willing to see it reduced if it meant he would testify against Fleer. Ultimately, she came to see Walker as one of the people who might help bring her son's killer to justice.

But Donald Walker meant something different to Jude; he had come to represent everything she hated. A woman she had met through Parents of Murdered Children was convinced Walker had murdered her son in cold blood after a disagreement at a party. One witness identified Walker as the killer; another said it was someone else. The police were left without enough evidence to file charges, and Walker went free. Jude could not stand the thought of a man like that being involved in her case, especially as a witness for the prosecution. She told Appelbaum repeatedly that she would rather take a chance and go to trial without Walker than give him a sweetheart deal that would secure his release from prison in exchange for his testimony. Appelbaum assured Jude that that wouldn't happen; all he had promised Walker was a letter to the parole board. But Jude still found Walker's involvement in this case another corruption of a system she already found lacking in integrity.

The fall was presenting other challenges to Jude's stability, too. In November, she moved out of Rick Pashia's house and found an apartment in Fenton for her and her daughters. The stress between Jude and Rick had been building for some time. She knew he was unhappy and had struggled to hold things together for her and the kids. But the time had come to do what was best for everyone in the long run. They would continue to see each other, and Rick promised to be at Jude's side through the rest of the ordeal they hoped would end with the trial in January. Leaving was difficult, but it was something Jude had to do. She wondered if there was a safe, peaceful place for her anywhere.

Jude and Mari worked hard to keep their emotions in check as the first day of trial arrived on Monday, January 22, 1990. They had talked to each other almost daily and spent those last months, weeks, days, and hours preparing for the end of this phase of their ordeal.

Jude literally marked off the days on her calendar. She worried about the lack of physical evidence proving Fleer was at the crime scene, but felt confident Appelbaum had put together a case to overcome that. She worried about jury selection, fearing that many residents of the mostly rural county might miss some of the subtleties of this difficult case. She even had awakened in a cold sweat after the words "not guilty" invaded her sleep and she thought she heard Geno Fleer laugh. She didn't think she could live with that.

Mari felt a new lift in her spirits as she sensed the approach of a cathartic event. She was attending AA meetings regularly, and the support from her friends buoyed her immensely. She had spent days in Appelbaum's office reading every page of every report in the file and was confident the case was there. She could see no way Fleer could escape his destiny in the gas chamber.

The women had not missed even one pretrial hearing, driving down to Hillsboro for court sessions every time one was held. That was part of their promise to their departed children; they would be there every step of the way and there would be no letup until it was over. They hoped that once Fleer was convicted, they would restore some order, some sanity, to their lives. Perhaps they could complete the grieving they knew could not end until Fleer had paid.

At one of the hearings, Mari's emotions had overpowered her reason and she finally had taken her hate for Eugene Fleer right to his face. During a recess in the hearing, Mari was returning to the courtroom and Fleer happened to look up from his seat at the defense table as she walked in. Their eyes locked—perhaps for the first time—and Mari erupted. She charged to the railing that separated her from this man by only feet, leaned as far past it as possible, and spat out with as much venom as she could muster, "You're a dead man."

The unexpected attack rocked Fleer back in his chair, and his eyes widened. Mari wheeled and hurried to her seat next to Jude as Marsha Brady pointed at Mari and complained to the shocked bailiff, "She's threatening my client."

Jude whispered to her friend, "You really blew it this time." Mari was afraid she might have done just that, but her anger had been beyond control. The defense attorneys complained to the judge about Mari's verbal assault several times later, and Appelbaum would do his best to explain the behavior. She had given the defense extra ammunition to use against the women, but she couldn't help it. She had to have at least one chance to let him know, from her own mouth, what she hoped would be his fate.

As the trial approached, John Appelbaum seemed to be getting more excited, perhaps more nervous. The women knew it was the biggest case of his growing career, and they could see that their faith in him actually weighed heavily on him. They had told him he was their only hope, and that was a terrible burden for such a young man.

Appelbaum had talked to the women extensively about their upcoming appearances on the witness stand—not coaching, just practical advice on how to get their important message across to the jury clearly and succinctly. Stay calm and talk directly to the jurors. Listen carefully, answer only the question asked, and don't volunteer any additional information. Speak loudly and clearly. And, most important, be absolutely truthful.

Jude didn't sleep a wink the Sunday night before jury selection was to begin. She was sitting nervously with Rick Pashia on the steps of the courthouse in Hillsboro by six o'clock Monday morning. She had to see the potential jurors as they arrived; she had to judge for herself the congregation from which this choir would be called. When the building opened at seven o'clock, she positioned herself on a bench just inside the front door. Every time it opened, she examined the entrant closely to see if he or she carried a jury notice or gave some other clue to membership in the select group. As the time crept by, she was surprised that traffic was not heavier and that she was unable to pick up any indications that the few people she saw were the ones who would decide the issue so close to her heart.

Mari awakened excitedly that morning, feeling her heart pounding the moment she opened her eyes. She kissed Bob a quick goodbye as he left for work and wished her good luck during the jury selection, which was expected to last three days; he would join her for the trial after that.

By the time Mari arrived at the courthouse about eight-fifteen, Jude had decided the jurors must be using a special entrance, another door to the building that would allow them to go directly to some assembly point. The women went to the second floor to wait outside the courtroom where the important events were about to unfold.

Appelbaum had been up past midnight the evening before meeting with investigator Chris Borgerson about a new witness—William Smith, another convict, who had been in a cell with Eugene Fleer shortly after his arrest in 1986. Smith recalled Fleer pacing the cell nervously and worrying aloud that a sample of his pubic hair taken by police could link him to the murders. Fleer referred to Lester Howlett as his partner, adding with relief that his death had taken the heat off Fleer. Appelbaum gave a copy of the statement to Clint Almond first thing Monday morning, but was not planning to use Smith as a witness if it would require a delay in the trial.

While Almond conferred with Fleer about the new development, Appelbaum stepped into the hallway to meet with his confidants—the two women who had been such a driving force behind this case. As they chatted, Appelbaum checked his watch—nine-fifteen by then—and wondered why the 125 jurors called for service were not crowding the halls, milling about in the normal routine before a big trial. He asked a bailiff how many jurors had arrived, and the bailiff said none.

"What do you mean, none?" Appelbaum shot back.

"We don't have any jurors yet," the bailiff responded.

Appelbaum asked the bailiff to check with the circuit clerk's office, which was in charge of the jurors, and before long the prosecutor found himself faced by Circuit Clerk Howard Wagner. The 125 jury summonses had never been sent by the sheriff's department, Wagner said solemnly. He assured Appelbaum that the clerk's office had done its job; the system had failed in Sheriff Buerger's office.

Appelbaum was too shocked and confused to respond; the import of the words sank in as he felt his chin drop. Without the summonses informing each juror to report on the specified date, there would be no jurors arriving today. Without jurors, of course, there would be no trial. Appelbaum had spent months preparing his case and psyching himself up for this difficult trial, and he finally was ready for the biggest case he had handled. This was a chance to prove himself in a trial that would be tougher than either of the death penalty cases he had won. And he might be about to hear that it wasn't going to happen because there was no jury. How could this be? There had to be a way around this debacle. A delay always benefited the defense, the old legal axiom said, and Appelbaum believed that. Surely this kind of freak lightning bolt shouldn't be allowed to help Eugene Fleer.

Appelbaum and the others soon assembled in Judge John Anderson's chambers to face the staggering reality. The judge was dismayed as he explained, "I ordered one hundred and twenty-five notices sent out on January 9, but the sheriff says no one knows what happened to them."

"Judge, we've got fifteen days set aside for this trial,"

Appelbaum began. "Why don't we send out summonses today for jury service two days from now. That's enough time. Or let's start in a week. I've got witnesses coming in from out of town. We're ready to do this. We can work later or do whatever we need to do to go to trial."

Anderson shook his head. "No, we're going to do this right. We have to do this with proper jury notices. We'll meet in a couple days and discuss a new trial setting."

Appelbaum thought Clint Almond and Marsha Brady were eerily quiet about the events. "I can't believe this," was all Almond had to offer.

Appelbaum's disbelief was evolving into anger as he stepped into the hall and walked slowly over to Jude and Mari. How could he break the news to these women who already were beginning to read the look on his face as trouble?

"You're not going to believe this," he said apprehensively. "The jury summonses didn't get sent out. The sheriff's department somehow didn't send them out."

"What?" the women gasped in unison. "What happens now?"

"Nothing. There aren't any jurors."

Mari screamed, "Then tell them to get some."

Appelbaum shook his head. "It doesn't work like that, Mari. There won't be a trial."

Mari and Jude burst into tears and fell into each other's arms. They were surprised to hear that this was a duty of the sheriff's department—the agency that had seemed to be their nemesis for so long and now was rising again to frustrate them.

Appelbaum could feel his face turning red and the anger pulsing through his temples; he was livid now. He had never been this angry over a case; he felt as if he couldn't talk or think straight. There was no excuse for this. He turned on his heel and stalked toward his office. As he walked in, the frustration exploded and he slammed his fist into a file cabinet. Mari and Jude hard the "boom" echo down the hallway. John didn't realize how hard he had swung until he saw the blood on his knuckles.

Mari and Jude were crushed; Rick Pashia felt as if someone had dropped a ten-ton weight on his head. All those months spent agonizing over this day, and it had come to nothing because of some bureaucratic blunder. As the women held each other, they wondered aloud how they could keep going now.

"I can't do this again," Jude sobbed. "I haven't slept for five days. My God, we've had to push and push for everything we've gotten in this case, and now someone else has screwed it up."

Mari was nodding angrily. "It's been like waiting for surgery without an anesthetic. We just keep waiting to put our lives back together again and no one ever gives us the chance to do it. But I know one thing. We're going to find out what happened here."

Judge Anderson called everyone into the courtroom minutes later to announce that he would select a new trial date as soon as possible. He turned to the two women who sobbed loudly on the bench at the front of the courtroom. "I've been on the bench for twenty years and we've never had this happen before," he said with a quiet voice that conveyed his frustration. He looked directly at Mari and Jude, and added, "On behalf of the State of Missouri, I apologize."

He explained that he was ordering Sheriff Buck Buerger to investigate and determine why his office had failed to get the notices in the mail. Mari and Jude were shocked that the judge was ordering the sheriff to investigate himself. Didn't that strike anyone else in the room as ridiculous?

But then the judge added that he would hold a hearing on February 2 to determine if the delay warranted setting bond for Eugene Fleer, the man who already had spent nearly a year in jail awaiting trial. The anger gripping Jude and Mari exploded into outrage. They and their children were being abused by the system, and the only real suggestion the judge could offer was the possibility that this screw-up would lead to Fleer's release on bond? There could be no decisive remedy so the trial could continue, but there had to be this consideration of the defendant's rights. The woman had hoped their difficulties with the sheriff's department had been left behind when the case moved to court. But this made them wonder if the almighty courts were any better. If the judge was worried about rights, where was his concern for the children's rights or

their mother's rights? Why should this unforgivable blunder—if it truly was something that innocent—accrue to the
benefit of the defendant and punish the victims?

As the crowd left the courtroom, Jude Govreau blew
down the hallway in tears. "I'm going to find Buerger," she
snapped over her shoulder as people leaned back to stare
at the passing tornado. The sheriff wasn't hard to find; he
was stepping off the elevator as Jude started to get on, and
the confrontation was immediate.

"Buck, what the hell happened?" she demanded angrily.

Buerger wasn't the least bit intimidated and just as angrily waved the jury list in his hand in front of Jude's face.
"Why didn't you get this to trial sooner?" he shot back as
he turned and started down the hall.

Jude followed his footsteps. "We're not the ones who
delayed this, Buck. We're the ones who have been pushing
you. I want to know what happened to those summonses."

"I'm not going to listen to any more of this," the sheriff
said with a wave of his hand as he strode away, leaving
Jude trembling in rage behind him.

"I'd like to *listen* to my daughter's voice one more time,
Buck," she screamed at his back.

Jude felt the walls closing in on her. She had to get outside; she turned and stepped onto the elevator. As the
doors closed, she pounded her fists against the wall and
screamed wildly, letting out all of the anger and defeat and
disappointment. Not until the doors opened and Jude saw
a little man scamper out behind her did she realize she had
not been alone. My God, she thought, I probably frightened
that poor man to death. He must have figured he was
trapped in an elevator with a crazy woman.

Mari had her own confrontation with Buerger in his office later. With a friend in tow for support, Mari stormed
in, hysterically screaming that she would not stop until she
learned what had happened. Her first call, she vowed,
would be to the FBI, which might be interested in her suggestion of a number of illegal activities underway in Jefferson County. Buerger bristled, telling her he could have her
arrested for such a threat. She thrust out her wrists in a
challenge. "Go ahead, Buck. That'll look real good on the
news tonight." She then stormed out of the room, only to

return to collect her startled friend, who sat there unsure of what to do after witnessing such an exchange.

Those verbal jousts paled, however, beside the confrontation a short time later when Steve Winzen arrived at the courthouse. After he was told what had happened, he charged into Buerger's office and the men ended up nose to nose. Winzen said later that the sheriff had exploded into a fury and grabbed and shoved him, and had had to be restrained by deputies. Buerger denied that and said the men had only shouted at each other and he had pointed his finger in Winzen's face before ordering some deputies to escort the man from his office. Winzen threatened to sue Buerger, but it never happened.

By the time the crowd left the courthouse, the reporters had arrived and were trying to catch up with the startling events. The circuit clerk explained that 125 names had been drawn by lottery from the list of registered voters on January 9, Judge Anderson had signed the list that day, and it had been delivered to Buerger's department for mailing of the summonses. Buerger vowed to find out exactly what had happened, but it was clear to him that a clerk in his office had made a mistake; he said he would accept responsibility for the mishap. The clerk who normally handled the summonses was ill, he said, and he would talk to her later. It was a mistake, he allowed, but it didn't mean Fleer would go free.

Bill Johnson told the press he was disappointed and upset by the delay. Almond and Brady said they and Fleer had been ready for trial and were distressed and frustrated that his time in jail would be prolonged by this turn of events.

But the reporters were more interested in the mothers' reactions, and the two women unloaded on them. Through continuous tears, they demanded a public apology from Buerger for deepening and extending their pain. "He owes our kids an apology for his stupidity," Mari snarled. Jude added, "We have nobody who seems to give a damn except the prosecutors. How long do we have to go through this nightmare, over and over again?"

The day seemed to last forever for the devastated women. They retired to their homes to pace and cry. Jude was too distraught to go to work that night. Mari once again was faced with breaking the bad news to her son, Brian. That was hard enough, but then she stumbled badly; she called her doctor and got a prescription for ten Valium tablets, filled it immediately, and took all ten that day. She was feeling sorry for herself and did not even want to deal with the new reality. She felt so guilty the next day, however, that she contacted her friends in Alcoholics Anonymous and confessed her transgression. It was a slip, they said, and they urged her not to let it become more than that. She took their advice.

For the men from the Major Case Squad who had worked so hard on the case, the disappearance of the summonses looked like another bad rap for the guys in Buerger's department. For the cops in the department, the episode was an embarrassment to everyone who had been associated with the Price-Winzen investigation. Captain Wally Gansmann was convinced the whole case was "snake-bit." He never would have believed this could happen and was sure it was something more than an accident. Sergeant Leo Burle thought the department finally had the case made, after all the pressure and criticism from the mothers, and then this had to happen; it was a terrible blow. Ed Kemp, now a captain, wanted to believe it was a horrible accident, a breakdown in the clerical system somewhere before the cards went into the mail. He wanted it to be that simple, and he knew the office was lax enough for it to happen. But he was cynical enough to know that he could not rule out the possibility that someone had made this happen for a selfish reason. Just the icing on the cake for this investigation.

On Wednesday, two days after the catastrophe, Sheriff Buerger was taking a somewhat harder line. He told reporters he was convinced his office had done its job; there was no negligence. The three tied bundles of cards either had been lost, perhaps falling off the mail cart after they were picked up in his office, or had been stolen. The clerk had shown him notations she normally made on the jury list before placing the cards in the mail basket to be picked up by a different clerk from the purchasing department who handled the mail. The sheriff believed she had done her job.

Appelbaum personally questioned the clerk from purchasing and was convinced the summonses had never made it to the mail basket. He wanted to talk to one of the secretaries in the sheriff's department, but she wouldn't see him. Five minutes after Appelbaum had called her, Buerger called and, through what sounded like clenched teeth, essentially told Appelbaum to back off. The sheriff would take care of problems within his office. Appelbaum didn't want to put the detectives on the spot, so he didn't press them for answers. In the end, he lacked enough evidence to determine what had happened or to accuse anyone of a misdeed.

And it soon became apparent that each side would blame the other. Both sides mumbled about free access to the department and how easy it would have been for someone to pick up the bundles of jury notices from a desk and walk away with them.

Within two weeks, the clerk assigned to mail the notices resigned and disappeared. To some observers, that suggested something more sinister than an accident. Jude met with an attorney to see if she and Mari had any legal recourse, any way to sue the sheriff or the courts for incompetence that inflicted more emotional stress on them. The attorney was sympathetic, but explained there really was no route to attack the courts through the very same courts.

On February 2, Judge Anderson set a trial date of May 15, delaying the case yet another four months and delivering yet another blow for Mari and Jude to absorb. Four months seemed an eternity to them, and they wept even more as the judge explained there was no open date before that. They had waited long enough, and they wondered why this forty-month-old case failed to merit priority treatment. But again, the system would not respond and they would have to wait. Their only salve that day was the judge's decision not to consider releasing Fleer on bond.

To keep their sanity, the women threw themselves into an unrestrained crusade to determine what had happened to those damn jury summonses. If their disappearance was a scheme designed to inflict another injustice on this case, Mari and Jude would find out and make sure someone paid for it. They wondered why no one else seemed to find it curious that Buerger had offered three different explanations. Had his clerk done it? Had the summonses been lost? Or had they been stolen? Which scenario was the truth and who was behind it?

The mothers spent weeks working the phones and writing letters. They called the Missouri Highway Patrol, and an officer explained that the patrol had to be called in by another police agency before it could investigate; he referred them to the U.S. Postal Inspection Service. A postal inspector was very interested, but explained that his agency could get involved only if the summonses had disappeared after they were in the postal system, not before they were mailed. The inspector seemed anxious to get involved and talked to the women several times before deciding there simply was nothing he could do. They spoke repeatedly with an assistant attorney general for the State of Missouri. He was as helpful and concerned as he could be, but there was nothing he could do. They called state senators and legislators. They even wrote to a justice with the Missouri Supreme Court to tell him they believed a crime had been committed and that someone outside the agency where it happened should be conducting the investigation.

When the women later met with Buerger to see if he could clear up the case, his inability to provide a final answer threw them into a rage. In hope of intimidating Buerger, Mari falsely boasted that she had talked to a justice with the Missouri Supreme Court, that he knew all about Buerger and was investigating him. Buerger's temper flared, too, and he called Mari's bluff with a call directly to the justice; Mari was relieved when he was unavailable. Buerger ended the conference by reminding the women again that he could arrest them for threatening the sheriff. They laughed off his warning and stormed out of his office.

What had been severe criticism and distrust of Sheriff Buck Buerger and his department suddenly graduated to something more, something on the next plane. Mari, Jude, and the sheriff had arrived on a new level of hostility from which they could never retreat.

The women had a difficult time believing Buerger had had nothing to do with the disappearance of the jury cards. But many others believed the fifty-nine-year-old sheriff, who had built a political career on a reputation as a "good ol' boy." He was a native of Hillsboro and something of a legend in the area. He had played outfield for the minor league teams under the Yankees and Braves for ten years and even had done a stint as a bartender before winning election as sheriff in 1964. Few people believed him to be capable of corruption, but many suspected his easygoing nature might allow him to look the other way if someone he liked was involved. Even Buerger admitted he tended to trust people too much and to let them get away with too much.

Amid all of that, Jude also was channeling her anger into more positive actions. She was becoming more active with Parents of Murdered Children and was out front when a coalition of such groups sponsored a march across the Eads Bridge in St. Louis designed to draw support for the rights of crime victims. Jude, Racheal, and Jackie Corey carried a banner for the Parents of Murdered Children; a picture of Jude and Racheal weeping as they comforted each other was featured on the front page of the *St. Louis Post-Dispatch* and its short-lived competitor, the *St. Louis Sun*. The papers quoted many of the 150 marchers as they complained that the system ignored the rights of the victims and their survivors, focusing only on the rights of people who inflicted horrible pain and suffering and death on others. The group demanded new legislation to give victims and survivors the rights that human dignity and justice demanded. The right to attend all court hearings. The right to be informed regularly by court officials about new developments. The right to be consulted before plea bargains led to reduced charges and lighter sentences. The right to be informed when the convicted offender came up for parole or was released from prison. The marchers wondered if any of that seemed too much to ask for the people whose lives had been destroyed by criminals who had rights guaranteed by state and federal constitutions.

To end the march, the group dropped flowers into the Mississippi River and released balloons into the air—gestures of loss and hope.

The strain of the jury summonses episode was taking a terrible toll on Mari Kane. She remained confident in John

Appelbaum and the case he had assembled against Eugene Fleer, but she worried that the system never would give the prosecutor the chance to do his job. A new sense of despair took hold and made her doubt Fleer would ever go to trial. He seemed destined to escape the punishment he so richly deserved. Mari knew she could not live if Fleer was free; if he escaped punishment, she would have to die. Seeing that he paid for what he did soon became a matter of life and death for her, literally, and she decided she would do whatever was necessary to accomplish that. Her course seemed clear.

Mari would have Geno Fleer killed.

In a replay of her obsession with the movie *Sudden Impact,* Mari had been spending hours watching a videotape of a television show called *Getting Even: Victims Strike Back.* Her thirst for vengeance found some relief as she replayed again and again the scene of a man firing a bullet point-blank into the head of a suspect who had kidnapped and molested the man's twelve-year-old son. Mari would stop the tape and rewind it so she could watch again as the police escorted the suspect past the bank of telephones at the airport in Baton Rouge, Louisiana, and the father turned from one of the phones to blow the offender's brains out in full view of everyone. Justice from a gun barrel. Punishment in the muzzle flash. Execution in an instant. Mari could see everything she wanted for Geno Fleer in an incredible heartbeat of revenge, and it was almost exhilarating to witness.

She also was fascinated by the show's account of a man in South Carolina whose impatience with the court system led to a bizarre plot that reached through prison bars and killed the murderer of his mother and stepfather. Fearing that the death sentence on this killer never would be carried out, the man hired another death-row inmate to plant a bomb in a radio in the killer's cell; it exploded in his face and saved the courts the trouble of an execution. The man who had exacted his own vengeance was convicted of conspiracy and served an eight-year sentence.

He was on parole when Mari tracked him down by phone, told him her story, and asked his advice. He was sympathetic, but bluntly told her to give it up. Although he would not hesitate to do it again, he advised her to let the courts handle it. Besides, the man said, if Fleer was imprisoned for the murders, he probably would die at the hands of other inmates someday. Baby-killers weren't treated well inside the walls.

Her next step was to meet with one of the most prominent defense attorneys in the St. Louis area. What would happen to her, she asked, if she arranged the murder of the man who had killed her son? The attorney immediately counseled her against the idea, urging her to let the police handle it. But, he said, if she persisted, she should know that juries had no sympathy for someone who hired an assassin. She would fare better if she did it herself, killing the man in broad daylight in front of witnesses. She could plead temporary insanity and a jury probably would accept that, given the murder of her toddler son and what she had been through since then. She might serve six months or a year in a mental hospital, but the attorney was confident she never would go to prison. He talked to her for just under an hour and charged her the "discounted price" of $200 for the advice.

Though the desire for revenge—fatal, permanent, terminal revenge—remained overwhelming, Mari finally abandoned the murder-for-hire plot. She didn't trust the courts, but she could not yet find the will to go outside the system and commit murder herself.

As the second trial date neared, reporter John Auble began a new series of reports on Channel 2 unlike anything John Appelbaum, Mari Kane, or Jude Govreau had ever seen. At five o'clock on Wednesday, April 11, Auble told his viewers that reliable sources in the sheriff's department were convinced there was insufficient evidence to convict Eugene Fleer. There was no physical evidence and the state's case was built mostly on statements by "jailhouse snitch" Donald Walker. A page of transcript from a police interview with Walker flashed onto the screen as Auble said ominously that the evidence Walker had provided against Fleer was this statement: "Well, he . . . He did it. He told me."

Standing in front of the courthouse, Auble announced, "Some investigators feel Walker's story is too thin and prosecutors have done little to develop the case. One says

Walker is an unreliable snitch who will say anything to get a sentence reduction. He says he doubts that a jury would find Walker believable, that Walker's testimony may torpedo the state's case, and that Fleer may indeed be innocent."

Clint Almond was quoted as saying Walker's story was preposterous and his conversations with Fleer never included discussions of the murders. The prosecutors got one line; William Johnson believed the state's case was strong and he was seeking the death penalty.

Auble repeated the story at ten o'clock after the anchorman announced, "Jefferson County deputies say, 'We may have the wrong man.'" At the end of Auble's story this time, however, another reporter offered brief interviews with Jude and Mari adamantly defending the case and expressing confidence in a conviction. Mari explained that she had gone through all of the evidence in great detail to convince herself. The reporter wrapped up by saying, "The mothers anticipate a conviction despite today's developments."

What developments? a furious John Appelbaum wondered. He had never seen such slanted reporting designed solely to suggest prosecutors had fabricated a case against an innocent man using a "jailhouse snitch." Of course, Auble had omitted the parts of the transcript where Walker described a drunken, drug-sniffing Fleer crying about how he was haunted by his murder of the little boy or how he had delivered a fatal "hot shot" to the man who was about to go to the police with the truth, or how he wanted Walker to kill yet another man.

With barely a month before the trial, this strafing run by one of three network television stations could be prejudicial to potential jurors, the prosecutor worried. He had to admit, however, that there was a grain of truth in one of Auble's assertions. Appelbaum had heard reports of some patrol deputies saying Fleer could not be convicted or might even be the wrong man. They never said such things to Appelbaum's face, but he knew there was a whispering campaign. He was convinced it had been initiated by Almond and spread through his sources in the sheriff's department. Appelbaum was targeted directly by some of the slams—"You can't trust John. He eavesdropped on another

lawyer's interview." Although he was sure he had won over
the detectives, Appelbaum sometimes felt isolated inside
the court system; he wondered if he was the only guy there
who really believed, down deep, that Geno Fleer was guilty.

Auble's reports infuriated Jude and Mari. To them, they
were more proof of a system gone nuts. This was not the
truth they knew. Mari was amazed when Appelbaum explained that there was no law requiring reporters to present
only the facts. Mari and Jude could see Almond's hand in
the stories and wondered why no one realized they were
full of factual errors and distortions. How could Auble be
allowed to go on television and deliberately present a view
obviously designed to help the defense, to help free a man
they knew in their hearts was a baby-killer? Did no one
care about those kids, about their families, about the truth?

The next day, Auble raised the stakes by announcing
that Donald Walker actually was the second snitch. Auble
dredged up Michael Watson and incorrectly reported that
his note about Fleer's confession was the first evidence to
implicate him. Then Auble described how Watson admitted
lying in an interview with Almond while Appelbaum eavesdropped. An incensed Appelbaum then found another
"jailhouse snitch" in Walker, Auble explained.

There was more the next day as Walker called the television station to defend himself. His mug shot filled the
screen as his voice announced, "I know my testimony is
going to be the absolute truth and I know for a fact that
Gene Fleer did murder those children." Auble countered
by flashing another document on the screen and charging
that Appelbaum had approved a plea bargain recommending ten years for Walker instead of what could have been
a life sentence for robbery. Auble also disclosed that Walker's work as a federal informant targeted, among others,
Judge John Anderson. Auble noted that Anderson had
vowed to stay on the Fleer case despite requests by the
defense for another judge.

More garbage, Appelbaum fumed. The document was a
letter Appelbaum had written to Walker's attorney saying
the prosecutors would consider recommending a ten-year
sentence, but only if Walker won a new trial on appeal;
and there was no chance of that. Appelbaum offered a
double-edged response to the latest from Auble—a letter

from a U.S. attorney stating that Judge Anderson never was the target of any such investigation, and a subpoena for Channel 2's tapes of its phone call from Walker in case anything useful was omitted. The station objected, of course, and the judge refused to order the tapes produced.

The intensifying conflict with Auble reminded Appelbaum how easily the focus could be lost. Everyone was tearing off on tangents that had little to do with the essence of the case or the real effort to get to trial. But Appelbaum was at a loss for an answer. He couldn't control the news media or the reaction to their reports. He had to keep his eye on the goal—presenting a strong case to a jury in hopes of proving that Eugene Fleer was the man who had killed those children.

John Auble was covering a murder trial in Illinois on March 2 when Judge Anderson granted a motion by Almond and Brady asking that reluctant federal investigators provide transcripts of the eavesdrop tapes made by Walker during his undercover work. In a contentious hearing in which Appelbaum even had to take the stand to answer questions from Brady, the judge also ordered prosecutors to turn over everything in their file to the defense. Channel 2 gave the story good play as the anchorwoman injected her opinion that the order meant the state's case could be in jeopardy. But Appelbaum thought the transcripts actually built credibility for Walker, showing that Fleer's name had come up in several conversations that could have brought the two men together as Walker had claimed.

As Auble's onslaught continued on subsequent days, he turned to Lester Howlett by showing the autopsy report in which the Major Case Squad called him "a prime suspect." Auble displayed the diagram of injuries to Howlett's knuckles "as though he had been in a scuffle," and then added, "But of greater interest is that a portion of his body bore fresh teeth marks." He quoted the coroner as saying the marks could have come from braces and that Stacy Price wore braces.

At ten o'clock that night, Auble's report followed the anchorwoman's question "Is the wrong man in jail for a sensational double-murder four years ago?" and her partner's lead-in "At five o'clock, John Auble told us the actual killer may have died two days after those murders."

Jude and Mari stormed into Sheriff Buerger's office the next day to demand to know the identities of the sources inside the department who were feeding such distortions to Auble. Buerger said he didn't know and once again ordered the women out of his office. But they were so outraged by Auble's campaign that they enlisted Jackie Corey's help, drew up petitions, and gathered thousands of signatures vowing to boycott Channel 2 "if you continue to slant stories in favor of the accused criminal and continue to provide only partial facts on behalf of the accused." They arranged a meeting with the station's manager but, once again, got no satisfaction; the station stood by the reports. The women were angrier when they left than when they arrived. Why was it, they wondered, that everything related to this case seemed so warped, so demented, so upside down?

"John Auble has become the judge and jury in this case and is trying it on TV," Jude lamented in her journal on May 7, one week before the real trial was scheduled to begin.

Appelbaum had met with the news director and Auble, and had come away with the same response. In fact, Appelbaum thought Auble seemed pleased by the complaints. Appelbaum's only recourse was to stop talking to Auble.

Despite his anger and frustration over the stories, he had to chuckle when one of the sheriff's detectives tweaked him by altering one of his business cards to read "John Aublebaum."

Cute, he thought; real cute.

CHAPTER 14

This time, there were jurors.

John Appelbaum had personally checked to be sure the jury summonses were mailed, just as he had promised Mari and Jude. And bright and early on Tuesday, May 15, 1990, the first half of the two hundred jurors called for service swarmed into the courthouse; the second group of one hundred would report the next day. From that pool, twelve men and women would be chosen to hear the charges that Eugene Fleer murdered Tyler Winzen and Stacy Price nearly four years earlier. To avoid any additional problems with the jury, the judge had decided to sequester the panel throughout the trial.

After escaping a repeat of the January disaster, Mari and Jude allowed themselves to feel hopeful—if still somewhat nervous—on this day. Surely, they said, nothing else could go wrong now. The first trial had been cursed by an event unprecedented in Missouri history. Surely this case had seen all the catastrophes that could possibly befall it.

Judge John L. Anderson already had disposed of the pre-trial motions. He had refused defense requests that he step aside because Almond and Brady felt he was prejudiced against them and Fleer. Anderson had agreed to Appelbaum's request for a gag order to keep the attorneys, court officials, and police from discussing the case with the media during the trial. Appelbaum had justified his motion by alleging that someone was leaking to John Auble information from Walker's Secret Service tapes, which had been placed under court seal. Auble took to the camera to deny that; the information came from a law enforcement source.

Things really seemed to be going right for Mari and Jude when Appelbaum told them the judge had agreed to let them sit in the courtroom for jury selection. Appelbaum had nearly begged the judge to overrule defense arguments that the women's presence was designed only to drum up sympathy among the jurors. Jude had been extremely upset earlier that morning when Buerger barred her from the courtroom and told her to wait downstairs. Mari and a friend marched up the stairs anyway and stayed in the hallway until the jurors moved into the courtroom. The women were thrilled when Appelbaum sent word that the judge would allow them to observe jury selection, even though they were relegated to folding chairs between the sets of inner and outer doors. At least they were there and the trial was underway, finally.

The women agreed that there had been a drastic change in Eugene Fleer. He seemed smaller. He had lost weight and appeared much less menacing than the man they had seen before. He was dressed neatly in a shirt and tie that fit his smaller frame well, and he seemed rather average compared to the man who looked so bulky and muscular under the heavy sweatshirt the day he was arrested. That was a major disappointment; the women wanted jurors looking at an intimidating figure they easily could picture brutalizing his victims. The trim, slim Geno seated at the defense table didn't seem to fit that bill. Mari thought the defense had done a good job of disguising the sinister side of its client.

The first round of juror questioning by Judge Anderson focused on publicity. All but seven jurors had heard of the case. When Anderson asked specifically about stories on Channel 2, only a few could remember them. Mari had to smirk with a bit of satisfaction; Auble's efforts had been for naught, and maybe that explained why Channel 2 was a distant third in the ratings among the three network affiliates in St. Louis. The icing on the cake came that afternoon when Appelbaum told Mari and Jude that the news director at Channel 2 had been fired. The women doubted that it had anything to do with this case, but they had no sympathy for the man who had defended John Auble so staunchly. Channels 4 and 5—the CBS and NBC affiliates—interviewed Mari and Jude that afternoon, but Auble knew better than to approach either of them.

They were intrigued by the process of voir dire—the French term for jury selection that translates as "to speak the truth." They had to shake their heads as Clint Almond tried to impanel a pastor from a local church and a man awaiting prosecution for an unrelated crime; the judge dismissed the two men. By the end of the day, twenty-two of the jurors had been excused for various reasons.

The important task of qualifying jurors for the death penalty began the afternoon of the second day. Anyone with religious, moral, or ethical problems with the death penalty was excused. The others had to be willing to make the ultimate decision, and only a straight-on question could determine that. Appelbaum drilled each juror with an intense stare and asked if he or she could impose the death sentence if the evidence proved Fleer guilty. Anything less than a firm yes was unacceptable.

Mari Kane had to hold back the tears as Appelbaum asked that question. Hearing jurors asked if they could order death for the man who had brought death to her son was almost unbearable. But she held her emotions in check; she didn't want the jurors to mistake tears in Tyler's memory for grief over executing Eugene Fleer. Mari watched Fleer intently and saw no reaction to the repeated questions about sending him to the gas chamber. The only time she detected any discomfort was when Steve Winzen and Mark Gerber sat down in the courtroom; that seemed to agitate Fleer more than anything else she had seen. Mari had saved a special distaste for Gerber since she concluded he had tried to use her and Jude to get information for the defense. She would have found the presence of him and Steve irritating, too, but decided that Fleer's intensely nervous reaction was well worth that.

By the end of the third day, six men and six women had been chosen to decide Eugene Fleer's fate. Appelbaum, Jude, and Mari were quite pleased with the case, and the women were surprised that the jurors they liked had been retained. They seemed to be intelligent, conscientious citizens who would be able to listen to the evidence, separate the chaff from the wheat, and apply the kind of common sense needed to return the proper verdict. Mari and Jude were especially pleased that John Appelbaum had consulted them so often. He made them feel part of the system, and that was more important than ever now that the end was within sight.

*   *   *

The evidence in this case was simple, John Appelbaum explained as he stood before the jury Friday morning, May 18, 1990, for the opening statement he had waited so long to present. Eugene Fleer had killed the children in revenge for a bad cocaine deal involving Fleer, Steven Winzen, Lester Howlett, and others. Fleer had even posed that theory to friends during many incredibly knowledgeable discussions just after the murders. Killing children in retaliation for a drug rip-off might seem unbelievable to average citizens, Appelbaum warned, but it was not such a surprising development among those in the violent and vicious drug trade that claimed Lester Howlett's life barely forty-eight hours after the children's.

The prosecutor turned directly to Fleer. Witnesses would place him at the apartment complex just before and after the murders, and one would identify Fleer as the man going into Mari Kane's building. Fleer knew minute and undisclosed details he shouldn't have known unless he was the killer, and he was too convincing to be innocent when he expounded on the brutal reason such hot water was used—to wash evidence off the bodies. He even admitted killing the kids to Donald Walker in a barroom conversation. Appelbaum was careful to downplay Walker's role in the trial, however, casting his testimony as little more than confirmation of what the other evidence proved.

As Appelbaum described for the jurors the jarring scene in that little bathroom, his emotional attachment to the case betrayed itself and his heart caught in his throat. For just that moment, his genuine grief for the children of these women he now knew so well overcame his professional cool, and his voice trembled. As he took a deep breath, he looked across the faces of the twelve people listening so intently and hoped they would not interpret what was so real as being artificial or theatrical. His confidence in the jurors was confirmed when their eyes told him they accepted his emotion for what it was.

When Appelbaum finished his remarks and turned to his table, he noticed again the two white roses in a glass vase that Mari and Bob Kane had placed there that morning with a very personal note. Inside the card with a cover that said, "Be strong," Mari had written, "These two roses are symbols of our kids—one for Tyler and one for Stacy. Do your best for them." No one had done anything like that before, and it touched Applebaum deeply. The solemn gesture reminded him why he did this work and why he had dedicated himself to this case.

Marsha Brady delivered the opening statement for the defense and zeroed in on Donald Walker with such intensity that the uninformed could have thought Walker was on trial and Brady was the prosecutor. Walker was no more than a convicted robber turned snitch in search of a reduced sentence—a professional informant now under federal protection. Appelbaum had offered Walker help with his sentence in return for incriminating evidence. Brady even explained how Almond had defended Walker and might have to take the witness stand to refute the former client's testimony.

Brady dismissed the prosecution's drug thcory as lightly as she had Walker. Steve Winzen would testify that he dealt marijuana, but never cocaine, and, in fact, objected to Lester Howlett's cocaine deals and $700-a-week habit. "Steve Winzen will also tell you, if his son was killed to send him a message over his drug dealings, he didn't get the message because he never had a drug deal go bad," Brady said.

Mari and Jude paced nervously in the hall as the prosecutor and defender fired opening volleys before the jury. So much rode on the events about to happen over the next week or ten days, and it began with what the lawyers were telling the jurors in the courtroom at that very moment. Being excluded from the courtroom because they were witnesses was torture, so they smoked and trembled in the hall. Mari would be first on the stand, and she had the shakes. She was heartened, however, when her husband and her parents charged out of the courtroom to rave about Appelbaum's opening statement. Brilliant and powerful, they said, completely overshadowing the defense effort. Fleer should be convicted on the strength of the opening alone.

And then the bailiff called her—the moment she had awaited and dreaded for almost four years. She felt like a Christian being led into the Colosseum to face the lions. She sucked in her breath, walked with as much poise as possible into the courtroom, and took the oath to tell the

whole truth about the murders of her son and the girl she
had loved so briefly. As she sat down and looked across
the courtroom at Eugene Fleer, she felt a new resolve to
get through this. The defendant deliberately did not return
her gaze.

Recalling Appelbaum's advice, she listened carefully to
each question and answered it as directly and simply as
possible. She refused to let the embarrassment of her life
with Steve Winzen and drugs inhibit her as she testified,
and she tried valiantly to remember that all of this was
being done in Tyler's name. She was aware that tears rolled
down her cheeks as she talked, but she could do nothing
about that. She was pleased with how well she coped with
the pain as John Appelbaum led her through the events of
August 7, 1986, and showed her pictures of the chair cushion that had been in the bathtub, of Tyler's bedroom, and
of his toy box. She thought her heart would burst, but she
got through it and realized she had started to feel strong,
almost comfortable, on the witness stand as she spoke for
her son. When she felt nervous, she would find strength in
her mother's face in the audience.

And then John Appelbaum blindsided Mari with a move
that cut her legs out from under her. He handed her a little
yellow blanket she had not seen since that day in August
of 1986 and asked her to identify it. She had searched for
Tyler's security blanket in the days after the murders, want-
ing to bury it with the little boy who clung so tightly to it
every night. She never dreamed it had been held as evidence by the police, and she never expected to have it
dropped in her lap at this moment. Mari lost all of that
careful control and began to cry almost hysterically as she
clutched the blanket to her chest.

John Appelbaum looked at the jurors and then lowered
his eyes for a moment. He knew his surprise tactic would
throw Mari for a loop, but he wanted the jurors to see the
humanity, the real cost in grief and loss, that too often was
ignored in the midst of the legal maneuvering of the murder trial. This woman's son—her precious child—had been
slaughtered, and the jurors needed to see the emotional
wreckage left behind. That display had to be spontaneous
and unexpected. John hoped Mari would understand and
forgive him later.

After Mari composed herself, Marsha Brady began her cross-examination. Because of the natural hostility that had developed between the mothers and the defense lawyers, Mari expected Brady to rip into her with claws flashing. Instead, Brady was restrained to the point of being kind and considerate. Mari found it terribly odd when Brady asked her to draw a diagram on a blackboard to illustrate the location of the furniture in the apartment. That seemed to serve no purpose, and Mari was bothered that the blackboard was so close to Fleer's chair. But she complied and did her best to answer Brady's questions.

Before she knew it, she had completed her testimony after two and a half hours. A new wave of tears swept in—relief that all the waiting finally was over for her. She later confronted John Appelbaum about the stunt with the blanket, but accepted his explanation that the surprise was necessary to bring the real impact to the jurors. Although she was glad to be done, she still was frustrated at being barred from the courtroom.

The next few witnesses went quickly. The sheriff's dispatcher who lived in the apartment complex recounted seeing Lester near a Dumpster outside Mari's apartment windows early that morning. A woman who lived there remembered seeing Mari's screen ripped. And then Neil Myrick dramatically delivered his rock-solid identification of Fleer as the man he saw entering the building. Persistent efforts by Almond to fuzzy up the time failed as the witness insisted it was about 9:45 A.M. As Joe Indelicato said to Mari about Myrick's steadfast account, "Neil must have been seeing through God's eyes that day."

Then Racheal was called to the stand. She was nervous about testifying, and her mother feared it would only traumatize her even more. She trembled as she told Appelbaum how she had gone into the apartment looking for Stacy and heard the "click" of the lock on the bathroom door. She handled direct testimony fairly well, but cross-examination could not have started on a worse note. As Marsha Brady began, she called the witness "Stacy." Racheal felt as if she had been slapped in the face; she burst into tears. Brady apologized for a slip of the tongue, but the damage was done. Racheal was so upset she barely could answer any

more questions. When Brady finished, Racheal flew out of
the courtroom and into Jude's arms. Appelbaum was sure
Brady's faux pas had indeed been unintentional, and it certainly had not endeared her to the jury. There would have
been no advantage for Brady to do that on purpose, and
Appelbaum knew how easy it was to commit such a nervous verbal stumble in the middle of a trial. But Jude and
Mari were not inclined to see it that way, and they cursed
the defense again.

Racheal was followed by another strong witness, Sandy
Barton. As an acquaintance of Fleer's, her testimony carried added weight when she described seeing a noticeably
messy and disturbed Geno driving out of the apartment
complex only minutes after the murders must have happened. Mari's family reported again that the testimony,
coupled with Neil Myrick's memory, seemed devastating.

Then it was Jude's turn. Clint Almond drilled her repeatedly about the timing of events that morning, obviously
hoping to show that Fleer had left the complex before the
murders were committed. Jude was nervous, and she
couldn't avert her eyes from Fleer's hands folded on the
defense table. Those were the murder weapons, Jude kept
thinking as she tried to concentrate on the questions from
the attorneys. By the time she slumped in a chair in the
hallway, her predominant memory was Almond's insistence
on being sure whether Rick was wearing a shirt when he
ran to Mari's apartment. What difference did that make?
Jude wondered.

Rick was the last witness of the day and may have provided the most emotional testimony. Appelbaum had him
describe the discovery of the children's bodies and then
asked him to identity photographs of the scene in that bathroom. Rick had to struggle to retain his composure as the
pictures pulled him back to the day, that moment when he
looked into that bathtub. He choked back the tears as he
nodded that the photos accurately depicted what he had
seen. Then Appelbaum passed the photos among the jurors. Many of their eyes filled with tears, and some of them
shook their heads as they looked at a sight none of them
would have thought possible, let alone expected to see captured on film for their education.

And that was how the day ended. Mari and Jude were

buoyed by the confidence expressed by Appelbaum's team and Mari's family. They all agreed it was going very well in the courtroom and the jury seemed to be extremely attentive. The feeling was unanimous that the jury was leaning the right way. And Mari was glad that her mother had taken full advantage of an opportunity earlier that day to tell John Auble how despicable she thought he was.

John Appelbaum knew Saturday would be difficult for everyone; the testimony would focus mostly on the shuddery events in the bathroom as assistant fire chief Russell Million, Deputy Ron Speidel, the crime scene technician Bob Miller described what they had seen and done there. Appelbaum purposefully broke some of that grim tension by following them with the important testimony from the apartment's maintenance man, Bob Lutz. He described giving the news of the murders to Lester Howlett, whose blank reaction suggested to Lutz that Howlett already knew about them. Howlett then shot up with cocaine before calling Tyler's father in Las Vegas. Lutz also offered the crucial memory of running into Fleer outside Howlett's apartment later that day, telling him about the murders, and then watching him drive away. Appelbaum hoped the jurors would see that the details Fleer knew so quickly about the murders had not come from anyone at the apartment complex that day. He could have known those things only one way.

But Appelbaum's next witness unexpectedly inflicted a painful wound on the prosecution's case. The medical examiner, Dr. Gordon Johnson, delivered the grisly details of the children's deaths from the forensic reports just as Appelbaum anticipated. Johnson confirmed that the children's throats showed no internal damage from heat, proving that the children were drowned in cooler water before the hot water was run into the tub. Marsha Brady dwelled on the point so much during cross-examination that Appelbaum wondered if she had some explosive revelation on that coming later.

But Appelbaum really was surprised when Dr. Johnson quite willingly agreed with Brady's suggestions buttressing the defense's theory that Lester Howlett was the killer. Johnson said bruises on Stacy's knees could have resulted from being dragged off the couch and forced to the floor, abrasions on Stacy's face could have resulted from being rubbed against denim—such as Howlett's jeans—and that the injuries on Howlett's penis could have been inflicted by dental braces such as Stacy wore.

Appelbaum was furious; Johnson's testimony had just helped construct a scenario in which Howlett was trying to force Stacy to perform oral sex on him and killed her when she resisted. Appelbaum knew of no scientific grounds for that kind of speculation and was shocked to hear his own witness go along with it so cooperatively. On redirect examination, the prosecutor huffily cross-examined his witness and attacked the bite-mark suggestion by asking if teeth with braces wouldn't make a scar that would be shaped differently. Johnson agreed with that and was willing to concede that the injuries could have been caused in several ways and there was no conclusive evidence to support the defense theory. Appelbaum hoped the jury would not put too much stock in unsubstantiated and suggestive guesses, but he knew Brady had made some points by drawing such testimony from a prosecution witness.

Mari and Jude were shocked when they heard the accounts of Johnson's testimony, and Mari nearly became hysterical. Hearing that Johnson had helped the defense so significantly set off the time bomb that had been getting closer and closer to exploding in Mari's head. When Fleer's mother passed by and Mari thought she detected a sidelong glance, she turned the anger against the woman. Mari snapped angrily, "Your son is an animal. Did you hear what he did to our kids? How can you look at me?" Mrs. Fleer was hurried away by relatives, and Mari would regret the bitter words later when she thought about the anguish Fleer's innocent mother must have suffered every moment. Mari hoped people would try to understand how she felt amid the turmoil of the trial over her son's murder, how the pain made you crazy.

Steve Winzen's girlfriend, Patty Garner, was the last witness of the day, called to explain how she and Steve had been notified of the murders while they were in Vegas. Her testimony set up Steve's appearance before the jury first thing Monday morning.

Despite the good buzz among the spectators about the direction the trial was taking, Mari was upset after hearing different versions of Bob Lutz's testimony. She called Appelbaum at home Saturday evening and kept him on the telephone for two hours, quizzing him about every detail of the witnesses' stories on the stand. He assured her things had gone well, but she finally broke down. "I'm going crazy sitting in the hall, John," she cried. "You have to get us in there. If you really care about us, you'll get us in the courtroom."

Appelbaum really needed some rest and relaxation, not additional pressure. But he understood Mari's feelings and pled her case with the judge Monday morning. Though he was reluctant because of reports about Mari's outburst at Fleer's mother and occasional comments to other participants, the judge agreed. The prosecutor happily gave Mari the news that the mothers could sit in the courtroom for the rest of the trial. Mari shrieked in excitement and ran to find Jude; they returned to the courtroom and perched in the front row with Bob Kane and the rest of the Indelicato family. "There is a God," Mari rejoiced.

The judge tempered his decision by asking the victims' partisans to move back two rows because they were such a "rough bunch." Even that didn't bother Mari. She knew the presence of so many of her Italian uncles had the police worried a bit. The family had been amused to watch the security-conscious detectives try to follow the men around the hallways and eavesdrop on their conversations, only to be tuned out when they slipped into Italian to keep the cops guessing.

But the judge's decision irritated the state's first witness, Steve Winzen. He angrily complained about Mari's presence and wondered aloud if she was sleeping with Appelbaum to get such favored treatment. Appelbaum ignored the insults and, as the third day of trial opened, called Winzen to the stand. Mari shook her head as Steve walked into the courtroom; she wondered why someone hadn't spoken to him about his clothes—jeans and a T-shirt under a corduroy jacket with leather patches on the elbows, and thongs on his sockless feet. His long hair was twisted into a braid at the back and he wore aviator-style glasses just above the thick mustache.

But that was who Steve Winzen was; he lived on his terms. He offered no apologies for his choice of clothes and made no excuses for his outspoken, sometimes insulting manner. That was about to become painfully obvious.

In brief Q&A with Appelbaum, Steve explained that he had met Lester Howlett when they lived with their families in a trailer park; they had become friends and had some business dealings.

"What type of business dealings did you have?"

"I had a marijuana connection," Steve said with some nervousness. "Picked up the marijuana. I dropped it off at Lester's. Lester had the cash customers. He brought me the money back."

"Are you familiar with Eugene Michael Fleer?"

"Yes, I am."

"How did you know him?"

"The first time I ever seen Geno Fleer ..."

Appelbaum sucked in his breath, and Mari and Jude grabbed each other's hands to ward off a feeling of panic. They all knew this story, and Appelbaum had warned Steve Winzen not to tell it on the witness stand. It was inadmissible and could damage the trial.

"Well, I don't want you to ... Just answer the question," Appelbaum stumbled.

The judge sensed a problem and stepped in to assist. "Just rephrase it," he suggested to the prosecutor.

"Who introduced you to Geno ... Mr. Fleer?"

"His fist," Steve snapped.

Mari and Jude gasped, and both clapped their hands over their mouths. Appelbaum froze in the center of the courtroom, his march toward the stand halted by his witness's remark. The ice under the prosecutor's feet suddenly had become very thin, and his mind was racing.

"Who?" Clint Almond asked.

Appelbaum ignored the defense attorney and concentrated on Steve. Appelbaum had to keep him on the right track and away from very dangerous territory.

"What person introduced you to Mr. Fleer? Is there anyone that he ..." Appelbaum still was searching for the detour sign to guide Winzen away from the cliff's edge.

Mari was shaking her head no in a desperate attempt to stop what she feared might be next. Jude prayed silently, "Please, God, don't let him say it."

"Geno Fleer was beating the hell out of a woman," Steve spat out.

Steve had said it, and Appelbaum felt his stomach flip. Appelbaum had been sure he had made it abundantly clear that Steve was not to say anything about how Fleer had beaten the woman in the tavern parking lot. Descriptions of prior bad acts unrelated to the charges in the trial were strictly forbidden by the rules of evidence. They were prejudicial and inadmissible—legitimate grounds for a mistrial. Appelbaum had warned Jude, Mari, and Steve, especially, not to mention anything they knew or had heard about Geno Fleer's previous criminal record. Mari was cautioned not to say anything about Fleer's admission to her about his prison term. That was one of John Appelbaum's List of Ten Rules for Witnesses—do not mention other bad acts of the defendant. He had even reminded Winzen of the rule earlier that morning.

Mari and Jude had begun to sob and cry. In five minutes on the stand, Steve had jeopardized the trial the women had fought so hard and waited so long to watch. Mari stared angrily at Steve as he sat there, looking blankly at Appelbaum and the judge.

Almond and Brady already were on their feet as Appelbaum turned plaintively to the judge. "May we approach the bench?"

Judge Anderson ordered the jury escorted from the courtroom as the attorneys converged in front of him. Almond and Brady immediately moved for a mistrial, and Almond asked accusingly if the prosecutor had put Winzen up to this trick to prejudice the jury. Appelbaum angrily denied the insulting suggestion. He wasn't surprised by a low blow from Almond; in fact, Appelbaum had to admit he already was wondering if the other side of the aisle was behind this disaster—a clever way to win another delay, perhaps. The judge told the attorneys to prepare for a special hearing to determine what had happened.

Mari and Jude were descending rapidly into hysteria; neither of them could stop crying. Mari kept telling herself there still was hope, that the judge surely would find a way to salvage the trial. Surely, she reasoned, the judge would not want to preside over another fiasco in this case and have to start all over again.

But Jude was sure Steve Winzen had blown the trial, and she could feel a new tide of anger rising inside. John Appelbaum was in a rage, too, by the time he reached the women. "It's over," he said with a shake of his head. "I don't think this warrants a mistrial, but I'm sure that's what the judge will do. He's going to talk to some of the other judges and read some cases, but I know that's what he'll do. This is a mistrial."

Mari became so emotional that investigator Chris Borgerson invited everyone to gather in his office across the street to get away from the crowd and reporters who were moving in for comments. Mari and Jude felt as if they were running the gauntlet as they made their way through the crowd and into Chris's office.

Judge Anderson soon convened the unusual hearing to find out what had happened and what should be done. Steve was first on the witness stand and continued his record of surprising the courtroom with an unexpected explanation. He had approached Prosecuting Attorney Bill Johnson at the elevator just before testifying and asked what he should say if he was questioned about the circumstances of his first encounter with Fleer. Johnson had advised him, "Just tell the truth," and that is what he had done.

Steve knew Appelbaum had said to say only that he had met Fleer through Lester Howlett. But Steve didn't trust Appelbaum as much as the women did, and he believed the real truth, the whole story, should be told. When he asked Johnson for clarification, he was told exactly that— "Tell the truth."

Johnson, obviously angered by the turn of events and the suggestion that he somehow was responsible for this, testified he had indeed told Steve to tell the truth. But that innocent and entirely proper advice was offered generally, and certainly had not been meant to override Appelbaum's repeated warnings about previous bad acts. How could anyone interpret "Tell the truth" to mean he should disregard those repeated admonitions?

As the judge retired to make his decision, the prosecution's team was left to wonder how and why this had happened. Appelbaum had been told that Steve had said nothing he could do would bring back his son and there was little reason to ruin his own reputation in a trial now. Had he just been trying to avoid testifying about his drug deals and his criminal circle of friends? Mari knew Steve would be reluctant to discuss his marijuana business while his father sat in the audience. Had this been his way to avoid that? Even if that was true, Mari had a hard time believing Steve would purposefully cause a mistrial.

Jude and Rick Pashia decided Steve's comment was a function of his personality, not an attempt to manipulate the trial. To them, making that kind of statement fit the way Steve was; he just didn't care about consequences.

John Appelbaum had spent hours interviewing Steve Winzen, listening to his bravado and macho statements. Appelbaum couldn't disagree with Jude's and Rick's perspective. Maybe Steve had wanted to slam Fleer and the possibility of causing a mistrial was worth the risk. In one long interview with Appelbaum, Steve had recounted in harsh and profane terms how violent Fleer became when rejected by women; in fact, Fleer's friends were kidding him about being horny because his reputation for beating women was keeping them away. Steve guessed that Fleer went to the apartment to force Stacy into sex and lost his temper when she resisted; Steve's memory of the look in Fleer's eyes as he pounded a woman in a parking lot made it easy for Steve to believe Fleer had beaten and killed Stacy. If he had, was it difficult to see him killing Tyler to eliminate a witness? Steve was absolutely sure Lester Howlett couldn't kill Tyler, so it had to be Fleer.

After reaching that conclusion, Appelbaum wondered, had Steve been trying too hard to hammer Fleer from the witness stand?

The prosecutor and the mothers realized that this newest disaster would probably go down on the list of unsolved mysteries in this case—another chapter like "What happened to the jury summonses?" They might never know what was in Steve Winzen's mind when he blurted out the now infamous line—"Geno Fleer was beating the hell out of a woman." Winzen swore he simply was following Bill Johnson's advice to tell the truth, and no one could prove otherwise. While the judge was deliberating, Winzen even told a reporter from the *Jefferson County Journal* that he was sorry for his remarks.

But Mari and Jude found it suspicious when they saw Steve leaving the courthouse with Mark Gerber that afternoon. Later that night, the women and Appelbaum would be sure that Gerber was the man interviewed by Channel 2—his face hidden in the shadows—as he blamed Bill Johnson for the confusion.

Amid the turmoil, Appelbaum realized the incident had forced upon him another of those decisions he would not tell anyone else for a while. But it was certain that Steve Winzen would never get near the witness stand again as a prosecution witness. Appelbaum couldn't take the chance. The stakes were too high—for Tyler and Stacy, for Mari and Jude, for Appelbaum, even for Fleer.

Judge Anderson spent more than three hours considering the situation and discussing it with other judges before he reconvened the court to announce his decision.

"Error occurred in this case when a witness stated that the defendant was 'beating the hell out of a woman' when he met him," the judge told the jury. Appelbaum knew what would come next. The error was prejudicial to Fleer and was grounds for a reversal by an appellate court if Fleer was convicted. The judge was granting the motion for mistrial.

Mari was crushed again and buried her head against Bob's shoulder as she burst into tears. She had kept her hopes alive, only to have them dashed one more time. Jude threw her arms around Racheal and they cried harder then they had over the jury summons catastrophe in January. Jude wondered if the case was lost forever.

"Racheal, I'm so sorry you have to go through this again," Jude sobbed.

Racheal looked into her mother's face and whispered, "It's not your fault, Mom. I'll get through it."

Judge Anderson looked at the mothers and, once again, apologized. He turned to the jurors, many of whose faces were showing their displeasure with the events, and thanked them for their service; he apologized to them, too.

And then the judge surprised everyone in the courtroom by announcing that he was stepping down from the case. He no longer could be impartial and, after two calamities, had decided the case should be heard by another judge. He would assign one soon and a new trial date would be chosen.

Mari and Jude couldn't believe their ears. The mistrial was bad enough, but a change in judges could cause another lengthy delay.

But Anderson still was not finished, and he saved the last blast for the defense. In the judge's considered opinion, Clinton Almond clearly suffered a conflict of interest by his representation of Fleer after he had advised Donald Walker on the question of Fleer's statements in 1986. In light of the disclosures about all of that during opening statements and the possibility that Almond would be called as a witness, continuing to defend Fleer violated the ethical rules of the Code of Professional Conduct for attorneys, the judge said. He based his opinion on a recent decision by the Missouri Supreme Court, which granted a new trial for a defendant whose attorney took the witness stand. Anderson said Almond had made himself a witness in this case and, under the Missouri Supreme Court decision, that made it a conflict for him to represent the defendant. The judge suggested Fleer should get an opinion from an independent counsel about whether to hire a different attorney.

Mari and Jude were shell-shocked. What else could happen? They had been through so much and fought so hard just to sit in the courtroom; they had come so close to a verdict. They wondered how God could let this happen now. Did He not want this to come to trial? How could two such bizarre events happen in the same case?

Mari was too distraught to face the reporters, but Jude stood before the cameras to rip into Steve Winzen again. "We've been waiting for so long, and to have somebody's stupidity and ignorance like Steve Winzen's screw it up in just two minutes ..." She let the unfinished thought hang in the air. But she vowed to be there when Fleer was convicted, no matter how long it took. "They're not going to break me," she said through the tears.

Marsha Brady told reporters it appeared to the defense that Winzen was determined to mention the beating incident. "He wanted to get it in. He saw his chance and he slipped it in." And Almond solemnly slammed Bill Johnson, saying it appeared the prosecutor had urged Winzen to make the improper comment. "This mistrial was caused by Bill Johnson, the prosecuting attorney, by the way he talked to the witness," Almond insisted to reporters.

Appelbaum was caught off-guard when a TV reporter asked him if his boss had given Winzen bad advice. Appelbaum searched his mind quickly for the proper response to this upside-down situation. Johnson never would do such a thing on purpose, and Appelbaum wanted to be sure his answer conveyed that. Appelbaum smiled ironically as he responded, "He told him to tell the truth. I don't know if that's ever bad advice."

Meanwhile, Mari was frantically looking for Appelbaum. He was her savior and she was hoping he had some words to redeem this tragic situation. When Appelbaum finally found the mothers, Mari threw her arms around him and asked what they were going to do now. But Appelbaum was grappling with his own emotions, too. "I don't think I can do this anymore, Mari," he said quietly. "I can't get this case into court. Maybe some other prosecutor in the office could get it tried, but I can't."

Mari closed her eyes, trying not to think about what might happen if she lost Appelbaum to the same morass that had claimed so many of her hopes and dreams since 1986. This young man was the only cog in the bureaucracy that had performed every time, that had never failed once. He was her legal hit man, and she couldn't imagine finding anyone else as strong and dependable. She prayed that Applebaum was only reacting to the disappointment and frustration she understood so well.

This prayer was answered. Within minutes, Appelbaum was vowing to stay as long as it took to get to trial. He had had other job offers and had considered a change, but he could not think about that now. This case—his case—deserved to be tried in court, in front of a jury, and he would get it there, no matter how long it took to overcome the astounding obstacles that seemed to await around every corner. He was confident he had been convincing this jury of Fleer's guilt. Despite the discouraging loss of this panel, he simply would do it again with the next jury, he swore.

Mari dreaded returning home again with such a sense of hopelessness and failure, and having to break the bad news to her son, Brian—again. She had been telling him how well the trial was going and now she had to crush him one more time. She knew his faith in the whole system—the courts, the police, the adult world—was crumbling bit by bit. His childhood was getting lost in the death of his little brother and the consuming battle to find some justice for that. And his mother was the one who had to keep bringing home the bad news.

Mari and Jude spent another long, tearful night. As Jude had said to one of the reporters that day, "It's like a nightmare that never ends. It just goes on and on."

CHAPTER 15

With the anguish of the mistrial yesterday still fresh, John Appelbaum made one of the toughest and most perilous decisions of his career. On Tuesday, May 22, 1990, he resolved not to risk another gut-wrenching, perhaps fatal screwup in the procedural aspects of this case. Another cloud hung over a technical point in the case, and, after the jury summonses, and the mistrial, Appelbaum wanted to clear the horizon as much as possible. Judge Anderson had properly slammed Clint Almond for his conflict of interest, and Appelbaum knew that issue had to be resolved before Fleer had an opportunity to turn it to his advantage. If Almond remained his attorney and Fleer was convicted, he could ask an appellate court for a new trial on the grounds that Almond had been ineffective because of the conflict. Appelbaum wanted to eliminate that concern, and this was the time to act.

So the decision was made, even though Appelbaum knew it would lengthen the already intolerable delay in the trial and perhaps alienate the weary mothers. But he had no choice. He began preparing a motion seeking the appointment of a special independent counsel to determine if Clint Almond had a conflict of interest that demanded his removal. Judge Anderson had observed from the bench that it was unclear whether Fleer had waived any potential conflict, noting that he might need guidance from another attorney. Appelbaum would move for exactly that. Under this unconventional approach, Appelbaum would not be the one escalating the hostility between the attorneys by asking directly for the removal of Almond and Brady; he would just be seeking a review of the situation. If they were removed, it would be done by the judge on the advice of the independent counsel. Appelbaum had never heard of such a procedure, but a lot of things had happened in this case that he had never heard of before. Maybe this one would cut in the prosecution's favor.

But even the upheaval from the mistrial and Appelbaum's concerns about his new motion did not give warning of what was about to happen. On Tuesday, Judge Anderson appointed Judge Philip G. Hess to the Fleer case. Hess was about to retire, so he disqualified himself. Anderson then sent it to Judge Timothy J. Patterson. Three judges in less than a week; Appelbaum wondered if that was a record. But he still had no way of knowing what lay ahead.

After he filed his surprising motion on Friday, the defense team released a statement denying any conflict. Marsha Brady said her partner had not made himself a witness, as Judge Anderson had charged. The situation hinged completely on Donald Walker's testimony; he was the source of the conflict. And the defense attorneys added to their response with some new motions of their own. They sought dismissal of the charges on double-jeopardy grounds; the prosecutors had caused the mistrial that had robbed Fleer of his day in court. The new motions also sought a speedy trial and a change of venue, insisting the trial should be moved because of all the publicity that swirled around the bizarre events.

Mari and Jude were not pleased with Appelbaum's motion to remove Almond and Brady. The mothers had watched the jurors in the mistried case, and they had seemed to react negatively to the defense. With Appelbaum's superior skill and that kind of response by the jurors, the mothers thought a conviction seemed more likely with Almond and Brady in the courtroom. If they were bounced, they might be replaced by one of the high-powered defense attorneys from St. Louis, and that could increase Fleer's chance of acquittal. To Mari and Jude, that certainly was not a desirable development. Appelbaum explained his strategy and the women understood it, but that didn't make it any easier for them to contemplate a turn of events that might improve Fleer's position before a jury.

On Tuesday, June 5, Judge Patterson held the first of a series of hearings on these unusual motions from both sides. Appelbaum supported his request for an independent counsel by explaining that Almond's credibility would come under attack as a defense witness trying to refute Donald Walker's testimony that Almond had advised him to keep quiet about Fleer's confession. Intense questioning of Almond about his advice to Walker, and even the rest of his career, could reflect badly on Fleer; the jury could be prejudiced against him because of Almond's conduct. Fleer needed an independent attorney to help him decide what to do.

Marsha Brady rejected the suggestion and denied there was a conflict. Fleer had no money to pay another attorney, and he certainly had every right to retain those whom he had paid and who had prepared for this trial twice already. Forcing him to switch attorneys would create a "substantial hardship," she said, and that was one of the stated exceptions to the conflict rule in the Code of Professional Conduct.

Brady also recalled how the prosecution had dropped snitch Michael Watson as a witness; there was no certainty Walker would even testify or what he would say if called. She also suggested that the rules of evidence barred Walker from mentioning Almond on direct examination by Appelbaum and the defense certainly wouldn't raise the question on cross.

As the attorneys sparred over Walker's anticipated testimony, Appelbaum mentioned that the defense had failed to appear for the deposition with Walker before the January trial date. In his frustration, Appelbaum even asked the judge to order the defense to pay the costs of bringing Walker to Jefferson County. Brady shrugged off the incident; the defense had made a strategic decision not to depose Walker. Every time the defense discovered a witness to contradict Walker's statements to police, he changed his story. It was better to avoid the deposition and force him to appear at trial to testify. Brady suggested Walker had been brought to the county to appear before a grand jury anyway, so the cost of his trip was not wasted.

Appelbaum was incensed. There had been no grand jury appearance, and the canceled deposition had cost the county several thousand dollars for a pointless junket; he wanted the judge to know that.

"Judge, I have just one brief point on the deposition.

That's another blatant lie. You will get used to those in the course of this trial."

Brady spun angrily toward the judge. "Your honor, I object to that. That is extremely uncalled for on John's part."

Almond shook his head. "Dirty," he spat out.

But in the front row, Mari Kane and Jude Govreau loved it. They had come to despise the defense attorneys almost as much as they hated Fleer. Almond and Brady were Fleer's champions, and the mothers would not take a neutral view of them. There were precious few times when the women thought the naked truth was told amid the lawyers' attempts to cloak it to fit their purposes. But Mari and Jude felt they had heard it then from John Appelbaum. The slam from him had been one of the few moments the women could savor, and they did so with glee.

Appelbaum knew he had crossed another threshold. The battle was becoming quite personal; he had let Almond and Brady get to him and had snapped at them in anger. What should be routine give-and-take between opposing counsels had taken on a new, sharper edge. That was never a good development. He didn't look forward to the escalation of that kind of conflict, but he wouldn't run from it and he wouldn't back down.

The judge promised a quick decision on an independent counsel after the lawyers submitted case law by the end of the week. Then he moved to the defense motions. Brady took up the request for dismissal of the charges, and that made Mari and Jude tighten up as they listened to this new effort to free Fleer. Brady called John Appelbaum to the stand to explain how he had repeatedly told Steve Winzen not to mention any of Fleer's bad acts unrelated to this case, especially the beating he saw Fleer administer to a woman.

Prosecuting attorney Bill Johnson was called next to testify that an agitated Steve Winzen had grabbed his arm and complained about Mari being in the courtroom and then asked what to say if questioned about a fight in a parking lot. Johnson explained that he made it a policy never to get involved with witnesses in his assistants' cases. He had told Winzen that the prosecutors had restrictions on what they could ask and then advised him just to tell the truth.

Appelbaum, getting the rare opportunity to cross-examine his boss, asked simply, "Did you deliberately incite Mr. Winzen to commit this mistrial?" Johnson responded, "No, sir, I did not."

Brady insisted that Johnson's instructions implied a desire for Winzen to tell the jury about the beating. The prosecution had caused the mistrial; therefore another trial was barred as double jeopardy. Appelbaum dismissed that whole argument as ridiculous. Without any comment, the judge denied the request to dismiss the charges.

Mari and Jude wanted to celebrate. At least the debacle of the mistrial had not led to the utter disaster of dismissal of the charges against Fleer. The decision was gratifying to Appelbaum, too; it rejected the idea of a conspiracy of misconduct by prosecutors.

The next defense motion was easier. Appelbaum agreed to a change of venue; a jury could be picked in another county and brought to Hillsboro for trial. The judge took the speedy trial motion under consideration, but warned that he had a crowded docket for the summer. That was not exactly what Mari and Jude had hoped to hear. With the conflict motion unresolved and the judge's schedule tight, who knew how long this delay would be?

Judge Patterson took only a week, however, to rule on Appelbaum's unconventional motion. In a response that surprised most parties, the judge appointed the well-known and widely respected defense attorney Donald L. Wolff of Clayton as independent counsel on the conflict question. Wolff was an experienced litigator and lecturer on criminal law, the judge pointed out, and had agreed to serve without a fee. His commission was to review ethical codes concerning lawyers becoming witnesses, consult with Fleer, evaluate whether he could waive any conflict, determine whether removing Almond and Brady would be a substantial hardship for Fleer, and then report to the judge in ten days.

Wolff made an appointment to interview Fleer and the defense team, but only Brady appeared; she announced that Almond would not cooperate and that the attorneys had advised Fleer not to talk to Wolff. Wolff talked to Appelbaum, researched the issue, and filed his report on June 20, right on time. He withheld any conclusion, however, until Fleer could be questioned under oath in a court hearing that Wolff asked the judge to order. The judge could not make a final ruling without knowing whether Fleer really understood the conflict issue and was willing to waive it as an appeal point.

But in his thirty-four-page report, Wolff said he had never seen a case fraught with so many potential problems of conflicts and ethics. Walker had asked Almond to use Fleer's confession to make a deal on Walker's robbery case, but claimed Almond had only said to keep quiet about it. Meanwhile, Walker was trying to collect evidence for the feds on a number of people, including his own attorney. Now Almond faced serious ethical questions by being required to cross-examine and impeach a former client, and run the risk of violating attorney-client privilege by getting into information Walker had divulged confidentially. In addition, Almond would have to testify about his own legal advice to Walker.

Wolff ended his report with a call for Judge Patterson to hear directly from Fleer before deciding if there was a conflict and if Fleer's waiver could circumvent it. Patterson agreed and set a hearing for Monday, June 25. That day, Almond and Brady addressed the situation in an unexpected way—they filed a motion exercising the defendant's automatic right to a substitution of judges. Instead of moving closer to resolving the conflict issue, the case took another detour. Patterson had no choice but to step aside and ask the Missouri Supreme Court to appoint a successor. The defense explained the move as an attempt to get to trial faster; after all, Patterson had a full docket for the summer and fall and would be vacationing in the Soviet Union in September.

The move set the revolving door in motion again. After running out of judges in Jefferson County, the Missouri Supreme Court had to look elsewhere. On Tuesday, June 26, the court appointed Circuit Judge A. J. Seier of Cape Girardeau County some eighty miles to the south. This time, it was Appelbaum's turn to respond; acting on wary advice from other prosecutors who knew Judge Seier, Appelbaum immediately exercised his right to ask for a different judge.

The next day, the Missouri Supreme Court turned to Circuit Judge Frank Conley of Boone County, where Fleer had been living when he was arrested. It was a fateful appointment. Judge Conley was pleasant, but had a reputation for countenancing no nonsense or unnecessary delay. He was a tall, lean man with a full head of silver hair, and he carried himself with an elegant and confident air that marked a man who knew what he was doing.

Appelbaum was delighted with the appointment. Conley was known as a great judge who had never been reversed on appeal and was, in fact, a darling of the Missouri Supreme Court. That had to help amid these twisted circumstances. Perhaps Conley could restore some order to a case that had been assigned to five judges within five weeks.

Mari and Jude were almost overwhelmed by the rapid-fire developments. Their worst fears that the court system was nothing more than loosely controlled insanity uninterested in simple justice seemed to be confirmed by the events of May and June. Who was on first? they wondered. Did anyone know? Did anyone besides them care? Once again, it seemed to the women, Fleer's rights were given priority above the real point of this exercise—to try him for the murders of two innocent children. In their meetings in court and calls to each other, Mari and Jude wondered just who Eugene Michael Fleer was that he was able to spin the courts into such disarray and confusion. Why did he get so many free shots? Every time the case neared resolution, new roadblocks sprang up as if by magic. How could this happen over and over and over? the women wondered.

And Jude's personal life was about to get another blow. In July, she was fired from Tucker's after seven years on the job. Her boss said she had too many personal problems, so he handed her unemployment as another one. Trying to keep her head above the financial waters while she looked for a job now was added to her list of worries over the trial, Racheal, and Johnna's recent announcement that she was pregnant. Jude had found no peace in four years, and it was obvious life was not about to give her a break now. Weeks and weeks passed before she found full-time work at a nursing home and a part-time bartending job to try to make ends meet.

Behind the scenes, more changes were brewing in the courts in Jefferson County that summer. The primary election in August would determine the nominees for state and county offices, including prosecuting attorney. No one filed for the Republican nomination, so the winner of the Democratic primary had a lock on the general election in November. The Democrats were featuring a three-way race, however, with Bill Johnson seeking election to the post he held on appointment. Opposing him were Patrick Healey, a private attorney and former cop; and George McElroy, the public defender in adjacent Franklin County, who had been a prosecutor in Dallas, Texas. McElroy, whose silver hair and strong face gave him a distinguished air and whose accent offered more of Texas than southeastern Missouri, seemed honest and straightforward. He campaigned hard, even taking advantage of the Fleer mistrial in May to slam Johnson in an interview with John Auble of Channel 2 at Clint Almond's office. Jefferson County, McElroy said, deserved better than the inept performance demonstrated by Johnson's clumsy advice to Steve Winzen.

That blast was McElroy's only comment about the Fleer case during the campaign; although it was not aimed at Appelbaum, he took some exception to the remarks from this political unknown who had been a county resident only a couple of years. Appelbaum thought McElroy had less than a slim chance to win; he clearly was the third horse in the race. Johnson had the weight of incumbency, and even though he had not courted the party leaders, he looked like the winner.

But the voters disagreed and on August 7 handed the Democratic nomination and a free ride in November to George McElroy. The change in leadership in Appelbaum's office came as Mari and Jude commemorated the fourth anniversary of the children's murders. Juggling two brand-new jobs, Jude worked that day for the first time since the killings. Mari and Rick took Racheal to a mass for Tyler, and then Mari delivered flowers and little gifts to Stacy's memorial at Jude's apartment. That night, Jude wrote another poem to the kids, ending it with thoughts from the two women:

> Gone forever
> Our love, our life, our bundles of joy.
> My little girl and your little boy.

As the women looked back in pain, John Appelbaum really began to wonder about the shape of the future. Clint Almond obviously had courted McElroy during the campaign, and that troubled Appelbaum. He hoped McElroy was as experienced and as sharp as he seemed; surely he would see through a defense attorney's transparent overtures. Appelbaum wondered if the bizarre delays in this case would accrue to the benefit of Fleer and Almond now that McElroy had won. Was Almond hoping Appelbaum's dedication to the case would fail to sway a new boss? Would this prosecuting attorney want to risk a defeat in court in a capital case so early in a new term? Or would he consider dismissing the case honorably after announcing that a reevaluation had found it too weak to prosecute? Was that the agenda here?

Despite McElroy's campaign promises to retain Appelbaum, the young prosecutor also wondered if his job really was safe. And if he wondered, Mari and Jude worried. Was this the next calamity to befall the case? After the two false starts earlier this year, were they about to watch McElroy remove Appelbaum and set back the case again? Or could it be worse? After all of this agony, could McElroy drop the whole thing?

Before Appelbaum could discuss Fleer with the prosecutor-elect, Judge Conley called a hearing on a motion Appelbaum had filed a week before the election. Anxious to keep the conflict issue in play, he had upped the ante by asking directly for the removal of Almond and Brady. But Conley wanted to take the advice of independent counsel Don Wolff first and get Eugene Fleer's opinion. On August 16, Fleer testified under questioning by Wolff that he couldn't afford new attorneys, understood the potential conflict with Almond and Brady, preferred to keep them, and was willing to sign an official waiver that would surrender his right to raise the issue on appeal.

Arguing for the removal of the attorneys, Appelbaum disclosed that there really was more than the question of Almond's advice to Donald Walker. The prosecutor added that Walker had secretly recorded conversations with Almond as part of the Secret Service investigation into "certain corruptions" in Jefferson County, such as trafficking in stolen food stamps. Although no charges had been filed against anyone, Almond's credibility could suffer from that disclosure, and that could prejudice the jury against Fleer. Appelbaum didn't want a conviction overturned on that technicality. Brady found little worry there. The judge could prohibit testimony about that from Walker or Almond. Anyway, Almond's testimony would be needed only to refute the accusation about Fleer's confession, Brady told the judge.

The judge promised to rule quickly, perhaps within days. But the ruling didn't come soon, and the delay brought more agony for Mari and Jude. As days became weeks, the women's patience was used up and they began to search for someone in authority who could force a decision. Mari learned the name of a helpful contact in the attorney general's office, and he explained that a judge had ninety days to make a decision before anyone could complain to the Missouri Bar Association or the state's judicial review panel. When nearly a month had passed, Mari wrote a heartfelt letter to Judge Conley explaining the pain the women had suffered and how his slow response was twisting the knife in their hearts. Jude liked the letter, but Appelbaum predictably suggested not sending it; Mari sent it anyway.

The delay was taking its toll in other ways, too, the women had heard. Henry Garcia, one of Fleer's best friends and a man the authorities suspected knew the real truth, had been killed in a motorcycle crash. And another friend who would be a witness at the trial, Jim Main, was seriously injured in a separate motorcycle crash. "By the time we get to trial, all our witnesses will be dead," Jude worried in her journal.

Conley finally handed down his decision on September 20. Clint Almond and Marsha Brady were off the Fleer case, and the judge would consider appointing a special defense attorney to take over. But Conley delayed the removal of Almond and Brady until October 3 to give them time to file with the Missouri Court of Appeals at St. Louis. The defense attorneys confirmed they would do exactly that, adding that Fleer was not happy about the delay while he was racking up eighteen months in jail. Brady told a reporter she had never seen such a move by a judge, but she admitted she had never seen a case with so many wrinkles. She shook her head as she admitted, "I've heard someone refer to this case as 'snake-bit.' I guess I've got to cave in and say that was an accurate assessment."

Appelbaum had expected Conley to rule that way; there really was no alternative. But Appelbaum was surprised when one of the veteran lawyers in the county sent him a special gift that day. Knowing that Bobby Kennedy was Appelbaum's hero, the lawyer sent a copy of the book *Bobby Kennedy: In His Own Words,* by Arthur Schlesinger. Inside, the lawyer had written a note acknowledging the import of removing a lawyer from his case. "You've got a scalp on your lodge pole now. Good moe-joe, sir."

After Conley's decision, Mari and Jude were even more agitated. Jude had been completely surprised, and she and Mari feared that a top-shelf defense attorney such as Don Wolff would be appointed to represent Fleer. Appelbaum had warned the women to brace for another delay as the issue went to the appellate court. That proved prophetic as the appellate court immediately issued a stay of Conley's decision; Almond and Brady remained on the case until their appeal was decided. Appelbaum hoped an expedited hearing might bring a final ruling within weeks, but he knew that could not be promised. He was right again.

When the Kane and Govreau families spent Christmas together, there still had been no action by the appellate court. Mari and Jude passed the day reminiscing about the children who weren't there to share the holiday and never would be again, and bemoaning the unbelievable twists of fate since August 1986.

In January 1991, George McElroy took office as the prosecuting attorney. He had worked unofficially as an assistant under Bill Johnson for weeks to learn the ropes, and that had given him and Appelbaum time to get acquainted. Appelbaum hoped that would be beneficial when he and his new boss sat down for a serious discussion of some pending cases, including Fleer and Patricia Stallings; she was set for trial the end of January in the poisoning of her infant son. McElroy was not like Johnson, the assistant knew. Johnson listened to Appelbaum and almost deferred to him for major decisions. McElroy was stronger; he had a lot of trial experience and would not be led by an assistant when it came to analyzing cases. Appelbaum had gone from total control to no inkling of what would happen.

But Mari and Jude were not pleased when they met George McElroy for the first time, despite Appelbaum's assurances that he was a tough prosecutor who would take no bull from defense attorneys or stubborn sheriffs. The women sat down January 3 in McElroy's office to explain how important it was to them that Appelbaum stay on the case. McElroy didn't disagree, but the women were perturbed by what they felt were constant interruptions as they tried to present their views. They had been at this too long to be outtalked, so they grew louder and louder every time McElroy tried to interrupt; he eventually gave it up. Another superior know-it-all, Jude thought; she didn't believe he even showed much compassion for the fact that the victims were children. "We're in trouble," Jude snapped to Mari.

Mari was so frustrated and soon angered that she finally told McElroy to stay out of the case entirely. In no uncertain terms and without any concern for tact or his elected position, Mari stated absolutely that this was to remain John Appelbaum's case. He knew it and he knew how to communicate the women's pain to a jury. Mari and Jude made it abundantly clear they would not stand for any attempt to take Appelbaum off the case. McElroy agreed; it was John's case, but McElroy would be there to advise if needed.

The new prosecutor's first review of the evidence led him to the same conclusion many before him had reached— Lester Howlett had probably done it. But after Appelbaum presented his evidence and quoted his witnesses—almost as he would to a jury—McElroy nodded his agreement; he was convinced Eugene Fleer was the killer. McElroy left the next big decision up to his assistant. "You can try it alone, as you were going to, or I'll assist as second chair at the trial," McElroy said. Appelbaum didn't even have to consider the answer. Having an experienced litigator like McElroy on this case would have to help.

In fact, McElroy's advice was needed on a recurring problem that was flaring up again in the Fleer case—Donald Walker was threatening not to testify at the trial. Frustrated with Appelbaum's steadfast refusal to do anything more than write a letter to the parole board in exchange for his testimony, Walker had written a letter to Appelbaum stating that he might not cooperate as a witness. The man dubbed the "jailhouse snitch" by TV might not talk after all.

That really upset Mari. Walker had given her an interesting scenario for the murders, and she hoped he would repeat it for the jury. In his version, a local criminal named Tony Calloway* had given Fleer money to buy cocaine from Howlett and Steve Winzen. But the coke was bad and Calloway wanted Fleer to kill his two buddies for ripping him off. Instead, Fleer had decided to send a hideous message to Steve and everyone else about making that kind of mistake; Fleer would kill the son Steve was so proud of. But the plan backfired, and Calloway was furious at Fleer for the murders. Fleer was afraid for his life, and that was why he had tried to hire Walker to kill Calloway. Despite the insanity rampant through all of that, Mari thought a jury might find some kind of perverted logic.

Walker's letter threatening to clam up became an issue when a three-judge panel of the appellate court finally held oral arguments on January 7, 1991. Clint Almond and Marsha Brady argued that Walker's letter made the conflict issue moot; there was no conflict if Walker did not testify. Appelbaum, appearing for the first time in appellate court, fired back that Walker's wishes did not rule; a prosecutor always would subpoena a reluctant witness and force him to testify as long as the testimony was not used against him. Appelbaum told the judges that he had every intention of presenting testimony from Walker, and Almond's conflict remained a serious problem for them to decide before a trial could be held.

Attending that hearing was a different experience for Mari and Jude. The appellate chambers in St. Louis were not like the courtroom in Jefferson County. This room was lavishly appointed, with huge benches for the judges and incredibly plush carpeting. The women wondered, however, whether these judges would move any quicker than those they had grown accustomed to in Jefferson County.

The answer would be no.

On January 31, a jury in a different case agreed with John Appelbaum and George McElroy and convicted Patricia Stallings of murdering her son. The prosecutors argued that testimony by doctors and experts proved little Ryan had been poisoned with ethylene glycol in antifreeze his mother fed him. The prosecutors brushed aside a defense suggestion that Ryan suffered from the same genetic disease diagnosed in his little brother, David Jr., who was born after Ryan died. Although the condition, called methylmalonic acidemia or MMA, caused a buildup of dangerous acids in a child's body, two laboratories had confirmed that Ryan had died of the effects of ethylene glycol. That chemical, the prosecutors pointed out, could not have occurred naturally in Ryan's body. Stallings, just twenty-six and the mother of one dead son and another who was seriously ill with MMA, was sentenced to life in prison. Even before the trial, plans were underway for a television movie on the strange case.

CHAPTER 16

Mari Kane was about to learn that even she did not know how severely her soul had been damaged by her son's murder and the ordeal since then. What she was about to find would horrify her and change her life yet again.

In February 1991, John Appelbaum received another call from prison inmate David Powers. After being moved to a halfway house, he was more willing to talk about this drug deals with his lifelong friend Eugene Fleer. One interesting tidbit was Powers's memory that Fleer disliked kids; he was so impatient, almost hostile, toward Powers's kids that Powers had had to warn him to back off when dealing with them. But among the more useful information was Fleer's account to Powers of dealing cocaine with Lester Howlett. There had been a bad drug deal, Fleer said, and in retaliation, he and Howlett had stolen some cocaine that Steve Winzen had hidden in Mari's apartment. The ounce Fleer gave to police after Howlett's death actually had been stolen from the apartment.

That clicked in Appelbaum's mind; not only was it confirmation of his theory of a drug motive, but it meant Fleer had been holding two different ounces of cocaine at the time of the murders—one stolen from Mari's apartment and the other purchased in Rockford, Illinois. Fleer had turned in one ounce to the police after hiding it in the refrigerator; he had hidden the other under Pete Wendler's trailer and Wendler and Jim Main had retrieved it later. Now Appelbaum wondered about the morning of the murders. Had Fleer been looking for Steve Winzen's cocaine stash at Mari's when he killed the kids?

Appelbaum called Mari on Wednesday, February 6, to explain that someone had claimed Fleer had stolen cocaine left at her home by Steve. That could be the motive, John added, for Fleer's visit on that fateful morning.

Mari was stunned. No one had ever suggested that before, and she had never had any suspicion that Steve or anyone else had hidden cocaine there; actually, she knew, Steve hated cocaine. But in the hours after that call, the thought that Steve's drug dealing could have brought a homicidal Eugene Fleer to her home and cost the lives of her son and Stacy swept Mari to a new level of anguish. For the next two days, Mari couldn't rid her mind of this torment. Had Tyler's young life really ended because of drugs and because Steve brought them to her home? Mari had divorced Steve to get away from that life and to protect her son from it. Had Steve violated her home by using it as a drop for cocaine? Had Tyler's own father called down this destruction on his innocent son? Mari had been unsure of the drug motive, but it made more sense if Appelbaum's information was accurate. Revenge was less likely; she always thought it would have been exacted on Steve, not his son. But if Fleer actually was going to the apartment to get the precious cocaine, he could be capable of killing anyone that stood in his way or saw what he did. It made the call from Lester asking what time she left for work more logical.

Mari felt as if she and her home had been raped. Before this, she often had feared that each new disaster had pushed her to the end of her rope. But now, she could find absolutely nothing to hang on to. The shock and pain soon turned to anger, and she wanted some way to strike back at Steve; he had violated her home and she longed for a way to violate his. She now hated Steve as much as she hated Geno. This was eating at her as nothing had before. She wanted to confront Steve right then; Bob had to refuse to take her to Steve's trailer in Fenton to demand to know if he had done this horrible thing.

Mari and a friend went out for lunch and drinks that Friday afternoon, February 8, and Mari raged on and on about this new indictment of Steve and his life and his friends. The more the women drank, the angrier Mari became. They ought to blow up his house, the women agreed. The gesture seemed a perfect response to the destruction he had brought to her home. The women were driving home when Mari's friend mentioned that her husband had explained to her once how to make a firebomb. "Let's do it," Mari said suddenly. "Let's burn his Hoosier trailer."

Within minutes, Mari was locked in the grasp of something she would realize only later was the kind of temporary insanity she had heard about in books and movies. Nothing mattered but striking back at Steve, and nothing was too extreme. The women stopped at a convenience store and bought the simple but deadly materials they needed for the instrument of the revenge she sought so singlemindedly.

They drove to Steve Winzen's trailer—the same one where Mari had lived with him—and found his truck gone. Mari's friend knocked on the door and posed as a marijuana buyer; Steve's girlfriend explained that he wasn't home. On her hip, she carried the two-year-old daughter she'd had with Steve. But Mari's mind was not processing that kind of information now. Only revenge counted. Mari ran to the kitchen window, lighted her Molotov cocktail, and threw it through the glass.

John Appelbaum was enjoying a Friday supper with his family when Detective Rich Harris called to tell him about a little problem—Steve Winzen's trailer had been firebombed. "Was anyone injured?" Appelbaum asked.

"No, it hit in the kitchen sink, and they got the fire put out before it did any real damage. But we think Mari Kane did it."

Appelbaum's heart sank. His first reaction was to reject that possibility. How could Mari have done something like that with a child in the house? Even if it was true, he could find room in his prosecutorial heart to understand how this woman could have snapped after what she had been through. She could be impulsive, anyway, and this was the ultimate impulsive act. He felt terrible for her, knowing what she must have been going through to do something so drastic. But he had to stay as far away from this, and from Mari, as possible. He told Harris not to tell him anything else. The police should call George McElroy and tell him to handle it.

Appelbaum hung up the phone and collapsed into a chair. How could there be such another bizarre, unpredictable screwup in this case? And what would this mean to the Fleer trial? As he pondered the event, John realized that there was a chance to flip the situation to the prosecution's advantage if the defense tried to use it to impeach Mari. Surely the jury would be sympathetic to a woman whose sanity was stolen from her by the ruthless murder of her child. Who wouldn't want to punish the man who killed the boy and pushed his mother over the brink?

Mari had arrived home that night in a frenzy, running almost hysterically through the house and frightening Bob. He had seen her nearly out of control before, but this was a new level of delirium. She told him what had happened and how she had heard the fire engines roaring toward the trailer before she could even get out of Fenton. She couldn't believe what she had done and she knew she was in terrible trouble. She decided she would deny it all if the police called; she would construct some kind of alibi about being with friends. Bob could never remember feeling such a mixture of anger, disappointment, confusion, and sympathy.

By the time the sheriff's detectives asked Mari to come to the department for questioning two days later, the case against her already had fallen into place. The clerk at the convenience store had identified Mari as the customer with the incendiary shopping list, and Steve Winzen's girlfriend had given a complete statement about the women who had visited moments before the fire. The detectives confronted Mari with the evidence and explained that she was headed for a seven-year prison sentence. The cops she had accused of being so incompetent had put together a rock-solid case against her. She denied everything, but the police were unimpressed. She was charged with first-degree arson, booked, and placed in a holding room in the same jail where Eugene Fleer awaited trial for murdering her son. The overwhelming irony of that was almost unbearable, and she felt humiliated. After an hour in the cell, her father and Bob arrived and posted her bail, and she was freed.

Mari also had to break the news to Jude. Mari called her and chatted for a while before mentioning, in a feeble attempt to be casual about it, that Steve's trailer had been firebombed and the police had accused her. Jude thought at first how ridiculous such an allegation was, and then she considered just what she and Mari had been through and how angry she had been most of the last five years.

"You did it, didn't you?" she asked quietly.

"Yeah, I did it. God, Jude, I am so sorry."

Jude pondered the frightening effect this could have on Fleer's trial and felt a flare of anger at her friend. But she knew she had to extend Mari the hand she had held so often.

"Well, you can count on me. I'll definitely testify that you're crazy."

The women laughed, but they both knew the razor-edged truth that only those who had been there would understand.

A few days later, Mari checked herself into the hospital again. She needed help dealing with what she had done and how it related to what had been done to her and Tyler so long ago.

The incident was another blow to Steve Winzen, and he was furious. In his mind, he had done nothing to cause any of this—Tyler's death, the frustrating investigation, the mistrial, Mari's drug problem. He already had a misdemeanor record from an angry, profane call he had left on Mari's answering machine one night; the police in St. Louis County charged him with harassment, and he got probation. All of that just for mouthing off, he marveled. He was the one always blamed for causing it all, and now his daughter had been threatened with the same fate as his son. He had taken enough abuse, he decided; he was leaving town. He needed the change, and, apparently, he needed more distance from Mari.

Amid the squabble over the attempt to throw Clint Almond off the case, it now had become Mari's turn to worry about getting a defense attorney. And she found a way to make this terrible situation serve at least one useful purpose; she turned to Don Wolff. He was reluctant to take her case, explaining that Judge Conley already had written him a letter saying he might be appointed to defend Fleer if Clint Almond was removed permanently. But Wolff thought about it overnight, called Mari the next day, and told her he would take her case for $5,000 up front. Now she had a lawyer and she had eliminated one of the best defense attorneys in the region from Fleer's team. Two birds; one stone. Even John Appelbaum had to admit she had pulled off a fairly sophisticated move under the circumstances.

Mari understood that Appelbaum would be upset with her for an act that could jeopardize his case, but she had a hard time accepting his refusal to talk to her about Fleer while the charge was pending against her. She didn't see the connection. He explained repeatedly that he could not communicate with a defendant being prosecuted by his office. "I don't want to talk about my case, just about Fleer," she would cry. But Appelbaum would tell her again that it would be a conflict for him to talk to her about anything while she was a defendant represented by an attorney. That was hard for her to accept. She had drawn strength, comfort, and assurance from him for two years, and she still needed that daily contact while the case was at such a critical juncture. Instead, she had to be satisfied with updates by John's secretary and secondhand reports from Jude. For someone who had lost herself in the prosecution of Fleer, it was distressing to be excluded from the inner circle.

Months later, Mari admitted what she had done and entered a guilty plea in exchange for probation. She endured more humiliation as she stood before the judge and listened to his pronouncement of sentence. But she knew it was better to face up to what she had done and accept the discipline from the court.

The real sentence came from inside Mari, anyway. She would have to live with the realization that she had set fire to that trailer knowing that a two-year-old child was inside. In her deranged state, she had not connected her obsessed attack with danger to the child. She had thrown the firebomb through the window over the kitchen sink, knowing it would land where it probably would do little damage; her mind may have directed her subconsciously to the least vulnerable place. But she had known Steve's child was there. She was more ashamed of that fact than anything else she had ever done. She could deal with trying to destroy Steve's trailer and, in fact, felt almost no remorse for that. But the fact that she had nearly caused harm or even death to that child was a terrible burden. She knew that if the girl had died, some people would have compared her to Geno Fleer. The murder of her son had brought her to this place, but she had to live with what she had done. And she could never be the same because of it.

As Mari dealt with that, she and Jude also had to find new ways to cope with the agony of waiting for an appellate decision. They made almost daily calls to the court to ask about progress, and Jude wrote a letter to the judges explaining how the months of delay affected the lives of the people waiting for justice. Please, she beseeched them, think about that and enter a ruling. She was even pressuring John Appelbaum to withdraw Donald Walker as a witness to end the conflict. How many times do we have to be victimized? she asked. How much do we have to take? Where is some measure of justice?

Eliminating Walker as a witness actually had been discussed by Appelbaum and George McElroy while Walker vacillated over testifying. His motion for a new trial was denied on April 1, 1991, and that did nothing to make him more cooperative with the prosecutors. At one point, Clint Almond surprised McElroy by calling and announcing that he was going to withdraw; the delay was becoming intolerable for Fleer as he sat it out in jail, and getting to trial had become the paramount consideration. McElroy urged Almond to hold off, however; the prosecutor had decided to put Walker on the polygraph in hopes of buttressing his credibility. So far, Walker was refusing to take the test; if he wouldn't agree to it or if he failed it, McElroy would pull him from the witness list and that would resolve Almond's dilemma.

While that was in the works, however, the news from the appellate court arrived on April 23. In what turned out to be more of a nondecision, the court sent the matter back to Judge Frank Conley for more hearings and a more detailed finding of fact. Was Donald Walker's testimony a certainty at trial? If Almond and Brady were removed, would that inflict a substantial hardship on Fleer? The appellate court wanted Conley to gather more information and then reconsider his decision to remove the defense attorneys. In the meantime, the appellate court said, they stayed on the case.

That was the last straw for John Appelbaum and George McElroy. Six days after the ruling, McElroy announced that he had sent a letter to Judge Conley stating that Donald Walker would not be a witness in Fleer's trial. His testimony was important and McElroy believed him, but there was too little corroborating evidence to stand without the support of a successful polygraph. Walker's testimony wasn't worth the continuing delay; he was out. And since that eliminated the need for Clint Almond to appear as a witness, the defense attorneys no longer had a conflict. The motion before Judge Conley was moot, and they could proceed to trial. Almond commended McElroy's integrity, but couldn't resist taking a shot by cracking that Walker couldn't have passed a polygraph anyway.

The turn of events answered the prayers of Mari Kane and Jude Govreau, although Jude wrote in her journal, "A year for nothing." The women wanted Almond and Brady on the case; they knew Conley was fair enough to have appointed a very good defense attorney to replace them. But that wasn't an issue now. Mari hated to lose Walker as a witness; she was convinced he was telling the truth and ultimately would have helped nail Fleer. But she also had faith in Appelbaum's promise that the case remained strong without Walker. On to trial, Mari thought.

Not quite. Judge Conley's busy docket at home in Boone County kept him from setting a trial date. Several weeks passed with no action, and the women found themselves facing even more frustration. And that was before they learned of the new storm brewing on the horizon. On June 19, Clint Almond filed a suit seeking George McElroy's ouster from office, charging that the prosecutor had committed official misconduct by filing "frivolous warrants with the court for the purpose of furthering his political ambitions and to discredit and hinder his political opponents." The suit also asked for the removal of four assistant prosecutors because they did not live in the county. Appelbaum was a resident, so Almond sought his removal by charging that he had suborned perjury from Walker and other prison inmates who were offered deals to testify against Fleer. Almond claimed McElroy and Appelbaum were blanketing prisons in Missouri with offers for inmates to come forward with incriminating stories in exchange for beneficial deals on sentences. Those offers were grounds to remove both prosecutors, Almond insisted. He even offered to serve as special prosecutor to investigate these incidents of prosecutorial misconduct, if the judge so desired.

Channel 2 wasted no time flashing its footage of Appelbaum on the screen while announcing that he had been accused of misconduct. Appelbaum tried to consider the source and shrug it all off, but once reminded a reporter from the station that a prosecutor in Philadelphia had won a $1 million libel verdict against a newspaper. Actually, Appelbaum had become numb to these attacks from Almond and really was not worried. He responded to each point in writing to perfect the record for appellate review later. And he assumed Almond's charges would be seen for the smoke screen they were.

Ultimately, all of Almond's allegations would be rejected by judges. But it was clear that more than the Fleer case was involved in this newest attack. It was sprung amid an investigation by McElroy into activities in Sheriff Buck Buerger's department and some months after newspaper stories described how certain deputies were referring jail inmates to certain bail bondsmen who then were sending the inmates to a certain law firm—Clint Almond's. Investigators from the Missouri Highway Patrol, sent in at McElroy's request to search the home of the lieutenant in charge of the evidence locker, found jewelry, guns, and videocassette recorders that had been confiscated as evidence. As a result, three high-ranking deputies had just been arrested for theft and a fourth had resigned. Later, the lieutenant would plead guilty and get a ten-year sentence; the other officers would be cleared.

The investigation exploded in the middle of a long and very difficult period for Buerger. His troubles seemed to have started in March 1990 with a shooting at the home of one of Buerger's old friends, William Pagano, a former police chief in Festus who now operated a security company. In the garage of Pagano's luxury home, he had fired two shotgun blasts that killed Mark Todd, one of his employees. Pagano claimed he fired in self-defense while arresting Todd for trying to hire a hit man to kill Todd's wife. Buerger was one of the first officers on the scene and immediately announced that Pagano's story of self-defense seemed plausible. But Buerger's credibility took a devastating hit when his own detectives built a murder case against

Pagano; forensic analysis indicated Todd was shot once in the back of the head and then, after he had fallen, was shot in the face. The detectives also learned Todd was having an affair with Pagano's daughter. Todd had told his wife and others that he was afraid Pagano would kill him if he didn't marry the girl. A special prosecutor was assigned to try Pagano for murder. Buerger's defense of his friend sullied his reputation.

Before his travails ended, he also would be investigated by the FBI over allegations of corruption leveled by Donald Walker, but no charges were filed. He would not be so lucky later, in what had to be the most humiliating event in his career. A grand jury returned a three-count indictment on allegations of sexual misconduct with women. A felony count charged that Buerger had solicited a bail-bond agent for sex; two misdemeanor counts charged that he had offered a secretary in his office money for sex and that he had had sexual contact with a female deputy in a patrol car. Buerger angrily denied all the charges, and they later would be dismissed. His attorney declared him vindicated.

But all of the allegations reinforced Mari's and Jude's harsh judgments about Buerger and the way he ran his department. And the delay in Fleer's trial caused by Almond's round of charges against the prosecutors made the women wonder if anyone in the Jefferson County law enforcement system—aside from John Appelbaum—had the slightest interest in seeking justice.

Finally, at a hearing on July 18, Conley and the attorneys agreed to begin the trial on September 30, 1991. When Appelbaum noted that fifteen days had been set aside for the proceedings that had ended in mistrial, Judge Conley made his opinion clear when he put down his gavel and leaned over the bench. "Mr. Appelbaum, let me help you," he said with a kind, slightly impatient voice tinged with a bit of humor. "This court has never tried a lawsuit that took longer than nine days. That was an absolute disaster that it took nine days. Most capital murder cases that I've tried, and I supposed I've tried as many as any judge in the state of Missouri, are tried in five days or less."

When spoken to like that by a judge like Conley, Appelbaum knew, the best response was agreement. Five days it would be.

                    *   *   *

While the latest stumbling blocks were being dealt with
in court, Mari and Jude struggled to keep alive their hopes
that an end was in sight. Jude feared she was losing the
fighting spirit that had sustained her. She felt as if she were
watching the downfall of the American criminal justice system and she was powerless to stop it. Mari talked about
her despondency to Appelbaum, and he likened it to the
way a bottle of soda lost its fizz when the cap was left off.
He wondered how much longer Mari and Jude would believe him when he assured them everything would be okay.
In reality, he felt as if he were trapped in a Hitchcock
movie.

Mari found inspiration in the story of another parent who
had battled to bring justice to the man who killed his child.
This father, Freddie Kassab, dedicated years of his life to
the investigation into the murders of his daughter and her
two little girls. Her husband, a Green Beret doctor named
Jeffrey MacDonald, was charged despite his claim that the
family had been attacked in its Fort Bragg quarters by a
band of homicidal hippies. As with Eugene Fleer's case,
MacDonald had managed to delay the trial for years while
professing his innocence. "Always a hearing; never a trial,"
Freddie Kassab had said during those years of delays.
There was a trial, finally, and MacDonald was convicted.
The case was made famous in the book and television
movie entitled *Fatal Vision.* Kassab's courage and devotion
gave Mari the strength to persevere through the months of
additional delays. If this old man could do it for his daughter, she could do it for Tyler.

The days leading up to the third attempt to try Eugene
Fleer were marked by a couple of momentous decisions in
Jefferson County cases. Buerger's buddy Bill Pagano was
convicted of second-degree murder on September 24 and
was sentenced to twenty-three years in prison. But he was
allowed to remain free pending his appeal.

The other case that hit the news was a double-edged
sword for John Appelbaum and George McElroy. Patricia
Stallings, the woman serving a life sentence for feeding antifreeze to her son, had been granted a new trial in July on
grounds that her attorney had been ineffective. After that,

experts on genetic diseases came forward to convince the new defense attorney and the prosecutors that lab tests had mistakenly identified the substance in the baby's blood as ethylene glycol; it really was an abnormal but natural compound caused by the methylmalonic acidemia. Patricia Stallings had not poisoned her son; he had died from a chemical produced by his own body because of the same genetic disease that now afflicted his younger brother.

On September 20, 1991, McElroy dismissed the murder charge against Patricia Stallings and announced that she had been totally cleared of any wrongdoing; it was the right thing to do. John Appelbaum hoped the national publicity about a mistaken prosecution—even one that was corrected by the system—would not taint the trial of Eugene Fleer just ten days later. What else could go wrong? everyone wondered.

CHAPTER 17

Only five hours. After more than five excruciating years of waiting—two of them consumed by obscene delays in court—the selection of a new jury to hear the evidence against Eugene Fleer took only five hours. Five amazingly fast hours on Monday, September 30, 1991, compared to the three days it had taken to choose the panel for the mistrial sixteen months before. Clint Almond had surprised everyone earlier by dropping his request to move the trial to another county because of the publicity; Fleer was entitled to be tried in Jefferson County and that was where the trial would be, Almond explained.

So the cast of the familiar and increasingly combative characters assembled in the same courtroom for a third run at a trial. Mari and Jude had been pleased with jury selection last time, but this time they were amazed and frightened by the speed at which Judge Frank Conley blasted through it. Even John Appelbaum was concerned by how quickly the judge handled the issue of publicity. It had taken two days to deal with it when Judge Anderson tried the case. Conley gave it a couple of minutes, satisfying himself that the jurors were candid and honest when they said they could set aside anything they had read or seen and base their verdict solely on the facts presented in court. Unlike the last time, when many jurors were excused because of their exposure to publicity, Conley exempted none on that point. The half day Appelbaum had spent last time qualifying jurors on the death penalty shrank to ninety minutes. In the end, however, Appelbaum was satisfied with this jury of six men and six women.

From their seats in the back of the courtroom—again—Mari and Jude were less than impressed. The slow pace by Judge Anderson had given the women time to get to know each juror, to get a feel for each real person who would sit in judgment on this crucial life-and-death case. This time, the slam-bang process allowed the women no chance to assess these people. Mari didn't want to surmise too much based on appearances, but she worried that the look of the jurors and their manner of dress—some bib overalls and flannel—suggested a group of rural folks who might be less open to the subtleties of a circumstantial case and less willing to reach conclusions based on the solid application of common sense and life's experiences. She was concerned, too, that Judge Conley might cut too many corners in his zest for speed. She thought he had been terse, perhaps rude at times, during jury selection.

Jude, however, was giving Conley the benefit of the doubt; she would reserve judgment for a while. But she did tell reporters she was frightened by the blurring pace of the proceedings. It had taken five years to get there and only five hours to pick a jury; she wanted the case tried, but she wanted it done right.

Appelbaum assumed the judge would schedule opening statements and the first evidence for the next morning—a fresh start early Tuesday. Instead, Conley informed the prosecutors and defense attorneys at 2:50 P.M. Monday that he was going to send the jurors home to collect suitcases for their sequestration and have them return to hear the attorneys' opening remarks and some of the state's witnesses that evening. "We will get this lawsuit tried today, folks," he said.

Appelbaum hurried into the hallway to alert his first witness, Mari Kane. She was shocked again and realized she had dressed casually in blue jeans for what was supposed to be a day of informal proceedings. She placed a nearly panicked call to Bob to tell him to leave work early, go home, get her a change of clothes, and hustle to the courthouse. Jude sent a ride for Racheal to get to court as soon as possible in case she was among the witnesses to be called that evening.

At 5:41 P.M., almost before anyone could believe it, Prosecuting Attorney George McElroy stepped before the jurors to make his opening statement. McElroy and Appelbaum had meshed well while trying the Patricia Stallings case—despite its bizarre conclusion—and had developed a pattern of alternating duties before the jurors. Since Appelbaum had handled jury selection, McElroy would deliver the opening. Actually, under the deal between the prosecutors, McElroy would make Appelbaum's opening statement from the last trial, with a couple of personal touches.

In his soft Texas drawl, McElroy explained that the evidence proving that Fleer killed Tyler and Stacy was circumstantial; the prosecutor compared it to putting together a puzzle. The individual pieces didn't mean much, but all of them were there and, if assembled properly, completed the picture. He ran through the separate, oddly shaped pieces: drug deals by Fleer, Lester Howlett, and Steve Winzen; Fleer's access to Mari's house and car keys; Howlett's presence outside Mari's apartment the morning of the murders; Neil Myrick's view of Fleer entering the building; the "click" of the bathroom door when Racheal entered the apartment; Sandy Barton's sighting of the disheveled Fleer driving away shortly after the murders; Fleer's incredibly detailed descriptions to friends of the murder scene and his insightful theories about what had happened and why; Howlett's convenient and suspicious death before he could be reinterviewed; Fleer's web of lies to the police; and finally, Fleer's cogent comment to the cops in 1989: "I knew it was just a matter of time before you guys came and got me."

"Those are the various pieces of the puzzle, folks," McElroy concluded. "Maybe by itself, any one piece won't give you the whole picture. But those are the pieces that, when assembled, will be the evidence on which the state will base its case for a guilty verdict."

Marsha Brady chose a different simile. The prosecution's case was more like a cardboard box containing a mouse. When someone puts a cat into the box and the mouse disappears, a circumstantial case would suggest the cat ate the mouse. But the defense would provide a closer examination of the box, exposing to the jurors the hole through which the mouse escaped. The essence of the case was simple, she said. "There is no direct evidence as to who killed Stacy Price and Tyler Winzen."

Brady then moved to the defense theory, describing how Lester Howlett was found crying and reading an account of the children's murders as he vowed, "I'm never going to drink and do drugs again. I let Steve down." Howlett was the killer and that was his remorseful confession.

The defense also attacked the witnesses against Fleer. Their stories had changed as they were interviewed and reinterviewed by prosecutors. New facts were added and times were altered to fit a schedule that would put Fleer near the apartment about the time of the murders. What about rumors of a cocaine-deal rip-off involving Steve Winzen, Fleer, and Howlett, and how that had led to retaliation against the kids? Never happened. "Tyler's father will tell you he never participated in any cocaine deals. He and Lester dealt pot. Lester dealt cocaine, but not with Steve Winzen."

Brady recalled the $10,000 reward by the families and said it had helped attract some leads. Some of those came from prison inmates looking for deals and sentence reductions in exchange for their testimony against Fleer. Could that kind of witness be believed?

At the prosecutors' table, John Appelbaum was jotting down a note about Brady's cat-and-mouse line. He wanted to remember that for closing arguments.

And then an emotionally unprepared Mari Kane took the stand as the first witness—again. This was happening too fast; she had not had enough time to prepare herself to revisit the stand and the murders and Geno Fleer's gaze. As she sat down and looked at him again from this dramatic viewpoint, she could feel her body trembling inside, and the tears began to roll down her cheeks. This was more difficult and nerve-racking than the first time. Appelbaum had not told her what to expect from him, and she wondered anxiously how the defense would approach her after getting a free lesson at the mistrial. She still was shaking as Appelbaum moved quickly to an episode few people had heard about before. He had her describe how Steve Winzen came to her apartment about two months before the murders, carrying a briefcase he opened to reveal that it was packed with cash. He told her it was $50,000 (he later told the police it was half that much). When he left the room, she slipped three $100 bills out of the case; she used it to pay her rent, she explained. She hated admitting she had taken the money, but she understood why the jury needed to hear about Steve's flashing around that kind of cash. It was a dramatic way to establish the level of Steve's drug business.

As Appelbaum took her through a description of her life with Tyler, her knowledge of Steve's drug deals, her relationship with Stacy, and the morning of the murders, Mari started to settle down and regain some confidence about her testimony. And then he handed her the yellow blanket again. She had wondered if he would do that and how she would react. Surely the explosive surprise that sent her into near-hysterics the last time would be diluted now, the effect on the jury lost. But as she held Tyler's security blanket, every searing piece of the emotional shrapnel from that day and the years since tore into her heart again. The tears streamed down her face and she sobbed as she identified the blanket; some of the jurors and spectators wiped away tears, too.

But there was another bit of information that would be unfamiliar to most people this time. Mari described how Fleer had stared intensely at Tyler the night Fleer drove her to class. "That's an incredible boy you and Steve have there," he had said when she caught his gaze. The memory, reappearing long after the murders, had not been revealed to the defense attorneys before; it drew their objection, but the judge allowed it. Appelbaum hoped the jury would see the ominous implications as Tyler was caught in Fleer's icy stare two nights before the murders.

Appelbaum ended Mari's testimony by having her identify Fleer—pointing to the stoic figure in the blue shirt and tie—and then by having her identify a picture of her son. "That's Tyler," she said as her voice broke into more sobs.

Marsha Brady's cross-examination was mostly a replay of the mistrial, and again she handled Mari gently. She drew a brief comment about the obscene calls to Stacy at the apartment before Appelbaum's objections shut off that line of inquiry. Brady got the judge's permission to make an offer of proof—a more detailed explanation of the reason the testimony should be admitted—at a later recess when the jury wasn't present. Brady then turned to her next angle, asking if Mari had told Stacy that Lester was a friend. Mari denied that; she had said Lester was cute and Stacy agreed. Mari may even have had a crush on Lester, but she certainly had never admitted that to Stacy or told her he was a friend. Mari knew Brady was fishing for a way to suggest that Stacy would have trusted Lester enough to admit him into the apartment.

The women sparred a little over a couple of points, especially when Brady asked repeatedly if Mari and Lester Howlett had talked about his drug-abuse problem and if Mari had tried to get him to accompany her to AA meetings. Mari insisted she and Lester never talked about it and she never mentioned AA to him; she told the police she had thought about suggesting AA, but had never done it.

Cross-examination ended with Mari's admissions that she had taken up to fifty Valium a day and had thrown a firebomb into her ex-husband's trailer. Appelbaum wished Mari didn't have those blemishes on her record; you never knew how jurors might react to such things. But he hoped this impeachment actually would touch the jurors, showing them how distraught this shattered mother had been because of the actions of the defense attorney's client. No harm, the prosecutor decided. He used redirect questions to have Mari recount what Steve had told her about the source of the money in the briefcase: "Don't ask me about my business."

The worst moment for Mari arrived as she completed ninety minutes on the stand. Marsh Brady informed the judge that Mari should remain subject to recall for further testimony, a tactic that would exclude her from attending the rest of the trial. Mari shouted, "What?" as Brady broke the news. Appelbaum protested; Mari was the mother of the victim and deserved to be in the courtroom even if she was subject to recall. But the judge wouldn't make an exception; Mari would be excluded.

"They're doing this on purpose. They can't do this," Mari protested loudly from the aisle. "This isn't right. They're doing this on purpose," she wailed as her father nearly dragged her from the courtroom and restrained her in the hall outside. He nodded as she screamed, "They're doing this on purpose, Dad. They're keeping me out of the trial in my son's murder and it's not right." Joe Indelicato nodded and hugged his daughter. He was used to things that weren't and hugged his daughter. He was used to things that weren't right happening in this case.

When Mari told Jude the defense was going to keep her out of courtroom, Jude felt the adrenaline pumping. "The hell they will," she vowed. But she worried that Mari's anguished screams in the hallway would be heard by the jury. Would that be grounds for a mistrial? Jude wondered briefly.

Appelbaum was furious, but he couldn't dwell on Mari's predicament now. He called county jailer Tom Hawkins to recount leaving his apartment for work about seven o'clock that morning and seeing Lester Howlett sitting on a ledge near Mari's building. Hawkins knew Howlett on sight, but wasn't sure of his name. Howlett's clothes and hair were a mess; he was wearing jeans and a T-shirt. Later that day, Hawkins told the Major Case Squad about the encounter and the detectives asked him to find out for sure whom he had seen. He went to Howlett's apartment that night and got him to agree to talk to the police. Howlett said he had been getting his mail when the men saw each other that morning.

Brady drew a description of Lester Howlett from Hawkins—six feet, 180 pounds, mustache. Appelbaum winced; that painted Howlett as a fair candidate for the man seen by Neil Myrick.

Judge Conley dismissed the jury for the evening at seven-forty, and Marsha Brady demonstrated that her decision to keep Mari Kane on the witness list had had a purpose after all. With the jury gone, Brady called Mari back to the stand so the defense could make its offer of proof on the obscene calls. Mari recounted Stacy's version of the caller's comments, which seemed to suggest that he somehow had been observing Stacy. But Mari insisted Stacy had laughed off the calls without being too concerned. Appelbaum had no questions, but Brady surprised everyone, including the judge, by asking again that Mari remain under the rule excluding witnesses; Brady said more testimony from her might be needed later. The judge seemed annoyed and suggested that the defense subpoena Mari if she was needed again. Brady said that would be done.

Mari spent an anxious night, worrying about having a subpoena slapped into her hand the next morning and spending the rest of the trial in the hallway. She and Jude had done that for two days at the mistrial, and it was torture to be excluded from testimony about your children's murders. They were so close to the end now. How could it be fair to keep them out of the courtroom? Was that how the law operated in Jefferson County? Could someone murder your child and then keep you out of the courtroom while the criminal justice system decided how you would live the rest of your life? Mari imagined riding a bench in the hall while the rest of the world watched the trial. She didn't know if she could go through that again.

She didn't have to. The first thing Tuesday morning, McElroy and Appelbaum went back to the judge, armed with a court case that had led to a favorable ruling for the victim in a similar instance. McElroy argued that the national movement toward victims' rights weighed in favor of admitting Mari. "It is her child that was murdered," McElroy said. "She has been living with this for five years. It is very important to her. It would certainly go a long way to help her get through this traumatic ordeal if she was allowed to remain in the courtroom."

Clint Almond strenuously objected, even claiming that a spectator in the courtroom during the mistrial had been reporting to the prosecution's waiting witnesses after hearing testimony. When Appelbaum asked for a name, Almond ignored him. Brady told the judge there was a good chance Mari would be needed as a prosecution rebuttal witness after Steve Winzen testified. But Appelbaum said he was willing to take the chance of admitting her to the courtroom and losing her for rebuttal. Finally, the judge relented. He would allow Mari into the courtroom, but she had to sit in the rear and be quiet; one outburst and she was gone, he scolded. And if she sat in on the trial, she was banned as a rebuttal witness. Appelbaum nodded; fair enough.

Mari happily slipped into the back row and sat down; Sir John, her white knight, had ridden to her rescue again. But she was not about to remain at the back of the bus. At each recess, she would move a row or two forward, until she eventually ended up back with her family near the front. Shy and retiring was not her style, not after what she had endured. And after all, Geno Fleer's mother was allowed to sit in the front. Surely Tyler's mother should be granted the same privilege.

*   *   *

As the second pell-mell day of trial shifted into gear, the prosecution presented Sergeant William "Butch" Myers's description of how Neil Myrick had picked Eugene Fleer from the photo lineup. Almond's cross-examination attacked the procedure, getting Myers to agree that someone viewing the selection of six mug shots would be unable to discern whether the suspects were three, four, or five feet tall. Myers also agreed that videotape and photos of Fleer had been featured on television and in the newspapers when he was arrested, clearly implying Myrick had several opportunities to see the face he culled from the lineup. In a warning of things to come, Almond hit hard at Myrick's first description of the man he saw entering Mari's building as six feet tall, and heavyset; Myers said Fleer was five foot ten and weighed between 161 and 165 pounds when he was arrested. Almond also noted that the first police reports quoted Myrick as saying he saw the man at nine o'clock that morning, earlier than he told police after Fleer was arrested. The man had stayed in the apartment about four minutes, Myers remembered Myrick saying.

Appelbaum had to wince. Almond had been fairly effective in raising questions about the size of the man Myrick saw and the size of the defendant, and even had made the photo lineup seem a little iffy. On redirect, McElroy gladly had Myers describe another lineup conducted at Myrick's request in January 1990 at the sheriff's department. After Almond and Brady had spent three hours interviewing Myrick at a landmark restaurant in St. Louis called the Bevo Mill, Myrick had called the police and wanted another lineup. He wanted to be sure of what he had thought he had known until he talked to Almond—a common state of confusion after talking to this defense attorney, Appelbaum thought. So Fleer and five other men were brought into a room and, with the defense attorneys present, Myrick picked Fleer again. Myrick also said Fleer looked fifteen to twenty pounds lighter than he had been in 1986.

Appelbaum knew the slight discrepancies in eyewitness testimony that Almond had emphasized were hardly unusual or exculpatory, although jurors sometimes got hung up on little details. Appelbaum was more than happy to put all of those tidbits into perspective with the next witness—Neil Myrick himself. The prosecutor thought Myrick was perhaps the best witness in the case. He had no reason to lie and no ax to grind. He had received harassing phone calls at home since he came forward, but he still had done what was right.

As Myrick told his story again, Appelbaum thought he seemed even stronger than he had at the first trial. He nailed all of the important points, especially when he set nine-thirty as the time he had seen Fleer. Appelbaum carefully drew an explanation from Myrick about the corrections he had made to the detectives' report when he was interviewed by the Major Case Squad. The officer mistakenly wrote that the man Myrick had seen was in his late teens or early twenties; Myrick actually had used those terms to describe a couple of guys he had seen later. The officers listed Myrick's corrections on the back side of their report.

Appelbaum then took Myrick to 1989, showed him the photo lineup again, and had him point to his choice—Number 3; Eugene Fleer. Myrick also recounted the personal lineup in 1990; same result. And then Appelbaum had the witness tell the jury if the man he had chosen both times was in the courtroom. Myrick didn't hesitate as he pointed at Fleer. Appelbaum thought that was the most significant gesture this jury would see.

Almond hammered away again at the time, stressing that the detectives' report listed it as nine o'clock. But Myrick was resolute; it had been about nine-thirty and that's what he always had told the police. It was the time he had awakened after his wife left for work. Almond also concentrated on Myrick's description of the man as six feet tall, heavy build, flabby belly, and mustache. Not a dead-on description of Fleer, and there wasn't much the prosecution could do to massage it. Appelbaum opted for the direct approach. "Is there any question in your mind that the man you described going into this building is the man you identified in court this morning?"

After an overruled objection from Almond, Myrick said, "No, sir." Bingo, the prosecutor thought.

Racheal Nichols was fifteen years old now, and the maturity showed as she testified. She still was nervous and emotional, but she was a stronger young woman, not a child. She told her story well, and it took only a few minutes. But Almond immediately suggested that Racheal's mother had instructed her to say she first went to Mari's apartment about ten-fifteen that morning. Hadn't Racheal told the police originally that it was ten forty-five? When Racheal denied that, Almond produced her mistrial testimony in which she said her mother suggested the time to her. Racheal shook her head. "My mom did not tell me what time it was. When you're ten years old, you don't remember everything."

Appelbaum liked that answer, but the memory of the next witness was much more critical. Sandy Barton took the stand to describe seeing the disheveled Fleer driving out of the apartment complex about ten-forty. Her conclusion that Fleer looked as if he had been partying all night was stricken on Almond's objection, but Mari Kane smiled; the jury had heard it. And then Sandy Barton pointed out the nicely dressed Fleer at the defense table as the same man she had seen that day. Almond kept his cross-examination brief, hammering away at the time element.

But Appelbaum hoped that in just a few minutes on the stand, Sandy Barton had joined Neil Myrick in putting Eugene Fleer in the wrong place at the wrong time, and perhaps pushing him well down the corridor toward the execution chamber.

As Jude Govreau was called, she felt as if she finally had been caught up by that tornado she had feared for so long. Everything swirled in a whirlwind around her, moving so fast she could not comprehend it all. She was hyperventilating, and she struggled to calm herself so she could get a deep breath. She had been chain-smoking furiously in the hallway, much to the consternation of the kindly old bailiff, who kept gently reminding her that smoking was banned. She knew he was doing his job, but she also knew she would explode if she couldn't have her cigarettes. She finally decided she would let the police arrest her if enforcing the no-smoking policy was that essential. That would be another public-relations coup for the sheriff's department, she mused—arresting the mother of a murder victim for smoking.

She trembled as she retold the story of that morning. As

she completed the account, Appelbaum tried to anticipate one of Almond's angles. Had Jude ever told Racheal what times to give? "No, sir, I did not." Then he asked her to identify a photograph. "It's my Stacy," Jude whispered as a downpour of tears arrived.

For Clint Almond, the cross-examination of Jude was important as a way for him to show the jury how he believed prosecution witnesses had altered the times involved. He went right to work by asking what time it had been when she first sent Racheal to Mari's apartment. It was ten-fifteen, perhaps a couple of minutes later, Jude said. Hadn't she told Deputy Ron Speidel that it was ten forty-five? No, she hadn't. The exchange was the first in what would be Almond's nearly second-by-second analysis. He drew mostly on times listed in Speidel's first report, asking Jude if those were the times she had given the officer. Appelbaum checked the report and noticed the times came mostly from Racheal and Rick; Jude didn't always agree with them. Almond quizzed Jude about how long it took her to get dressed before she went to Mari's, asking for such detail that Jude finally said in exasperation, "Well, I only had to slip on a pair of shorts. I mean, it didn't take an hour."

"Well, if you just put the shorts on, what would that take you? Twenty seconds?"

"I guess. I don't know. I didn't time it."

"And then you left immediately?"

"Within a couple of minutes."

"Well, what did you do in that couple of minutes, Mrs. Govreau?"

Jude couldn't believe this. "Well, I have no idea. It was five years ago."

How long did it take to cross the road? A minute, minute and a half. Fast walk or slow walk? Regular walk. How long was the hallway outside Jude's apartment? Don't know. Twenty feet? She wasn't good with estimates of feet. Jude was becoming flustered and angry. Did Rick put on pants or shorts when he got up? Don't remember which. Didn't she tell the police it was shorts? Could have, probably.

"That wouldn't take him over fifteen seconds to put the shorts on, would it?"

Jude wanted to scream and claw Almond's eyes out. She glared at him and gritted her teeth as she snarled, "I don't know, Mr. Almond. I don't know how long it takes people to get dressed. I mean, he got up, put his shorts on, put his shirt on. However long that took."

She described Rick's discovery that the bathroom door was locked and how she had run outside to look into the window that turned out to be in the kitchen.

"And then after trying to look in a window which didn't exist, you came running back?" Almond asked with a tinge of sarcasm.

You rotten bastard, Jude thought. She wondered if she could hate anyone—other than Fleer—as much as she hated Almond at that moment. In the audience, Mari could feel steam coming out of her ears. She wanted to run over and slap Clint Almond.

After the basic story of the morning was completed, Almond asked who had helped Jude work out the time schedule. Jude caught the implication and was insulted again. "Nobody worked out a time schedule. I gave them the times," she said as she worked hard at controlling her anger.

Almond finished by pointing out that Jude had offered a $10,000 reward, gone on television to publicize it, and picketed the sheriff's department. The implication in that was clear, too; the police had to arrest someone, anyone, to appease this rabid woman. On redirect, Appelbaum simply had her explain that the reward had been offered through the defunct Child Find group, that it had never brought in any useful information, and that no one had ever tried to claim it.

Finally, Jude stepped off the witness stand to a feeling of relief she had not known for five years. At last, she had done everything she could to get justice for Stacy. Now it was up to the other players in this long-running drama. Jude took a seat in the audience without any objection from the defense.

As Rick Pashia sat on the stand, he looked at Geno Fleer. In the blue shirt and tie, he looked like a junior executive from Wall Street. He had lost weight since the day he was arrested. He didn't look as menacing, but there still was a striking coldness in the face, behind the eyes.

Rick still felt the shudder. He offered his memories of that morning and choked again as Appelbaum handed him the photograph of the kids in the bathtub. To blunt Almond's concentration on the times, which Appelbaum feared might be making some points with the jury, he closed by asking Rick if anyone had ever suggested to him what time to say Jude had awakened him. "No, sir."

Almond zeroed in on that immediately, challenging Rick's memory that the time was ten-forty or ten forty-five. Hadn't he told Deputy Speidel it was eleven o'clock? Rick didn't remember saying that, but he couldn't deny that he might have in the shock-filled hours just after the murders. He really hadn't paid that much attention to the time.

Assistant Fire Chief Russell Million testified about finding the bodies in the steaming water. Deputy Speidel checked his report for Almond to confirm that Racheal had said she had gone to Mari's apartment about ten forty-five and Rick had remembered waking him up at about eleven. Speidel also said he got the call to go to the scene at 11:04 A.M. Appelbaum hoped the jury would realize that it had taken Rick and Jude more than four minutes to go to the apartment, discover the bodies, go through the hysteria of the moment, get help from the Turners across the hall, and then make a call to police.

Sergeant Bob Miller was called next to describe processing the bathroom and later being called to Fleer's trailer to investigate Howlett's death. Miller also recounted finding a cellophane bag of cocaine and a set of scales there. Then he showed the videotape of Mari's apartment. Judge Conley had expanded the limits set by Anderson, who had barred any view inside the bathroom. Conley allowed just one pan of the camera across the bodies in the bathtub. It was a horrible sight, but it added a new dimension, and Appelbaum wanted the jurors to see it, no matter how briefly. They should really experience the essential point of this whole trial. The jurors didn't offer much reaction outwardly, but Appelbaum knew the average citizen had to feel something inside when viewing that scene. Appelbaum thought he saw one of the jurors glare briefly at Fleer as the tape ended.

From her hard-won seat in the courtroom, Mari Kane had turned and walked out before Miller began the tape.

* * *

John Appelbaum hoped Dr. Gordon Johnson could read the handwriting on the wall. The medical examiner had nearly torpedoed the prosecution last time, and Appelbaum and McElroy would not tolerate it again. As Johnson took the stand, Appelbaum hoped the prosecutors had covered themselves well enough with a new strategy. At the end of Johnson's testimony, McElroy got the doctor to agree that the injuries to Stacy's knees were consistent with striking a wooden coffee table, and he drew a conclusion from Johnson that the marks to her face were caused by blunt trauma from blows.

On cross-examination by Marsha Brady, Johnson testified that the children apparently had been drowned in cooler water because their air passages showed no burns from water as hot as the other witnesses described. And Brady focused intensely on the injuries to Howlett's hands and penis, the first serious step toward developing the defense theory. Johnson thought the marks were two to five days old, probably closer to two. But Brady didn't take the questioning as far as she had at the first trial. She knew what Appelbaum was planning as a response, and she was hoping to blunt his tactic; she did not ask Johnson if the marks on Howlett could have been from bites or if Stacy's face could have been roughed by denim.

On redirect, McElroy asked a question he hoped the jury would find intriguing. What was a hot shot? "It's a very concentrated amount of a drug that is administered in a lethal dose in the form of a murder weapon, essentially," the doctor explained.

"Is what you found in Lester Howlett consistent with a hot shot?"

"It could be, yes."

Brady asked if there was any evidence of a hot shot administered to Howlett? "No."

McElroy had to get approval from Judge Conley for the next witness. Although there had been no direct questions to Johnson about bite marks on Howlett, McElroy felt there was enough testimony to allow the defense to present that scenario in closing arguments. Therefore, McElroy told the judge, he should be allowed to call his next witness for rebuttal, even though the defense was complaining that it had not learned about the witness by the deadline set by the judge. For rebuttal witnesses, McElroy argued, that notice was not necessary. Brady objected to the witness, but the judge agreed with McElroy.

The prosecutor called Dr. James McGivney, the only forensic odontologist in the state of Missouri. As a dentist trained in the application of his science to criminal evidence, McGivney was uniquely qualified to offer an opinion on whether the mark on Howlett's penis was caused by human teeth or dental braces. "I don't believe it was," he said firmly. How old was it? "About four days old." Was it consistent with a wound suffered in a forced sexual incident? "I don't believe it was."

After a conference at the defense table, Marsha Brady had no cross-examination for Dr. McGivney. Appelbaum beamed.

McElroy moved to the next bit of scientific evidence. Roger Corcoran, the director of the Jefferson County Crime Laboratory, testified that the hair found at several locations in the bathroom came either from Tyler or Stacy. It did not match hair from Fleer, Mari, Jude, Racheal, Rick, Brenda Turner, or Lester Howlett. On cross, Brady also had Corcoran testify that a long blond hair found on Tyler's right thigh did not match anyone. Appelbaum hated that kind of unresolved evidence; it was easy for the defense to argue that the real killer was still unidentified, and Marsha and Clint surely would not miss that chance.

In the audience, however, one woman was convinced she knew whose blond hair suddenly had become an issue. Jude Govreau was outraged that, once again, the authorities had missed something so obvious. If they had checked with her about this piece of evidence, she could have explained that Stacy had been wearing a T-shirt that belonged to her sister, Johnna—the one with long, blond hair. If someone had thought to ask Jude such a simple question, the police probably could have matched the mystery hair to Johnna before the trial, thereby removing a weapon from the defense's arsenal. God, Jude fumed again, how many mistakes would she have to overcome to see justice done?

With the next witness, the prosecution turned the case more directly toward Fleer and even began hinting that he could have murdered Lester Howlett. Sergeant Tom Moore

of Ballwin testified that one of his duties with the Major
Case Squad had been to conduct the first interview with
Howlett. But Howlett had been so upset and nervous,
breaking down and crying, that Moore had asked him to
come back later. He never showed up. Why? "He was deceased." Again, there were no questions from the defense.

Then it was time to start telling the jury what Eugene
Fleer had had to say about the murders. Pete Wendler's
wife, Cathy, remembered being at John Cass's house one
evening and hearing Fleer start a conversation about the
murders of two children. Someone had slipped into the
apartment through a screen and murdered a little boy and
a girl, he said. The next Saturday night, Fleer visited the
Wendlers' home, chatted a while, made a phone call, and
left. Fifteen minutes later he returned, talked for a while,
and then left for ten minutes to get some beer. He came
back, talked some more, and then left with a television set
he was borrowing. Twenty minutes later he was back again,
asking to use the telephone in the bedroom. After the call,
Fleer told the Wendlers that Howlett was dead. Fleer and
Pete Wendler left and didn't return until much later. Appelbaum asked her to describe Fleer's demeanor that
night. "Quiet."

The prosecutor hoped the jurors would be struck by
Fleer's suspicious number of trips in and out of the Wendlers' house and by his cockamamie story about what had
happened that night. Would the jurors be sharp enough to
infer that Howlett was dead before Fleer's first trip to the
Wendlers' and that the rest of his activities had been designed to provide an alibi?

The defense had no cross-examination for Cathy Wendler, either.

Former deputy Ron Bartelbort and Lieutenant Bill Baldwin of Ladue told the jury that Fleer had lied to the Major
Case Squad about his activities before and after the murders, as well as about the events surrounding Howlett's
death. Almond went after Baldwin on the question of
whether Fleer had been shown pictures of the crime scene,
which would be an easy way to explain Fleer's knowledge
of the facts. But Almond drew the detective's terse insistence that the photos hadn't even been developed yet when
Fleer was questioned and that the police wouldn't have

shown them to him anyway. Baldwin could feel his temperature rising as Almond badgered him about the photos; Baldwin knew the detectives had had to nag the lab to get the developing done over the weekend. As he explained to Almond, he had never even seen the pictures before Tuesday, five days after the murders. That was too much of a delay in that kind of investigation, and the detectives had complained about it. And it infuriated Baldwin to have Almond insist the police had the photos within hours or a day to show Fleer. The argument was an odd juxtaposition of two negatives: the lab didn't get the photographs developed in time for them to be used in what would have been poor police work by showing them to Fleer.

Almond also pushed Baldwin about Fleer's drug arrest. Hadn't Baldwin and the other detectives promised many of the witnesses in this case, including Fleer, that they would not be prosecuted on drug charges if they provided information about the murders? Baldwin had to explain several times that he had never made any such promise, especially to Fleer.

Almond wouldn't take no for an answer; after all, his client insisted he had been sandbagged by the cops on the drug charge. "Isn't it a fact that you told Eugene Fleer that if he would tell the truth, you would make sure that he was not charged with cocaine? Did you tell him that?"

Baldwin took a deep breath as he repeated, "No, sir, I did not tell him that."

"And then after you told him that, he told you the truth, didn't he?"

Baldwin had to restrain himself as he glared at the defense attorney and said slowly and deliberately, "I did not tell him that, sir." As Baldwin left the stand, he felt the need of a shower.

McElroy called Tim McEntee, now a lieutenant, to provide more details about Fleer's lies. Captain John O'Rando had sent McEntee to interview Fleer after it became clear he was lying about too many of his activities to allow an innocent construction. But Brady and Almond called for a private conference at the judge's bench as McEntee described advising Fleer of his rights. The defense did not want the detective repeating Fleer's comment that he would not sign the waiver because experience had taught him that he had a better chance of "beating the rap" that way. That came too close to exposing his record of criminal convictions, a clear violation of guidelines on testimony. Appelbaum and McElroy argued that McEntee could repeat the comment as long as there was no specific reference to previous prison sentences. Judge Conley looked intensely at the attorneys and cautioned, "Let's not mistry this case at this point."

That thought made Appelbaum shudder. He asked if the defense would stipulate that Fleer refused to sign the waiver. Conley looked directly at Appelbaum and said, "Stop and think about that, John." McElroy shook his head and decided to err on the side of caution; no one wanted to slide into a disaster over this issue. "That's okay," he said. He hopscotched over the land mine by asking McEntee what had happened after Fleer was read his rights.

McEntee was only too glad to describe how Fleer admitted lying when he claimed he had been at home the morning of the murders. When confronted with the information from Sandy Barton, Fleer admitted he had been at Howlett's apartment all night after a cocaine-snorting party. McEntee also told the jury that Fleer's memory had been detailed and descriptive for the hours and days after the murders, but rather hazy and tentative, and even nonexistent in some cases, when it came to what had happened in the hours just before and after the children were killed. Appelbaum hoped the jury recognized such memory lapses as glaring evidence of guilt; it should be obvious that Fleer's recall was poor because he was making up lies to cover the time when he was committing a double murder.

The burly lieutenant also recounted Fleer's eager and full cooperation on the drug possession charge, even telling them where to find the cocaine he had hidden in the refrigerator panel and showing them where he had thrown the bottle of baby laxative powder used to cut the coke. McEntee enjoyed repeating Fleer's strange comment, "I'm not a baby-killer. I'm a cocaine dealer." And Appelbaum loved it when McEntee described Fleer's demeanor: "Hard as nails."

Almond tried to attack Myrick's testimony through McEntee, getting him to remember that Myrick had said he'd seen the man enter Mari's building about nine o'clock and that the man was six feet tall, weighed about two hundred pounds, and was in his late teens to early twenties. But McEntee also remembered that Myrick had told him he had written down some of the details incorrectly. McEntee had turned the sheet over and noted the correct description on the back—age in the twenties and wearing a speckled T-shirt. Just as Myrick had said, Appelbaum thought.

Tim McEntee stepped off the stand and took a seat in the courtroom near Mari and Jude. He shook his head, however, as he noticed something new in Jude's appearance. He had not seen her since she pierced her left nostril and added a gold ring. He had to chuckle; Jude certainly was her own woman, he thought. Appelbaum had asked Jude to leave the diamond stud or gold ring at home, but Jude rejected suggestions that she become someone else for the trial. This was about the kids and Fleer, and anyone who would let her pierced nose influence the outcome of this case shouldn't be involved.

McEntee was on vacation, but had decided to spend his time watching the rest of the trial. From the day he began investigating these murders, the case had never left him. The candle never got blown out on this one. He was certain Fleer was the killer, but was unsure why he had gone to the apartment. Maybe it was for drugs, as Appelbaum said. Maybe it was for sex, as the defense theorized. Maybe it even had started as an innocent visit to the family he had just met a couple nights before. But something had sent him there, something had pushed him over the edge once he was there, and something had made him kill those kids. Even if McEntee never learned exactly what that something was, he still wanted to be there when the end was written to this case. He remembered looking at the kids' pictures on the wall during the Major Case Squad investigation. He had worked for the kids in those pictures and he would be here for them when the verdict came in.

CHAPTER 18

The parade of witnesses John Appelbaum hoped really would sink Eugene Fleer was about to begin, and the prosecutor was anxious to see how they played in front of the jury. They had been a tough group to handle. Some of them flip-flopped between the prosecution and the defense, apparently unsure which side of the fence was right. They knew Fleer and didn't want to go against him in court. But they also had crucial testimony they knew they had to give.

The first one called Tuesday afternoon epitomized those difficulties. Jim Main—Fleer's friend, whose face carried the scars from a terrible motorcycle accident he had just survived—had vacillated between cooperation and reluctance. He rotated calls and loyalties among Appelbaum, Almond, and Fleer, and Appelbaum had to work continuously to keep him on track. Main even had taped several conversations with Fleer, but they had provided no useful information. If Main testified as Appelbaum hoped, however, he would offer great insight into Fleer, his friends, and his activities after the murders.

Appelbaum started Main's testimony with Lester Howlett's tearful performance the day after the murders as he sat on the floor of a garage owned by Fleer's friend Henry Garcia. Too bad, Appelbaum thought, that hearsay rules prevented Main from quoting Howlett's promise never to do drugs or alcohol again because he had let down Steve Winzen. But the jury had heard that from Marsha Brady's opening statement. At least the episode portrayed Howlett as remorseful enough to be ready to go to the police with his incriminating knowledge about Fleer's guilt.

And Main had more direct information for the jury about Fleer, too. During the two months Fleer stayed with Main after the murders, Fleer had engaged in detailed discussions about the crime that Appelbaum prayed the jury would see as Fleer's bragging about his clever plan. Fleer had told Main the kids had been murdered over a drug deal that had gone sour. The killer had known Steven Winzen was in Vegas. Tyler had been wearing pajamas when he was murdered. Stacy had been watching television. The victims had known the killer and let him in; there had been no forced entry. Stacy had been beaten so badly that the esophagus in her neck was destroyed. The killer had used hot water to wash off fingerprints, impressions, evidence like that. He must have stayed in the apartment a while to clean up, because there hadn't been any physical evidence. The Major Case Squad had shown him photos of the crime scene.

And then came the commentary that Appelbaum really wanted the jury to hear. Main remembered Fleer saying, "Whoever killed these kids must have killed them with their bare hands, placed them in a bathtub, and run scalding water over them." Fleer had said the same thing to several people, always in the same words, in the same order, in the same way. They were Fleer's version of his homicidal actions. They were part of his coded confession; he was describing what he had done but attributing it to some faceless killer.

Appelbaum also steered Main through an account of an odd, frightening incident about six weeks after Fleer moved in. While Main was in the shower, Fleer had managed to get through the locked door, and had reached through the curtain, grabbed at him, and then laughed. Appelbaum interpreted that as a threat to Main: don't tell anyone what I said because I can reach out and get you, too.

On cross, Almond brought out Main's indecision about his friend and had Main confirm going to Almond's office to ask if there was any way to help Geno. "If he's innocent, I wanted to see him innocent. If he's guilty, I wanted to see him pay," Main explained. Appelbaum's objections kept Almond from asking if Main had said he thought Fleer was innocent. But Almond hoped the jury would see how unreliable the prosecution's witnesses were.

Almond also had Main recall an arrest on a marijuana charge just after he had become annoyed at the prosecutors and threatened to stop cooperating with them. He denied the marijuana was his and said he thought it had been planted. And Almond seemed pleased as Main confirmed that he had made a deal with the prosecutors—dismissal of the charge in return for his continued cooperation.

Appelbaum thought it should be easy to deal with the defense's troubling suggestion that Main had lied to get a deal. Had his story about Fleer's comments changed after Main was arrested? No. When had Fleer said hot water took impressions and fingerprints off skin? When he lived with Main right after the murders, years before Main's arrest. Okay, Appelbaum thought, those were the only points that really mattered.

The next witness buttressed Jim Main's testimony and then expanded on it with additional and important details. Carol Thompson had met Fleer while he was living with Main and had spent a year after that as Fleer's girlfriend. Fleer had attributed the murders to a drug deal that had gone bad. He and Howlett had gone to Illinois to buy cocaine, but had realized when they returned that something was wrong with the product. They had tried to contact Steve Winzen because he had made the connection in Illinois, but they couldn't find him. Fleer had not offered speculation on the identity of the killer.

But Carol Thompson quoted Fleer as saying Howlett had died while they were cutting the stuff, making one pile of pure cocaine and one pile that was diluted. Fleer claimed he had made a trip to the store for drinks and found Howlett dead when he returned. "His theory of it was that the piles of cocaine were switched and Lester hit the wrong pile," Thompson said. More support for Fleer as Howlett's killer, the prosecutor hoped.

Marsha Brady handled the cross. Wasn't it true that all Fleer had said was that it was his theory that the kids had been killed because "someone" had had a bad drug deal in Illinois? No, Geno had said he and Howlett had had the bad deal, Thompson insisted. Brady read from a transcript of a taped interview between Thompson and the police, who asked, "Did Fleer say somebody or did he say the killer?"

"He said somebody. He said somebody went to Illinois to do a drug deal."

"That's who killed the kids? Just somebody?"

"Yes."

Brady wanted to play the tape for the jury, but Appelbaum stipulated that Thompson had indeed quoted Fleer as saying "somebody." Thompson explained that the police had never asked her if Fleer had been referring to himself. She insisted now that Fleer had named himself and Howlett as the "somebodies" who had had the bad drug deal. Appelbaum hoped that would convince the jury.

But Brady also asked Thompson to describe what had happened after Fleer was paroled on the drug charge. They had dated in Columbia and she had let him baby-sit her seven-year-old daughter while she worked on Saturday mornings; she hadn't worried about leaving her child with Fleer, even after what he had told her. Did that seem logical if she knew Fleer had killed the kids in Jefferson County?

On redirect, Appelbaum prodded Thompson's memory of Fleer's comments about the use of hot water. They had been watching a movie, she said, where a body was put in a bathtub. That had prodded her to ask why scalding water would be used on the bodies of people who were already dead. He had explained that the water would take off fingerprints.

Appelbaum had one more round of questions.

"You indicated on cross-examination that when you were in Columbia you left your daughter with Fleer and he treated her very well. Is that correct?"

"Yes."

"You never ripped him off for drugs, did you?"

"No."

Appelbaum wanted the jurors to understand that Fleer was dangerous only to people who messed with his business and that they shouldn't expect their ideas about what was normal to apply to drug dealers.

Fleer's "theorizing" about the murders was recalled by the next witness, too. Tom Hudson, with whom Fleer had lived for about three weeks before he went to prison in late 1986, quoted his guest as saying he thought the murders were repercussions from a drug rip-off in Illinois. Fleer had said he had been questioned by the police and they had shown him photos of the crime scene, Hudson remembered, and Fleer had called the use of hot water to remove fingerprints and other evidence proof that the murders were "a professionally done job." Appelbaum thought it was obvious; Fleer was bragging.

Hudson agreed with Almond that all of that was just talk. "It wasn't that he told me this for sure. It was just in theory."

Hudson left the witness stand at seven-thirty Tuesday evening, and Judge Conley recessed court for the day— after twenty witnesses and more than ten hours of testimony.

Mari and Jude could hardly believe what was happening. After all the delays, the trial was blowing by faster than they could comprehend. They thought the witnesses sounded pretty convincing. But Jude and Mari had been watching one juror, an older man in the back row, who seemed to be having a lot of trouble staying awake. "The narcoleptic juror," they dubbed him. They were getting angrier by the minute, worrying that his dozing could cause another mistrial.

Appelbaum was fairly happy with the way the case was playing out from the stand, and he could only hope the jurors weren't getting lost in the jumble of witnesses and stories coming at them so fast. He worried, however, that the jurors were being influenced by the defense's persistent attacks on the witnesses from Fleer's circle of friends and the many suggestions that prosecutors were manipulating them. That defense tactic always bothered him, and he wondered how jurors reacted to it.

At 9:05 A.M. on Wednesday, Pete Wendler took the stand and told the same stories his wife had told about Fleer's description of the murders hours after they happened and his bizarre visit to their trailer the night Howlett died. Fleer had asked him to lie to the police and say they had been together when they found Howlett's body. Wendler agreed; after all, they were longtime friends. They went back to Fleer's trailer, hid the cocaine, called the police, and lied. But Wendler later told the truth; he had no reason to lie now.

Almond stung Wendler on a recurring weakness among the prosecution witnesses. Hadn't Wendler plea-bargained an armed robbery charge down to theft? Yes. Hadn't the

Wendlers been using drugs in August 1986? Yes. Hadn't they both been afraid they would be charged in the deaths of Howlett or the children? Yes. The police had even implied they might charge Pete with the murders, hadn't they? Uh-huh. And then he told the truth? Yes. More testimony bought and paid for, Almond thought.

Appelbaum was not terribly bothered by all of that. He would put Wendler's testimony into perspective later when the jurors heard about Fleer's encounter with the maintenance man at the apartment complex, Bob Lutz. But all of that was part of another facet of Appelbaum's strategy and the jurors would have to wait.

The next witness started a new chapter. William G. Smith was the first of several who would testify about Fleer's comments behind bars. Smith had been in the Jefferson County Jail with Fleer in 1986 when he claimed he was getting a bum rap. Later Fleer had said he was in for the murders of two kids in a bathtub—a little boy and a baby-sitter. His partner had "OD'd" on drugs. "He said he was kind of glad in a way because it took the heat off of him," Smith remembered. But Fleer still was nervous because he had given the police a pubic hair sample. "He said he shouldn't have done it. He kept pacing the floor. Said he shouldn't have done it. He said they will pin it on him now, is what he said."

Almond went for the jugular with the first question. "Mr. Smith, are you related to a very famous Smith?"

Appelbaum was expecting that and was ready with an objection. There was no relevancy to Smith's relatives, he said; the judge agreed. Almond would not get to identify the witness as the brother of Gerald Smith, a murderer who had been executed more than eighteen months earlier for using an iron bar to bludgeon the girlfriend he said had given him a venereal disease. Gerald even had earned a second death sentence for killing a fellow death-row resident.

Almond's attempt to smear William's credibility with his brother's record had one unexpected consequence: William Smith's wife fled the courtroom in tears. Jude felt a pang of sympathy for the woman and started to go after her, perhaps to offer some bit of comfort. But she held back; it might not look right for the victim's mother to console the wife of a man whose brother had been executed for murder. What a tangled web, Jude thought, and there wasn't room in this system to be a human being.

Almond turned the attack on William Smith's record, dragging it out in agonizing detail while suggesting he had received a sweet deal for testifying against Fleer. The maze of charges in St. Louis, St. Louis County, and Jefferson County included resisting arrest, carrying a concealed weapon, violating parole, and a long list of drunk driving counts. Theft and assault charges had been dismissed. Almond had Smith describe the cell where the conversation took place, but cross-examination ended without getting into the essence of Smith's memory.

Witness number 25 was David Wayne Powers, the former convict whose story about cocaine hidden at Mari's apartment had sent her to Steve Winzen's trailer in a flaming rage. Now Powers could tell the jurors about buying cocaine from Fleer, the first time they had heard Fleer linked directly to coke deals in a case that hinged on stories about bad coke deals. Powers related Fleer's theory that the kids were killed in retaliation for a "bad drug deal and drug rip-offs." He said the cocaine he had turned over to the police after the murders had come from Mari's apartment. Fleer had said the children had been sexually molested, bound, tied, and put in scalding water.

Appelbaum asked, "Did he ever indicate anything about the evidence in this case?"

"That there was no evidence."

"And why was that?"

Even from Powers, the answer sounded hideously ominous. "Everybody was dead."

Almond leaped upon Powers's record—four armed robberies and two armed criminal actions. Hadn't he talked to prosecutors from prison in return for a plea bargain and an early release? Bill Johnson had written a letter to the parole board that did no good; Powers's minimum sentence was fifty-two months and he had served fifty-nine.

Appelbaum had a few more questions he thought might give the jurors something to think about when it came to testimony from jailhouse snitches, as some in the media so loved to call them.

"Mr. Powers, what's it like in prison after you talk to authorities or testify in court?"

"You're a snitch."

"And what happens to snitches?"

"A lot of things. You can get killed. You can get beat up. Nobody will talk to you; that kind of thing. Your things will get stolen. Your locker will get broken into."

"It is not something that prisoners want to do, is it?"

"No."

Detective Rich Harris made a quick trip to the witness stand to recall Fleer's comment when he was arrested in 1989 for the murders. "He knew it was only a matter of time before we came after him." It was not the kind of thing an innocent man said; it carried a "consciousness of guilt" that Appelbaum was sure the jurors could grasp.

And then he put on his last, and he thought perhaps his most powerful, witness. Ronald Eugene Boyer, Jr., a slim young man serving forty-two years in prison for robbing Domino's Pizza stores, took the stand to tell what he had heard Fleer say in the Jefferson County Jail in August 1989. Boyer had been using the toilet when he heard Fleer and another inmate talking in a cell fifteen feet away. Powers had seen Fleer through the bars as he was asked if he was guilty.

"And what did Mr. Fleer respond?" Appelbaum asked.

"He responded with, 'Yes, yeah.' "

Had he heard Fleer say anything during a telephone conversation later? "More or less, just that he would get out of this any way he could."

There it was—an honest, simple, straightforward, sincere story without embellishment or exaggeration. Appelbaum had believed Ronald Boyer even before he passed a polygraph on Fleer's comments.

Almond stuck to his plan of attack against such witnesses, pointing out that Boyer had six felony convictions and a release date in the year 2033. Wasn't he looking for any break on his sentence that he could get? "I guess you could say that," Boyer agreed.

But then Almond turned up the heat. Wasn't Boyer more worried about serving time than most prisoners because he had some problems when he was in the St. Louis County Jail?

"I did at one time," Boyer said cautiously.

"Mr. Boyer, you were raped in the St. Louis County Jail, isn't that true?"

Jude and Mari gasped, and Appelbaum registered his objection on relevancy grounds. Almond shot back that Boyer's fear of being in prison was relevant. Judge Conley overruled the objection.

"Is it true or isn't it?"

"Yeah," Boyer said as he began to cry.

"And you were hurt pretty bad up there, weren't you?"

"Yeah."

"Now, you're actually having some mental problems, too, aren't you, Mr. Boyer?"

Appelbaum's objection was overruled again.

"You're having some mental problems, too, aren't you?" Almond demanded again.

"When, when?"

"How many times have you attempted suicide, Mr. Boyer?"

Boyer's hands covered his face as he cried; in the audience, Jude dissolved into tears, too.

This time, Appelbaum's objection was sustained. "Let's proceed," Conley said tersely.

Jude and Mari were furious as they watched Boyer suffer humiliation such as they had never seen another human being endure. Jude had never seen anyone treated so cruelly. How devastating it must have been to admit being raped by other men and to have that bandied about publicly as punishment for telling the truth. Surely this man was being truthful. Why else would he subject himself to such humiliation?

Appelbaum could not believe what he had just seen happen in a court of law. Almond's abuse of Boyer had been vile, unconscionable, and dehumanizing, and Appelbaum was ashamed to have witnessed it.

But to Almond, Boyer had placed himself in harm's way with false testimony intended to buy a sentence reduction. And Almond was not done yet; he returned to the attack. Hadn't Boyer been seeking assignment to the protective-custody section in the prison? Not at the Jefferson City

Correctional Center, where he was serving his time now; he had sought it at other prisons, but not recently. Wouldn't it be easier to get protective custody—PC, they called it—if he was a snitch and in danger in the general population? Yes, but Boyer insisted he didn't want PC now; conditions there were actually worse than in the general population.

Almond kept up the barrage. Boyer had heard Fleer confess in 1989, but had waited to go to prosecutors until just weeks before the trial. "Now, are you coming forward because you just wanted to be a good citizen? Is that right?"

"A little more than that," Boyer said firmly. "I've had to live with this two years, knowing what I heard, and it kind of eats you alive, at times, inside."

Boyer's sincerity rang through, but Appelbaum wondered if the prisoner's account of Fleer's confession had been weakened by Almond's merciless assault.

The time had come for a momentous announcement, and John Appelbaum stepped before the bench. "At this time, your honor, ladies and gentlemen of the jury, the State of Missouri rests."

Boyer's testimony had not come off as the dynamic end to the prosecution's case that Appelbaum had planned. But on the whole, he thought the evidence had sounded good from the stand, perhaps better than he really had expected. And no matter what happened next, at least Appelbaum had won the right to put this case to a jury. Now everyone knew there was a valid evidence to support the charges that Eugene Fleer had murdered these children. This case was not filed to appease two women, and now everyone would know that. He had accomplished that much and had kept his vow to two children and their mothers.

In the audience, Mari and Jude squeezed each other's hand. The evidence was in, and, even allowing for their enormous prejudice against Eugene Fleer, it seemed enough to convict him if they were sitting on the jury. But what had those twelve people heard? How effective had Almond's relentless tactics been? Neither woman was confident about the jurors, and they were worried about the defense case yet to come.

Appelbaum also was expecting something dramatic; surely Almond and Brady would put on quite a show. There had been some hints: the defense's preoccupation with the timing of the events that morning; the attacks on Myrick's identification of Fleer; the repeated strafing of prosecution witnesses with checkered pasts; the bold insistence that Howlett was the killer. Appelbaum still had a couple of tactics tucked away himself, but he was more than a little worried about what this pair of defenders had up their sleeves.

CHAPTER 19

Calling a detective from the Major Case Squad as the first witness in defense of Eugene Fleer was a pretty slick move. The jury had to appreciate the irony even if it was just a gesture. But Detective Tom Brennan actually had information that could be essential to Clint Almond's strategy. The detective was there to offer a significantly different account of what Neil Myrick claimed to have seen. According to the original report Brennan had written and was using to refresh his memory on the witness stand, Myrick had seen a six-foot, 180-to-200 pound man in his late teens or early twenties, wearing a blue T-shirt. The man was only walking *past* Mari's apartment building.

"And do you recall what Mr. Myrick said about whether or not the gentleman he saw went into and then came out of the building at 200 Stillbrook?" Marsha Brady asked.

"He said he saw him walking south toward 190 Stillbrook, that he thought he had come out of 200. He didn't see him come out of 200."

"Did he indicate whether or not he was even sure?"

"He was not real sure."

What time? Nine o'clock.

"He didn't tell you nine-thirty or quarter till ten?"

"No, ma'am. Nine o'clock."

Had he described a jogger with a towel around his neck? No.

Appelbaum had some serious reconstruction to do if he was going to save Myrick's testimony, and there was only one way to do that. Did Brennan's memory of Myrick's description rely solely on the report he had just read? Yes. How had the report been written? By Brennan with notes taken by either him or Tim McEntee. Still have the notes? No, they probably were destroyed.

"Have you been able to find those notes and look them over and see if there were any corrections made on the back?"

"No, sir."

Jude shook her head. Another screwup that shouldn't have happened in a case that could have been solved sooner. If only those corrections had been preserved, noted, and compared to Fleer.

Appelbaum hoped he had erased any concern over the missed details, so he switched gears. Had Brennan shown Fleer any photographs or given him any details of the murders while he was being interviewed? "No, we wouldn't give him any specific details." Once again, Appelbaum had been able to make a crucial point through a defense witness.

The second one up for the defense was another man Mari and Jude had grown to despise. Mark Gerber—the good-looking man with black hair and almost hypnotic blue eyes—had tried to play them for fools, pretending to help them look for the killer during those dark days before Fleer was arrested. Gerber had introduced himself to Jude at the second memorial service for Stacy, and the women had wanted desperately to trust him. He had been friends with Fleer, Howlett, and Steve Winzen, and that meant he knew ways to get information about them and their activities. He seemed anxious to help solve the murders, so they traded tips with him, hoping his entree into those circles would lead to that elusive bit of incriminating evidence. And then they learned that Gerber had been taking what the women told him back to Clint Almond, who happened to be his own attorney.

Almond employed a touch of showmanship by having Fleer walk to the witness stand and pose so Gerber could size him up. "Does he look any different as far as weight is concerned than he did when you knew him back in 1986?"

"No, not really."

"And has he shrunk any?"

"No."

"Has he gained any weight?"

"No."

"Now, in 1986, did he have a mustache?"

"No, he did not."

How had Gerber known Lester Howlett? They had dealt marijuana and cocaine together. Was Fleer a dealer? No, he just used drugs. Where did Gerber and Howlett get their marijuana? From Steve Winzen.

Then Almond moved to the essence of Gerber's testimony. With how many people had Gerber discussed the murders in the week after they happened? Seven or eight. Did they know about a torn screen? Yes, Steve Winzen had mentioned that and the scalding water; a lot of people were talking about those murders.

Almond then had the witness turn his guns toward Appelbaum. Gerber had been on probation when Appelbaum interviewed him and the prosecutor had mentioned that he personally handled probation revocations to send violators back to prison. Almond was boring in again on his complaints of witness manipulation.

What tripe, Appelbaum fumed; he objected on hearsay and relevance grounds. Almond argued that he should be able to present evidence of prosecutorial misconduct. The judge sniffed, "Well, if it's a matter of misconduct, there's a commission you make a report to. The objection will be sustained."

Rebuffed, Almond ended his questioning and Appelbaum jumped in. Did Gerber know anything about drug rip-offs around the time of the murders? Yes. Was Dave Helmond one of the dealers ripped off? Yes. Had Gerber been in Howlett's apartment the night before the Helmond rip-off? Yes. When he awoke from sleeping, had he seen Howlett pass something to Fleer, who stuck the object in his pants? Yes. What was the object? Gerber assumed it was a gun.

"How well did you know Howlett and Fleer?"

"I had known them pretty well."

"Did you ever confuse them?"

"No."

"They looked a lot different, didn't they?"

"Yes."

"You pled guilty to several stealing counts?"

"Yes."

"And your attorney was Mr. Almond?"

"Yes."

Appelbaum loved cross-examining guys like Gerber.

*   *   *

After lunch, Marsha Brady made another offer of proof on testimony that the Major Case Squad had lied to Fleer about the results of his polygraph. Although testimony about polygraphs was barred at trial, Brady believe the fact that the police had lied about the results should be admitted. Those lies had caused Fleer to talk about the case incessantly, part of the conduct the state called incriminating. Brady called Officer Dennis McGuire to recall administering the test to Fleer and concluding that he was truthful. On cross-examination, George McElroy had McGuire agree that experts might differ on the result of a test. Would it surprise McGuire to learn that one of his colleagues, whom McGuire said had an excellent reputation, had disagreed with McGuire's conclusion? Yes, it would. Would a sociopath be more likely to lie and still pass a polygraph than a normal person? Yes, sir.

The judge refused Brady's request; no polygraph evidence.

After Brady questioned the woman from the apartment complex who saw the torn screen on Mari's window that morning, Clint Almond called the name that made John Appelbaum's day: Bob Lutz. Appelbaum had taken a calculated risk by not using the maintenance man as a prosecution witness, gambling that the defense would have to call him, and that would give Appelbaum much more freedom when he questioned Lutz on cross-examination. A good chess move like that was part of the joy of litigation, especially if it worked.

Lutz said he had talked to ten or fifteen people in the complex by the end of that day and had heard some of them talking about the cut screen and scalding water. But Appelbaum's hearsay objections stymied Almond's attempts to elicit more about the gossip. At a sidebar conference, Almond insisted that Lutz should be allowed to relate what details were circulating freely that day. After all, he said, the prosecution's case rested mostly on Fleer's knowledge of those tidbits. But Appelbaum had been waiting for that argument. Fleer had not been around the apartment complex that afternoon, and Lutz's testimony proved that. What the residents might or might not have discussed was irrelevant to what Fleer knew, and that was the crucial test of Fleer's guilt. The judge agreed; Almond was looking for hearsay testimony beyond the details of the screen and the scalding water, and it would not be permitted. Appelbaum tightened his fist; that ruling was a major victory, and it justified his chancy decision to play Lutz as a defense witness.

Almond pushed ahead, having Lutz describe running into Fleer at the complex about noon and discussing the murders. Lutz told how he had visited Howlett right after the murders were discovered and had seen Howlett injecting cocaine.

Appelbaum had eagerly anticipated this cross; it was a linchpin in his case. When and where had Lutz seen Fleer the morning of the murders? Sometime around noon or twelve-thirty outside Howlett's apartment. Then Appelbaum began a series of the simplest, but most crucial, questions he had ever asked on cross.

"And you told him that the children were killed? Is that right?"

"Yes."

"That's the only discussion you had with him?"

"Yes."

"You didn't know at that time that the screen was cut, did you?"

"No."

"You didn't know at that time that the kids were put in hot water, did you?"

"I didn't know for a fact, no."

"And you didn't discuss that with him, did you?"

"No."

"And in fact, he left the complex then, didn't he?"

"Yes."

"Got in his silver Granada and drove off, right?"

"Yes."

"Didn't stop and talk to anyone else."

"No."

"Didn't come back the rest of the day."

"Not that I saw."

"And the rest of the people that you talked to all were around that complex that afternoon. Isn't that right?"

"Yes."

"In fact, some of them probably walked around and saw the screen. Isn't that right?"

"Yes."

"So, the way they got their information was that they were all gathered at the scene talking. Isn't that right?"

"Yes."

"So you would have to have been on the scene to know those things. Isn't that right?"

"Yes."

There was the key to the state's case, and it had been delivered by a defense witness. Eugene Fleer hadn't learned the details about the screen and the scalding water, about the kids' clothes and their injuries, about anything at all by talking to other people. He had left the apartment complex without hearing any of that from Lutz or anyone else, and had gone directly to John Cass's house, where he told Cathy and Pete Wendler all about the cut screen and the scalding water. He hadn't been shown the pictures of the scene, because the cops hadn't even had the photos developed yet. So, how had he known these things? Because he had been there; he had done it.

Appelbaum's strategy with Bob Lutz had worked as well as he could have hoped. The defense had been forced to put him on the stand, and Appelbaum—given extra latitude on cross-examination—had been able to pose a series of leading questions that defined Fleer's knowledge of the crime: he knew because he was there.

Jude and Mari were thrilled, and Jude felt almost shocked by the testimony just provided by a defense witness. In the women's eyes, the cross-examination of Lutz had provided more than enough ammunition for the jury to blast Fleer with a conviction—if this jury was like the first jury. But the women were left wondering if Appelbaum's masterful touch would be appreciated by this panel.

In an attempt to tear the drug-dealer label off her client, Marsha Brady called Billy Schwartz to describe how he had bought cocaine once a month from Howlett, but never from Fleer. Schwartz had seen Howlett use cocaine and marijuana, but Appelbaum's objections kept Brady from getting an appraisal of Howlett's drug use. Schwartz needed a little help from Brady, but he remembered talking to Howlett on the phone the night of the murders; Howlett had quite a drug-induced buzz. Howlett asked him to make a trip to Illinois to buy cocaine the next day; Schwartz declined.

Appelbaum used a defense witness again to make an important point. Schwartz said Howlett was such an experienced cocaine user that it was unlikely he would make a mistake like overdosing. Surely the jurors could draw the incriminating inference from that. But Appelbaum's questions about Howlett's experience opened the door on redirect by Brady; she got to ask again how much Howlett was spending per day on his cocaine habit. "Probably two to three hundred dollars," Schwartz guessed.

Brady then called the woman who had helped police prepare a composite drawing of the man she had seen walk out of Mari's apartment building that morning. This could provide another suspect, and Appelbaum hated this kind of loose end. When Appelbaum turned to look at approaching witness Lisa Nelson, whom he had never seen before, he was startled. He quickly looked back at the document in his hands. This was too good. With a signal to McElroy, Appelbaum indicated he would handle cross-examination.

Lisa Nelson was the wife of a deputy sheriff and the sister-in-law of another officer. She had been driving by the apartments between nine-thirty and ten-thirty when she saw a young man with shoulder-length sandy blond hair come out of 200 Stillbrook. Brady handed her the composite she had helped the police put together; it was a good likeness of the man she had seen, she said.

As Appelbaum approached the witness, he looked hard at the composite drawing in his hands. He had been looking at it, thinking how effeminate the subject looked, when Lisa Nelson walked in.

"Would you agree that this composite has very effeminate features?" he asked the witness.

"Uh-huh."

"In fact, would you agree that, if you put glasses on it, that it would resemble you?"

"Uh-huh," she agreed readily.

In just a few questions, Appelbaum believed he had neutralized the composite and the suggestion of a blond killer. The drawing looked so much like the witness that it was uncanny. When she walked into the room, Appelbaum's

chin had dropped as he thought, It's her! He didn't mind
a bit as Brady had the composite circulated among the
jurors; let them see the resemblance.

The defense attorneys asked for a conference at the
judge's bench. They had two missing witnesses. Deputy
Speidel couldn't get free to testify, and no one could find
Steve Winzen, even though he had been subpoenaed. They
would learn later that Winzen was attending a St. Louis
Cardinals game at Busch Stadium—a businessman's special.
Steve wasn't about to be used as part of the defense for
Eugene Fleer. There had been no bad cocaine deal involving Steve, but he had decided to let the prosecution run
with that theory if it helped convict Fleer. Fleer was guilty
and should be convicted, and, as far as Steve was concerned, the theory used as the basis for the conviction was
irrelevant. Let them find me at Busch Stadium, he decided.

After some discussion among the attorneys, Appelbaum
agreed to stipulate that Speidel would have testified that
no one could have entered through the cut window screen
without disturbing the cobwebs he saw. No damage there,
Appelbaum thought.

The stipulation on Winzen's testimony was a little more
dangerous, but Appelbaum was willing to accept it. Marsha
Brady read for the jurors some comments Winzen had
made during the taped conversation with Fleer on August
22, 1986. Winzen rambled through some speculation about
what had happened at the apartment, and the defense
hoped that would suggest he had been the source of Fleer's
information about the scene. Winzen said Stacy had been
beaten, and he wondered if Tyler—still in his pajamas—
had awakened and interrupted her murder. Maybe the
killer was someone Tyler knew through his father, so Tyler
had to be eliminated as a witness. Appelbaum didn't think
the short passage was that effective.

It was three o'clock when the judge asked Brady to call
her next witness. She stood and announced, "Defense rests,
your honor."

Appelbaum and McElroy were shocked. They had been
sure there would be some grand surprise before Almond
and Brady finished, and Appelbaum certainly never would
have allowed his case to end on testimony as anticlimactic

as the composite drawing. Appelbaum had guessed that Fleer's felony record would keep him from testifying, but there still had been a chance the defense would go for broke by putting him on the stand. Appelbaum had looked forward to that; he even had consulted FBI experts for advice about cross-examining someone like Fleer. They suggested keeping him on the stand for about four hours so all the factors pressuring him—being drug-free and in jail for so long, and his intense hatred of Appelbaum— could cause him to break and reveal the ugly side of his personality to the jurors. Although Appelbaum would have loved to cross-examine Fleer, he would not quarrel with the decision to keep him off the stand. So much the better, he thought.

But there was something else to consider. John Appelbaum was not ready to make his closing argument. He had sat for three frustrating hours the night before with a pen and legal pad in his hands and had ended up with a blank page. His wife had brought him back to reality. "You know this case, John. You have lived it for three years. Just get up and talk to the jury." And with that moment about to arrive, that was what he would have to do.

Before closings began, however, Judge Conley had to make a record on a point that would be important if an appeal was needed later. With the jury on recess, the judge called Fleer before the bench to confirm his decision not to testify and to affirm that he was pleased with his attorneys' performance.

Just before four o'clock on Wednesday, October 2, John Appelbaum stepped before the jury for the last time. He held up the pictures of Stacy Price and Tyler Winzen that had been seen so often on television and in the newspapers.

"On August 7, 1986, Stacy Price and Tyler Winzen were living, breathing, dreaming children. On August 7, 1986, they fought for their lives, and they lost. Innocent children, who had neither the will, the desire, nor the power to harm anyone. Lives snuffed out by this man. Why? Drugs. Revenge."

He pointed directly and angrily at Eugene Michael Fleer. "That man's quest for revenge, his lust for the almighty high and the almighty dollar, cost them their beautiful lives.

His rage for revenge overpowered their ability to fight for their lives. Make no mistake, it is evil and evil alone that cost them their lives."

Appelbaum turned and set the children's pictures on an easel so the jurors could see them while they listened to closings. He then held up a picture of the bodies in the bathtub and called on the jurors not to look away from the graphic testimony and the descriptions of lifestyles that were so foreign to average people. The government was waging a war on drugs, a war that had cost two children their lives. "And you can do your part today," he said as he looked at each juror.

He asked them to imagine a scene. "This man—after he's killed those children—on his hands and knees in the bathroom, wiping the place clean, as their lifeless bodies— his prey—lie in their reservoir of death." Deliberate, cool reflection—as specified in the charges.

What about Marsha Brady's mouse-in-the-box image? "Folks, we have our box. The mouse is dead. The cat is in the box. We have turned the box over for the last three days and there is no hole in it. The defendant is guilty of two counts of the most brutal murders you will ever hear about. And how do we know that there's only one person on the face of this earth that could have caused this crime? Let's review the evidence."

Appelbaum began an intricate dissection of the facts, applying his theory of how the puzzle pieces fit together. When Neil Myrick saw Fleer jogging through the rain about nine-thirty, Fleer was casing Mari's apartment. He went into the building but came out quickly when he encountered two men leaving about that time. They drove away in a car that witnesses had seen parked there often, so they weren't suspects. Fleer then returned to carry out his grisly plan. He knew Steve Winzen was in Las Vegas, maybe even spending the money from the drug rip-off. And Mari's innocent request for a ride to class played into Fleer's hands perfectly, giving him access to her apartment key in case he needed it later. Howlett helped with the plot by calling Mari to confirm what time she left for work. And then, on a rainy day when the construction crews weren't around, Fleer made his move.

Appelbaum analyzed the timing. He estimated it would

take thirty or forty minutes to complete the horrific activities in the apartment, from about nine-thirty to ten-fifteen, when Racheal made her visit and heard the ominous "click" of the lock on the bathroom door. When Jude arrived later, the killer was gone. Just enough time for Fleer to go back to Howlett's and then be seen driving away at ten-forty by Sandy Barton. And remember her description of Fleer's appearance. "This egomaniac who wouldn't allow a hair out of place—his hair was all messed up. Looked like he had a horrible hangover, I believe, were her words."

The prosecutor's eyes narrowed. "The time is not only coincidental, it is succinct. It is perfect. It is the truth."

Fleer went home to shower, shave, and set up his alibi. He went back to the apartments about twelve-thirty and ran into Bob Lutz. And that was where his plan fell apart. Lutz gave him none of the details Fleer was passing on to his friends less than an hour later.

What about Lester Howlett and his breakdown during the police interview? Why had he died before he could return to be questioned again on Sunday morning? "We know why. Because if he had, Geno Fleer would have been arrested then for the murders and not two and a half years later."

Appelbaum recalled the trip to Rockford, Illinois, for cocaine the night after the murders. The men were cutting it at Fleer's trailer Saturday night, and that gave the opportunistic Fleer the chance to solve his problem with the nervous Howlett. Just switch the piles of cut and pure coke, and Howlett's threat to Fleer was over. Among Fleer's obvious lies and schemes was the drafting of Pete Wendler as an alibi, except that Wendler later told the truth.

Were the murders really drug-related? Appelbaum held up Lester Howlett's telephone bills for July and August 1986 and ran down the list. Twenty-six calls to Rockford between July 16 and August 7. And then, on the morning of the murders, calls to Rockford at 5:46 A.M. and 5:38 P.M. "Does that sound like just calling a long-lost friend?"

And when Fleer went into Pete Wendler's bedroom the night Howlett died, where did he call? Rockford, Illinois.

What about the cocaine itself? More evidence linking Fleer to Mari Kane's apartment. David Powers testified that Fleer said he and Howlett got cocaine out of the apartment; that was the ounce Fleer turned over to the police. The ounce Howlett and Fleer bought in Rockford the night after the murders was hidden under the trailer next to Pete Wendler's. Two ounces—one from Rockford and one from the murder scene.

Fleer had virtually confessed during his conversations with his friends. All of those details. He even assumed Stacy's esophagus was broken, since he knew how much pressure he had used when he strangled her. He knew hot water was used to wash off fingerprints, and he was right; it worked. He talked about drug rip-offs and said the murders were in retaliation. He told Carol Thompson the killer probably thought Steve Winzen was in on the rip-off and was in Vegas spending the proceeds.

And what about that comment to Jim Main? The killer murdered the kids with his bare hands, put them in the bathtub, and ran scalding water over them. That could be just a description gleaned from newspaper accounts. But it also was exactly the correct order, as described by the medical examiner. The kids were not drowned in hot water. After they were drowned in cooler water and while Fleer cleaned up the room, he ran the hot water over them to destroy evidence. "He didn't just tell you what he heard on the streets. He told you subconsciously exactly the order that these children were murdered."

Appelbaum took a deep breath. "Now, it would have been nice if we could have brought in twelve Jesuit priests to say that they heard Fleer make statements. But, ladies and gentlemen, this kind of man doesn't hang around with Jesuit priests. He hangs around with Dave Powers, William Smith, Tom Hudson, Jim Main, and, yes, Ron Boyer. We play with the cards we're dealt. And in this case, we've got a winning hand."

Those witnesses had come forward because they knew the truth and couldn't live with the secret of those children's murders. Even prison inmates didn't want that on their consciences, and Dave Powers was willing to risk wearing a "snitch" label in prison to tell the truth. He and the others stepped forward, although the way they were treated in court would make it understandable if they kept quiet. "The way Mr. Boyer was treated in this courtroom was atrocious. And you should be appalled that kind of behavior had to happen in front of you."

It was time to close. "Tyler and Stacy gave up fighting for their lives that Thursday morning. But they're still looking to you for justice, crying out for what they know in their spirits to be right."

In the audience, Mari and Jude found even more tears to cry for their children.

"And they will not rest until justice is served. It has been a long, turbulent five years. You need to give them some rest. Give them their justice. Convict Eugene Fleer of these brutal murders and let justice be done."

As Appelbaum sat down, he felt years of tension melt away. Every ounce of energy drained from his body was replaced by a new exhaustion. But it felt terrific. He had wondered what he would say, but the argument had poured from him as if he were on autopilot. His heart and mind had taken over, and he had felt as if he almost were able to observe himself in action. He thought the jurors had responded well, even throwing the occasional glare at Fleer. John worried that there had not been much of the kind of emotional reaction he had seen from jurors in other cases. But now, for John Appelbaum, the long battle was over. He had done all he could, and the final answer now lay in someone else's hands.

The mothers felt something similar to that, too. John Appelbaum, their hero, had touched them again in a way no one else had as he argued on behalf of their children. He made Stacy and Tyler real again. The kids weren't just names, victims, toddler or baby-sitter, statistics or autopsied evidence. They had been special little people with wonderful lives ahead of them, and now with family left behind to mourn them forever.

Marsha Brady had to diffuse the emotional plea made by Appelbaum and jolt the jurors back to hard reality. She reminded them that this was not *L.A. Law* or *Perry Mason* or *Murder, She Wrote*. The defense attorneys could not beat a confession out of the real killer at the last minute. The reality was that the jurors could not convict Eugene Fleer on circumstantial evidence unless it was inconsistent with any reasonable theory of innocence. And there were many reasonable theories of innocence here. What about the man Lisa Nelson saw coming out of the building? He had long blond hair, and the state's evidence expert had testified that there was an unmatched long blond hair found on Tyler's thigh.

What about the motive suggested by prosecutors for these murders committed in broad daylight? Why would a vengeful drug dealer kill an innocent baby-sitter instead of Mari? "You want to get even with Steve, do it that way."

If Fleer let himself into that apartment with a key, while Stacy was on the couch, why didn't she scream? Surely she was nervous about the obscene calls that suggested someone was watching her. No, it was more likely that Lester Howlett knocked on the door and Stacy let him in. They may have sat and talked; there were cigarette butts in the ashtray that weren't tested, so no one knew whether they were Mari's, as she claimed. Brady noted that Mari emptied the ashtrays every night, so they surely had been put there the morning of the murders.

Brady offered her theory. Wasn't it reasonable that Lester had cut the screen while he was outside Mari's apartment early that morning, but abandoned his attempt to get in that way after he was seen by the county jailer? He went over to have sex with Stacy, as he had with the previous baby-sitter, Bobbi Turner. He hadn't intended to kill, but things went terribly wrong. He took her into the bathroom and forced her to her knees on the hard floor, explaining her bruises. The marks on his penis and the abrasions on her chin could have resulted from his attempt to force her to perform oral sex; she clenched her teeth and he rubbed against her braces. The state's expert had offered an opinion based only on photos; Dr. Johnson had examined Howlett and concluded the marks could have been from a human bite. If Stacy bit Howlett and he struck her, that could explain the injury to her head. If he had struck her in the mouth, that could explain his injured knuckles.

Was Lester drowning Stacy when Tyler wandered into the bathroom to empty his full bladder? Wasn't it reasonable that Lester, already in a panic, had grabbed Tyler and pushed him into the bathtub, too? Then Lester cleaned up the bathroom to remove his own blood from the genital injury. He went home and acted as if nothing had happened, to keep his overnight guest, Fleer, from becoming suspicious. Brady noted that Howlett's phone bill also showed a call at 10:37 A.M. to Leesburg, Missouri, where Howlett was known to be going later. That time was important because that was when Fleer got up and went home, seen by Sandy Barton as he drove away at 10:40 A.M.

Brady suggested that Howlett then returned to the apartment and ran scalding water over the bodies. That would explain why the water was still so hot when authorities arrived at 11:11 A.M. The water couldn't be that hot if it had been in the tub since ten-fifteen, when Racheal originally told police she heard the click. Howlett was the one who locked that bathroom door then, but he came back later to run the scalding water. Brady said Stacy's family had changed the times so they fit with the time Fleer was seen leaving.

"Ladies and gentlemen, we're very sympathetic toward the families of these children. It is a hard thing to lose a child for anybody, for any reason. But for no reason, it's even worse. But, ladies and gentlemen, we can't convict an innocent person. We can't take that chance just because the families think it will make them feel better. It won't bring the children back. It won't do justice to their memories to convict someone who's not guilty."

What about the prosecutors' speculation that Howlett was killed to keep him from cracking? First, there was not enough room in that little bathroom for two grown men to be involved in the murders. Second, the medical examiner said there was no evidence of a "hot shot." And third, why would Eugene Fleer silence Howlett by killing him in Fleer's own trailer, automatically focusing suspicion on himself? No, a remorseful Lester Howlett had overdosed, perhaps because he couldn't live with what he had done.

Brady referred to Jim Main's recollection of a weeping Howlett reading the newspaper and vowing never to do alcohol or drugs again because he had let Steven down. But an objection from McElroy was sustained by the judge, who ordered the comments stricken and disregarded by the jury; the judge had barred those comments during Main's testimony as hearsay.

Finally, Brady asked, where was the evidence that Fleer or Howlett ever had any grudge against Steve Winzen? The state hadn't found that evidence in five years because it wasn't there.

As Brady turned the floor over to her partner, Judge Conley called a brief recess, the first Appelbaum had ever seen during closing arguments. Appelbaum thought Brady had been fairly effective. She had hammered away mercilessly at Howlett, perhaps overselling the point. But she had presented a good argument for an alternative theory, and Appelbaum wondered if she had planted enough doubt in the jurors' minds to overcome the evidence he thought stacked up high against Fleer.

Mari and Jude weren't buying it, of course. They never had found enough evidence to consider Howlett the actual killer, although there was a chance he was an accomplice.

Clint Almond stepped before the jury at 5:24 P.M. to begin his remarks. "Now, we all know there is not one iota of physical evidence against defendant Eugene Fleer, not one iota. Now, as far as Mr. Howlett is concerned, there is physical evidence." But even that, Almond warned, was inconclusive. "I don't know who killed those children. I wish I did. From what I've seen in this court, I don't think anybody knows who killed those children."

Then Almond launched into a lengthy attack on the prosecutors and their prison witnesses. "McElroy did not pay these witnesses any money. He gave them something much more valuable, something much more precious. He's given them time off their sentences." McElroy's objection was overruled, and Almond dived even deeper into a tirade about the inmates. A ten-year-old wouldn't believe Boyer, the man with mental problems who attempted suicide three times. If his information about Fleer bothered his conscience so much, why did he wait three and a half years before reporting what he heard? Did the jurors want McElroy influencing the parole board to release Boyer so he could stick a gun in their faces and rob them next? The prosecutors had put out the word in the prisons, trolling for anyone who would come forward and testify against Fleer. Who could believe any of the inmates who came forward after that? Giving plea bargains to prisoners for that kind of testimony was the worst thing a prosecutor could do.

This won't work, Appelbaum was thinking. The jury

doesn't want to hear this. They want the defense to present evidence, not attack witnesses.

What about Neil Myrick? Almond continued. Who could believe him? He changed many parts of his story, from the times to the description of the man. He even added that the man was jogging in the rain. Obviously, Almond pronounced, Myrick was quite confused.

Using a blackboard, Almond began to chart the timing to show how the prosecution's witnesses had changed their stories on the times. For each element described by Racheal, Jude, and Rick, the defender assigned specific times. Thirty seconds for Rachel to run home after hearing the click. Thirty seconds for Jude to go to Mari's apartment. Another thirty seconds for Jude to double-check Mari's address. Thirty seconds to run back to get Rick. Thirty more for Rick to accompany Jude back across the street. Almond's final estimate was seven minutes. He subtracted that from the time Brenda Turner's call was received by the police—11:04 A.M.—and mistakenly ended up with 10:47 instead of 10:57. The fire chief found steaming water at 11:11, Almond continued, and it was unlikely that the water would have stayed that hot for thirty to forty minutes shown by the times on the blackboard.

Jude and Mari were looking at each other in bewilderment. Appelbaum was almost as perplexed as he dropped his chin into his hand and stared at Almond and his blackboard; he had to squelch a grin at the machinations underway before the jury.

Almond plugged on. If Fleer drove away at 10:40 A.M., then he had left Howlett's about 10:37. "He was long gone before this ever happened," Almond concluded.

Jude and Mari looked at each other again. "What?"

Almond insisted again that Jude, Racheal, and Rick had altered the times of their activities since their original statements to the police. Racheal at first said she went to Mari's apartment at 10:45 and Rick had said Jude awakened him at 11:00. Racheal had to be back up her time to 10:15 and Rick had to slide back to 10:40 or so to construct a time period that would put Fleer in the apartment before he was seen driving away. Even Myrick changed his time from 9:00 to 9:30. But the correct times had come from the officers

Almond said. Surely the jurors could see the prosecution's scheme to turn back the clock.

What about all of the drug accusations? Fiction; a way to smear Fleer in front of the jury. Appelbaum had spent five minutes talking about the murders and the rest of the time talking drugs, drugs, drugs, and what a terrible man Fleer was. "Now, you can say he sold cocaine and he had a ton and hauled it around in his eighteen-wheeler. He is not being tried for that, ladies and gentlemen. I know the prosecutor has tried him for it, but it is not right."

What about the idea of a revenge killing for a drug rip-off, a message to Steve Winzen? Where was the message? "Why would a drug dealer want to kill two beautiful children and then not even send a message? What good would it do him? It wouldn't do him any good."

Could the jurors imagine Jude Govreau picketing the detective division? Almond asked incredulously. These two women had kept up the publicity and the pressure with rewards and television interviews, and the police had gone looking for a goat. Almond asked the jurors to send the message that sacrificing a goat was not done in Jefferson County.

Demand physical evidence, he urged. There was none against Fleer, but look at the marks on Howlett; look at Howlett's presence outside the apartment building. Overlook concerns about Fleer's lifestyle and give him the constitutional right due everyone in this democracy. Find Fleer not guilty.

Prosecuting Attorney George McElroy rose slowly to deliver the state's rebuttal. After a long, dramatic pause, he surprised the courtroom with a booming voice, dripping in mocking sarcasm, as he drawled, "Let's blame the dead guy. That's what he would like for you do. Blame the dead guy. That takes the heat off everybody."

Jude and Mari were among the most startled people in the courtroom. McElroy's dynamic response to the defense argument was shockingly effective; it pulled everyone back to the real issue and away from the red herring named Lester Howlett.

Wouldn't that have been the easy thing to do? McElroy asked. That would have solved the problem for the police, for the families, for the prosecutors. "There's just one problem with that theory. The dead guy didn't do it." It wasn't the dead guy who cased the apartment, who stared at Tyler Winzen, who had Mari's keys, who made up half a dozen lies and alibis, who went into the building shortly before the murders and drove away minutes after Racheal heard the click, who told all of his friends so many details about the murders, whose partner was found dead under suspicious circumstances before he could talk to the police.

And McElroy added an unexpected factor as he pointed to Howlett's phone bill. At 10:26 A.M., when these murders were underway in Mari's apartment, the dead guy was in his apartment accepting a collect call from Las Vegas. Brady sprang to her feet to object and to claim that the call was listed in Las Vegas time, not St. Louis time. The judge overruled the objection.

What about the defense's incredible speculation about Howlett and a sex crime? Where was the evidence to support that? No residue of a rape. No clothing in disarray. The experts said Howlett's injury was not a bite mark and the abrasions on Stacy's face were consistent with pressure from a hand. Who could believe the theory about Lester committing the murders at seven-thirty or eight, and then going back more than two hours later to clean up? Ludicrous.

Why would Fleer use his own trailer to commit Howlett's murder? You use what you have. Fleer had Howlett and the cocaine together there the night before Howlett was going back to the police. He had to act then. A "hot shot" doesn't have to be applied with a needle, McElroy cautioned the jurors; somebody switched the cocaine piles.

Who knew where the long blond hair could have come from? Who knew how màny people went in and out of that building that day or who Lisa Nelson saw before she helped with the composite that looked like her mirror image?

What about Neil Myrick? He had no vendetta against Fleer; he was just a good citizen doing what was right. Who knew what details he had corrected in the officers' notes on the back of the report—times, clothing, size, age? But even errors in such details by a witness couldn't change the basic facts. And the important point was that Myrick identified Fleer three times—in the photo lineup, in the personal lineup, and in the courtroom.

A motive? Prosecutors aren't required to prove a motive, but the facts led to a reasonable conclusion. Fleer told Carol Thompson that Steve Winzen made the connection in Rockford and something was wrong with the cocaine. The murder of Tyler certainly sent a message to Mari, and McElroy was sure it got to Steve, too. "You bet he got the message; you bet he did." Don't try to look inside the criminal mind and find reason, he warned.

Why was there no physical evidence? Because Fleer cleaned it all up. Don't reward him with acquittal because he was smart enough to run hot water over the bodies. Don't speculate about a wild sex angle when Fleer provided the drug motive with his own words. Why did he talk about the murders so much? "People like this just can't keep quiet, and it is those confessions that made the difference. It's those confessions that begin to fall into place, that finally close the door. Put the puzzle together. We're asking for a verdict of guilty on both counts."

The mothers of Tyler Winzen and Stacy Price held their breath in the audience. That was it; at 6:29 P.M. on October 2, 1991, it finally was over. Everything they could do, the police could do, the prosecutors could do, the defense attorneys could do, the judge could do—all of that was done. Now it was up to that unknown quantity called the jury.

CHAPTER 20

The wait for a verdict in the darkened courthouse hallway
was eerie for everyone. Groups split off and staked out
their own turf. Mari and her large family were unable to
observe what some thought should have been a churchlike
quiet and often broke into boisterous conversation. They
coped with the pressure and anxiety that way, and it
seemed to help Mari keep from going crazy as she waited.
Jude and her small group gathered at the other end of the
hall, trying to find some insulation from the noise; the din
was getting on Jude's nerves. Eugene Fleer's family stayed
as far away as possible and kept quiet. They had been the
target of Mari's anger before, and they obviously wanted
to avoid that. But at one point, they offered to bring back
coffee and doughnuts for Jude's family. A gracious gesture
at such a strange time, Jude thought.

John Appelbaum, his wife, and the prosecutors' squad of
supporters had joined the mothers' contingents for dinner
at Munzert's Restaurant across the street from the courthouse. The mood was high, almost jubilant, in hopeful anticipation of a conviction. The groups had begun drifting
back about mid-evening to take up their positions.

The first note from the jurors had come quickly, barely
thirty minutes into their deliberations. At 7:03 P.M., they
asked for some of the exhibits, photographs, and an easel;
the judge complied. At 7:52 P.M., the second note arrived—
a request for the time frames from the prosecution and
defense for when Jude sent Racheal to the apartment, the
time when the Turners called the police, and Howlett's
phone bill. The bill was sent, but the judge explained there
was no document containing the times.

About mid-evening a squad of sheriff's deputies arrived;
Buck Buerger's life had been threatened and security was

being beefed up, the word was. Mari's brother had a disagreement with the police and was escorted out of the
building. The tension was growing for everyone.

Mari and Jude began to get even more uneasy as the
hours ticked by. John Appelbaum tried to reassure them.
He was confident of a conviction by midnight; deliberations
of five to six hours in this case were just about right. When
twelve o'clock arrived and there was no word from the
jury, Mari and Jude began to take their worries seriously.
Mari was really frightened, and Jude wondered if a hung
jury would be the next foulup for this cursed case. Appelbaum still was calm; a long deliberation would not be
unusual.

But, as more time passed, Appelbaum began to wonder
why Judge Conley was not breaking deliberations for the
night and sending the jurors to a motel for some rest. They
had been through three long, exhausting days of testimony
and were edging into the wee hours of the morning. At
least, he consoled himself, there had been no notes suggesting the jurors were having trouble with deliberations.

A note finally arrived at three in the morning. The jurors
wanted to get some sleep and resume in the morning; the
judge agreed.

No one knew if the jurors were able to sleep, but when
everyone else reassembled Thursday morning about nine
o'clock, it was agreed none of them had slept at all. The
concern Mari and Jude had begun to feel now was joined
by creeping exhaustion. And John Appelbaum soon turned
terse and crabby. Even though he was supported now by
more of his family members, he was snapping at everyone,
including the women he had tried to console the night before. When Mari and Jude asked his assessment of deliberations after the jury resumed about nine-thirty, he snapped,
"I'm not in the jury room. How should I know?"

About noon, George McElroy called Appelbaum into his
office for a personal conference. "John, you know you
could lose this case. I'm not saying you're going to, but you
could. You need to be ready for that. It wasn't that strong
of a case, and you did the best you could. There wasn't
any more you could have done."

Appelbaum nodded; he already had told himself the
same thing. Later, he suggested Mari and Jude be prepared

for the possibility of a hung jury. That message was hard for John to deliver and hard for the women to contemplate.

Mari—the fear and exhaustion showing painfully in her face—glared into the prosecutor's eyes as she cried, "I will not accept that from you, John Appelbaum. You *will* win this case and I refuse to accept any other outcome from you! You *will* win this case and I refuse to accept *any* other outcome from you."

She caught her breath and then added in a quieter voice, "You must win it, John. Our very lives depend on it."

Although Mari knew Appelbaum's heart went out to both women, she still could detect some resentment in his eyes as she heaped the extra pressure upon him.

The hours passed Thursday as people paced the halls, slumped on benches, collapsed on the floor, stepped outside for a cigarette, or wandered across the street for a meal at Munzert's.

Lieutenant Tim McEntee stayed right there, too. He had never sat in on closing arguments before, and it had been a chilling experience to hear all the evidence pulled together by the attorneys. But McEntee had a more personal stake in this, too. He wanted to wait with the mothers for the end of this saga they had started together five years earlier. After all, McEntee had been on the Fleer case longer than anyone else, since the shoot-out during the robbery in 1974. And he also wanted to be here at the end for the eighteen detectives who had worked the children's murders for the Major Case Squad; they all deserved to be represented.

Jude felt as if she were sitting on a bubbling volcano. For her and Mari, this was life and death. They wondered aloud how they would go on if Fleer was acquitted. They knew they couldn't live if he was free. Mari had been through this contemplation before, and she knew exactly what Jude meant when she said in deadly seriousness, "If he's acquitted, I'll kill him." They both fantasized about standing over his lifeless body.

Appelbaum gathered with his sisters and other relatives in his office that evening and they threw darts at a board bearing Clint Almond's photograph; it was a therapeutic gift from Mari and Bob. Drilling the photo with darts was small consolation, but fun.

The note came at 11:15 P.M.; the jurors asked to break for the night. They sent no official word on progress, but they wanted to resume deliberations Friday morning.

In the judge's chambers, there was time for some fairly good-natured joking. Appelbaum asked if the jurors' note indicated how close they were.

"Do you think if I knew I would tell you?" the judge said, grinning.

Clint Almond offered his analysis that the split was nine to three, for acquittal. The judge turned to Appelbaum: "So that tells you that you probably ought to have plea-bargained the case."

"Okay. My apology," Appelbaum dead-panned.

The judge grinned again and claimed Almond had made an offer; if prosecutors dismissed the charge and apologized, Fleer might accept it. Appelbaum grinned and shook his head; no deal.

There would be no sleep Thursday night, either.

The jurors began fairly early Friday, back at work by 8:20 A.M.

John Appelbaum was in his office at 10:05 A.M. when the buzzer from the jury room sounded. One buzz would mean there was a note from the jury. A second buzz would mean there was a verdict. There had been several notes, and Appelbaum was used to the solitary report of the bell. When the second buzz came, John's heart began to pound. The verdict was in.

After almost twenty-three hours of deliberations—a record for the county and nearly as long as it had taken to hear the evidence—the verdict was in.

Jude and Jackie Corey were sitting in the women's lounge drafting a victim-impact statement Jude might be allowed to deliver as part of the evidence at sentencing—if Fleer was ever convicted. Rick Pashia threw open the door and said those magical words—"The verdict's in."

Mari was chatting with her mother outside the courthouse when a police officer told them the news. Mari felt the same wave of shock she remembered from five long years ago. The sensation began at her feet and coursed through her body to her head.

The mothers arrived at the courtroom at the same time,

and, as if by order of God, the crowd parted before them like the Red Sea. The women lurched through the doors and were surprised to see the jurors already seated in the box. The women hurried to their benches near the front of the courtroom and dropped into their seats. Jude held her hands over her mouth and gasped for air as she began to rock back and forth. She looked at Eugene Fleer and was amazed that she still could find nothing in his face to read.

The first count was for Stacy's murder, and Jude knew she had to hear the right word at the very beginning. Please, God, she prayed, let me hear guilty.

Mari clenched her fists in pure fear and prayed just as hard for the second verdict in Tyler's name.

Appelbaum arrived just behind the women and was as shocked that everyone else was in place already. As he walked past all of the people outside the doors and strode into the courtroom, he felt an odd sense of power. His entry into this scene struck him as so dramatic, almost theatrical. One of the women jurors was crying, and Appelbaum could not remember this kind of palpable tension awaiting a jury's verdict. It seemed that the future of Jefferson County was riding on this decision.

About ten uniformed deputies filed into the courtroom and took up positions in front of the women and at other points around the room. Mari and Jude looked at each, both of them wondering who was being protected from whom.

Judge Conley turned to the spectators to issue the traditional warning against any outburst. He acknowledged the high emotions on both sides of this case, but added sternly, "I don't want anyone creating any type of scene in the courtroom that will make it more difficult for us."

The judge had the jury foreman hand the verdict forms to the bailiff, who delivered them to Conley. Appelbaum followed the papers intently as they changed hands. He knew what to look for: two lines on the "guilty" verdict, one line on the "not guilty." He thought he could make it out, but as the judge stared at the forms, Appelbaum began to doubt his own eyes. What had he really seen?

"As to Count One," the judge read, "we, the jury, find the defendant, Eugene Michael Fleer, guilty of murder in the first . . ."

Jude Govreau screamed and turned to Rick. "Oh God, they did it. We got him," she screamed.

Tim McEntee spun in his seat in front of her, grabbed Jude's hand, and squeezed it hard in celebration, and then he pushed her down onto the bench as Rick piled on top of her, too. Racheal collapsed in tears into Jude's lap and also was crushed by the bodies that formed around them. Rick and McEntee knew they had to restrain Jude or face the wrath of Judge Conley, who had paused to watch his orders violated so flagrantly in the frenzy.

Mari Kane was screaming, too, as she squeezed her husband's arm; Bob was warning her to stay quiet, but he knew it was useless.

On the other side of the courtroom, the scene was as emotional if not as jubilant. Geno's mother collapsed into the arms of her husband as she lamented, "Oh God, they want to kill my son."

On the bench, the judge resumed his announcement. ". . . guilty of murder in the first degree. As to Count Two, we, the jury, find the defendant, Michael Eugene Fleer, guilty of murder in the first degree."

Mari kept screaming, "We got him," as she and Jude finally hugged each other in the moment they had awaited so long. "He's going to pay," the women said to each other.

At the defense's request, the judge polled the jurors, and each one confirmed the verdict. Mari and Jude grinned and shook with excitement as they reveled in the music of hearing "guilty" twelve more times.

John Appelbaum had a death grip on the edge of the table as he heard the verdicts. He was trying to remain composed, but he wanted to jump and scream like Mari and Jude. He turned and flashed them a thumbs-up.

And then Mari vaulted over the back of the bench, hugged a supporter, and made a dash to find a telephone to begin sending the word to friends. Jude also ran for a phone; she had to get the news to Johnna.

The women paused momentarily before the television cameras, where their unrestrained celebration was captured. Mari and her mother hugged, and Mari fought tears as she said, "We got him. He's going to pay for what he did to my baby." Did she want the death penalty? "I want him to die the way he killed my son," she vowed.

Jude later regretted that she had talked to the media too soon after the verdict, while she still was giddy. She felt embarrassed as she watched herself on television shouting, "We're happy. We're damned happy."

Fleer's family vowed to continue efforts to clear his name and distributed copies of the report showing that Geno had passed the polygraph. His father said there was much in the trial that was not "kosher" and he hoped to find justice for his son.

But there was more work to do on this day. The judge sent the jurors to a recess before the parties returned to being phase two—the death penalty. Then he called the attorneys into his chambers. Clint Almond's anger was almost unrestrained as he blew into the room. He ranted about the perjury by prosecution witnesses, the misconduct by the prosecutors, and the injustice done his client. Appelbaum had expected Almond to be furious, but this was beyond all bounds. The defense attorney threw his note pad across the room and vowed to do everything in his power to right this wrong. The judge told the attorneys to be ready for the penalty phase in fifteen minutes and released them.

But as they left the chambers, Almond continued his verbal assault on George McElroy, calling him a son of a bitch who had bought a conviction with "perjury deluxe" from lying convicts. Almond would file ethics charges against McElroy with the bar association, he fumed.

"You shut your mouth," an angry McElroy finally shot back as he stepped toward his opponent. The men began to shove at each other, and deputies rushed over to drive a wedge between them. The deterioration of the attorneys' adversarial roles in this case finally had hit bottom.

At the home of his parents, Steve Winzen anxiously watched the television for news of a verdict. When the word came, he cried for joy the first time in five years. He had been crucified by the prosecutors in the courtroom and by the press, which reported every day how a drug deal involving Steve Winzen had caused his son's brutal murder. He had lost friends. His life had dissolved into something hardly worth living. But now, at this moment, the pain had been worth it. It had been Steve's privilege and honor to be Tyler's father for the short time he was on this earth, and now Steve could remember Tyler that way. When Patty Garner looked into Steve's face, she knew the man she had loved before was back.

The intense emotions released by the guilty verdicts had not diminished when everyone returned to the courtroom to decide whether Eugene Michael Fleer—now officially the murderer of Tyler and Stacy—would be executed for his crimes. Neither side presented witnesses, leaving the attorneys to argue their positions. It was clear that Fleer qualified for the death sentence, Appelbaum told the weary jurors. Three of the aggravating circumstances listed in the law were present here: multiple murders, a defendant with a record of assault and violence, and the presence of torture or depravity in the commission of the murders. What case could fit better than the strangulation and drowning of two innocent children by a man with a record of armed robbery, assault with intent to kill, and cocaine possession? This was the jurors' chance to send a message to criminals about strong law enforcement. "We don't need to rehash the evidence," Appelbaum said quietly. "The images of Stacy and Tyler will be emblazoned on your minds and will haunt us all forever. This is not an easy thing that we ask you to do. It is the right thing."

Clint Almond's fervor had not diminished, either, and he opened his argument with a surprising statement. "My client has instructed me that he would just as soon die. He does not want a defense; however, he has given me permission to say a few words." Almond said Fleer and the defense attorneys did not blame the jurors for the verdict. He pointed at the prosecutors and snapped, "However, we blame the people who abuse the system and flagrantly use perjury."

Almond turned his argument into a diatribe against the prosecutors, pointing and gesturing angrily at them as he accused them repeatedly of misconduct and bringing in perjured testimony from prisoners and ex-cons. Almond even stood in front of the prosecutors' table to wave his legal pad in their faces and announce he wasn't afraid of either man. He urged the jurors to go to a judge if there had been some deal made during deliberations to persuade hesitant jurors to vote guilty in exchange for life in prison for Fleer. The defense was entitled to know that, he pleaded. Fleer's record was being exaggerated by the prosecutors to turn him into a bad guy while the prosecutors overlooked their own politically motivated misconduct.

McElroy objected often, but tried to hold his temper until Almond mentioned that Fleer had passed a lie detector test. McElroy pounded the table, shouted his objection, and then asked the judge to hold Almond in contempt of court for violating one of the clearest prohibitions in rules of evidence. Judge Conley sustained the objection and ordered the jury to disregard Almond's comment; the judge said he would rule later on the contempt issue. Eventually, it would be denied.

In his rebuttal, McElroy told the jurors they had nothing to apologize for and they should hold up their heads. They had done their duty, and no attack by defense attorneys could change that. Now, he urged, they should do their duty again and order Eugene Fleer's execution for his horrible crimes.

The jury deliberated through the afternoon, and, as word of the scuffle between Almond and McElroy leaked out, reporters asked repeatedly for details. The men admitted the confrontation, but McElroy tried to minimize it. They had had words, he said, but he added, "It has been a long trial and tempers are frayed." Appelbaum denounced Almond's conduct and argument in the penalty phase as ludicrous. Almond said he would renew his efforts to oust the prosecutors from their jobs for misconduct.

Just before seven o'clock, after six hours of deliberations, the jurors returned their final decision. The mothers' groups were eating at Munzert's when the word came, and Rick Pashia almost had to laugh as a dozen women in high heels ran awkwardly back to the courthouse. The scene in Munzert's had turned ugly not long before that, however, when Sheriff Buck Buerger chafed under continuing criticism from Mari. He had approached her and offered his congratulations, saying, "We got him." But Mari couldn't find room to include Buerger in the "we" she believed were responsible. "We got him in spite of you," Mari snarled. Buerger's anger flashed as he slammed a bar stool across the room and threatened to turn Fleer loose that very minute. Buerger's daughter tried to pull him from the room, and Rick Pashia thought he might have to punch the sheriff to protect Jude and Mari. But Buerger left before it came to that.

The scene in the courtroom for this verdict was almost as tense, but there was no outburst when the jurors ruled against executing Fleer; they recommended a life sentence without parole. The judge set final sentencing for November 15. After the drama of the verdict, this seemed strangely anticlimactic. The prosecutors and police thought death would have been justice, but they could accept the jury's decision. And one of the other judges summed up many people's speculation when he cracked to Tim McEntee, "He'll die a thousand deaths in prison."

Jude had held out little hope for execution; she didn't think that the jury had the stomach for it. She had come down from the high of the conviction by then, anyway, and she realized that none of it would bring Stacy back. Jude still had to face life without her precious daughter, and nothing that could be done to Fleer would change that. Jude was angry that he would be allowed to breathe the air that Stacy couldn't, but she would work on accepting that as another part of this story of injustice.

For Mari, life in prison was not complete justice, but it was enough. George McElroy approached Mari to apologize for the sentence, but she grabbed his face and said, "I don't care, George. He's guilty." Now that Fleer would go to jail, Mari could be set free as his prisoner; God had freed her from the prison sentence Fleer had given her on August 7, 1986. She still hated Fleer with all her heart, but she could end her obsession with him. He would spend every day in prison, perhaps being sexually abused by other inmates and waking each morning to wonder if someone would stick a knife in his belly that day to show him how prisoners felt about baby-killers. He would have years, decades, to think about what he had done to Tyler and to know that Mari and Jude and Appelbaum and the others had got him for it. "He'll never be able to hurt another child again," she told reporters.

Almond summed up his angry reaction by telling the media, "I do not believe there is any way to get a fair shake with these prosecutors in this county. They are very

politically ambitious and this has been a political trial from
the time it started."

In another exclusive interview with John Auble, a sub-
dued Eugene Fleer said, "It's a real tragedy when the prosecutors can abuse the power and influence of their office to
buy perjured testimony, and that's exactly what they did."

Jude went home to change clothes so she could go out
and celebrate the conviction. But her sister called, and Jude
filled her in on the incredible events of the day. By the time
Jude hung up, she was so drained she decided to stay home.

Mari's evening ended in another eerie parallel to Jude's.
Mari and Bob joined the rest of her family at their favorite
Mexican restaurant for what was intended to be a great
celebration. But the refreshments had just arrived when
Mari realized that all she really wanted was to go home.
She was exhausted and she could not find the spirit for
a celebration. She and Bob left before they finished their
first drinks.

For both women, some time alone was the only appropriate commemoration on this night. What had just happened didn't call for drinking and boisterous partying. It
called for quiet reflection, private thoughts, and grief. Jude
had some talking to do to Stacy, and Mari had to make
sure Tyler knew she had kept her promise to him.

CHAPTER 21

Eugene Fleer would suffer more in prison.

That was the rationale offered by one of the jurors for the decision to reject the prosecutors' call for the death sentence. In a newspaper story the week after the verdict, juror Reldon Pyatt said the panel as a whole had agreed to impose a life sentence as a way to make Fleer suffer more. Juror Eileen Cook agreed with Pyatt and said she was insulted by Almond's implication that the jurors had convicted Fleer because they didn't know any better. During their very lengthy deliberations, they had discussed everything in great detail and considered all the evidence carefully before reaching a verdict, she insisted.

The other ten jurors refused to talk with the reporter. But Pyatt provided a number of other interesting revelations. The jurors discounted the much-maligned testimony by jail inmates—those "jailhouse snitches" some people had been so obsessed with—and convicted Fleer on the word of other witnesses who had nothing to gain or lose by testifying. And the most damaging evidence had come from a defense witness, Pyatt confirmed. Bob Lutz's testimony that he hadn't provided any of the details Fleer was repeating to friends had indeed sunk him, as Appelbaum had predicted. The jurors had agreed that the only way Fleer could know those particulars so soon was to have been the killer.

The first vote the jury had taken had been about evenly divided between guilt and acquittal. But by the end of the first day of deliberations, the tally had swung dramatically to eleven for conviction. The rest of the time had been spent dissecting the case minutely and convincing the holdout to go for guilty.

*　　*　　*

In their motion for a new trial, Clint Almond and Marsha Brady reprised the familiar refrain about prosecutorial misconduct and perjured testimony, but added an interesting new chorus—four affidavits from jurors challenging the verdict they had helped deliver. In sworn affidavits, the jurors charged that their foreman had made notes during recesses—after the judge told him not to take notes in the courtroom—and the others often relied on the notes during deliberations. Only after the verdict had the jurors discovered that the notes had been incorrect; the foreman had quoted Bob Lutz as saying Fleer had told him that Stacy had been strangled and her esophagus was crushed, when that testimony actually had come from Jim Main. The four jurors also complained that the trial was conducted so fast that they had difficulty keeping track of the witnesses and testimony, and were exhausted by the time the lengthy deliberations produced a verdict.

One of those jurors, Linda Reifstech, had been the last holdout for acquittal and would say years later that she was convinced Fleer had been convicted amid tainted deliberations. As she had weighed the evidence, she had kept wondering what it was that all of those nice people saw that she did not. She had cried for weeks after the verdict and would always feel remorse for caving in to the others under incredible pressure. One man even told her—incorrectly—that a hung jury would force the judge to ask each juror to declare his or her vote publicly; she would be revealed as the one who had thwarted a verdict. The foreman, a very religious man, had used Biblical scripture to try to convince her that God wanted the blood of these innocents avenged. Another man said all of the characters in the case were into drugs and Fleer surely had done something deserving of conviction. A woman revealed she knew Fleer's grandmother—a fact she had never reported during jury selection. Another juror had slept during much of the evidence.

Reifstech said the jurors were too inexperienced to know they did not have to deliberate for such long hours and could have asked to break before three in the morning during that first session. The early mornings and late evenings left them exhausted and compromised their abilities to analyze the evidence and debate their positions.

All of that clashed head-on with what Appelbaum had heard from other jurors, including the published comments of Reldon Pyatt and Eileen Cook. They were confident of their verdict and comfortable with what they had called careful deliberations. Appelbaum wondered how these people could have such different views and what this might mean to the appellate process.

The hearing on the motions and the final sentencing for Eugene Fleer arrived on November 15 and—with Mari and Jude in the audience for the finale—was just as combative as the rest of the proceedings. Almond complained of "an enormous amount of misconduct" peppered with perjured testimony and subornation of perjury by the prosecutors. He first went after Ron Boyer's testimony from an odd angle, insisting it should have been barred because the man Fleer was talking to in the jail had been placed there at Appelbaum's request; Fleer's cellie was, in effect, an agent of the state sent there to get more jailhouse evidence. Almond presented testimony from a sheriff's lieutenant who was in charge of the jail; he had brought the cellie to several meetings with Appelbaum in the detective division and had been told by someone to put the man in the cell with Fleer. On cross-examination, however, the lieutenant said he was not present for the conversations and had been told by the inmate that he was working with the prosecutors on a different case. The officer also confirmed that he had been paid to serve process papers by Almond and Brady, and had paid them for legal services in the past.

Almond criticized the prosecution's endorsement of some fifty witnesses when fewer than half were called at trial. That lengthy list had sent the defenders off on wild goose chases and made it impossible to prepare for trial. The judge shrugged and noted that Almond had not asked for a delay; he could have had one.

Almond also complained that the judge had allowed the prosecutors to bring in Ron Boyer and Dr. James McGivney after the deadline for endorsing witnesses. McElroy explained again that Boyer had come forward just three weeks before trial, had been endorsed as soon as he was found, and had been approved by the judge. The dental expert was a necessary rebuttal witness who did not have to be endorsed before trial; the judge had approved him, too. Neither witness was a surprise and Almond had had time to prepare for their testimony, McElroy insisted. The judge agreed.

Informants Michael Watson and Donald Walker came in for criticism from Almond, too, but McElroy angrily noted that neither of those men had even testified. That was the point, Almond said. Appelbaum's unethical eavesdropping on the defense interview with Watson had sent the prosecution in search of other witnesses, completely changing the defense's strategy. The prosecutors' misconduct had undermined the defense and resulted in an unfair verdict. But the judge wasn't interested in pursuing that, either. "I do not want to rehash matters we already have dealt with."

The defense attorneys also failed to gain any ground when they turned to the jurors' complaints. Although the jurors were present under subpoenas, the judge refused to hear their testimony. "I am going to continue to follow the case law in the state of Missouri, which is that we do not impeach the verdict of the jury by the testimony of jurors," the judge said flatly. He agreed that he had admonished the foreman about taking notes during the trial. But the judge said he was unaware of any rule that prohibited jurors from making notes at other times. Almond argued insistently that the reliance on inaccurate notes as evidence corrupted the verdict, but the judge was unbending. He thought this was one of the most impressive juries he had seen. The jurors had worked at their own pace, never seemed disgruntled or angry, indicated when they wanted take recesses, and told the judge they were ready to return to the motel or wanted to eat, even when they wanted a soda. He didn't think they had been fatigued during deliberations.

"I've looked at all the allegations and I know that tempers are hot down here in this county. I don't know why that is. I don't pretend to know why you all are angry with each other down here, but that's your business to decide, not mine. But I believe that the defendant got a fair trial in this case." Without further ado, he denied the request for a new trial; the conviction stood.

And then he unceremoniously called Eugene Michael Fleer before the bench and sentenced him to two consecutive natural life sentences without parole, as the jury had recommended. Fleer never flinched, and he answered, "Yes Your Honor, I am," when the judge asked if he was satisfied with his attorneys' services.

The moment was sweet for Jude and Mari. They had fought for this and now they could savor it. They watched Eugene Fleer led from the courtroom in handcuffs, officially denied another breath of free air for the rest of his life. Now, they hoped, they could begin to get on with the rest of theirs.

Appelbaum also relished the sense of finality. Fleer should have been executed, but spending the rest of his life in prison could be worse for him. And Appelbaum could live with that.

In November 1992, Sheriff Buck Buerger retired from office at the end of his seventh term. Although he had served for nearly three decades—bringing the department from a part-time operation in a rural area to one of the state's largest departments in a growing, metropolitan community—his last term had been marked by incredible controversy. Some said he went out under a cloud. He said he was proud of his record and was going out with his head held high.

Eugene Fleer's petition to the Missouri Eastern District Court of Appeals met the same fate as his post-conviction motion. In February 1993, despite assertions by Clint Almond and Marsha Brady of ten reversible errors at trial, the appellate court affirmed the convictions and sentence.

Meanwhile, Appelbaum still couldn't shake loose of the Fleer case. In March 1993, Donald Walker sued Appelbaum on allegations that he had reneged on his promise to make a favorable recommendation to the parole board for Walker in exchange for his testimony against Fleer. Appelbaum responded that doubts about Walker's credibility had prevented his testimony; he was owed nothing. In March 1994, Walker dropped the suit.

Eugene Fleer's foray through the courts continued on the established course. On May 25, 1993, without any comment, the Missouri Supreme Court refused to hear his appeal.

The end of the appellate process was a relief to Mari and Jude. But they still wonder about a motive; as time passes, they still have trouble finding it in Appelbaum's story of vicious drug revenge. They know Fleer was guilty, they just don't believe they know why he did it. A sexual assault on Stacy seems more likely, they believe. Geno had heard Lester Howlett talk about sexual activities with Mari's baby-sitter, not knowing a new sitter had been hired. When Stacy resisted, Geno's violent reaction to rejection kicked in and he quickly and viciously overpowered her. Tyler wandered into the middle of that homicide and became the next victim. That made more sense to the women.

It certainly made more sense to Steve Winzen. He insisted he had never been involved in a fractured cocaine deal that caused the murders, even though that scenario helped convict Fleer while crucifying Steve. Geno was the killer, Steve agreed, but the motive had to come from somewhere else, and the sexual assault fit everything Steve knew about Fleer. But even that left one bothersome question for Steve and Patty Garner. What about the collect call from the hotel in Vegas to Lester's apartment at 10:26 A.M. the day of the murders? Who placed that call, and why? Steve has tried to move on with his life, but many unanswered questions nag at him.

Other loose ends that arose during the long years of the Winzen-Price case were tied up in surprising ways after Fleer went to prison.

On August 23, 1994, the Missouri Court of Appeals upheld the murder conviction of Sheriff Buerger's friend, William Pagano. Already disappointed by the decision, Pagano was stunned by the unannounced arrival of deputies at his door later that day to take him to prison. Unable to face the loss of his freedom after three years out on bail, he stepped into a closet, picked up a .357 magnum revolver, and shot himself in the head.

Another murder case returned to the headlines with a vengeance, too. Patricia Stallings—cleared of any wrongdoing in her son's death and living quietly in a beautiful home built with proceeds from a substantial settlement with the medical labs—contributed some of her newfound wealth to thwart the men who had convicted her in error years earlier. In the primary election in Jefferson County in August 1994, Stallings donated $10,000 to George Wilkins, the man running against George McElroy for the Democratic nomination as prosecuting attorney. With support from Stallings, Buerger, Clint Almond, and others angry with McElroy, Wilkins won handily. Wilkins went on to win the general election in November and replaced McElroy in December.

John Appelbaum also had decided to launch a political career and won the Democratic nomination for state representative in the August primary election. But just days before the general election, Stallings made a sizable contribution to John's opponent and sponsored a mailing to voters, criticizing Appelbaum's involvement in her case. Appelbaum lost his election, too. He was expected to enter private practice, perhaps ending his career as a prosecutor.

From a cell at the Potosi Correctional Center at Mineral Point, Missouri, Eugene Fleer still insists he is innocent and that his trial had nothing to do with the truth. The jurors simply voted for the side with the smoothest words and the best story.

Now, at thirty-nine years old, Fleer has a life in prison. "It's not much of a life, but I do have a life. I keep up with my nieces and nephews and sisters, and Mom and Dad."

There are days when he doesn't want to get out of bed, when he feels like snapping at another inmate over little details, when he feels like staying in his cell instead of playing handball or exercising in the yard or going to the law library. He can call friends and relatives collect; he can write letters or watch television or read. It's a life.

Having lost all appeals in state court, he is uncertain how he will proceed. Clint Almond and Marsha Brady are out of the case now; they did not contract with him for appeals beyond the state courts. So he is studying about federal appeals before deciding how to proceed and whether to look for another attorney versed in the federal appellate system. He knows he must plead some violation of his civil rights, some abuse of discretion by prosecutors or the trial judge. And he knows there is no great hurry. So for now, he is just biding the ample time on his calendar.

EPILOGUE

The anger that sustained Jude Govreau and Mari Kane for more than five years has not subsided. Just below the surface, it always simmers and can explode furiously as they recount what they believe was the indifference and incompetence of many in the system that was supposed to bring them justice. Although their journey led to a measure of justice—incomplete and less than satisfactory—what they remember in their hearts is abuse that turned already crushing grief into a burden few people could imagine. Those who have not endured the murder of a child and what follows at the hands of the system can only try to envision the experience—as someone standing by the fire wonders what it must be like to be consumed by the flames.

John Appelbaum was the exception, of course. He gave the women the respect, dignity, consideration, information, dedication, and participation they deserved. He made sure the jurors understood that Stacy and Tyler were real people who had died horribly, children loved and missed greatly by those left behind in emotional carnage. He persisted in that effort against the other cogs in the system that callously crush any suggestion that real people are involved, are damaged, are battered, are abused by those who see the court's work only in terms of case numbers and files and charges and motions and rulings and defendant's rights.

John did all of those things for the women even though he didn't have to. Part of what still angers them so is exactly that—he didn't have to. "Unless you get a good prosecutor," Jude says, "your child can leave this world without an identity." Every prosecutor should be mandated by law to do all of the things that John Appelbaum did because he knew they were the right things to do and he knew the women and their children had every right to expect him to do those things. Instead, before Appelbaum joined the cause, Mari and Jude found a system that offered them little sympathy or little else.

They still deal with their grief in different ways, but remain connected by their children's deaths and their absolute certainty that Eugene "Geno" Fleer was the killer. They still wish he had been executed and admit they would not mourn his death. Jude awaits the day when she hears the news that he no longer breathes the air that Stacy stopped breathing in 1986. Mari accepts his life in prison on different terms, hoping each day, each hour, each moment, is an eternity of suffering for him.

The women have good thoughts about the Major Case Squad and its efforts. But Sheriff Buck Buerger and some of his men are suspended in angry memories; the women refuse to believe the jury summons fiasco was an innocent mistake. They can find no room in their hearts to understand why some defense attorneys behave as they do, or why judges tolerate tactics so obviously designed to frustrate justice, not assure it.

Mari and Jude ask, What kind of country coddles the criminal and abuses the victim? Shouldn't the coddling be saved for the damaged, battered victims or their survivors left behind? They kill our kids and then the people in the system treat us as though we're making trouble for them, inconveniencing them. Why does the system work so hard to protect cold-blooded killers and their sacred constitutional rights, while ignoring, if not trampling on, the rights of the victims and their families whose pain and grief are aggravated by the very people charged with dispensing justice on their behalf?

The women understand what a tragedy it would be to execute an innocent man. But they ask if there is not just as great a tragedy in paroling a convicted murderer so that he can so often—as statistics show—commit more crimes and perhaps take more innocent lives. Why can parole boards escape any consequences when they release someone who kills again? What sense does it make to strain so mightily to protect the rights of the guilty when the result is the sacrifice of even more innocents? What kind of trade-off is that? Where is the justice in that?

* * *

"Justice delayed," William Ewart Gladstone wrote, "is justice denied." The British prime minister of 130 years ago understood that truth then, and Mari and Jude had five years to learn it. For these women, the abuse and delays they suffered at the hands of the system were, indeed, justice denied.

Defense attorneys bar victims' relatives from the courtroom during jury selection and even during trial with transparent tactics. For Mari and Jude, that is justice denied. Other than the defendant and the jurors, who has more right to hear the evidence than the family of the victim? A defendant's mother is allowed to sit in the courtroom, but the victims' mother must beg for what should be an inalienable right.

The courts do not have to inform the victims and their families about any legal proceedings, hearings, or plea bargains. Justice denied.

The police and prosecutors refuse to allow the family of victims to see police reports or other documents the defendant can see. A driver in an automobile wreck gets a copy of the report, but the parent of a murdered child does not. Justice denied.

The courts may decide arbitrarily whether the families are allowed to make victim-impact statements. Justice denied. Those statements should be the families' option without interference from anyone. Jude said George McElroy would not allow her to make a statement to the jurors because he thought they already had heard enough emotional testimony. "This is not about the jurors," Jude fumes. "This is not about the judges. This is not about the defense attorneys or the prosecutors. This is about Stacy and Tyler."

Unless sentenced to life without parole, violent criminals and even convicted murderers serve only a fraction of their sentences and the victims' families may not even be informed when the criminal is paroled. To Mari and Jude, returning to freedom a person who was proved to be a killer, and giving him the ability to kill more law-abiding citizens, is reprehensible. What could be justice more dangerously denied?

Anyone who has not suffered loss or a loved one at the hands of a murderer cannot begin to imagine how deep the pain goes, how ugly the scar is, how that one act of violence haunts every waking minute for the survivors. Parents left to mourn a murdered child carry open wounds that penetrate their very souls and never heal. And, like the ripples in a pond from one stone, the pain rolls out and over the parents, the grandparents, and every other relative, until it reaches the friends, schoolmates, coworkers, and everyone who ever knew the victim.

And Mari and Jude watched it exact a terrible toll on other children who had lost one of their own so unnaturally. Their innocence fell victim to the violence just as surely as the murdered child did. What had been a wondrous world became an ugly and dangerous place seen in a way no child should have to see it. They became fearful, cynical, and angry. A letter that one of Tyler's friends sent to Mari the night before the trial began told that story. "I hope you win," six-year-old Felicia Weiss wrote. "I love you very much. I hope I see you soon. Everybody hopes you win, even my friends. Everybody hopes Fleer goes to *hell*! I know you do, too. P.S. I love you. Love, Felicia."

Even after the trial ends and the sentence begins, the injustice continues. Mari and Jude wonder why convicted murderers eat well, enjoy air-conditioned comfort, have access to handball and basketball courts, and can pump iron until their bodies develop into even more dangerous weapons. They can read in the library, watch television, see a movie, or make telephone calls. They can get free college educations, free medical and dental treatment. All of that is paid for by the taxpayers—including the families of the victims, who may be going without those benefits because they cannot afford to pay for them. The children who were murdered are buried, never go to school, never get counseling, and are barely remembered by the state. Except for a few scholarships, law-abiding citizens and kids do not get free college educations.

Justice denied.

Mari and Jude want those luxuries for prisoners ended and the money used for good causes, such as programs to help poor kids avoid drugs or find an alternative to a life of crime. The women are convinced that fewer ex-cons would risk a return to prison if the prisons returned to the idea of pure punishment in a cold, sterile environment devoid of creature comforts.

The women have tired of hearing about the rights of the accused and the evils of society that forced them into crime. They believe Justice Clarence Thomas of the U.S. Supreme Court was right when he urged judges and legislators to stop blaming society for crime and start blaming criminals. He was right when he said that falling back on excuses such as racism and poverty has contributed to the soaring rate of violent crime.

The national movement for victims' rights has led to passage of important legislation in some states giving the victims the rights Mari and Jude were denied. Missouri's Victims Rights Law, passed in 1993, provides some of those rights. Governor Mel Carnahan of Missouri signed a bill in 1994 that requires dangerous criminals to serve at least 85 percent of their sentences before they are eligible for parole—another improvement Mari and Jude support. But few of the states have gone far enough, according to these women, who have become "experts" the hard way.

Jude remains active in groups such as Parents of Murdered Children, one of the organizations that pushes for such legislation. Mari has found special affection and admiration for people such as Hyman Eisenberg, who founded the chapter of Parents of Murdered Children in St. Louis; his work for victims' rights has been instrumental in legislative successes.

Mari had shared her experiences with those groups and heard horror stories about the system that have made her ill. She always comes away thanking God that John Appelbaum drew the Winzen-Price case.

The day after Eugene Fleer was sentenced, Mari found herself facing a new emptiness. Since August 7, 1986, her whole life had been aimed at finding the killer and then getting justice. When that was over in 1991, she wondered what she could do now with her life. Routine, daily existence, didn't seem enough. Where was the purpose, the passion? Finally, her therapist provided the insight she needed. "Do something positive in Tyler's name to keep his spirit alive," Dr. Larry Kiel told her.

Now Mari has found the way to put her passion for justice to work. She is finishing her college education and plans to attend law school to become a prosecutor. She is driven to make straight A's, and has earned an academic scholarship from the Phi Theta Kappa Society, a national honors society.

As their mothers continue the fight, the memories of Stacy and Tyler may find justice yet.